Totally Five Star: Marrakesh

CHAMELEON

ASHE BARKER

Chameleon
ISBN # 978-1-78430-414-0
©Copyright Ashe Barker 2015
Cover Art by Posh Gosh ©Copyright January 2015
Interior text design by Claire Siemaszkiewicz
Totally Bound Publishing

Published in 2015 by Totally Bound Publishing, Newland House, The Point, Weaver Road, Lincoln, LN6 3QN, United Kingdom.

Totally Bound Publishing is a subsidiary of Totally Entwined Group Limited.

Totally Bound Publishing books by Ashe Barker:

Carrot and Coriander
Red Skye at Night

The Dark Side
Darkening
Darker
Darkest

Sure Mastery
Unsure
Sure Thing
Surefire

The Hardest Word
A Hard Bargain
Hard Lessons
Hard Choices

A Richness of Swallows
Rich Tapestry
Rich Pickings
Rich Promise

Collections
Paramour: Re-Awakening
Jolly Rogered: Right of Salvage

What's her Secret?
The Three R's

Totally Five Star
Chameleon

CHAMELEON

Dedication

Chameleon is dedicated as ever to my family, John and Hannah, and to Danny who showed an uncommon interest. And most of all, to the nameless woman riding a donkey through the desert of eastern Turkey, who was the inspiration for all of this.

Chapter One

Christ, it's hot.

Ethan straightened. Scowling, he ran his fingers across his brow and flicked off the moisture. He leaned into his car to retrieve a liter bottle of water and took a long drink. The liquid was warm, but still wet enough to help—a little. He returned to stand at the front of his car, leaning over the large geological chart spread out across the bonnet. He studied the details on the map, resting his hands on the curling paper in an attempt to smooth it out, only to wince as his palms flattened on the scorching metal of the car. He stood up again, fast, shaking his hands and cursing the heat, the dust, the general desolation that was this place.

Forty degrees Celsius and rising, and still not nine in the morning. He had maybe an hour's work to do here before he could head back to the blessed, air-conditioned cool of the Totally Five Star hotel in the center of Marrakesh but that was eight miles away to the north. Here, in the arid desert—in the foothills of the Atlas Mountains—was where his friend James

Conroy had it in mind to construct his latest project. It was why Ethan found himself out in the already searing heat, parked in the dust at the side of the long road leading from Marrakesh to Tahnaout, boiling his nuts and squinting at the glowing metal of his hire car.

James was CEO of the Totally Five Star chain of hotels, internationally renowned playgrounds of the rich, the famous and just occasionally the infamous. The Marrakesh Totally Five Star was without doubt the best hotel in the city, arguably in the whole of Morocco. Constructed in the style of a series of Arabian *riads*, it offered its exclusive clients a rare blend of privacy and luxury, an oasis of Western efficiency set against the backdrop of exotic Eastern tranquility. The Totally Five Star was a slice of authentic Eastern promise, but the water ran hot, the electricity never failed and the newspapers were in English.

Despite all this, James wasn't satisfied with it. He loved horses and saw no reason why his guests should be denied this fine Arabian tradition. But downtown Marrakesh was not the right location for an equestrian themed leisure spa. For this, James would need space — lots of space. Ethan looked around him, turning a full three hundred and sixty degrees. No shortage of space here. Flat, endless, timeless space, shimmering away to the horizons in every direction. James had acquired an option to purchase several thousand acres of scorching desert, intending to transform it into an annex to his opulent hotel chain, this time catering to horse lovers. There would be the usual other spa facilities too, of course — swimming pools, Turkish baths, massage, beauty and health treatments — all the pampering that money and an abundance of leisure time could make possible.

But only if Ethan said so. James needed Ethan to complete the geological survey and tell him if this site was suitable for what he had in mind. He needed to be sure there were no hidden deposits of toxic substances, no subterranean instability rendering the location unsuitable for a major development. So he'd called his old school friend, Ethan Savage, now heading up his own company specializing in geological surveys. Savage Geo was just the firm James required to start this ball rolling, to help him take the first steps in turning his dream into reality.

This is what had brought Ethan here. This was why he now found himself sweltering in the morning heat of the Moroccan desert, his eyes scrunched into tight creases behind his dark Ray-Bans as he peered at the charts before him, matching the diagrammatic representation to the reality of the actual contours and hollows of this barren landscape. He'd need to do some bore holes, sink some test probes to check what was actually going on below the surface, but so far, he'd seen nothing to cause him any real concerns. This scheme of James' might just work. Though Christ only knew how James would manage to recreate the lush cool of the Totally Five Star out here, where the very air vibrated in the heat.

On that thought, Ethan straightened again and took another long drink. As he bent to place the bottle back in the car, something caught his eye. A glimmer, a slight tremble of motion in the distance. He squinted back along the road as it snaked away across the hillside, shading his eyes to focus. Something glinted, shimmered, right out there on the horizon. He walked around to the boot of his car, where his field equipment lay stowed, and opened it to grab his binoculars from his rucksack. He raised them to his eyes, adjusted the focus and blinked in surprise as the hazy vision solidified.

A head. A woman by the look of it, heavily cloaked, emerging slowly over the horizon. Her pace slow, sedate, rolling slightly. Ethan watched, puzzled, but soon understood the reason for the curious gait. Another head, this one gray with long ears pointing straight toward the heavens—a donkey. As they crested the hill, Ethan saw that the cloaked woman sat astride the animal, perfectly in tune with its leisurely pace as the beast ambled placidly along the ribbon of tarmac. Neither the woman nor her mount appeared to be in a hurry. As Ethan watched through his binoculars, a pair of shoulders appeared, also shrouded in a heavy cloak, the fabric enveloping her small figure. She didn't appear to be guiding the donkey. She had tucked her hands inside the drapes of her clothing, perhaps for protection from the searing heat. Her feet, too, were swathed within the cloak. The ethnic details in the brightly colored fabric crystallized as he watched. He suspected the multihued woolen fabric to be hand-woven. When the pair came fully into view, Ethan could make out panniers swaying on either side of the beast, one with a small, rolled up carpet peeking from it.

As they made their slow, unruffled progress down the road toward where he stood, Ethan dropped the binoculars onto the passenger seat, preferring to watch them with the naked eye. He stared, unashamed, as they drew nearer, taking in every detail of this pair, so incongruous almost anywhere else yet so perfectly placed here in this unchanging landscape. Ethan strolled to the rear of his car, resting his hip against the boot. He made no pretense of disinterest, not so much as a passing nod. His fascination was total.

The woman and donkey would not have looked out of place in Biblical times, and it struck Ethan that in many ways not much had changed here in over two thousand years—at least on the face of it. He watched as the woman reached up to rearrange her cloak slightly to cover most of her features, the traditional modest feminine gesture so common hereabouts. Now she gave off no clues at all, there was no way he could surmise what might lie hidden beneath the heavy shawl. Long minutes crawled past as the pair covered the distance separating them from Ethan. He regarded them solemnly during the whole of their journey.

At last, they were close enough for him to make eye contact. On impulse—and because it seemed impolite not to—Ethan removed his Ray-Bans and met the woman's gaze. She looked him in the eye, direct, unafraid. And certainly not so much as hinting at the timid modesty he might have expected. Her eyes were dark, lined in the local kohl, but her Berber heritage was evident. Despite having no other clues to tempt him, Ethan found her eyes oddly beguiling. Intrigued, he would have liked to know her, to chat perhaps. But that would never happen, not here. In this magical, timeless place, worlds passed within inches of each other, beings such as she and he might co-exist, but their lives did not touch, would *never* touch. They were a million miles apart.

The woman and donkey drew alongside, and Ethan greeted her in the way that seemed natural to him. He nodded, offering her half a smile—polite, distant, acknowledging her presence in this remote place, and his. The woman inclined her head slightly, the movement almost imperceptible but enough. Just enough. As she passed, she dropped her gaze from his, returning her attention to the road in front of her as the donkey carried her onwards.

The innate submission in her response to him affected Ethan powerfully. His cock twitched and leaped to attention with a degree of enthusiasm that even he felt was unseemly in the circumstances. With his erection straining the front of his faded jeans, Ethan turned, following her with his eyes as she moved away from him, relieved that she could no longer see him, as the effect she'd had on him would have been difficult to conceal. From the back, she appeared even more mysterious, even more inscrutable—a small, still figure swaying gracefully with the motion of the donkey.

Ethan shook his head slightly, intrigued, mesmerized, though he couldn't say why. Where else in the world could two people so different in every respect meet, pass each other, nod a greeting, neither one in the least surprised to see the other, and both with a perfectly good reason to be there?

What was it about the small woman that fascinated him? He knew nothing of her life, nor she of his. They would never meet again and he doubted he'd even recognize her if they did. Still, he stood transfixed, watching as she slowly receded from his sight.

It was perhaps twenty minutes before she finally disappeared over the next slight brow in the road and dropped out of view. At last with a sigh, Ethan tore his gaze from the now-deserted road and back to the matter at hand—his geological survey of the spa site. He grabbed his tripod from the boot and quickly snapped the legs out, locking them in place and securing his camera on the top. He proceeded to position the equipment before capturing a few dozen images. He moved the camera about, photographing the site from every angle, also recording distances and gradients with a view to constructing a three-dimensional section model at a later stage. He worked quickly, keen to complete his site investigations and be able to return to the cool, air-conditioned comfort of his suite at the Totally Five Star to input the data into his laptop and start analyzing the information. He hoped to be able to provide James with preliminary survey results within a few days, sufficient for his friend to take a decision regarding further, more detailed work.

Satisfied at last that he'd completed all he could do here, today, Ethan dismantled his photographic equipment and put it all back in the boot of his hire car. He refolded the charts and tossed them in as well, took one last swig of his water then gratefully slithered back into the driver's seat. He slammed the air conditioning on full blast as he reversed the car off the dusty roadside and back onto the asphalt. He turned the nose toward Marrakesh and headed for home. Or, at least, this week's home.

He caught up to her maybe two miles farther on, still walking sedately along the dusty road, swaying gently on the donkey's back. The animal struck him as the most placid of creatures, but still Ethan slowed as he came up behind them, careful not to over-rev his engine as he drew close. He passed them at a dead crawl, leaning down and forward to make eye contact again with the woman through the passenger side window. He lifted his hand in greeting this time, as did she. Once past, Ethan accelerated again but not hard. He flicked his eyes up to watch her in the rear-view mirror, enjoying his last vision of her before she slipped out of his sight.

He should have been watching the road ahead, not ogling a beguiling Berber peasant woman behind him. If he had been looking where he was going, he might well have spotted the pothole before he crunched his front nearside wheel straight into it. Amid the grating clatter of his suspension bottoming and the powerful jolt as the shock reverberated through the axle and up the steering column, Ethan fought to regain control of the vehicle. He might have succeeded if the tire had held out. But it didn't, and he found himself hurtling off the road, out of control and heading with unerring accuracy toward the only obstacle for miles around.

He hit the olive tree with less force than perhaps he might have feared but still enough to spin the car around. Ethan lost his grip on the steering wheel and hurtled forwards, his last thought before he hit the windscreen that he really should have used the seatbelts provided. Pain exploded in his head, and the world went black.

Idiot tourist!

Fleur kicked a reluctant Agwmar into a canter as the squeal of brakes died away. She rounded the bend in the road seconds after Ethan to find the stretch of tarmac ahead empty. A sweep of her eyes to her right located him—or rather his gas-guzzling car—still rocking from its impact with the innocent olive tree. At a glance, she saw that he was still inside, unmoving.

Fleur hurled herself from the donkey's back and sprinted across the dusty, hard-baked earth to reach the car. Hampered slightly by her cloak, she hiked it up around her legs for greater speed. She had a terrifying vision of the crashed car exploding in flames before she could reach it. Him. The man might be a foreigner and altogether too inclined to stare but he was still gorgeous. And she didn't want him going up in smoke. That would be such a waste.

Reaching the vehicle, she was amazed and relieved to note that the damage seemed to be a lot less than she had initially feared. And importantly, there was no ominous smell of leaking petrol. Rushing around to the driver's door, she yanked it open, leaning past the inert form of the man inside to turn off the engine. Instinctively she pocketed the ignition key, slipping it inside the voluminous folds of the cloak now swirling around her in the dry desert breeze.

She turned her attention to the unconscious man, placing two fingers against his neck to check for a pulse. Steady and strong. Fleur heaved a sigh of relief. She examined his head wound, visually at first, then carefully laying her fingers on it. He groaned, his eyelids flickering. He started to turn his head, but Fleur took hold of his face, her palms on his cheeks.

"Ne bouge pas, monsieur." She instructed him to remain still, her tone sharp. She waited a few seconds until he subsided into still silence once more, then she took a chance and left him. She ran around to open the boot. Scanning the contents, she located his first-aid box and dragged it out. She opened the box, but found neither the immobilization collar nor the small torch she sought. She looked into the boot again and this time pulled out a rolled-up chart.

It would have to do. She flattened the cylindrical shape to create a rigid length and grabbed a roll of bandage from the first-aid kit. Returning to the driver's door, she leaned in again. The man's eyes remained closed but his head wound was no longer bleeding, his pulse still steady. Fleur slid the makeshift collar behind his neck, pulling the two ends around to cross at the front, and wrapped a bandage around to hold it in place. One could never be too careful, and a spinal injury remained a possibility.

"*Monsieur, pouvez-vous m'entendre?*" Her tone was softer now, less urgent as she peered up into his unmoving features. *He really is very attractive.*

"*Monsieur?*" she repeated.

He muttered something. She didn't catch it.

"*Pardonnez-moi, monsieur, comment vous dites?*"

"English…"

His low voice was muffled but this time she did catch his words.

"I apologize. Can you hear me, sir?" Fleur switched easily, her English accented but otherwise perfect.

"Yes, I can fucking hear you. Stop shouting. Please." His final word was delivered with considerably less venom than the first sentence.

Fleur smiled to herself. In her experience, belligerent patients were rarely in serious trouble.

"What is your name, sir?"

"What…?"

"Do you know where you are?"

"For fuck's sake, stop shouting at me."

More belligerence. A promising sign. Fleur battled on.

"Sir, do you know today's date?"

"Yes."

Fleur sighed. He was not making any of this easy. But at least the Englishman did not seem unduly confused. That would have been much more worrying than mere rudeness. She tried one last tack.

"Do you know the name of the President of the United States?"

"Of course I fucking do."

"Then perhaps you would tell me, sir." She hoped she was managing to keep the edge of irritation from her tone. He really was most trying.

"Barack fucking Obama. Are you happy now?"

"Perfectly. Do you have a torch, sir?"

"A what?"

"A torch, sir. Do you have one?"

"In my bag." He still seemed disinclined to open his eyes but at least he appeared reasonably coherent. Fleur scrambled to her feet again and headed back to the car boot. She found the rucksack, opened it and dug around inside it until she located his pen torch. Exactly what she needed. She rushed back to the front and leaned in again through the open driver's door.

"Can you open your eyes, sir? Can you look at me please?"

No response.

"Sir, can you hear me?"

"Yes, I fucking said so."

Ah, belligerence again. Fleur kept her amusement to herself as she shoved the constraining folds of the cloak back from her face to lean in close. She laid her fingertip gently over the man's right eyelid and peeled it upwards, shining the torch directly in his eye.

"Fucking hell!"

Undeterred by the angry expletive, Fleur repeated the process with the other eye, satisfied to note that each pupil dilated evenly. No obvious signs of concussion there. And his eyes were the most brilliant shade of blue.

Her makeshift collar held his head still. He'd live. At least until she could get him to a hospital.

"That's better. Much prettier."

His low tone had a quality to it that caused a curious sensation in her lower abdomen. Fleur wasn't sure she liked it exactly. His words perplexed her.

"Excuse me?"

"Better without the veil. Nice hair."

"Ah. It was not a veil, merely a cloak. To keep the sun off."

"It covered your face."

"I *chose* to cover my face. The sun was in my eyes. Also, you were staring. It was not polite."

"I'm sorry. I meant no offense. But I still prefer you without the…whatever."

Fleur relented. "I took no offense." She stopped, unsure what to say next. She settled for a murmured "Thank you" before returning to the more pressing problem facing them. "You have crashed your car, but you do not appear to have sustained any serious injury. You do need medical attention, though. I am going to get help."

"No!"

"I need to—"

"Don't go."

"I am not going. I just need to get my phone." Fleur turned and hurried back across the dusty plain to the main road, where Agwmar still stood exactly where she'd left him. She lifted the lid on one of her panniers and pulled out an iPhone. She hit the on switch and peered hopefully at the screen. No signal. She might have guessed. She glanced back toward the crashed car. Perhaps the man had a phone. He might be on a different network. *It's worth trying.*

"My phone is dead. There is no signal so far out of the city. What about you?"

"Me?" His eyelids fluttered now, cracking open to reveal those gloriously deep blue eyes again.

"Your mobile phone. May I try with that please?"

"What? Yes... It's... It's..." He appeared confused, puzzled about something. He began patting at his jeans.

"In your pocket?" Fleur guessed. "No, keep still. Allow me." She placed her hands over his to stop his movements. "If you would just excuse me..." She closed her eyes and slid her hand into his front jeans pocket, feeling about in it for his phone. No joy, but she did find something else of interest. A solid, thick erection, growing harder by the second.

"Fucking hell, girl," the man growled at her.

Fleur was not at all sure he was complaining. And, *girl?*

"I apologize. Perhaps the other pocket..." She withdrew her hand quickly and leaned across him to investigate the other side before her courage failed her entirely. Her patient groaned but remained still while she fished his smartphone from his pocket without further undue embarrassment. Aware now of his baleful gaze fixed on her, Fleur hit the on switch and scanned the screen for some glimmer of a signal. Nothing. She shook her head in frustration.

Fleur turned to crouch beside the car, looking up at the man, who was now fully conscious and attempting to sit up. He had noticed her attempts to immobilize his head and clearly was somewhat less than appreciative of her efforts.

"What the fuck's this?"

"You might have a neck injury. Keep still, please." Her tone remained calm, professional. She'd perfected her cool, confident voice. It worked as a rule, but not this time.

"You'll be the one with a fucking neck injury. Take it off. Now."

"No, sir. It stays. And please do not swear at me — or threaten me." She tried her best stern voice, less practiced but still effective. Usually.

His beautiful azure eyes drooped closed again and he leaned his head back against the headrest. He may have groaned, though Fleur was not certain.

"I apologize. That was unforgivable of me."

"That is quite all right, sir. How does your head feel?" Back to her cool professional persona once more.

"Sore. But I'm okay. Really. And my neck's fine too."

"I expect that you are right, but the collar must stay. At least until you have been X-rayed. And for that, we need to get you to the hospital."

He pinned her with a glare again. "No collar and no hospital. I'm fine. I'll just go back to my hotel and see the doctor there."

It was clear he meant it, the idiot, misguided man. Fleur got to her feet and stood beside the car, looking down at her grumpy patient. She made one last attempt to talk some sense into him. "Your hotel will not have an X-ray facility and that is what you need right now."

"The Totally Five Star has every fucking facility known to man…"

Fleur stiffened, her gaze reproachful now. It was enough to halt the tirade.

"Sorry. No swearing, right. But no hospital. That's final."

Fleur gazed into the distance and thought it just as well that his injuries were not more severe, because regardless of his wishes on the matter, she had no idea how she was going to get him anywhere near a medical facility any time soon. No phone signal meant no ambulance. Another vehicle would come past...eventually. But there was no way of knowing how long they might have to wait and it was going to get a great deal hotter out here before much longer. She had just half a bottle of water in her pannier and she'd spotted the two empty bottles in this tourist's car boot. He might have more supplies but she would not wish to rely on that. No, waiting it out was not an option.

She could leave him here and go for help. That was probably the most prudent plan. From the best of her recollection, the nearest property was about four kilometers away. They would have a phone and probably a serviceable vehicle. She could have help back here in an hour, two at the most. Seriously considering that option, she glanced back at her patient, who had already started easing himself from the car.

"No, stay there..." She rushed back over to him and placed her hands on his shoulders, intending to push him back into his seat. She might as well have tried to shove the car back onto the road single-handedly. He just continued getting to his feet. In moments, he towered over her. At five feet four, Fleur was not especially small, but this man had at least a foot on her.

He had already begun to untie the bandage she'd used to secure his collar.

"You should..." One hard stare from those glinting blue eyes silenced her. She watched as he removed her carefully crafted handiwork. She was ready to accept that her cautious approach was not needed after all, but even so, she embarked on salvage plan B.

"Do you have more water?"

"One bottle. You?"

"Half a bottle. I will be no more than two hours.

"Two hours? What are you talking about?"

"I will go and phone for help. I will leave you all the water and as long as you stay in the car, it will be hot but you will have a little shade."

He shook his head firmly. "No need. The car's not too badly damaged. I'll change the wheel and drive it back." He crouched to study the wreckage of the ruined front tire, then he turned his attention to the buckled bumper. "Lost a headlamp, could have been worse. It's broad daylight. I'll manage."

Fleur had never heard such lunacy. *It is not happening. Definitely not.* She took advantage of the fact that he was crouching by the car to rise to her full height and glare down at him.

"Oh no you will not. You have had a serious blow to the head. You could have sustained a concussion or some other head injury—anything. You are not safe to drive. I cannot permit it."

He glared at her, incredulous. "You cannot—? I beg your pardon." He tilted his head upwards, furrowing his brow ominously.

Fleur shivered inwardly, but stiffened her shoulders. She was right about this and would stick to her guns.

"You are not in a fit and safe condition to drive your car. I cannot agree to this idea."

"No? I don't recall asking your permission. Look, miss, er... I appreciate your help and concern, genuinely. But I'll manage from here. Thank you." He turned on his heel and headed for the boot of the car.

Fleur followed, maintaining a distance of a few meters between them now. "No, sir. You must not."

He muttered something under his breath and Fleur strongly suspected his 'no swearing' promise was already in tatters. She didn't much care. She had heard worse, probably, and soon would again. She stepped forward as he straightened, pulling out the car jack. He staggered slightly.

"You really do need to sit. Please get back in your car, out of this sun. I will be back as soon as I can with help for you."

He didn't answer her. His scathing expression did his talking for him as he proceeded to the front of the car and bent to peer underneath.

"What are you doing?"

He glanced up at her sharply. "Looking for a jacking point. Care to help rather than standing there telling me what I can and can't do?"

"I am happy to help you, sir, but you are *not* driving. That is final. I will go fetch assistance. A tow truck, perhaps." She turned and headed back toward the patient donkey, now idly chewing the scraggy tufts of wiry grass poking through the hard earth as he watched them with solemn eyes.

"Please don't trouble yourself, honey. I won't be here when you get back."

The idiot man called the words at her retreating back, and Fleur curled her lips in private amusement. He would be there. He was going nowhere. She knew that, as he would soon enough, when he realized his predicament. The ignition key safely secreted in her pocket would make sure of it. She turned to face him, bowed slightly then turned away.

Perhaps it was her unruffled confidence that alerted him. Or maybe some other sixth sense made him check his dashboard. Whatever it was, his sudden shout halted her momentarily in her tracks.

"Where's the fucking key?"

Fleur started running. If she could reach Agwmar and persuade the elderly donkey to exert a little more than his customary effort, they could probably outrun this ridiculous foreigner. Then he would have to see sense. She could do the sensible thing, return with help, then he could soon be enjoying a nice lunch in the safety of his hotel. He would thank her…eventually. She hiked up her cloak and sprinted, hard.

It was no good. She knew almost instantly she had no chance of reaching the donkey before the man did. His pounding footsteps were behind her, gaining, and in seconds he seized her from behind and lifted her off her feet. He clamped an arm around her waist, the other across her chest and swung her round to face the car again.

"My key, if you please?"

Fleur was unused to being manhandled and should have been more scared than she actually was. Her reaction was more outrage than fear as she kicked, squirmed and struggled in his arms. "Let go of me. I insist. Put me down. Put me down!"

The man chuckled in her ear, holding onto her effortlessly, despite her frantic wriggling. He made no attempt to search her clothing, she noted, though he could have easily overpowered her and retrieved his key. Instead, he carried her back to the car. Once there, he turned her in his arms and bent her over the bonnet, her cloaked back against the hot metal.

"Is it burning you?"

"No, sir." Fleur shook her head, though she could have lied and said yes. He seemed concerned not to hurt her, despite the determined gleam in his eyes.

"I'll let you go. You are free to walk away whenever you like. But there's no way you're leaving here with my key. I don't want to take it from you by force, but I will if it comes to it. I normally make it a rule not to lay my hands on any woman who hasn't asked me very, very nicely, but I'm ready to make an exception with you. I *will* have my key back. Do I make myself clear, girl?"

Fleur went still, staring up into his eyes. The blue was dazzling, clear, almost turquoise. She shivered, despite the heat, and her pussy moistened. She clamped her knees together, wishing the intense feeling away. She didn't even like this obstinate foreigner, so how could he affect her in this way just by suggesting that he might lay his hands on her? Correction, he was already doing just that. He gripped her wrists, his fingers against her flesh where her wide sleeves had fallen away. He made no attempt, though, to lift them above her head, which would have spread her out under him, making her feel even more vulnerable. That seemed not to be his intent, as he allowed her to keep her hands clutched in front of her.

All in all, she had to admit, he treated her incredibly gently.

"Do I?"

"What? I do not know…" Fleur blinked up at him, confused

"Do I make myself clear?" he clarified, lowering his voice to a growl.

Fleur nodded. "Yes, sir. I understand."

"And?"

"I will return your key to you, sir."

He nodded, straightened then helped Fleur to her feet. Stepping back from her, he held his hand out to her, palm up. Waiting. Fleur slipped her hand inside her cloak and into her pocket, her fingers closing around the small key. Despite his demanding, impatient gesture, she didn't immediately pull it out to hand it over.

"I have another suggestion." She raised her eyes to his, squaring her shoulders. She was just as determined as he was to have her way, but she wasn't above compromising.

"No deals, girl. You hand the key over, or I take it from you."

Clearly, this man was not inclined to negotiate but Fleur ignored his stern, implacable tone.

"I have said I will give it to you. There is no need for threats, sir. And please, do not call me girl. My name is Fleur. Fleur Mansouri." She managed to keep her voice blessedly even, keen not to betray how intimidated she actually felt. Negotiations were better conducted from a position of strength, or at least the illusion of it.

She had perhaps succeeded, or at least given him something fresh to think about. He narrowed his eyes at her.

"Fleur? What sort of a name's that?"

She stiffened, well aware that he meant what sort of a name is Fleur for a Berber peasant. More unwarranted assumptions on his part. She was starting to become irritated by his continual inferences, though, in fairness, she had done little to clarify the situation. "It is a French name, sir. It means flower. Please feel free to use it."

He smiled and bowed his head slightly. "I know what it means. It suits you. I'm delighted to meet you, Fleur Mansouri. I'm Ethan Savage. Now, the key, please."

"I will give you your key back, Mr. Savage. And I will help you change the wheel and get your car back onto the road. Then, if it is indeed drivable as you say, I will drive you back to your hotel."

"You? You can drive?"

He couldn't have looked more astonished if Agwmar had taken to the air and she'd offered to convey him back to the Totally Five Star on a flying donkey.

Fleur managed not to smile, though she found his reaction this time both amusing and mildly annoying. Her appearance today was traditional, dressed appropriately for a long ride in the hot sun rather than for making the acquaintance of stranded foreign motorists. Even so, his assumptions regarding her abilities were beyond arrogant.

She kept her tone deliberately level. "Yes, Mr. Savage, I can. And I will drive you. Now, shall we proceed? The tire?"

He did not move initially. He stood, regarding her, obviously considering her proposal. He could still have his own way—she knew that—and he must realize it too. But it was equally obvious that he preferred not to manhandle her if it could be avoided. After all, she mused, she had not asked him very, very nicely.

Not yet.

Her solution would give them both what they wanted. He really should accept it.

It would seem he arrived at the same conclusion, because he nodded curtly. "It's Ethan. Very well, Fleur. We have a deal." He extended his hand to her again and this time, she took it. They shook briefly before he stepped past her and once more crouched in front of the car. "So, jacking point. Can you see it anywhere?"

Chapter Two

Ethan watched Fleur, his amazement growing by the minute. The small Berber woman did indeed know where to find the jacking point on a car and she proceeded to attach the jack to it. He stepped in, though, when she lifted her foot to start pumping the car off the ground.

"No, let me do that. Could you find the spare wheel, please?"

The girl — Fleur — nodded and scurried around to the boot. Her brief absence allowed Ethan, and his rampant cock, some respite. Christ, she was lovely. His first thought as he had opened his eyes after the bang on his head was that he must have died and was meeting his first angel. Then his beautiful guardian spirit had shined that fucking torch in his eyes. Christ, what was that about? She did seem to have some medical knowledge, because the collar she'd improvised was effective, if unnecessary. She'd insisted on checking his pulse and repeating her trick with the torch a couple of times since, and for now, seemed satisfied that he was not about to expire.

However, that could change if he didn't get out of this heat sometime soon.

Ethan raised the vehicle up slightly then went around to the battered wheel while it still rested on the ground. He knelt beside it and loosened each of the four wheel nuts then went back to pumping the jack.

"Tell me when the wheel's clear of the ground, Fleur."

"Yes, sir." She stationed herself beside the car to watch.

Sir. He liked the sound of that from her, though he knew she meant it merely as an appropriate term of respect for a stranger. There was sir, and there was Sir.

But alas, not with her. Ethan knew better than to mess around with local women. There was no surer way to screw up a promising international career than to outrage local sensibilities. He'd worked in enough Muslim countries over the years that he knew the score. He had no intention of compromising himself or of upsetting pretty little Fleur. Not that the girl seemed especially daunted by him, even at his sternest.

He shook his head, giving himself a mental telling off. He must stop thinking of her as *girl*. That would never do.

"It is clear now. Shall I remove the nuts?"

Ethan loved the sound of her accented English. He noticed that she never used contractions. It was sweet. And vaguely exotic. He couldn't fault her English, though, nor her French, from what little he'd heard of it. She was clearly well educated.

"Sir? Ethan? Your nuts?"

Shit! He groaned as the nuts in his jeans tightened. "What? Oh, yes. I already loosened them."

"Thank you, sir."

"It's Ethan." He was trying to rein in his natural dominance, but some habits die hard and he detected a distinct growl in his tone. She could not have missed it.

She seemed disinclined to comment, thank God. Fleur nodded and set to removing the wheel nuts. She shoved each one in her pocket, probably to keep the car key company, he mused. Ethan heaved the wheel off and carried it around to drop it into the boot before slotting the replacement onto the four screws. He held out his hand and Fleur dropped each of the nuts back into his palm, as he needed them.

"So, what about your donkey? If you insist on driving me back into Marrakesh, you can't just leave him here and I don't see him fitting in the back seat somehow."

"No, sir — Ethan."

He noticed that she added his name in response to his raised eyebrow and he couldn't help wondering how strong her urge to obey actually was. His cock twitched maddeningly.

"As soon as I locate a phone signal, I shall phone my cousin, who will come to collect him."

"What about you? How will you get home?" Ethan knew he could arrange a taxi for her, or even call on the hotel's private transport. But he was interested to know how she intended to tackle that problem.

"I will be fine, sir. Please do not concern yourself about me."

Ah, but I will. It was the least he could do. And the most.

* * * *

"Where did you learn to drive?" Ethan asked as they made their way sedately along the still empty road, heading back in the direction of Marrakesh.

He'd had his doubts—he couldn't deny that—but his enigmatic little Berber chauffeuse with the sexy French name handled the car skillfully. She'd taken her rolled-up carpet from the pannier on her donkey's back and dropped it into the boot along with the damaged wheel and his field equipment. She'd tethered the donkey to the olive tree, where he could take advantage of the shade, then she'd slithered into the driver's seat and started the engine. It had coughed a bit but then it always had. Ethan had had to wrench a stray piece of the bumper back to stop it scraping against the wheel. With that done, they'd seemed good to go. Kicking up a lot of dust, Fleur had carefully maneuvered the car back onto the road, then they'd set off.

She was cautious—he understood that. Another blowout would be disastrous, and it was just possible that he'd damaged the vehicle in the collision with the olive tree back there. Fleur had observed that the steering felt rather stiff to her, though, of course, she had not driven the car previously, so could not be certain.

Ethan was considerably less inclined to doubt her opinion than he had been even a few minutes ago. She was a bundle of surprises.

"Edinburgh," she uttered the one word, then returned her attention to the road ahead.

"What?" Ethan stared across at her from his unaccustomed position in the passenger seat. "What about Edinburgh?"

"That is where I learned to drive."

"What the fuck were you doing in Edinburgh?" Yes, full of surprises. But he didn't doubt her word.

Fleur glanced at him briefly. "I've asked you not to swear at me, sir." She faced front again. "I went to university in Edinburgh."

"And I've asked you to call me Ethan." *Though Sir would be acceptable in some circumstances.* "I'm sorry. University?" He managed not to let his growing astonishment become too obvious—he hoped. "Is that where you learned such excellent English too?"

"Thank you but no. I learned English at school, though I expect my vocabulary improved whilst I was studying in the UK."

"I see." He didn't, really. He was totally at a loss. In what world did Berber peasant women on donkeys have degrees from Russell Group universities? And speak God knows how many languages fluently? And drum up the courage to stand up to an angry Dom and manage to get their own way? Mostly. Perhaps she was right about that head injury. He fell silent, studying her profile, pondering.

She was lovely, without doubt. He'd seen that, he reflected, even before she removed her headdress at the crash site. Just her eyes, lined with that sexy kohl so popular with Eastern women, were alluring and evocative. Her eyes put him in mind of sensual nights filled with long, soft sighs, gentle and not so gentle caresses. Her eyes were dark, almost black. Would they darken further as she came?

Not that he was likely to find out. *More's the pity.* If she had a degree, she must be in her early to mid-twenties at least, and in this part of the world, that was well past marriageable age. She probably had a husband who dealt with all that stuff for her. A husband who had the right to watch her pupils dilate as she orgasmed.

"Are you married, Fleur?" *Christ, why did I just ask that? What business is it of mine?*

"No, sir. Ethan, I mean. Not anymore."

"Oh, what happened?" Too many questions. But he couldn't help himself. She fascinated him.

"My husband died. A year ago."

"I'm sorry."

"It was — difficult. He was not an easy man. And much older than I. Older even than you, Ethan." She smiled at him, a hint of mischief in her expression.

Ethan felt that she did not appear unduly distressed at the passing of her husband, but he wasn't letting that slur about his age pass.

"I'm thirty-four."

"Ah, then you have seen life, I think. You seem older. More stern perhaps."

You're right there, sweetheart.

"I have my moments. How old was your husband?"

"Youssef was fifty-one when he died."

"And how old are you?"

"I am thirty years old."

He'd thought she looked younger. "Quite an age gap, then."

"Yes. But Youssef was a good friend of my father. I knew him all my life."

"But?" Ethan really should let this drop and he knew that. He couldn't, though. He had to know."

"But it was a long time ago and it is over. Now, I am a free woman who spends her time rescuing stranded tourists."

Okay, have it your way, sweetheart. "I'm not a tourist."

Now he had the vague satisfaction of seeing her expression alter in surprise.

"Oh, so why were you out in the desert taking photographs and looking at your map?"

"It wasn't a map, it was a chart. I was working. I do geological surveys."

"I see. Why would you need to conduct a survey in the desert?"

Ethan couldn't tell her that. Client confidentiality prevented him from broadcasting James Conroy's plans for his hotel development. He shrugged and remained silent. Fleur did not press him.

As they neared the outskirts of the city, Fleur pulled up and reached for her phone, now concealed somewhere within the intriguing folds of her cloak. She dialed a number then chattered to someone in rapid Arabic, the conversation brief. She finished her call and made to shove the phone back inside her clothing. A low hum signaled the arrival of a text, so she paused to read that before slipping the phone back into her pocket.

Flashing Ethan a brief smile, she explained, "Agwmar. My donkey. He needs a lift home. I have asked my cousin to collect him. Now, we need to get back to the Totally Five Star."

"Ah, right." Ethan nodded, and she did not elaborate further. It pleased him that she cared for her animal when so many in this part of the world did not. Ethan liked animals and hated cruelty in any form. And he was starting to find that he liked Fleur a lot more than he'd imagined he might, though perhaps liked was not the right word. She enticed and tempted him. She made him consider doing things to her best left unexplored. He'd done his best not to grope her when he'd wrestled with her over his key, but couldn't help noticing how slim and light she seemed under that voluminous costume of hers.

Almost boyish in physique but totally feminine even so. Christ, he wanted her.

There, he'd admitted it. Much good would it do him. Widowed or not, she wasn't for him. She would never agree to the things he wanted to do with her. To her. It was almost certainly illegal here in any case and the last thing he needed was a confrontation with the Moroccan authorities. No, he'd thank her politely, call her a taxi from the hotel and rule a line under it there.

Fleur turned the car into the narrow entrance to the Totally Five Star underground car park as though she knew the way. "Do you have a designated parking spot, Ethan?" She glanced at him expectantly.

He told her the number and she steered the car into the correct bay. She shut off the engine and extracted the keys. She handed them to him. "Yours, sir."

"Thank you." Ethan opened his door and got out. Fleur did likewise and they regarded each other across the roof of the car.

"I need to get my carpet from your boot."

"Of course." Ethan opened it for her and passed her the roll of hand-woven matting. He peeled back a corner to examine the intricate design. "This is beautiful. Did you make it?"

"I helped. But it is my grandmother's, really. It has been sold. I still need to deliver it. I could not leave it at the roadside. She would have never forgiven me."

"I see." Ethan smiled warmly at her, though he felt slightly saddened to be parting from his enigmatic companion. "If you would come with me into the reception lounge, I'll arrange a taxi for you."

Fleur offered him a mischievous smile. "Are you in the habit of inviting women you do not know to accompany you into your hotel? Or only those whom you ask very nicely?"

Ethan couldn't help the answering grin spreading across his features. She was quite delightful—sassy, beautiful, intelligent, witty, and clearly not at all what she had originally seemed. Maybe...

"You haven't asked me nicely. Perhaps you should. You wouldn't regret it."

She regarded him for a moment, appeared to be considering his offer. "I think not, sir."

He'd expected as much, but Ethan's cock still hardened in his jeans. If she called him sir just once more...

"In that case, I'll just see to it that you have transport to—wherever you need to be."

"Thank you, Mr. Savage, but that will not be required. I am already where I need to be. Shall we go up?" She didn't wait for him to respond, simply turned and headed straight for the internal lift, as though she knew exactly where it was.

Ethan caught up with her as the lift doors opened. They stepped inside. He had questions, but refrained from firing them at her. He was fast coming to the conclusion that nothing about this 'Berber peasant' he'd met out there in the desert was as it had originally seemed.

"*Salaam a laykum,* Doctor." The smart-suited hotel employee bowed slightly as they entered the courtyard that served as the main reception area for the Totally Five Star hotel.

Ethan opened his mouth to explain that his was an academic title only. He usually went by simple Mr. Savage. But Fleur beat him to it.

"*Valaykum salaam.*" She returned the universal Muslim greeting with a polite smile, obviously conscious of her companion's astonished gaze on her back as she made her way across the courtyard to take hold of the phone discreetly secreted in an alcove. "Mr. Savage has met with an unfortunate accident. His injuries appear to be superficial but I will need to examine him to be sure. I received a text to say I was needed here. What suite number, please?"

The receptionist answered her, then glanced at Ethan, noting the swelling and bruise on his forehead for the first time. "Mr. Savage, are you in pain? Would you like to sit? Do you require an ambulance?"

Ethan waved away the other man's concerns. "I'm fine. I'll just have my room key, please"

"Of course, sir."

Despite Ethan's request, the man still looked to Fleur for confirmation that this was indeed the course he should take.

It was clear to Ethan who would have the final say, at least as far as the hotel staff were concerned. Fleur shrugged and nodded. The man slipped into the small office leading off the courtyard and returned moments later with Ethan's key card. He handed it to him. Ethan took it absently, his attention on the rapid-fire French Fleur now spoke into the desk phone. She replaced the receiver and turned to him, the very epitome of cool medical efficiency.

"I need to attend to another guest who also requires medical attention, but I just spoke to them and have established that your need is the more urgent. I would like to rule out the possibility of more serious injury. Please, come with me."

Ethan narrowed his eyes and made no move to follow her as she set off across the vast expanse of marble flooring. She turned after a few paces.

"Mr. Savage, please…"

"I don't know about you, Fleur, but I'm going to my suite."

"You need a proper examination. In my office."

Ethan bowed politely. "I hope to see you later then, *Doctor* Mansouri, but not in your office. You know where to find me." He turned and strode off in the opposite direction.

Shit! The hotel doctor. She must be, but how? And what the fuck was a bloody doctor doing out in the desert on a donkey? Ethan's head ached like a bitch, and not just owing to the impact with his windscreen, though that certainly hadn't helped. Half an hour in the scorching sun changing the wheel and sparring with his little Berber *pretend* peasant had added to his discomfort, and now he just wanted to lie down somewhere cool and dark. He needed to sleep. And think.

He let himself into his *riad*-style suite and dropped the key card into the slot inside the door to activate the electrical circuitry. The air con whirred comfortingly to life. Ethan paused to relish the sudden cool draft from above his head, tilting his chin up to let the chill wash over him. He needed a shower, fresh clothes—a beer perhaps. But first, he just wanted to turn over the morning's events in his head. He strolled across the lobby and out of the double patio doors facing him to find himself in the private, secluded courtyard. The sound of running water attracted him and he perched one hip on the edge of the raised pool in the center as he reached out to let the fountain trickle across his fingers. This reminded him of just how thirsty he was, so he went back inside to grab a bottle of cold water from one of the several drinks fridges arranged throughout the rooms allocated to him.

Back out in the courtyard, he dropped into a low outdoor seat. He propped his feet on the edge of the water feature and took a long drink. He let his gaze range around the peaceful space and, not for the first time, marveled at what his friend had managed to create here.

James' instruction to his architects had been very specific. He wanted a hotel that would transcend what was normally expected of the five-star trade. Elegance, efficiency, luxury would be taken as read. The finest standards in service and cuisine went without saying also. But the Marrakesh Totally Five Star's uniqueness was rooted in the architecture and design of the place. James had set out to meet and exceed the demands of even the most exacting guest, whilst sacrificing nothing in terms of local tradition. His hotel captured the very essence of the Moroccan lifestyle and showcased the finest local craftsmanship. Although Ethan's own expertise was far more concerned with what lay under the foundations than above the ground, he knew that this was quite simply a beautiful place.

The entire resort was designed around a central courtyard that served as a reception area. The various restaurants, souks, a massive internationally stocked library, bars, a theater, a health spa and other entertainment facilities led off from that, and all were totally enclosed within a perimeter wall. Access was closely controlled — only guests could gain entry — so peace and tranquility were guaranteed — as were privacy and anonymity, should those be required.

The guest accommodation consisted entirely of a number of *riads*, the traditional Moroccan design for private residences, each rising to two or three floors and arranged around private and absolutely secluded open-air courtyards. The design provided a cool interior space in which to relax and enjoy the Moroccan climate, shielded from the heat of the sun and from any external intrusion. Only hotel staff had access to the *riads*, so guests could rely on not being disturbed. It suited Ethan admirably.

His pounding headache began to settle and he could at last bear to contemplate further exertion. He stood and strolled back inside, heading up one flight of stairs to his bedroom, one of three in this suite. Traveling and working alone, he had no need for such spacious surroundings, but James would hear of nothing less, so Ethan left the spare rooms undisturbed. In the master bedroom, he quickly shed his sweat-soaked white T-shirt and faded jeans. He tossed them in the hotel's laundry basket to be followed by his boxer shorts and socks. He hated wearing socks in such a climate, but they were needed for his desert boots, a requirement for tramping across rough terrain.

Naked, he stepped into his adjoining wet room and jabbed the switch to set the jets off. Hot water hit him from all sides. He adjusted the temperature downward slightly before bracing his arms against the tiled wall and leaning in. The steaming water ran across his back and buttocks in warm rivulets, and for long minutes he just stood there and let it wash over him, swilling the desert dust away. At last he straightened, reached for the shampoo and quickly lathered his hair. Maybe a little on the long side, it was a rich, dark brown in color and slightly wavy. The informal cut suited his globetrotting lifestyle, requiring nothing in the way of fuss. Wash it. Comb it. Forget it. That suited him. He had other things to concentrate on.

Like strange little Moroccan doctors who masqueraded as Berber peasants. He wondered if he would see her again, but felt certain that he would. If nothing else, her sense of duty seemed to require that she examine him thoroughly to convince herself he was not about to expire. He looked forward to that.

Ethan killed the water jets and stepped naked from the wet room back into his huge sleeping area. He grabbed a bath towel from the stack in his wardrobe and wrapped it loosely around his hips, not bothering to dry himself more thoroughly. The sun would quickly accomplish that. He was soon back in the courtyard, this time collecting a bottle of the local Casablanca beer on the way.

It was perhaps ten minutes and half a bottle of beer later that he heard the discreet, understated tinkle of the doorbell. He hadn't ordered anything from room service, and the daily maid service had already been to turn down his sheets. That only left...

Ethan got to his feet and strolled to the outer door. He opened it to find the gorgeous Doctor Fleur Mansouri on his doorstep. Gone were the peasant cloak and headdress. She stood before him now, the very epitome of professional correctness. She'd caught her long dark hair back in a severe chignon, and she wore a pair of glasses. He thought those quite adorable, especially as her luminous eyes appeared even larger behind them. Her tight-fitting medical jacket buttoned right up to her throat. Beneath that, her slacks were plain black. A medical bag completed the ensemble, her stethoscope looped around her neck.

Ethan smiled pleasantly at her, leaning against his doorjamb. He did not invite her in.

"Fleur, how nice. I almost didn't recognize you."

She took in his near-enough naked form and stepped back. "I am sorry. Have I caught you at a bad time? I would be happy to return later."

"Not at all. How can I help you, Doctor Mansouri?"

"I am here to find out how you are, Mr. Savage." She kept her tone cool and polite. She was clearly not rising to his bait.

"I'm fine. And you?" He still didn't move to allow her in. She would have to ask him. Nicely.

"I need to examine you, Mr. Savage. May I come inside, please?"

Result!

"As you've asked so nicely, please do." Ethan stepped to the side and gestured her to pass him.

"If you'll excuse me a moment... Please help yourself to a drink if you'd like one." He slipped past her and up to his bedroom to drag on a pair of jeans. He was all for discomfiting attractive women, but tended to find that he had better results if he were clothed and she was not. He was entertaining no false optimism regarding the likelihood of getting beneath the good doctor's cool professional façade to the delectable body underneath, at least not at this visit. But he had to start his campaign somewhere. He zipped the jeans, dark gray denim this time, but didn't bother with the button. He grabbed a dark gray T-shirt and took that with him as he strolled back downstairs.

He found her in his courtyard, staring into the raised pool. He would have given a lot to know her thoughts in that moment as he watched her from the dimness of his lobby. Perhaps feeling his gaze on her, she turned to look directly at him.

"Would you prefer me to check you over inside? It might be a little cooler." She grabbed her bag from the paved area at her feet and started toward him.

"I don't mind. There's no need. Really. I *am* fine." He walked across the courtyard to retrieve his beer, noting her scowl of disapproval as he finished the bottle in one long swig.

"Let me be the judge of that, Mr. Savage. I am a doctor, and while you are here in the Totally Five Star, you are *my* responsibility. You really shouldn't be drinking with a head injury. And you should put that shirt on while outside. The sun is very hot."

You don't say.

Ethan shrugged. She was probably right—about the beer and the shirt—but in his dealings with beautiful women, he preferred to be the one barking out orders. Still, he let it pass, and decided that letting her do the physical she seemed so set upon might not be such an onerous chore. If nothing else, she could no doubt supply him with some pain relief for his nagging headache.

"Right. What do you need to do?" He turned to her, his smile open and, he hoped, guileless.

"I just need to check your heart, breathing, blood pressure. The usual routine. I will dress that head wound too."

He lifted his hand to probe the sore lump on his head with his fingers. "It stopped bleeding ages ago."

"Yes, I will just clean it and apply some antiseptic. If you would sit, please, either out here or inside. Your choice." All cool efficiency, she appeared unperturbed by his bare-chested male presence. Ethan quite liked that about her, marveling yet again at the transformation from when he'd first set eyes on her.

He sat on the seat alongside the water feature. "Here then. Do your worst, Doctor."

No words were exchanged as Fleur went about her checks quickly and efficiently. She listened to his breathing, his heart, pronounced his blood pressure fine, his temperature normal. Minutes later, she announced that he'd been very lucky, though she really would prefer him to be X-rayed, just to make absolutely certain. Ethan just smiled and shook his head, and she abandoned that notion finally.

"Tilt your head to the side. Let me have a proper look at this." She came up close, leaning in to examine his head wound properly. Her fingers were cool and gentle as she positioned his face to catch the light. "Does it hurt much?"

"No, not really. I have a headache, though. Do you have anything for that?"

"Yes, sir, I can leave you some analgesics. But *no alcohol* while you are taking those. You have to promise me that."

Ethan grinned, preferring the slightly pleading tone to her earlier imperiousness. "Yes, Fleur. If you say so. And it's Ethan." He wasn't that fond of alcohol in any case. It would be no real hardship. He did like to hear her asking him nicely, though. And he really didn't object to her calling him sir, but he'd rather she properly understood the significance of it.

He wasn't sure at just what point his intentions toward Fleur had shifted, but they definitely had. He wanted her. More specifically, he wanted her naked, tied to his bed and orgasming on command. He hoped that prospect would be one she could find herself drawn to, and instinctively he felt she would. Her manner, her gestures all screamed submission to him.

He wanted to test the waters, but it was too soon. And this was neither the time nor the place. She was in clinical, professional mode. Ethan could be persuasive, quite compelling when he set his mind to it, but he somehow did not see the seductive doctor coming to his room to treat his injuries, and agreeing to strip for him and suck his cock in the same visit.

And he wouldn't want her to. He liked that she took her work seriously, as he did his own.

He needed her to be off duty. Receptive. Free to respond.

"So, tell me, Doctor, how long have you been a hotel medic?"

"Not long. I'm a locum, just filling in while the permanent hotel doctor is on a sabbatical."

"Do you work here full-time?"

"There are two of us and we split the week."

"I see. When do you have some time off?"

"Not for a while. Why would you ask that, Mr. Savage? Please be assured I will be here if you need me, or my colleague will. He is very good too."

Not for what I have in mind, sweetheart.

"I don't want you to bandage me up. I want you to have dinner with me."

He was gratified by her start of surprise. He would have expected nothing else. And he was ready for her quick refusal too.

"I cannot. I am sorry."

"Cannot? Can't?" He kept his tone deliberately light. He needed her to explain, intended to push her to justify her reaction. Either she'd talk herself into agreeing to meet him, or he'd find out what he was up against. Either was good.

"No, I am afraid that is impossible. I do not socialize with hotel guests. It would be unprofessional."

"Is that all?"

"Yes. No. It is enough. I just cannot. Do not."

"Do you live here? At the hotel?"

She dabbed at his head with antiseptic-soaked cotton wool. "Yes, mostly. I have a staff apartment."

"Do Totally Five Star staff apartments include a nice space to tether your donkey then? Plenty of grass?"

"Do not be ridiculous. Agwmar is not my donkey."

Ah, now I'm getting somewhere. "Agwmar? Is that his name?"

"Yes. It means stallion in the Berber language."

Now Ethan did grin. She was really opening up. "Stallion? Sounds about right. Whose donkey is he, then?"

Fleur glanced up at him, meeting his eyes. She knew full well she was being drawn out but didn't seem to mind. He sensed no withdrawal from her.

"He belongs to my grandmother. She lives on a farm close to where I met you."

"I see." He let that lie, enjoying the silence between them for a few moments. She seemed relaxed just now and he was taking care not to push too hard or too fast. He waited to see if she might volunteer more, but when she did not after a few minutes, he ventured a little further.

"Agwmar looks like a fine beast, but I can't really imagine you were intending to come all the way here on that donkey, stallion or not…"

He caught her small smile and noted the uncomfortable effect it had on his cock. He really should have been less casual about his attire. He might live to regret not fastening that top button on his jeans. As he shifted slightly in an attempt to redistribute his swelling length, she murmured her reply.

"No. I was not on my way here. Today is my day off—or it should have been. My co-worker is ill, so I am working an extra day."

"So, where were you going when I saw you out there on the road?"

"I was delivering that carpet for my grandmother and exercising Agwmar. He's lazy and getting fat in his old age. He needs to get out more. I will drop the carpet off later."

"But you did come here. And back there in the entrance courtyard, you were expected. Another guest was ill..."

"Yes. I had a text. It arrived just after I phoned my cousin to ask him to collect Agwmar."

Ethan thought back and remembered. She *had* received a text message, though he'd assumed it was nothing significant. But if she was the doctor on call...

Enough on that, though. He had other questions, lots of them. But his main mission was to get her to agree to have dinner with him. He returned to the fray.

"So, no socializing with the guests. What about the staff?"

"Staff? I beg your pardon, Mr. Savage?"

"Ethan. Yes, staff. Do you eat with colleagues? With people who work for the hotel?"

"I... Well, yes. Sometimes."

"Would you have a meal with me if I wasn't a guest? If I was staff too?"

"But you are not." She gestured around them at the superb courtyard and beautiful *riad* suite he enjoyed. "This is not staff accommodation, Mr. Savage."

He didn't correct her use of his name, though he was starting to be of the mind to firm up his expectations of her. But first...

"Would you?"

The moment of truth—the acid test. Fleur dropped her gaze from his and crouched at his feet on the pretext of searching in her bag for some additional piece of gauze or other irrelevance. Ethan was not about to relent. He reached for her, placed his fingertips under her chin and tilted her face back up to his.

"Would you?" His voice was little more than a whisper as he leaned down to her, his lips now just inches from hers. He caught her gaze, held it. And waited.

"Yes." Her reply was faint, more a breath than spoken. But he heard it, and he knew he had her — or he would.

"I work for James Conroy. He's a friend of mine, which is why I get the star treatment. But I'm here on business for the hotel, like you. So now, Doctor Mansouri, I'll ask you again. Will you have dinner with me?"

Her eyes widened and she looked apprehensive. Rather late in the day, in Ethan's view. Much too late, in fact.

"I-I cannot. Not tonight. I am working."

Yes!

"It doesn't have to be tonight. Tomorrow, then."

She just gazed at him, not answering. But not refusing, either.

Ethan pressed his advantage. "Tomorrow, in *Le Jardin Français*. Eight o'clock. I'll book a table." He smiled. Then, on impulse, lowered his head farther and brushed his lips across hers. Not quite a kiss, but the gesture was both intimate and sensual — and sufficiently suggestive that his cock took on a life of its own. He had to end this now and make for his rooftop and the plunge pool before something extremely unfortunate happened to undermine his otherwise sterling efforts.

"Have you finished disinfecting my head?"

"I… Yes. Yes, you are fine now."

"Thank you. Until tomorrow evening, then. Can you see yourself out?" Ethan didn't wait for her to reply. He released her chin, smiled at her once more and stood. She might have spotted his erection as he rose to his feet. She was, after all, a doctor. But neither of them saw fit to remark on it as he strode away from her and back into the cool lobby to make his way up to the roof.

Chapter Three

Fleur watched Ethan Savage's retreating back and wondered what had just happened. *Did that rude Englishman just kiss me? Was that a proper kiss or just…?*

It had been a long time since anyone had not quite kissed her. In fact, Fleur could not readily recall another such instance and she was convinced that such an event would not have slipped her mind. Not if the wetness in her knickers was anything to go by. He had been affected too. She could see that. And she knew exactly where he was headed off to in such a hurry. Pity *she* couldn't just take off and sink into a cool plunge pool whenever she felt like it.

It was all right for him. He might not be a guest, but he seemed to enjoy all the privileges of one. Whereas she, she had to work. Fleur closed her eyes, lifting the glasses from her nose to press her thumb and forefinger to her eye sockets. What had she done? What had she agreed to?

Not a guest, he had said. Well, that was easily checked. A personal friend of the CEO. Less straightforward to check that claim, but it might be wise not to antagonize him, even so. That was not why she had agreed to have a meal with him, though. In truth, she was not at all sure why she had agreed. Now that he'd gone, now that his commanding, intimidating presence no longer loomed over her, she had no inkling at all what had compelled her to say yes.

Surely she couldn't want to spend time with him. He was arrogant, presumptuous, bossy, obstinate. Not at all the sort of man she liked, not the sort her family would like. Would accept.

She shook her head in irritation at herself. Her family was not going to be troubled at all by Ethan Savage, as they would never know. There was nothing *to* know. A meal with a colleague, a friend. That was all it was. Nothing more. And she might not even go.

Except she knew she would. If she did not, he would come looking for her, and that would present her with a whole lot more trouble to deal with.

Fleur repacked her medical bag and slipped from Ethan's *riad*, closing the door softly behind her. Working or not, she definitely needed a shower. *Another* shower. And fresh underwear.

* * * *

Fleur spent the rest of that day in uneventful scurrying around. She dealt with sun-induced complaints for the most part, generally advising that her patients should drink lots of bottled water and stay in the shade. Her advice was rarely heeded. She had one child with chickenpox to treat—not a serious complaint, but very uncomfortable in this heat. She prescribed a soothing lotion for the spots and asked the parents to bring the little girl back the day before they were to fly home. She would need to issue a certificate to say that the child was past the infectious stage or she might not be permitted to board an airplane.

That evening, Fleur felt torn. In good conscience, she knew she should visit Ethan Savage again. He might have a concussion. She admitted it was unlikely, but the danger would be present for up to twenty-four hours. He really should be checked at least once more overnight, preferably twice. And as she was the only medic available in the hotel today, that responsibility would fall to her. At eight thirty, she gave in to temptation, or maybe she just stopped shirking her duty. Whatever... She made her way back along the rabbit warren of internal staff corridors to reach his suite.

She pressed the doorbell and waited. No answer. She pressed again, waited again. Still nothing. She hoped that was a good sign. Perhaps he was well enough to be out and about. Or maybe he was ill, inside his suite. Perhaps he needed help. But surely, he would have called reception. She turned, took a few paces away before spinning on her heel and marching back to the door. She gave herself no further time to consider before she'd pulled her passkey from her pocket and slotted it into the door mechanism. The lock clicked and she pushed the door open.

Stepping through the entrance, she called out to him. "Mr. Savage? Ethan? It is Doctor Mansouri."

Silence. Total silence. She knew immediately that he wasn't here. She would have felt his presence, would have known if he was nearby. Even so, she took a few steps farther across the lobby. She peered into the courtyard, now bathed in the soft balmy darkness of a Moroccan evening. She listened, but the only sounds were the constant splashing of the fountain and the high-pitched hum of a million cicadas, evident everywhere, but largely unseen.

She quickly glanced into the dining area and the wide expanse of the lounge, both deserted. That just left the bedrooms. Should she? Fleur supposed that if he were ill, the most likely place to find him would be in bed. For reasons she preferred not to examine at this time, that prospect was distinctly unsettling. But she was here. She was a doctor. Her patient might need her help. She had no choice.

A quick check of all three upstairs rooms and it was obvious which bedroom he was using. That too was deserted. His rucksack, which she remembered from earlier in the day, rested on the floor, his camera and a lever arch file on the bed. The rolled-up map she'd improvised as a neck collar was there too and, on impulse, Fleur unrolled it now. It was indeed a chart of some sort and not the tourist road map she'd originally thought. That being so, Ethan Savage's claim to be an employee of some description seemed more plausible. Not that she had seriously doubted that. She trusted his word. Fleur rerolled the chart and placed it back on the bed where she had found it. He was not here. That much was clear. She could ask the hotel reception to let her know when he returned and she would look in later. She was to be on duty all night.

Fleur turned and screamed.

"Did you forget something, Doctor?" Ethan blocked the bedroom doorway as he lounged against the doorframe, watching her, dressed in smart gray trousers and a pale lemon sports shirt, obviously ready for an evening out.

How long has he been there? Fleur splayed her hand across her heart, felt the furious pounding in her chest. She sat on the bed abruptly.

"You gave me a shock," she accused him, choosing to disregard the fact that he was exactly where he had every right to be.

"And you're a day early, honey. We're having dinner tomorrow."

"I am not here to eat. I came to see you."

"Do you usually let yourself into the guest *riads* and wander around the bedrooms?"

"Of course not. I thought you might be ill."

"Do I look ill?"

In truth, he appeared to be about as healthy and robust as anyone she'd ever set eyes on. Disgustingly, disconcertingly so.

"No, you look fine."

"Thank you. So do you. And now we've got that sorted, could I offer you a drink?"

"I told you, no alcohol with the painkillers." Fleur fell back on her stern medical persona.

"Juice? Water? A coffee, perhaps?"

"Nothing, thank you. I really should go." She stood and walked purposefully toward him, expecting him to step aside and allow her to leave the bedroom. Ethan seemed to have other plans and remained exactly where he was.

"Why were you looking at my chart?"

"I was interested, that is all."

"You were checking."

"Checking what?"

"Checking that I was telling you the truth, about being here to work rather than for pleasure. Though, of course, I could always manage to combine the two."

His smile could only be described as wicked. She had to put a stop to this now.

"Do not be ridiculous, Mr. Savage. Why would I want to check on you? What interest would I have?"

"What indeed?" His grin widened.

With an angry, exasperated sigh, Fleur moved to push past him. This time Ethan did shift to one side to allow her through. The corridor was narrower than perhaps she had realized and she brushed against him, caught that wonderful, musky aroma of freshly showered, sexy male—a scent she'd not savored for some time, perhaps had never come across in quite such a potent form. Ethan Savage evoked strong sensations in her, uncomfortable, unsettling feelings, an awareness buried deep, where her pussy dampened at her merest thought of him touching her again. Of not quite kissing her again.

If she ate with him—*when* she ate with him—she knew she would not be satisfied with that. She wanted more from the wickedly smiling Ethan Savage than a five-star gourmet dinner. She wasn't yet ready to give a name to it, this yearning, though she suspected he might be able to. Something in his manner told her that he knew, that he could see and feel her longing for—for what?

"Excuse me. I should not be here." Fleur muttered her excuses and scuttled toward the stairs. Suddenly, for reasons she could not even start to fathom, she stopped. She turned to look back at him, still lounging in the bedroom doorway. He watched her, one eyebrow raised, a slight smile on his mouth.

Fleur dropped her bag to the floor, the solid clunk echoing across the room. Then she ran the few steps back to him. She reached him, placed her palms on his cheeks and raised herself on her toes to lay her lips across his. This was no almost kiss, nothing not quite about this kiss. Fleur opened her mouth, drew her tongue across the seam of his lips and pushed through the unresisting barrier to taste him. He placed his hands at her hips, then she was vaguely conscious that he had wrapped his arms around her to draw her in close as she deepened this full and proper kiss, plunging her tongue inside his mouth in a way she'd only ever really read about.

But she was actually doing it and doing it well, if Ethan's reaction was any indication. He lifted her, never breaking the kiss, and carried her back across the room to the bed. Moments later, they were on it, rolling together among the camera, lever arch file and chart. Fleur managed to end up on top—she had no idea how—but this was where she wanted to be, needed to be. Ethan's smart gray trousers did even less than his jeans had earlier to conceal and contain his solid erection. Still in her doctor's uniform, Fleur's black cotton trousers were the only barrier between her and whatever it was he could offer. She wanted her trousers gone, his too. She reached down to unfasten Ethan's pants, but he covered her hand with his, preventing her.

"No, love. You first."

Fleur frowned, baffled. "What? I do not understand. You want…"

"I do want. I do indeed want. But not yet. First, we deal with you."

She frowned, opened her mouth to argue, but he sealed it with his, flipping her onto her back. Now Ethan was the aggressor, now he took the lead, and Fleur was carried along as he deftly slipped the buttons on her medic's tunic top. He opened the front to find just a vest top underneath and her white lace bra.

"Mmm, pretty." He smiled at her, briefly glanced up to meet her startled gaze before he dipped his head to nudge the bra cup down and reveal her nipple. He flicked his tongue across it and Fleur's pussy squeezed in response. Her underwear was moist, becoming wetter all the time as he opened his mouth around her nipple, to suck, to scrape it with his teeth. The sensation was intense, almost overwhelming. Fleur cried out, her moan one of surprise mixed with joy. Ethan did not let up, releasing her other breast to subject that hard little bud to the same exquisite treatment. Fleur writhed under him, her words a confused tangle of French, English and Arabic as Ethan ramped up the pressure.

He unfastened her trousers and slid them down her legs. Fleur lifted her bottom helpfully then kicked the trousers away. All the time Ethan peeled her clothes from her body, she was conscious of what was happening, what she was doing, what Ethan was doing. She had never behaved like this before, never even contemplated doing anything like this. Not even when first married — especially not then, perhaps.

She knew with absolute certainty that this madness was rooted in the knowledge that soon he would be gone, she need never face him again. In a matter of days, all this would be a memory. And she wanted this memory more than anything. She was not stopping now.

With a few deft movements, Ethan slipped her tunic and vest from her shoulders, and unfastened her bra. In moments, all her clothing lay scattered on the floor, yet his seemed uncannily intact. When Fleur would have made a further attempt to even things up, Ethan

Ashe Barker

just chuckled and slid from her reach. He worked his way down her nude body, trailing open-mouthed kisses along her abdomen. He swore in appreciation of her waxed, naked mound, and Fleur breathed a belated sigh of relief. Not all Western men liked this particular custom. Her husband had insisted on it, and she'd realized she preferred her body this way and had opted to maintain it in the years since his death.

Ethan trailed the backs of his knuckles over the smoothness as Fleur clamped her legs together in sudden self-consciousness. Ethan dropped a brief kiss on her navel then turned his head to smile at her. Their eyes met and held.

"Open for me, honey." He uttered his command in a low, sexy tone, his voice gentle, but he expected to be obeyed.

And Fleur wanted to obey, she wanted this, wanted him to touch her. It was just—more than she'd ever done before with a man not her husband.

"Close your eyes, sweetheart, and open your legs." Ethan's tone was, if anything, even lower. But it had hardened too, the timbre of command now unmistakable.

The desire to do as she was told became irresistible. With a conscious effort, Fleur lowered her eyelids, raised her hands to lay her arms back on the pillow behind her head. And she parted her thighs.

Ethan placed his palms on her inner thighs and gently opened her legs farther. Fleur did not resist. Her breath hitched as he trailed his fingers across her inner thighs to her sensitive folds. He stroked, parted her with aching tenderness. She knew he was looking at her, could feel his gaze on her as surely as she felt his fingers. And she loved that knowledge, loved the intimacy of this moment with this virtual stranger.

His breath feathered across her clit, a riffle of air as he blew on her. She might have murmured something—or perhaps it was just a purring in her throat. She did not know, did not care. She lifted her hips, offering herself to him now as he spread her inner lips wide open with his fingers. His tongue, when he at last laid it across her clit, felt hot. Soft, yet firm at the same time. Now she did vocalize, though she had nothing coherent to say. It was just a sound of need, of longing. Of having waited far too long.

Ethan seemed to get it, seemed to know what she needed. He flicked her clit with his tongue, at the same time sinking one finger deep inside her pussy. Fleur surged her hips upward, and Ethan responded by laying his arms across her stomach, holding her still. He was not rough, just determined—and knowing. He leaned in, increasing the pressure with his clever mouth, licking her clit hard then drawing it between his lips to suck it as he had her nipples just minutes earlier. That had been heavenly. This was just divine. Sheer bliss.

Ethan withdrew his finger then drove it back in again, two fingers this time. She was tight, could feel the friction against her sensitive inner walls. Ethan seemed to know just how, just where...

Fleur gasped as he found her G-spot and rubbed. Her orgasm started to uncoil, deep within her, building, gathering strength.

"I feel, I... That's..."

Ethan increased the speed of his thrusting, finger-fucking her expertly as she writhed against his restraining arm. He increased the suction against her clit, only slightly, but Fleur let out a low moan. A scrape of his teeth, and she screamed as her release grabbed and swept her away. Fleur's entire nervous system crackled as her climax washed over her, pulsing waves of pleasure starting at her pussy and sweeping along her limbs. Her body shook under the onslaught, and Ethan spread his fingers inside her to increase the sensation and draw out her release, dragging every last shuddering tingle from her.

At last, it ended. Her body stopped pulsing, her senses reassembled. Fleur lay still as Ethan lifted his head to drop a kiss onto her stomach, his fingers still inside her, but unmoving now. Slowly, Fleur opened her eyes, stared at the ceiling above her, idly admiring the traditional Moroccan artwork decorating the room. She ought to speak, should say something. What was usual at a time like this? And what would happen next?

He would fuck her. That always came next. Foreplay, then fucking. He'd pleasured her, now it was his turn. Fleur wasn't entirely sure what *she* wanted, though, what she hoped for next. Or even whether she was entitled to object, given what he'd just done for her.

"You're tensing up again, honey. Why is that?"

Ethan's question took her by surprise. How did he know what she was feeling, hoping for? Not hoping for?

"I am not. I…"

"You think I'm going to drop my pants and fuck you now, and you're not quite sure that's what you want. Am I right?"

"I…" Speechless, Fleur had no response to that. He *was* right. He was spot on. And, incredibly, it seemed to be okay.

Ethan shifted, drew himself up to lie alongside her, leaning up on one elbow. He raked her naked form with his eyes, idly brushed her right nipple with the backs of his fingers. He glanced at the hard, pebbling nub then met her eyes.

"That's not how this is going to be. You *will* be sure. I'll make you sure, then I'll fuck you. Not now, though. Now, this, was for you. Just you. Because you needed it. That's all."

"All?" Fleur did not understand. She was mystified. Surely a man, any man, would want his due? Apparently not Ethan Savage. He lay beside her, pulled her into his arms and simply held her. And it no longer mattered that she was naked and he still fully dressed.

Long minutes passed before Fleur spoke again. "What must you think of me? I do not usually do this." She paused. "I *never* do this."

He chuckled, nuzzled her hair. "What I think is that you don't do it very often. Maybe you should."

"I cannot believe I did this. It was not planned, I never intended…"

Now Ethan laughed. "Ah, but the best plans are the ones you don't make. You just know the next step when you see it. You saw it, and you took it. Opportunism."

"But I hardly know you. I only met you today. I cannot believe this has happened between us."

"Well, I admit I wouldn't have put money on it, either, the first time I set eyes on you on that donkey. I'm glad it did, though. You know, you're even more beautiful when you come, the way your body stiffens and your breath stops for a few moments."

Fleur considered this. "You were obviously paying close attention. I am mortified."

Ethan dropped a kiss on the top of her head. "I was. Always do. And no, you're not. You're surprised, perhaps, maybe a little embarrassed. But nowhere near mortified. Get used to it, honey. I'm nowhere near finished with you yet."

"I thought—"

"I intend to provide you with many more orgasms, but we'll discuss it tomorrow. Over dinner. Now, I was just headed over to the bar. Would you care to join me?"

More orgasms? Fleur's pussy tightened at the mere mention. What was happening to her? "I cannot. I am on duty."

"If you're needed, the hotel can call you. Or we could stay here, if you like. I'd even let you get dressed, though I do prefer you naked." He trailed his fingers along her shoulder then down to her breast, gently cupping the soft mound by way of illustration.

Fleur's eyes drifted shut as he caressed her. "I want… I want…"

"I suspect you might. But not tonight. Think about it. And tell me tomorrow, over dinner, what it is that you want, lovely Fleur. Are you sure you have to leave?"

Reluctantly, she opened her eyes. She smiled at him—a genuine smile, no longer anxious, no more crippling modesty to mar this intimate moment. "Yes. I do need to, really. But—I am looking forward to tomorrow."

"Me too, sweetheart. Now, I'll help you find your clothes."

Ethan walked Fleur as far as the corridor leading to the hotel medical facility. By unspoken agreement, he didn't touch her or kiss her as they parted. She was a professional woman in an environment where she still had to battle every day to be taken seriously, and she knew he wouldn't compromise her in public. Instinctively he seemed to realize that this was important to her. His handshake was polite, impersonal. The wink, as they went their separate ways, for her eyes only.

Chapter Four

The next day was busy for Ethan. His mishap of yesterday had resulted in a delay in his project so he had time to make up. He had intended to make another field trip yesterday afternoon but had abandoned it. Instead, he'd had to sort out a new hire car and fill in countless forms for the insurance to cover the damage wrought by the little olive tree. And his head had hurt. By the evening, he was feeling more his old self again, so the visit from his sensual little Moroccan princess had been especially welcome.

Her unrestrained response to his presence had been unexpected. He'd replayed that scene in his head over and over and apart from a distinctly lustful grin or two, he had definitely not been the instigator. It had all come from her—all that pent-up passion and untapped sensuality. His cock had been hard pretty much permanently since and he knew he needed to get some relief soon. Oddly, the prospect of a quick hand job in the shower lacked its usual interest and he had no appetite at all for other women.

He suspected that, with a little effort, he could locate an establishment locally to cater to his particular preferences, but he had no real hankering for that either. An anonymous BDSM encounter with an experienced submissive would usually hold far more appeal for him, but it seemed he wanted only one female tied to his bed at the moment. And currently she was dishing out sunburn cream and dealing with cases of Moroccan tummy back at the Totally Five Star.

Ethan swore to himself as he hoisted his rucksack from the boot and set up his photographic equipment to record the landscape from a different angle. He wasn't even completely sure she would agree to what he wanted. He thought she might be amenable to a little gentle fucking—in fact, he was quietly confident about the prospect of vanilla sex. With just the slightest bit of pressure, she'd have done that yesterday. He wasn't into pressuring women, though. He required a considerable degree of enthusiasm for what he had in mind, so he was prepared to wait.

And vanilla was not a bad offer, he might still settle for that. He might have to. He'd seen the innate submission in her expression, in her demeanor, the way she lowered her eyes when under pressure, her instinctive tendency to call him sir. But she wasn't yet ready to acknowledge her desires, and he was only here for a few more days. She might need more time than that.

He was looking forward to dinner this evening. He'd have a much better idea then how the land was lying with the lovely Fleur.

By late afternoon, he'd finished for the day and had written up his notes in the cool luxury of his *riad*. The searing heat had just started to mellow into the balminess of evening, and Ethan decided to take a stroll. This was his favorite time of the day to explore the city, before the streets became crowded with evening diners and shoppers, and the souks were transformed into heaving masses of humanity. He had a couple of hours at least before he needed to shower and meet Fleur in the restaurant. Time to think, to walk, to soak up the local color. And maybe do a little shopping.

He made his way along the intricate corridors to reach the central courtyard, where he left his key card with the impeccably dressed attendant. He exited the hotel's main gate to be instantly caught up in the buzz of the city. By no means as crowded as it would be later, the tiny winding streets still bustled. Ethan loved cities like this much more than the elegance and stately architecture of some European showcases. Marrakesh was timeless, life moved at a snail's pace here, unhurried yet teeming with vibrancy. Moroccans were a hard-working, industrious people, and this ancient city had a perpetual air of frenzy about it. Always deals to be struck, wares to be made and sold, a living to be dragged kicking and screaming from the desert. The colorful, crowded souks typified that, the raucous merchants trading everything from hand-woven carpets to leatherware, to copper and gold. Always gold, and lots of it.

And no deal was easy. Every transaction had to be haggled and negotiated, from the most modest pile of beans to the richest jewelry. This was the Moroccan way of life, to barter and to trade, to arrive eventually at the final price all could feel satisfied with, however long that took. The process was as vital to the life of this city as oxygen. Ethan didn't mind bartering—he was a negotiator too, both in his professional life and in the more personal aspects of his existence. He'd negotiate limits, agree the boundaries, stretch those when he could, when it was right to, and respect them otherwise. He understood the nature of compromise, the art of persuasion. He suspected both would be tested in the near future.

He made his way to the silk souk, where glorious fabrics of every color and quality were draped over the close-packed stalls. He wanted scarves—at least four, maybe more. A blindfold and a gag could always come in useful. He hadn't entirely made up his mind yet how to approach his lovely doctor but it paid to be ready for any eventuality or opportunity. He'd never felt minded to join the Scouts as a boy—too regimented for his taste—but their credo 'Be Prepared' made sense to him. Ethan was, and always would be, prepared.

He ran his fingers over some particularly beautiful lengths of sheer silk, but discarded those. Silk could tighten, especially if it became moist. Not the best fabric to use. His interest shifted to some squares of a light cotton, still sheer, still pliable enough to tie a slender wrist to his headboard. He might take half a dozen or so...

"Good evening, Mr. Savage."

Ethan turned, to find the bearer of the wrist in question at his side. She wore Western style jeans and a long-sleeved T-shirt, but she had shrouded her head in a loose cotton shawl in deference to the local tradition.

He smiled, genuinely pleased to see her and even more delighted that she would approach and acknowledge him in public. She'd seemed much more reticent as they parted yesterday in the hotel, though on reflection, perhaps she had still been reeling from her orgasm. He suspected it might have been the first one in a while. She was not reeling now. Her smile was bright and confident, her hand outstretched in greeting. He took it, shook briefly, only then noticing the older woman at her side.

Also dressed in Western style, her companion was obviously European, though she wore the same modest head-covering common to all women in Morocco. She smiled, though her expression was one of curiosity. Fleur turned to her.

"May I introduce you to Monsieur Savage. He is a surveyor, contracted to the hotel for a short while."

The older woman smiled at him, also extending her hand.

"Ethan, this is my mother, Yvette Mansouri."

Her mother! Ethan couldn't contain his surprise, though of course he should have realized something of the sort.

"Enchanté, Monsiour. Serez-vous à Marrakech pour longtemps?"

"Mr. Savage is English, Maman. He does not speak French."

Actually, he did, pretty much, but saw no point in correcting that just now. He was studying Yvette Mansouri with undisguised interest.

"You are French, madame?"

"I am, but I have lived in Marrakesh for over thirty years. How long will you be visiting us for, monsieur?"

"Ah, not as long as that sadly. I have a few more days here before I return to London."

"I see. And are you shopping now, perhaps? Are we disturbing you?"

"Not at all. I'm delighted to meet you, Madame Mansouri."

"Yvette, please. We were just about to stop for a coffee. Would you perhaps care to join us, Mr. Savage?"

Ethan glanced to Fleur then, to gauge her reaction to this. Acknowledging him in the souk was one thing — going for a coffee with her mother quite another. She seemed relaxed at the prospect, though, smiling calmly at him. He turned back to Yvette.

"I'd be delighted."

A few minutes later, they sat at a small roadside table outside a coffee shop, tiny thimbles of strong coffee in front of them. The potent brew was not entirely to Ethan's taste, but he could manage the occasional mouthful. Any more than that and he feared he might never sleep again.

"I understand now why you have such a beautiful French name." Ethan watched Fleur across the table, taking his lead from her regarding how much of the nature of their relationship to share with her family. Not that he was particularly certain himself what that was, though Fleur seemed to be going for the 'just friends' look today. Ethan wouldn't rock the boat.

"Yes. She is named after my mother. Though her middle name is Tilleli, which is Berber in origin, after her other grandmother."

"I see. Both lovely names." His murmur was the epitome of polite. Ethan sipped his coffee, and waited.

"Indeed. We call her Lily at home, though."

Ethan smiled into his tiny cup. *Lily*. It suited her, though she would always be Fleur to him.

"What is the nature of your work here, Monsieur Savage?" Yvette inquired.

"Please, call me Ethan. Everyone does, including your daughter on occasion. When she remembers." His guileless smile belied the true nature of his barb, and it amused him to observe the slight flush creep up her face. Almost unnoticeable, but it was there. "My company does geological surveys, investigating ground conditions, that sort of thing."

"You are an engineer then, Ethan?"

"A mining engineer originally, more specialist now."

"My husband would be fascinated. He lectures in mechanical engineering at the university here in Marrakesh. If you are in our city for a few more days, perhaps you would have a meal with us? He would love to meet you."

Ethan felt rather than saw the jolt of alarm from Fleur seated to his left. He never took his eyes from Yvette as he inclined his head and smoothly accepted her invitation. "Thank you, Yvette, that's most kind. I would love to have dinner with you one evening. Perhaps you would like to come to the hotel? The restaurants there are superb."

"No, no, I wouldn't hear of that. You must come to our home, enjoy traditional Moroccan hospitality."

"There is nothing traditionally Moroccan about our family, Maman. You will give Mr. Savage an entirely false impression of our culture," Fleur interjected, perhaps a little too hastily in Ethan's view. It hadn't been his intention to rattle her, but it did seem her mother was set upon such a course, despite his own good intentions.

Ethan said nothing as Yvette regarded her daughter in silence, her shrewd gaze seeming to take in Fleur's slightly flustered appearance. The older woman nodded, apparently satisfied. "Monsieur Savage will be welcome in our home. Would the day after tomorrow suit you, Ethan?"

"Yes, that would be fine. Thank you again for your invitation. I'll look forward to it."

"Excellent. Lily will give you the address and directions to our home. And now I am afraid I must leave you. I am due at the hospital in half an hour." She turned to Fleur. "Will you be at home tonight, *ma petite*, or are you staying at the hotel again?"

"I will not be finished until maybe eleven, perhaps even later, and I am on duty again from seven in the morning, so I think I will use the staff accommodation again."

Yvette stood to leave, bending to give Fleur a brief hug and a kiss on her cheek. "Do not work too hard. Your hours are long. You should rest and you should play more. I will see you soon, *cherie*." She turned to Ethan, now also standing politely to hold out his hand to her. Yvette ignored the hand and instead kissed him lightly on each cheek. "Please try to convince Lily that there is more to life than medicine and work. I will see you in two days, Ethan."

"Indeed, Yvette. It's been a delight meeting you."

With a flurry of fluttering fingers and a swirl of her headscarf, the bubbly Frenchwoman was gone, swallowed up in the milling throng of people bustling through the souk.

Ethan sat again, picked up his tiny cup and checked the remaining contents before turning to study Fleur. She had the look of a woman desperately wishing the earth might open up and swallow her. As a geological engineer, he thought that unlikely but couldn't resist stoking the flames a little.

"Your mother is lovely. It was kind of her to invite me to your home."

"She is meddling. She means well, but should not concern herself with my relationships."

"Do you have relationships, Fleur?"

"No, of course not. I did not mean that. I simply meant…"

Ethan waited in silence for Fleur to clarify exactly what she *did* mean. No further information was forthcoming. Eventually he broke the silence.

"We do have a relationship. I think so, certainly. Your response to me last night suggests you might think so too. If you let yourself."

Fleur shook her head quickly but didn't meet his eyes. "That was an isolated incident, quite out of character for me. It will not happen again. I should apologize to you for my behavior. And I wish to thank you. For what you did."

"No thanks required, honey. It was entirely my pleasure."

"We both know that is not true. I had the pleasure and you had none. I appreciate your forbearance. Most men would have been more…insistent."

If they had not been in such a public setting, Ethan would have cupped her chin and forced her to meet his eyes. He was conscious, though, of the inappropriateness of touching her in public so instead, he simply told her what he wanted.

"Look at me, Fleur."

His tone brooked no disobedience, and got none. She lifted her gaze to his.

"You may be a widow and a doctor, but you have a lot to learn about male sexuality. There are few things more erotic for a man than a woman's orgasm, especially when he caused it. You did give me pleasure last night. I sincerely hope it *will* happen again." He paused to allow that to sink in then delivered the rest of his salvo. "When you're ready — and if, when you ask me very nicely — I'll fuck you, which will give both of us even more pleasure. Do I make myself clear, Fleur?"

She didn't answer, seemed bewildered by his words. Ethan would settle for that. The key thing was, she was not arguing with him, not protesting, not insisting he was wrong. That would do for now. In a smooth shift of gears, he changed the subject.

"I hope your mother's not ill."

"Ill? No, why would you think so?"

"She said she was due at the hospital."

"She works there. She is a pediatric consultant."

"Ah, I see." The daughter of a French doctor and a Moroccan academic, herself a medic, fluent in at least three languages. Who would have thought it? That cloak and donkey had a lot to answer for.

"I need to return to the Totally Five Star. I have some calls to make before I can shower and change for dinner. Did you say the table is booked for eight?" Fleur smiled her thanks at the waiter, who collected their empty cups, and reached for her bag intending to pay for their drinks. Ethan beat her to it, tossing a fifty-dirham note on the table. The waiter snatched it up almost before it landed. Fleur would have insisted on the change, but Ethan shook his head. The waiter took no more persuading and was gone.

"Yes, eight o'clock. Is that convenient?" Ethan's tone was smooth, faultlessly polite. Who would have thought just moments before he was offering to fuck her?

Fleur tried to ignore her seriously wet pussy as she inclined her head. "Yes, perfectly convenient. Now, I must leave."

"I'll walk back with you."

"No, I could not ask you to do that. You were shopping. We disturbed you." His company would be oddly welcome, but she knew full well he would be cutting short his visit to the souk if he were to return with her now. She was reluctant to inconvenience him.

"I was just buying some scarves. Maybe you could help me to get the best price. Then we'll go back. I can always put the table reservation back half an hour if you have work to finish."

"No, no that will not be necessary. Are the scarves a gift?"

"Yes." He offered no further explanation, and Fleur hesitated to ask. Surely he would have told her if he was married or otherwise involved. Eventually she felt she had no option, not least given his clearly stated intentions toward her.

"Who are they for?" Her voice was soft but clear. She met his eyes as she waited for his answer.

"They're for you, Fleur. One for each wrist, one for each ankle, and maybe a couple more to make life especially interesting."

She'd steeled herself to hear of a wife, or girlfriend, perhaps. She had not expected that. Speechless, she stared at Ethan as the significance of his words sank in. Surely she'd misunderstood, misheard him.

"You mean... You want to... I do not think that would be..."

Ethan interrupted her stammered response, a slight smile lifting the corners of his beautiful mouth. "Yes, I do mean that. I do want to buy several of these beautiful scarves and use them to tie you up. Then I intend to do some truly wicked things to you. With your permission, of course. We'll discuss it over dinner. But first, I'd welcome your assistance in making my purchases."

Under his gentle but determined shepherding, Fleur found herself at one of the stalls, a handful of brightly colored scarves thrust at her. She took them dumbly as Ethan leaned in to murmur in her ear.

"What should I offer for these? I want to buy all eight."

Eight scarves! What on earth could he have in mind to do with eight scarves?

"I, er, perhaps..."

"Is finest cashmere, very fine workmanship. Please, look at the exquisite stitching, sir."

The vendor broke into Fleur's reverie, bundling more scarves at her.

"Very pretty scarves for your pretty lady, yes?"

"Indeed, very pretty. I want eight. How much?"

Fleur was unsure whether he was talking about the scarves or her, not that it really mattered. No way was she going along with this madness.

"We do not need them. I am sorry." She tried to hand the bundle of vividly hued fabrics back to the stallholder. He was having none of that.

"A thousand dirhams each, sir. Very fine work." The vendor was determined. A sale like this didn't happen along every ten minutes

"That's far too much. A hundred dirhams each, and I'll take eight." With a friendly smile, Ethan entered into the spirit of the negotiation, but Fleur knew the vendor had already noted his Tag Heuer watch and expensive clothes. The price would have been trebled already. Ethan would have to bargain hard to get anywhere close to a reasonable price.

Serves him right. Sadism should not come cheap. Fleur watched dumbly as Ethan progressed the negotiation, responding equably to the stallholder's heartfelt pleas not to starve his innocent babies, not to break the heart of his wife and parents, all of whom had apparently not eaten for days and had forgotten what shoes looked like. He could accept perhaps nine hundred dirhams for each scarf.

"A hundred and fifty. And I'll take ten."

Ethan leveled his gaze at the enthusiastic salesman, and Fleur had to admire his skill at this. The stallholder seemed to recognize a worthy opponent too, and reduced his price to seven hundred dirhams.

"Two hundred, no more than that," Ethan stated his offer firmly. He made to walk away as the vendor continued to bemoan the parlous state of his nearest and dearest.

"You buy ten. I make you good price. Very cheap price. Five hundred each. No cheaper anywhere in Medina, anywhere in Marrakesh." The trader draped yet more scarves over Fleur's arms, in the apparent hope that this hard-nosed tourist might be parted from a few more dirhams.

"Two hundred and fifty each, and that's my final offer." Ethan pulled a wad of local currency from his pocket and proceeded to peel off two thousand dirhams in notes. He held the cash out to the stallholder. "Ten scarves. So I expect a further discount for buying in bulk. Two thousand for the lot. Take it or leave it."

"Ah, you are a hard man. You do not look like a Moroccan but you barter like one. You have Moroccan in your family, yes?"

"No. At least, not yet." He shot a sidelong glance at Fleur, whose knees threatened to give out entirely. Her pussy cramped and moistened at his words and she dropped her gaze quickly. It was the work of moments for the money to change hands and the ten admittedly gorgeous scarves to be wrapped and safely tucked under Ethan's arm. At two hundred dirhams each they were not so outrageously over-priced, though Fleur might have purchased the goods for less if she'd conducted the haggling in the Moroccan dialect of Arabic. Still, her companion had not done badly and seemed content. And they were exceptionally lovely scarves.

At Ethan's gesture, she fell in step beside him, strolling back through the labyrinth of souks that made up the medina. Fleur might have expected to have to give directions, but Ethan seemed to know his way, and they passed the journey more or less in silence. Fleur's head spun, whirling with images both tantalizing and utterly terrifying. She had no idea what occupied Ethan's thoughts. His expression, each time she risked a peek at him, was inscrutable.

It seemed that they reached the hotel quickly, each presenting their pass card to the attendant at the outer gateway to gain admittance. Once inside, they stopped in the huge central courtyard.

Ethan requested his key from the reception staff then turned to Fleur. "Will you meet me at the restaurant or would you prefer me to come and find you?"

"I will meet you there. At eight o'clock." She managed not to slip a 'sir' in. Only just.

"I look forward to it. We have much to discuss. Until eight o'clock then." He bowed to her, the gesture swift, curt almost. She noted he did not offer her the scarves, despite having made it clear for whom he was buying them. Fleur hugged her tummy, gave one last despairing squeeze of her aching, desperate pussy muscles, and headed for her staff apartment.

Chapter Five

What was she going to say to him? How would she explain? She had to make him understand that this was not happening. Could not happen. Even an affair was too much to contemplate, though she could have been tempted. Sorely tempted. But the wicked, unspeakable things he had in mind. Now those were quite out of the question.

Whatever Ethan's intentions for this evening, Fleur knew she would not be discussing this mad notion at dinner or anywhere else. It would not be spoken of. It was too dangerous to voice aloud. She knew that from bitter experience.

As she shampooed her hair under the shower in her staff accommodation, she allowed her thoughts to drift back to her wedding day, nearly twelve years ago now. She'd been just eighteen, only recently out of school and not sure what she might like to do with her life. Youssef had offered for her and for reasons she could hardly fathom at all now, she'd convinced herself it would be a good match. He was wealthy and he had a distinguished air to him that she had found fatally attractive. Add to that he was kind, generous, a close family friend. It had all seemed so natural, so right to her.

Yvette had been horrified at the prospect of Fleur marrying so young, her father only marginally less so. They had tried to dissuade her. They'd begged, pleaded, threatened, cajoled. They had advised her to wait, to study, to travel — not to rush into such a decision. With the impetuousness and arrogance of youth, Fleur had not listened. She had known best. She loved Youssef, or so she'd thought. And he'd loved her.

Her parents had eventually bowed to what seemed to be the inevitable and the marriage had taken place. Fleur had moved into Youssef's *riad* with him and his children from his first marriage, themselves of similar age to her. She'd expected to get on famously with them, especially his daughters Fatima and Sara. Instead, she had been met with a wall of resentment and hostility. She had been shunned by them, largely ignored even by Youssef, treated as an unwelcome outcast. But she hadn't minded. Or, rather, she had managed to put up with it. Because she had Youssef and he loved her.

Given this love, what could have been more natural than to express her deepest and most secret desires to him, invite him to help her fulfill them? What man would not want his wife, his young and beautiful wife, to submit to him in all things? Fleur had yearned to feel his firm hand, his stern touch exerting his will over hers. She had made this clear, shy about explaining exactly what she wanted from him, even though it was fairly clear in her head. So she had settled for telling him that she recognized his dominance and wanted to respond to it. That she welcomed it. Her words had been coy, but she'd gotten her meaning across. It would have been far better if she had not.

She had been wrong. Horribly, fatally and profoundly wrong about Youssef. What she had taken for dominance was no more than insecurity and swagger. Her husband had been a bully—intolerant and overbearing. He'd wanted a pretty young wife as he believed that would make him the envy of his friends and colleagues, but he had no wish at all to make her happy. He had been indifferent at best to her desires and downright hostile to those traits of hers he considered less than suitable. The first time she had tentatively suggested he might like to spank her, he had been aghast and his shock had soon grown to become outrage. He had found her desires both disgusting and unacceptable, described them—and her—as perverted and sinful. If she craved beatings, he'd happily supply them and, as a result, she might learn to behave like a proper Muslim bride.

Fleur had grown up in a family where her mother's Roman Catholic heritage and her father's Muslim culture intermingled. Her own faith, on the days she entertained any at all, straddled both. But she knew enough of Islam to be quite certain that Youssef's rage had had nothing at all to do with the teachings of the Prophet and a great deal to do with her husband's own inadequacies. He was a thug. A frightened bully, who thought he could make Fleur conform to his notion of the ideal wife by beating her almost senseless.

He had applied this solution frequently throughout all the months of their marriage, and Fleur had quickly regretted her obstinacy in not listening to her parents' advice. If she had waited she might have seen, might have realized, what sort of a man was hidden under her husband's urbane, sophisticated façade. But it was too late. Too late even to ask her parents for help, as she had chosen this course in the face of their concerted opposition. Why should they intervene now, even if they could?

By the time she had been married six months, Fleur was almost completely isolated from her old life. She never left her husband's home, never saw her friends or family. If they phoned or called at the *riad*, her husband would make some excuse or perhaps she would. She couldn't face people. She was miserable, ashamed, could see no way out. And all because she was a dirty little pervert, a whore, a woman who was somehow impure and in need of punishment to cleanse her, to make her fit to live in her husband's home, to mix with his family.

It all had ended as abruptly as it began. Her husband had left on a business trip and within an hour of his departure, Fleur had heard a commotion in the courtyard outside. There were raised voices, one of them a man. A familiar voice, calling her name.

Her father had been there. Baffled, disbelieving, Fleur had peeped from behind the blinds shielding her bedroom from the light, reluctant to greet anyone, even her father, with her face a mass of bruises, her body hunched in pain from her freshly pummeled ribs. She had seen him, tall and determined, almost glowing in the strong midday sunlight, managing to ignore the outraged shrieks of Fatima and Sara as he paced around the courtyard, throwing open blinds as he strode from room to room looking for her.

Of course, he had found her. It was the work of just seconds probably, then he was in her room, cradling her in his arms and whispering sweet, reassuring words to her, first in Arabic, then in French. His remarks for Fatima and Sara as they attempted to insist he leave had been less choice, but effective. They had rushed off to phone their father, or the police, or the imam. Said Mansouri had been unimpressed by any of their threats. He had simply lifted Fleur in his arms and carried her from her husband's home. Outside the main gate of the *riad*, he had placed her carefully in his car then driven her away.

She never returned. Back at her parents' home, her mother had treated her injuries and Fleur had taken to her bed. Days later, she'd emerged to learn that her father had 'spoken' to Youssef, who apparently had perceived no difficulty in a quick and quiet divorce. Such possessions of Fleur's as had been left behind at her husband's home had been returned to her and the matter was closed.

Her parents had urged her to return to her studies and apply to university. They'd suggested she combine study with travel, maybe attend a university abroad. At first uninterested, Fleur had allowed them to nudge her along that path, agreeing that the UK might be nice and Edinburgh a beautiful city. Paris might have been simpler. She had grandparents and other family there, but the very anonymity of Scotland appealed to Fleur. She knew no one, had no history there. She could start over, reinvent herself. That was exactly what she had done, emerging five hard, long years later as the newly qualified Doctor Mansouri.

Yvette and Said never asked Fleur what was behind her husband's violence, and if he ever tried to justify his behavior in any of his conversations with father, nothing of it ever reached Fleur. But she knew. She knew full well the consequences of airing her submissive desires and she would never fall into that trap again. Ethan Savage was attractive, without doubt a Dominant, and yes, he could make her pussy damp with just a look. But that was not good enough. Appearances could deceive and people were often not as they seemed.

His hints and thinly veiled promises were evidence of a more welcoming attitude. She suspected he would respond positively to her natural urges. His purchase of the scarves was a clear indication of the way his mind was going, the path he sought to entice her down. But she could not — simply could *not* — take that risk. He would have to return his lovely scarves to wherever he lived and tie some other woman to his bed. Fleur's interest in such antics had been well and truly scotched and she was never going there again.

On further reflection, she might sleep with him, vanilla-style. If he asked, if that was what he wanted, if he would accept it from her. She had had lovers since her divorce, admittedly in the UK, where such matters seemed simpler — not here in Morocco. Even so, they could be discreet and he would be gone in a few days in any case. She had not had a great deal of experience, but enough. And it had been good mostly, fulfilling, enjoyable — and entirely physical. No one had ever engaged her emotions and she doubted anyone ever would. No matter, she was not looking for that. She was happy as she was — independent, respected, doing a job she loved. And she was safe.

* * * *

Ethan was already at *Le Jardin Français* when Fleur arrived. She caught sight of him, lounging against the bar nursing a drink and chatting to the barkeeper. He had his back to her so she was able to observe him unnoticed for a few moments, collect herself before joining him. His hair covered his collar at the back, curling softly from the shower. As always, she could see that he was smartly dressed, his clothes informal but expensive. His short-sleeved navy sports shirt revealed arms that she already knew to be hard, firmly muscled, and lightly tanned. His coloring was paler than hers but not much so. He clearly led an outdoor existence. Despite his subsequent misadventure, she'd been struck by how at home he had looked out there in the desert, as though he found himself frequently in such rough terrain and was at ease in that environment.

He had broad shoulders, and she could just make out the ripple of muscles as he reached across the bar to pull a newspaper toward him. She watched, amused slightly, as he turned it over and went straight to the back page, the sports news. What would his interest be? Rugby? Motor racing? Cricket? Did he play any sport or was he a spectator? Or just an enthusiast? For herself, she enjoyed playing and watching tennis, and was not averse to a round of golf. Her father loved football, and Fleur entertained a passing interest in the fortunes of the local heroes, Kawkab Marrakech. If Ethan had been staying a little longer, maybe they could have watched a match together.

Except she knew that he had an entirely different idea of fun. And she needed to make her position on that perfectly clear.

Drawing in a deep breath, then another, she squared her shoulders and approached him. Perhaps he heard her. Perhaps he sensed her nearness. He turned, his smile of welcome quite dazzling.

"Fleur, right on time. I like that. I do appreciate punctuality." He took her outstretched hand and shook it briefly, gesturing to the high stool at his side. He waited until she had scrambled onto it and arranged her long cashmere skirt to cover her legs completely before he offered her a drink.

"Just water, please."

Ethan requested a carafe of iced water and two glasses before turning to regard her carefully. His expression seemed appreciative.

"You look stunning, Fleur. Cashmere suits you."

Heat flamed in her cheeks as the inference in his choice of word hung in the air between them. *What an idiot!* She had walked right into that one. Why hadn't she worn something else?

"Thank you," she murmured her reply, scanning the bar for any sign of the waiter returning with their iced water. Nothing. She had no excuse not to look at him.

His dark, warm gaze held hers and her pussy dampened instantly. So much for her resolve to set him straight. She needed to start by having a stern word with herself, get her wayward cunt under some semblance of control.

Except that is his job.

Where did that come from? Her blush intensified as her thoughts spiraled rebelliously into the danger zone.

"Are you all right, Fleur? You look a little hot. Should I ask if the air conditioning can be adjusted?"

"No, thank you. I am fine." Her tone seemed forced, even to her. The clink of glassware heralded the arrival of their water, so she had a few moments to re-gather her composure as Ethan poured her a glass and one for himself. She held her chilled glass between her palms, drawing on its welcome coolness to calm herself. Ethan seemed content to let her relax for the time being, though she knew he could have easily found ways to keep her off kilter. Happily, that did not seem to be his intention. Quite the reverse. In fact, he seemed to be at pains to put her at ease now.

"Did you finish off your duties in your clinic? You do have a clinic or some such thing here, I assume?"

"Yes, we do. And I did. Nothing very pressing today. I had plenty of time to shower and change."

"I'm glad. The results are worth it."

He ran his admiring gaze up and down her body once more, his smile soft and knowing as Fleur's pussy dampened further. She would stain the delicate fabric of her skirt if this continued for much longer. She shifted in her seat, grateful at least that the dark purple color she'd chosen to wear would help camouflage the worst effects of his scrutiny. For a while, at least.

He flicked his gaze back to meet hers again. "I understand the food here is excellent—two Michelin stars, I think."

At last, something safe to concentrate on. "Yes, the chef is much in demand. You were lucky to be able to book a table here at just a day's notice. Maybe they had a cancellation?"

"Not that they mentioned. It pays to be well in with the management, I expect. Would you like to stay in the bar for a while and order our food here, or would you prefer to go straight to our table?"

The tables were arranged in secluded booths, altogether too intimate, too private for her liking right now. Fleur needed more time in the relatively public setting of the bar to compose herself—and to think.

"Here, please. If that is all right with you, Mr. Savage."

"Quite all right. And if I want you to call me Mr. Savage, or even Sir, you can be assured I'll tell you. It's Ethan this evening. I *insist*." He eyed her, his expression hardening. The shift was subtle, indefinable almost, but it was there in his tone, a glint in his eye, a tightening around his mouth. When Ethan Savage decided to insist, he meant it.

Fleur shivered, her pussy clenching madly. Her wet knickers put her skirt in mortal danger. How did he do this? She was not even interested in — *that*. She might have been once, but not now. Never again would she venture into such perilous terrain. Even the most attractive, most likable of men could turn in an instant. She had experienced that once and was not risking it again. Ethan Savage might seem different. He might seem to bear not the slightest resemblance to her husband, but it was not worth taking the chance.

Glancing sharply at him, Fleur was torn. She knew she had no alternative but to set him straight regarding her intentions, even if that required a confrontation with him. Her head insisted that she just say what she needed to say, just tell him she was not interested, would not appreciate further barbs. Her instincts were having none of that. Every fiber of her being screamed *caution*. She might *need* to set him straight, but she *wanted* to submit.

"I apologize. I meant no offense. Ethan." She hoped her response struck the correct note of courteousness. She was going for polite — not too formal. But not familiar either. Definitely not that. This evening was going to be a trial. She needed to get it over with, eat her meal, remain calm and collected, avoid that stern air he seemed to evince effortlessly, and above all remain firm in her resolve.

She was a professional woman, mature, and she was on her home turf. She should be able to manage that.

"That's fine, then. Have you eaten here before? Is there anything on the menu you could recommend?"

"The food here is all superb. The menu is in French, though. Would you like me to translate?"

He opened the finely embossed leather folder on the bar in front of him and glanced at it. "No, that's fine. Do you like seafood, Fleur?"

"I do. They serve a very good dish with mussels, *moules au Roquefort*. It has cheese…"

"Mussels, excellent. We'll have that for a starter, then. What would you like for your main course?"

Fleur scanned the menu before her, hardly taking in any of the delights on offer. She quickly landed on one of her personal favorites, a traditional dish made from monkfish "Could I have the *Lotte a L'Imperatrice*, please?"

"Good choice. I'm going for the lobster myself. Wine?"

"Anything. You choose."

With a small nod and an almost imperceptible lift of one finger, Ethan summoned the maître d'. The man bustled over to them smiling profusely, the wine list in his hand and his immaculately pressed white linen tea towel draped across one arm

"Bonjour, monsieur, soirée, madame. Bienvenue dans Le Jardin Français. Etes-vous prêt à commander ou voulez-vous que je vous recommande nos meilleurs plats?" Fleur started to respond, intending to thank him for the kind offer that he might recommend the specialties of the restaurant, but Ethan beat her to it.

"Merci, mais non. Nous aimerions les moules, puisla lotte pour mon compagnon et moi, je suis allant avoir le homard."

Fleur stared at him as he ordered their food in more or less flawless French.

"I thought you spoke only English. In the car the other day you said…"

"I told you I was English, not that I couldn't speak or understand French. I'm not at your standard, of course, but I get by." Ethan smiled at her before turning his attention once more to the maître d', who had concluded his frantic scribbling on his order pad.

"*Nous aimerions un vin blanc bon. Que proposez-vous?*"

The waiter beamed, flicking open his wine list. Clearly in his element when asked to make suggestions, he rattled through the dizzying collection of fine white wines, all priced at amounts that Fleur privately thought might wipe out the national debt of several Third World nations. Ethan seemed unconcerned and simply asked the maître d' to bring something suitable for them with their mussels.

Left to their own devices once more, as their effusive host rushed in the direction of his beloved wine cellar, Fleur found herself again the sole focus of Ethan's attention.

"So, I've impressed you with my French, and I've demonstrated that I can deliver a decent orgasm. What else will it take?"

"I beg your pardon." Fleur splashed her water across her lap as she juggled her glass in suddenly trembling fingers.

"I want you in my *riad*, naked, on your knees. What do I need to do, or say, to get you there?"

"I… I…" Completely thrown by this sudden and direct approach, Fleur reached blindly for her glass again, her fingers fumbling over the polished mahogany of the bar. Ethan reached across and placed his hand over hers, stilling her movements.

"Pay attention to me, Fleur. Answer my question."

She wanted to set him straight. Here was her chance, the perfect opportunity. She just had to say no. He might protest. He might seek to persuade her. But eventually, he would accept her word. She just had to say it.

"You could just ask me." *What? Where did that come from?* Fleur looked up at him, met his gaze now and managed not to waver.

"I'm asking."

"Very well. I would like that. The naked part, that is. I will not kneel, though."

He lifted one eyebrow but made no comment. He had no need to. His expression said it all. His gaze conveyed his doubt and disbelief. Fleur felt compelled to make her point, to put matters beyond doubt or misunderstanding now.

"I will sleep with you. Tonight, if that is what you would like. But those other things you mentioned, the scarves, and…and…"

He raised his eyebrow further, clearly enjoying this, despite her resolve to thwart the plans he had been making for her. Fleur's face flamed, the heat creeping upwards, but she was in now, she was set on her course and determined to get her point across, however difficult he made it.

"I am not that sort of woman. Honestly. I want… I mean, I like…"

"You'd like me to fuck you but not tie you up?"

She drew a deep breath. "Yes. Exactly." *More or less.*

"And my tongue. Would you like to feel that again on your sweet, hot pussy? Are you wet now, Fleur, thinking about what I might do to you?"

Another deep breath, then, "Yes."

"Yes, what? Yes, you'd like my tongue on your pussy, or yes, you're wet."

"Mr. Savage, you are very…forthright."

"I am. And it's Ethan. I already told you that. And you're playing for time, which I won't allow. Now, which is it?"

His gaze hardened, again that oh so subtle glint, that flash of something vaguely metallic and wholly inflexible in his deep blue eyes.

Fleur abandoned any attempt at prevaricating. "Yes. To both questions."

His smile broadened and he inclined his head to her politely. "I'm so pleased. And I do want you tonight, Fleur. All night."

"I see. Very well. But not to… I mean, you won't…"

"I would never do anything to you without your agreement, your consent. You will be safe with me, Fleur. And you'll have fun."

As easy as that? No pressure? No coercion? No threats or false promises? It never occurred to Fleur to doubt his sincerity or his ability to deliver. She *would* be safe and she *would* have fun. So she *would* be spending the night in Ethan Savage's *riad*.

Chapter Six

"Now that we both know exactly where this evening is headed, you can relax and enjoy your meal." Ethan leaned in to murmur the words into Fleur's ear, amused at the bright flush still staining her face and neck. She blushed so easily. He loved it. He intended to make her blush a lot. It was a pity he wouldn't get to redden her arse too, but he accepted he couldn't win them all.

He was puzzled, though, and more than a little surprised. The signals were there, he'd not imagined those. Nor had he been mistaken. He didn't get those things wrong. Yet Fleur was adamant that she did not want to explore that aspect of her nature, determined not to lift the lid on that particular can of worms. Her inner submissive would remain untroubled, at least by him. He had no intention of trying to persuade her otherwise. In his view, a submissive needed to embrace her role freely, with enthusiasm. Reluctance, ambivalence—none of these boded well. Maybe Fleur just wasn't ready yet. Ethan envied the Dom who was to hand when she did finally acknowledge her desires.

But for now, he was blessed with a beautiful companion for dinner and the promise of delightful vanilla sex later. Not a bad outcome at all. He turned the full gleam of his dazzling charm on Fleur.

"Would you like to go to our table now?"

"Yes, that would be nice. More private. A little quieter, perhaps."

"Perhaps."

He offered her his arm as she made to hop down from the bar stool. Fleur took it with a grateful smile and dropped to the floor. She was light, he thought, and nimble. He'd already noted the delicacy of her fingers as she'd patched up his head wound. Now she seemed delicate, frail almost. Perhaps it was just as well... He dismissed that notion—he'd never inadvertently injured a submissive and he didn't imagine he'd start with Fleur Mansouri. Not that she'd give him the chance.

They strolled together across the restaurant, her hand tucked neatly in the crook of his elbow. He liked the feel of it there. A waiter followed them, their half-full carafe of water and glasses on a silver tray. At the table the waiter discreetly deposited their drinks, shook open their neatly folded linen napkins then made himself scarce.

The maître d' had followed his instructions diligently, Ethan noted. They were shown to a suitably isolated corner, dimly lit and secluded but offering a decent view of the rest of the room. Ethan ushered Fleur to the best seat. She could observe her fellow diners, but wouldn't feel unduly crowded or hemmed in. He wanted her to relax, to enjoy her evening with him as the prelude to a truly breathtaking experience later. He intended to take a lot of time and trouble over her and his instincts told him his care would pay off.

It wasn't just that he wanted her response. He liked Fleur, genuinely enjoyed being with her. She was beautiful, but funny too, amusing, intelligent, a pleasure to be with. She deserved a man who would appreciate her and he fully intended to do just that. He leaned across the table to top up her water glass, his smile open now, friendly.

"Are you comfortable? Not too warm?"

"It is perfect, thank you." She sipped her water, and he noted her hands were no longer shaking. That pleased him. Perhaps now she might satisfy his curiosity.

"Tell me about yourself, Fleur. Did you grow up here, in Marrakesh?"

Her frown was brief. She seemed surprised to be the topic of conversation, but not disinclined to share a little about herself. "Yes, mostly. We lived here in the city. My father teaches at the university, and my mother's work is here."

"Yes, Yvette said. So you went to school here?"

"At the international academy, yes."

"You must have done well at school, to be accepted to study medicine at Edinburgh."

"I suppose so. I was able to meet their entry requirements for overseas students, and I am qualified to practice in the UK. I did, for a while."

"Oh? Where?"

"I worked in the accident and emergency department at the Royal Victoria Infirmary, in Newcastle. I was there for four years, but decided to come back home for a while. I have been back in Morocco for nearly a year now."

"Do you intend to remain here? The work you do now must be very different from what you did in Newcastle. Totally Five Star clientele are a far cry from a bunch of drunken Geordies out on a Friday night binge."

"Drunken...?" She looked puzzled.

"Geordies. People from the northeast of England. It's a slang term."

"I see. Yes, the hospital could get a little chaotic at times. But most patients are quiet, perfectly sober and just glad to receive help. Guests here are exactly the same. Except for you, of course. You were very hard to help, Mr. Savage."

He noted the mock sternness in her tone, and his smile to himself was rueful. She would make a truly perfect submissive.

"I'm sorry to have disappointed you, Doctor Mansouri. But if you want me to lick that pretty little clit of yours later, I must insist you call me Ethan."

She blushed again, lowered her gaze. And muttered her apology.

Absolutely fucking perfect. "I get the impression you remain keen to have my tongue on your pussy. Are you perhaps feeling a little aroused, Doctor? Panties wet again?"

Her complexion darkened, taking on a delicate shade of something close to puce.

Ethan leaned across the table to place his palm on her burning cheek. "Very wet, I'd say. What am I going to do with you?"

"Please stop. You should not talk to me in this way. It is not—decent."

"I'm not trying for decent. Now, indecent...?

"I am a respectable woman." Her words were perfectly articulated, her expression almost haughty.

Ethan leaned back, studying her still-flushed face, though now he wondered how much of the high color was owing to mounting anger rather than embarrassment. No, on further reflection not anger, more like... He considered for a few moments, groping around in his head until he had it.

Defensiveness. That was it. *Methinks the lady doth protest too much.*

Ethan watched as Fleur retreated back into herself, her brief display of defiance evaporating before his eyes. He found he did not much care for that. He wanted her bristling, answering back. He liked sassiness in a submissive, was always drawn to the more assertive types. But with Fleur it was something more, something he couldn't easily define underlying her response to him. Something she was hiding, suppressing. And it had to do with this image she seemed to need to project, this façade of decency and respectability.

Is it a façade? He thought not. In truth, Ethan was a little in awe of Fleur—of what she'd achieved. Although hers was not a traditional Moroccan family, still it was not easy for a woman to succeed professionally here, as Fleur seemed to have done. She'd worked hard, was clearly intelligent, dedicated. Of course she was respectable, how could he not respect her? How could anyone?

"I hope that nothing I've said or done to you has created the impression that I believe otherwise. If so I apologize, that was not my intention."

She shook her head quickly, as if trying to clear it. "I know that. You would not insult me. Not when you, when you want..."

"Do you think I'm trying to sweet-talk you into bed, Fleur?"

"I… Perhaps. That is what men do."

"Why would I need to do that? You've already agreed to spend the night with me. I've promised to fuck you very nicely and to lick your clit for you, as long as you call me Ethan. Why would I need a charm offensive for that? You're a done deal, honey."

"You make it all sound so sordid."

"Not sordid. Not at all. You're a beautiful, sexy woman, and I'm looking forward to sinking my cock into your tight cunt. I think you might be looking forward to it as well. Are you?"

"No… I mean, yes, but…"

Ethan had the good sense not to interrupt. He sat still, silent, waiting for her to unravel her thoughts. It paid off.

"I am not a whore."

"I see. Did I give the impression I thought you might be? If so, I apologize unreservedly."

"Is that not what men always think? When a woman wants sex? When she demands pleasure? Even without all that, that…"

Her tone was bitter, not something he had heard from her previously.

"Even just vanilla?" Ethan prompted gently, sensing he was close to something important now, and keen for her to continue to open up. In a flash of inspiration, he continued softly. "This concerns your husband, doesn't it?"

Fleur nodded, her eyes fixed on the spotless tablecloth. Her hands in her lap, she twisted her napkin violently. Ethan made no attempt to calm her. She might not be a submissive, or she said she was not, but all his Dom instincts were on red alert. She needed to articulate this, whatever it was, and he needed to hear it. So he waited, and eventually she rewarded his patience.

"He said it was disgusting. He said *I* was disgusting." Her voice was a mere whisper now, tears streaming unchecked down her face.

From the corner of his eye, Ethan spotted the waiter approaching with a tray of food. He gestured the man and his mussels away and leaned across the table to take Fleur's hand.

"He sounds like a fucking idiot, but tell me anyway."

"I cannot."

"You can. You can tell me anything."

"Why? Why would I tell you about this? This is private."

"Because you want to tell someone, and I'm on your side. And you already agreed to fuck me, so you've nothing to lose."

Fleur peeped up at him through spiky, wet lashes. And seemed to arrive at the same conclusion. Slowly, haltingly, she told him about her disastrous marriage, those few months of violence and fear, shame and degradation as her fragile sexuality was crushed and trashed by her bully of a husband. She told of her months of self-loathing and of the years since. She'd learned to set her inappropriate urges to one side, to adopt a lifestyle that would not attract comment or criticism. She lived quietly now, discreetly, her sexuality under firm control. She intended to enjoy Ethan, would not regret their time together, but never again would she make the mistake of assuming that it was okay to be kinky.

What a waste. What a fucking crime. As he listened to Fleur's account of her marriage, Ethan knew that if the vicious bastard had still been living, he might have considered killing him. Or perhaps her late husband was to be pitied. Youssef had been offered a precious gift, something beyond price, and he couldn't fucking see it. He'd attacked it, wrecked it, trampled it into the dirt. Ruined her. No, on reflection, Ethan *would* have killed him.

It was too late now, though. The damage was done. Fleur was set on her course, hiding under her vanilla comfort blanket. Given more time together, he might have coaxed her back out from under it, but he didn't have that luxury. The best Ethan could offer her was a night of shit-hot sex.

Satisfied at last that his companion was under control again and ready to resume her meal, Ethan signaled the waiter to bring their mussels in Roquefort sauce. The food was delicious and the mini army of serving staff attentive and discreet. Always appearing out of thin air to top up a water glass, to pour wine, to clear empty plates, but never in evidence otherwise. This was the peculiar quality of the Totally Five Star. The hotel prided itself on offering absolute luxury, comfort, privacy, peaceful, quiet efficiency. The surroundings were palatial, the architecture inspired, but the true quality of the experience lay in the impeccable service offered by the highly trained staff. Exuding competence, always in just the right place, where and when needed and invisible otherwise. It was a fine art, the product of meticulous training, carefully honed over years of practice. The staff melted into the very walls of the place. They were its lifeblood.

The lovely woman sitting across the table from him was a part of all this, yet seemed separate from it too. Perfectly at home, yet set apart. There was a rare and unique quality to Fleur Mansouri. Submissive or not, she truly fascinated him. He looked forward to having her to himself later but was in no particular hurry to get her back to his *riad*. He was content for now to watch her, to listen, to enjoy.

"Tell me about your family. Do you have brothers or sisters?"

"I have both. Two older brothers and a younger sister. You will meet Yasmine when you come to our home the day after tomorrow. She is twenty-five."

"I see. Is she a doctor too?"

"No. A lawyer. Like my eldest brother, though he practices in the USA. Omar works for an organization called Amnesty International. You may have heard of them?"

Ethan nodded. "I do know of their work. They campaign on behalf of political prisoners, yes?"

"That is correct. My other brother is an electronics engineer, here in Morocco. He owns a telecoms company based in Casablanca. You would have much in common with Anas. You would like him, I believe."

"I expect I'd find all your family as fascinating as I do you. Are any of the rest of the brood given to riding donkeys in the desert?"

Fleur laughed. "I can tell this bothers you. Poor Agwmar does not fit your image of me now, just as my iPhone and the fact I could drive your car did not fit your image of me yesterday morning."

"Agwmar? Ah yes, I remember. Named after a stallion. Did he get home okay?"

"He did. My cousin collected him and he is safely back at my grandmother's farm."

Ethan entertained the notion that he would like to visit that farm himself, reacquaint himself with that noble beast and try to understand this facet of Fleur. He contemplated extending his stay in Morocco, but knew that it was not realistic. He could delay his flight for a couple of days, but no more than that. He was needed back in the UK and he had meetings the following week in Faro, then on to Seville. It was a pity, though.

Their main courses arrived, and the conversation gave way to appreciative tasting and sharing. Ethan offered Fleur a sample of his lobster, his cock solidifying nicely as she wrapped her lips around his fork. *Would she? Maybe?* He thought so.

He accepted the offer of a forkful of monkfish, not a dish he'd tried previously. It was good, so he mentally chalked it up for another time. They lingered over their meals, enjoying the delightful flavors, the efficient service, the perfectly chilled wine — and each other.

Fleur asked about Ethan's family, his business, his life in the UK. He answered her questions, told her of his childhood, growing up in an ex-mining village in south Yorkshire. Ethan only vaguely remembered the miners' strike of 1984 having been just five years old then. The miners' struggle was a doomed attempt to preserve a dying way of life. The pit had closed and his father had never worked down a mine since. Robert Savage had retrained as a warehouseman, but he'd always hated that work. His bitterness had never ebbed, divided pretty much equally between the Thatcher government, which he'd felt had decimated his life, and the handful of miners who'd broken the strike and had never never forgiven. Although the mining industry was gone forever following the strike, the life had been bred into Ethan, and he'd found his way back into it by training as a minerals engineer. He didn't dig for coal, but he dug all the same, extracting a good living from the bowels of the earth as his father and grandfather had. His father would have been proud of him, he thought, had he not died of emphysema just ten years after he'd been forced out of mining. Robert had always blamed Margaret Thatcher for his illness too, though Ethan had privately felt that was stretching a point somewhat.

Their main courses were cleared away and the dessert menu discreetly presented. Ethan convinced Fleur to share a *crème brulée* with him. They dawdled further over coffees. Ethan called for refills, still in no rush to get Fleur's clothes off. He knew, as she knew, they had all night.

Fleur regarded the handsome, charming man across the table and wondered whether perhaps she might have been mistaken. Could she have taken the chance? He knew what had happened with Youssef. He knew all about her so-called perverted habits and was apparently unconcerned. He seemed to consider her preferences perfectly acceptable. His anger at Youssef's treatment of her had been palpable, not unlike her father's reaction. She had never told Said the whole truth, but she had little doubt that he had pieced it together from what her husband had told him in a pathetic, self-serving attempt to justify his brutality. Her father's attitude toward her had been unwavering, as had her mother's. The whole family had closed ranks around her. Then, when she was healed, physically and emotionally, enough to contemplate picking up her life again, they had encouraged her to get out there.

The Mansouris were wealthy—she knew that and realized that this made a difference. But it was more than just the money and the freedom that provided. Her parents were enlightened, tolerant, forgiving.

They loved her, as they loved all their children. So it was simple to them. She had made a bad decision. She had suffered as a result, but they had picked her up, dusted her off and put her back on course again. Maybe one day she would have children of her own. She hoped she'd be half as good a parent.

But in the meantime, she was in for a night of hot and fulfilling sex of the purely recreational variety. She appreciated Ethan's laid-back approach, the fact that he didn't hurry her. She wasn't prevaricating or playing for time—in truth, she was as keen to go back to his *riad* with him as he was to have her there. But it was good to savor, to anticipate, to enjoy the company of an attractive, attentive man. Ethan made her feel special. She knew she was attractive enough, but he made her feel beautiful. It was there in his words, but also in what he didn't say, the way he looked at her, the heat that glowed in his eyes. She had long since given up worrying about the state of her wardrobe. Her skirt was surely ruined and her pussy was quite simply out of control. She needed him to take action. Her desire was getting urgent now. She was ready.

"More coffee?" He made the offer, but she was quite sure neither of them wanted to eat or drink anything else.

"No, thank you. I am finished."

"Are you ready to leave?"

"Yes." She smiled at him, a curious tingling starting in her lower abdomen as a flock of butterflies took flight. It was now. And she was ready. Excited, nervous, but ready.

Chapter Seven

Ethan dropped a healthy tip on the table as they left *Le Jardin Français*. He'd welcomed the discretion of the staff earlier, when Fleur had been struggling to get her story out, and he liked to reward good service. There was much to appreciate here at the Totally Five Star. The pair made their unhurried way through the rabbit warren of corridors leading to his private *riad*. There, Ethan unlocked the door and gestured Fleur inside. He dropped the key card in the designated slot and followed her through the foyer and out into the courtyard.

Fleur's outline was dimly lit by artfully subdued floodlighting as she leaned against the central water feature. Ethan could make out her slender figure outlined by the soft folds of her skirt, now fluttering in the late evening breeze. The warm desert wind rippled the surface of the pool where the fountain didn't reach, balmy and rich, itself almost a caress. Ethan watched as Fleur stretched, easing the kinks from her muscles after having been seated for nearly two hours. The time had flown by. He'd lost track certainly and rather thought she might have too.

Fleur turned to face him, her small hands going to the top button of her blouse. Despite the heat here and the thoroughly Westernized backdrop of the hotel, she still covered her shoulders and arms in traditional fashion. It added to her unique allure. She'd loosely captured her long hair in a claw, tendrils trailing seductively across her neck and breasts. Before she could open her button, Ethan closed the distance between them.

"Not yet, honey. I want to unwrap you myself, but let me look at you first." He framed her face with his hands, sweeping the loose wisps of dark hair back from her cheeks. Fleur tipped her head back to continue to meet his eyes, and seemed faintly surprised not to be undressing immediately. Whatever she might have anticipated, Ethan had no intention of rushing.

He lowered his head to nudge the end of her perfect little nose with his as she reached up to place her now redundant hands on his shoulders. He smiled then lightly brushed his lips across hers. He felt rather than heard her sharp intake of breath. He settled his mouth fully over hers. She parted her lips immediately and he slid his tongue between her teeth. She widened her mouth to accept him and he slanted his head to deepen the kiss. She reached higher, now tangling her fingers in his hair. He returned the compliment by releasing the clasp and letting her thick tresses fall as they would across her shoulders.

Ethan tunneled his fingers through the mass of almost black silk, musing that it reminded him of the deep Moroccan night. The perfect darkness of the desert. It suited her, and she suited him. She was perfect.

He dropped his hands to her hips and lifted her to place her bottom on the waist-high wall surrounding the fountain. Then he returned his hands to her hair to tilt her face up for his kiss again. He explored her with his tongue, tasting and teasing until she joined in, twisting her tongue playfully around his. Ethan was delighted, loved the artless response, the sense of fun as well as the heady sensuality of the kiss. He was aware of the spray from the fountain speckling the backs of his hands—it must have been wetting her clothing too, but she didn't seem to notice. Or if she did, she didn't care.

Ethan trailed his fingers across her neck, the backs of his knuckles caressing that tender spot below her ear. She shifted, tilted her head to allow him access. He replaced his fingers with his lips, trailing wet, open-mouthed kisses across her throat.

"Ethan…?"

"Mmm?" He didn't lift his head, just growling his response against her neck.

"Please be quick. I cannot wait."

"Somewhere you need to be?" He muttered the words against her ear, pulling the lobe into his mouth to suck on it.

"No. But I need this now. I need you. Quickly. I want to come. And I want you to be inside me when I do."

"I will be inside you. Eventually."

"Now. Now, *please*." Her tone held a growing note of urgency.

For a moment, Ethan considered doing this her way. He dismissed that notion quickly. She was no virgin, but he'd back his own experience against hers any day. She might think she needed quick. He knew better.

"Hush, love. Let me do this. You'll love what I have in mind for you, I promise."

"But I..."

"Honey, we agreed just vanilla but if you prefer me to tie you up and gag you, I'd be just as happy with that."

Shit, where did that come from? He had not intended to make any reference to the great elephant in the room. He'd promised himself that he would leave all that well alone. Amazingly, though, his words had the desired effect.

"That will not be necessary. I apologize."

Or did it? He wanted the playful lover, not the contrite, whipped puppy.

"No apologizing now, love. You can say anything you like to me. Do anything you like. But we go at my pace. Yes?"

He lifted his head to look into her eyes, needing to know she was all right with this, with him. He was rewarded by her slight smile.

"Yes. Yes, Ethan. Your pace."

He could think of nothing especially pertinent to say to that. So he kissed her again.

I might faint. I might just dissolve into a puddle, right here at his feet. Or I might simply trickle away into the fountain.

Fleur's head whirled with a kaleidoscope of emotions and sensations as Ethan returned to kissing her, seemingly in no rush to divest her of her now soaked knickers. She shifted in his arms, felt the warm wetness of the spray from the fountain seeping through the light silk of her blouse. The fabric clung to her skin, cooling as the water evaporated. She could not suppress a shiver.

"Cold?"

"No. Just wet."

"Ah. But you've been wet all evening." Despite the warmth of the evening, his low, sexy voice caused her to shiver as he made the intimate but accurate observation.

Her pussy clenched again, as it had been spasming almost without let-up for the last two hours. She would have to be patient since he was obviously not to be hurried. But she needed him inside her—fast.

"I know." And more to the point, she no longer felt hesitant about admitting it. Ethan desired her response. He demanded her honesty. Her arousal was his goal and he was working his way toward it with consummate skill. She was close to melting and so far, not a button out of place, not a zip lowered.

"I would like to be undressed. Please."

"Mmm, I'm beginning to think that might be nice. Please feel free." He released her from the circle of his arms and lifted her from the wall. He set her on her feet and stepped away. Just a couple of paces, enough that he could lean against an ornamental pillar and watch her. She saw him fold his arms and regard her from under his lowered eyebrows.

"I thought you said... I mean, did you not want to unwrap me?"

"I did say that. But now I find I'd like you to unwrap yourself, if you don't mind. And I'll watch you."

Oddly, she would have been less self-conscious before he had kissed her nearly senseless. Now, this was hard, more intimate somehow—more studied and deliberate. She had no doubt that he was perfectly aware of this as he lounged a few feet away, his gaze intent, unwavering.

"Problem, Fleur?"

"No. Not a problem, exactly. But I am not accustomed to doing this."

"You did it yesterday. In my bedroom. I seem to recall on that occasion you displayed a degree of enthusiasm best described as sluttish."

Fleur started to bristle, opened her mouth to protest, but Ethan's upraised finger silenced her.

"Sluttish is a good word. Sluttish is what I want from you. For you. Your modesty is natural, but inhibitions have no place here. They'll get in your way. Leave them by the fountain. With your clothes."

Long moments passed as they gazed at each other, neither looking away. At last, Fleur was the first to move, turning slowly so her back was to Ethan. She lifted her hands to her top button again, but this time she flicked it open. She continued down the front of her blouse, opening each button before slowly sliding the sheer fabric from her shoulders. The silence behind her told her that Ethan was not moving. He remained motionless, watching her across the courtyard. Resisting the urge to look back over her shoulder at him, Fleur continued with her quest. She unfastened the waistband of her long skirt and lowered the concealed zip. She hesitated for just a moment then allowed the soft material to fall to her ankles with a soft whispering sound, landing in a pool of dark purple around her feet. She stepped over and away from it and wondered if she should lose her strappy sandals at this stage too. She decided she was more comfortable barefoot. It was her preferred and natural state for the most part, so she toed them off.

Wearing only her underwear now, she wondered if she should turn to face him. She decided against it and reached behind her, intending to unclasp her bra. Her fingers fumbled with the fastening. It was awkward, especially as her hands were now shaking.

A footstep, a rustle of movement, and he covered her hands with his. "Allow me." He unhooked the bra expertly but left it to Fleur to slide the cups forward and away, freeing her breasts.

The night air provided a cool caress on her naked skin. She knew this to be a totally private place, absolutely secluded, but still she felt exposed, decadent. To strip for a man was daring enough — well, for her it was. But to do so in the open air was quite outrageous.

Even so, she was doing it, *loved* doing it. Her awareness of his attention on her body aroused her. She knew that he watched, admired, that he took his time as he explored her visually. Soon he would be touching her. She wanted that, craved it more than anything. Fleur murmured her thanks for his assistance with the bra, then hooked her thumbs in the waistband of her matching white silk panties. She drew those slowly down, past her hips, her knees, bending slightly. Then she let them go, dropping them to her ankles before stepping out. She did not bend to pick them up, preferring instead to turn to face Ethan.

He had retreated to his pillar, his arms folded across his chest. Her pupils had adjusted sufficiently to the dimmed light to be able to make out the heat of his gaze and the obvious bulge of his erection beneath the expensive Chinos. He looked less comfortable than she now felt, in fairness.

"You like what you see?" She opened her hands, inviting him to comment. She knew by his expression that he liked, but she wanted to hear him say it.

"I like. I like very much. Come here, Fleur." He continued to cup his elbow with his left hand but he raised his right hand to beckon her to him. Fleur stepped forward, unhesitating, to stand right before him.

"I thought yesterday that you were lovely. Now I see I was mistaken. You're exquisite. Breathtaking."

"I..." She wasn't quite sure what the correct and appropriate response to that might be, so fell silent again. She allowed her eyelids to drop as he drew the tip of his finger along the outer edge of her left breast, tracing the outline before brushing the backs of his fingers across her nipple. The bud puckered, tightened. He shifted his attention to her other breast, repeating the process. Fleur remained still, her shoulders back as she displayed her body to him with pride, enjoying his pleasure in her. She fully intended to enjoy him in the not too distant future.

"I intend to fuck you here, under the stars."

"Yes." He could fuck her anywhere he chose. Fleur just hoped he would not take too long over it because her knees were close to giving up the struggle to keep her upright. She was fast arriving at the conclusion that vertical was overrated.

"Don't move." He turned on his heel and marched away, back into the lounge area of the *riad* now. He re-emerged moments later with his arms full of cushions from the low sofas ranged around the suite. He dropped the pile at her feet, crouching to scatter them across the cool tiles that made up the flooring. He stood, strode back indoors, and this time came back with his arms full of pillows from the spare bedrooms.

These soon joined the scatter cushions. At last, he seemed content that all was ready. Standing again, he scooped Fleur into his arms and sank to his knees with her, leaning forward to lay her in the nest he'd fashioned. Only then did he lie alongside her and finally kiss her again.

Fleur couldn't remain still. She rolled toward Ethan, wrapping her arms and legs around him. She felt an overwhelming urge to be as close as she could get, to surround him, to hang on tightly. He rolled to his back and she was on top, the aggressor now, her lips open on his, her tongue thrusting into his mouth. He seemed content to let her force the pace, and didn't object when she tugged the hem of his shirt from the waistband of his trousers. Not even bothering to undo his buttons, she shoved her hand underneath and upwards to scrape her fingernail across his flat nipple. She was gratified by the soft hiss of pleasure, sufficiently encouraged to do it again—and again. Then she withdrew, reaching now for his trousers to flick the waistband button open. The bulge of his swollen, hard cock was throbbing against her naked thigh, the heat seeming to penetrate even through his trousers. She wanted no barriers now, wriggling off him to be able to push his Chinos down.

Ethan was ahead of her. Sitting up, he hauled his shirt, still buttoned, over his head and tossed it in the direction of the fountain. Fleur took a moment to admire the hard planes of his torso, so unlike hers, but couldn't resist watching as he shoved his trousers and boxers to his knees in one swift motion. He kicked them off, along with his shoes and in seconds, he stood as naked as she was.

His thick, long cock jutted proudly at her. Every instinct screamed at her to touch it, to wrap her fist around it. She reached for him and did just that.

Her fingers could not quite meet around the thick girth of the shaft. Fleur lay alongside Ethan, propped on one elbow, admiring the beautiful cock in her hand. She'd seen others. She was a doctor, for goodness sake. But this was different.

There was nothing even remotely clinical about what was happening here. Frowning in concentration, Fleur slid her fist up the shaft as far as the pink, shiny head. She ran the pad of her thumb over the smooth surface, spreading the moisture already gathered there right across the top. She knew the most sensitive part was at the front, just below the rim, so she paid particular attention to caress him there. His muffled "Holy fuck" confirmed that she was on the right lines as he threw his forearm across his eyes.

Managing to ignore the furious clutching of her pussy, Fleur concentrated fully on the responses she could coax from Ethan. In fairness, he was not playing hard to get. Each thrust of her closed fist along the length of his shaft earned her an appreciative groan or an occasional oath. He rewarded each pass of her thumb over the engorged, slick head of his cock with a sharp thrust of his hips. It reminded her how badly she wanted him inside her, but for now she was intent on giving him pleasure. Without thinking, acting on pure instinct, she leaned forward and placed a kiss on the moist tip. She angled her head toward him, opened her eyes wide to be able to meet his gaze. Ethan's eyes flew open and he looked directly at her.

Shall I? Should I? Ethan said nothing, but Fleur knew. She knew exactly what he wanted from her. Turning back to his cock, she drew the tip of her tongue across the head, experimenting with the sweet saltiness of the juices she lapped from him. It was a pleasant taste, she decided, sort of savory and uniquely him. She tasted him again, lapping more vigorously now. She increased the pressure, using the flat of her tongue to massage the underside of his cock. Her fingers were still wrapped tight around the shaft, and he hardened even more in her hand.

She started to pump his cock with her fist, slowly at first but gathering in speed and strength as Ethan's gasps and moans of pleasure spurred her on. She set up a rhythm, using her mouth, her lips and her tongue to concentrate on the head whilst her hand worked the shaft. She slid her other hand between his legs to caress his balls, and her efforts were further rewarded by his muttered, "Fuck, Fleur, you're good at that."

She hoped she was. She was certainly going to give it her very best shot. She continued to caress, to lick, to pump her fist. Ethan's hand lay on her head, his fingers tangled in her hair. She hesitated, half remembered, wondered if... But no, he stroked her scalp, encouraging but not forcing her forward. She relaxed, leaning over farther to take more of him. She widened her mouth around him, loving the feel of his cock against her tongue, edging toward the back of her mouth.

He writhed under her, his movements hard and fast, his breaths short. She sensed he was near and wondered if she should stop. A tightening of his hand in her hair answered that for her, and she was determined not to let up until he came in her mouth.

She did not have long to wait. Only seconds after she had resolved to swallow his semen, his cock twitched violently, his balls seemed to tighten under her palm, and the warm, salty liquid gushed across her tongue. She swallowed it fast, ready for more. There was a second spurt, less this time, then a third. Fleur continued to lap, to suck, to pump, until at last she sensed that he was fully spent.

Slowly she released her grip on him, loosening her fingers one by one. Lifting her head, she drew back from his cock and wriggled up to lie alongside him once more. His eyes remained closed but he reached for her with his hand, caressed her cheek.

"That's not what I was planning."

"Perhaps it is best not to always control everything. A surprise is nice, *n'est-ce pas?*"

He slowly raised one eyelid, then dropped it again. "Perhaps. But if you tell anyone, I'll deny we ever had this conversation."

"My lips are sealed, Mr. Savage."

"Your lips are fucking wonderful. But they won't be sealed for long. I intend to make you scream."

"If that is your intention, perhaps we should go indoors."

He chuckled, the sound sexy and low in the near silence of the night. "Perhaps we should. We don't want the staff worrying. Calling for a doctor, even. Come on."

With an agile ripple of muscles, he rolled to his feet, reaching back to pull Fleur to hers. Towing her behind him, he made for the open doors leading back into the *riad*. She followed him, silent, as he crossed the foyer, headed for the stairs to the bedrooms on the first floor.

At the top of the stairs, Ethan paused, turned to Fleur. His lip quirked, she thought he intended to speak, but instead he backed her against the wall and kissed her again. Fleur could still savor the salty tang of his semen in her mouth, so surely he could taste it too?

"Mmm, so sexy." Apparently, he could. He angled her head to dip his tongue deeper into her mouth, clearly loving the flavor as much as she had. He ran his hands through her hair, tangling them in the inky locks, holding her still. Not that she was seized by any great desire to move right at this moment. Her brief flirtation with sexual aggression was at an end. She was entirely in his hands now, both figuratively and literally.

The hard, cool plane of the wall was at her back, her shoulders pressed against it as Ethan leaned in, deepening the kiss. He adjusted his stance slightly so his hands were now braced on the wall on either side of her head and he continued to plunge his tongue between her lips. Fleur had never dreamt a kiss could be so sensual, so all consuming. Was it possible to orgasm just from a kiss? She hadn't thought so, but now, she was not so sure. Perhaps. If he didn't let up.

He did let up, and Fleur was not sure if she was relieved or disappointed. Ethan broke the kiss, but seemed disinclined to straighten and continue on to the bedroom. He leaned his forehead against hers, framing her face between his hands.

"God, you're lovely…"

"So are you, Mr. Savage." It seemed a reasonable response to Fleur, the best she could come up with at short notice, certainly. It seemed to please him.

"Why thank you. I should explain that I intend to kiss every inch of your body. No part of you will be hidden from me. Are we clear?"

"Of course." She could not resist adding, "Should we not make a start?"

"Impatient girl. You've had your turn to set the pace, so it's my show now. Is that clear too?" He rubbed his nose playfully against hers, taking the sting from his words. He need not have bothered. Fleur's pussy tightened in delighted anticipation. She would allow him to lead, naturally, since Ethan seemed to wish it and was clearly very good at this. But still she could not help wishing that he would get a move on.

As though reading her mind, he straightened and took her hand again to tug her along the short upstairs landing toward the one door that stood open.

The master bedroom.

His bedroom.

The space was every bit as perfect as she remembered, quite palatial, the utmost in traditional Moroccan opulence yet underscored with the most modern facilities available anywhere in the world. An iPod and mobile phone docking station had been built into the wall over the dressing table, air conditioning of course, top of the range coffeemaker, every variety of tea imaginable, minibar, room service offering everything from a portion of hand-cooked crisps to a four-course dinner for twelve. The fresh fruit came as standard, as did the flowers, which were changed daily. The Totally Five Star knew how to take care of its guests. And its consultants who happened to be friends of the CEO.

The bed dominated the room. She estimated it to be at least seven feet wide, floating on a small platform and lit from below. Cedar wood panels made up the floor, the cool surface broken by stepping stones of hand-made Berber carpets. These drew Fleur's expert eye as she appreciated the thousands of hours of nimble-fingered artisanship that had gone into the weaving. Each carpet was unique, each as much a statement about the woman who had created it as the location it would eventually grace.

Ethan drew her into the room but not immediately to the bed. He led her instead to the deeply upholstered window seat overlooking the courtyard where they had cavorted just minutes ago. He seated her then turned to take a bottle of chilling champagne from a cooler on a low table alongside the window. He poured them each a half glass, handing one to Fleur. She accepted it, sipping the light bubbles daintily. Ethan took his place at the other end of the seat and leaned forward to clink his glass against hers.

"It's good to have you here, Fleur."

"Yes, I know. I mean…" She shook her head, trying to get the words right. Usually her command of English was so much more sophisticated. He somehow managed to confuse her, without apparently even trying. "I mean, I am glad to be here too."

He smiled, understanding perfectly. "No second thoughts? No regrets?"

"No. Absolutely none." Over the rim of her champagne flute, she eyed the huge bed with a mounting degree of impatience. That was where she wanted to be, but her host seemed not to share her sense of urgency. With a resigned sigh, she knew that this was not to be a hurried encounter. She leaned back, noting with amused interest how little her nudity now concerned her. His too. On the contrary, she felt oddly liberated by it. She sipped her bubbles and allowed her gaze to wander around the luxurious surroundings.

On her rounds taking care of the sick and the sunburned, Fleur had seen many of the *riads* that made up the guest accommodation at the Marrakesh Totally Five Star. All were different, each one unique, but all offered the ultimate in comfort and style. Even so, she thought that this must be one of the finest suites in the hotel. Hangings of pure silk adorned the walls, bright splashes of burnt orange, vibrant reds, earthy browns perfectly complementing the natural tones of wood. The soft lighting was provided by two chandeliers, one directly above the bed, the other above the dressing table and seating area. The illumination was controlled by a remote dimmer switch. Ethan adjusted the level until he achieved what he must consider the optimum blend of practicality and intimacy. She thought he had it just right as she glanced at her companion, his eyes glimmering a deep, dark blue in the muted illumination.

"We have a candle-lit bathroom I thought might be nice later. I'm minded to experiment with the house specialty – rose petals. How does that sound to you?"

Fleur smiled mischievously, entering into the spirit of his easy seduction. She was, after all, sold. "It sounds wonderful. I do not think I have ever had a rose-petal bath before."

"No? Me neither. I'm sure I'd have remembered. Music?"

Fleur shrugged. "If you like. What do you have?"

"Everything, I should think." He stood, walked across the room to the dressing table to activate the inbuilt sound system. Moments later, the soft strains of Chopin drifted from the concealed speakers. "Okay?"

Fleur nodded and sipped her remaining champagne quietly. Waiting. Patient. She set her empty flute back on the low table and turned to Ethan.

"May I kiss you?"

He raised one eyebrow and placed his flute next to hers. Leaning back against the wall he regarded her levelly. "Trying to force the pace again, Fleur?"

"No. Yes. It is just—I want you." She hadn't intended to say that, exactly, though as soon as the words were out, she knew them to be true. She drew in a deep breath. "I want this, you, more than I ever have. Anyone else. Before." Not especially articulate, but she blamed her clumsiness on the fact that English was her second language. She could tell by his expression that he understood her perfectly, which was, after all, the main requirement in any act of communication in any language.

"I told you already, you can do anything, say anything you like."

Fleur took that to be a yes and turned to kneel on the seat, facing him. She leaned forward, placing her palms on his cheeks. She took a moment to gaze into his eyes from a distance of just a few inches before lightly brushing her lips across his. Ethan remained perfectly still, allowing her this moment. Fleur slanted her head to deepen the kiss, slipping her tongue between his lips to explore his mouth. Ethan parted his lips, his mouth softening under hers. Fleur sucked on his lower lip, drawing it into her mouth to nibble it between her teeth.

He slid his hands into her hair, sweeping it back from her face. He made no attempt to hold or take control of her, though, encouraging Fleur to shuffle closer to him. She snaked her hands around his neck and pressed her breasts against his chest as she laid her body against his, seeking contact now. Fleur broke the kiss to murmur in his ear, "Now. Oh please, now…"

He stood and scooped her from the window seat. Two strides later, he laid her across the wide expanse of the bed, the crisp cotton of the coverlet cool against her back as she settled there. Turning from her for a moment, Ethan drew a low stool up beside the bed and sat on it. Catching her gaze, he beckoned with the fingers of both hands. "Wriggle toward me, honey. And spread your legs."

Fleur knew exactly what he wanted her to do. Despite her eagerness just a few moments ago, now that he had shifted the pace, gone up a few gears, nerves took over again. Ethan's expression was intense, purposeful. His position meant that he would be looking at her, at all of her. He expected her to place herself before him, to open herself to him. And she was about to do just that.

Any remaining shreds of modesty were ruthlessly swept aside as Fleur shifted toward the edge of the bed. She brought her knees up, her feet planted at the edge closest to him. Then she let her knees fall to the sides, presenting her pussy to him. She closed her eyes—despite her determined efforts, there were still limits to her precociousness it would seem—but she had no need to look at him to know he was watching her. Admiring her, she hoped.

"God, you are so beautiful."

Yes! Fleur lay still, intensely aware of his gaze on her pussy, the lips moistening yet more under his scrutiny. She swore she could feel her clit swelling, throbbing, pulsing. But still he did not touch her. Still he looked.

"Please. I need…"

"Tell me what you like."

"I do not understand."

"Is this good?"

Despite her level of anticipation, Fleur jerked wildly as he pressed the pad of his thumb against her clit, circling it in a gentle rubbing motion. He did it just once, then stopped.

"Well, is that good, little Fleur?"

"Yes." Her voice was a fractured whisper as she stiffened, desperate for him to do it again.

He did. Twice.

"And this? Is this good too?" Now he drew the tips of both his thumbs along the length of her labia, delicately opening the inner lips to reveal the entrance to her pussy.

"Yes." Fleur was unsure how she was managing to get the words out, but sensed that he expected answers, that he would demand them.

Leaning in a little, Ethan blew on her exposed inner lips, his mouth just a fraction away. If she shifted, lifted her hips the merest fraction, he would kiss her. She wanted that, yearned to feel his mouth on her, his tongue in her.

"Tell me what you want me to do."

Fleur hesitated, searching for the words. "Lick me. Please."

"Like this?" He drew his tongue around her pussy, tracing the shape of her inner lips before moving up to her clit and flicking that.

Fleur jerked sharply, unable to suppress a small cry of pleasure. "Yes, yes, more please."

"More of this?" He lapped at her pussy again, poking his tongue inside her opening now, then returned his attention to her clit. "Or more of this?"

He flicked the sensitive bundle of nerve endings, and Fleur cried out in earnest. She recalled, dimly, that he'd promised to make her scream. He was certainly making good on that promise now.

"I'm guessing that's a yes, then." He leaned in farther, spreading her lips with his thumbs as he dipped his tongue inside her again.

Fleur lifted her hips, thrusting toward him as he speared her more deeply this time.

"Yes. Yes *Yes!*" Fleur thrashed on the bed now, desperate for more as the sensations mounted. He had hardly started and already she was on the verge of orgasm. She didn't want it all to be over so quickly, but she had no idea how to contain herself—or if she even wanted to. In moments, it was out of her hands in any case as her first climax swept her along on a shuddering wave. She let out a sharp cry, her hips gyrating wildly as she sought more friction, greater penetration.

Seemingly aware of every sensation pulsing through her, Ethan waited until her orgasm started to ebb before plunging two fingers deep into her pussy and reigniting the firestorm. Now he transferred his oral skills to her clit, scraping his teeth across it before drawing it between his lips. He sucked, just slightly at first, gradually increasing the pressure as Fleur tensed under his onslaught. Moments after her first orgasm, she knew she was about to come again. Not over then, not by a long way.

The second climax was, if anything, more powerful than her first. Fleur's entire body seemed caught up in it as the intense waves of pleasure washed through her, right out to her fingertips. She was sure her entire nervous system was alive, vibrating, her pussy clenching strongly around his fingers as he slid a third digit inside her to join the first two.

He drew out the pleasure for her, slowing his thrusts as he finger-fucked her, angling his hand to find her G-spot and caressing it with every stroke. Fleur was dimly aware of what he was doing, her medical training having provided her with a vocabulary of sorts to describe what was happening. But none of her experience to date had come close to this, the sensual honesty of what had been merely words before. Now the feeling was real, authentic, and happening to *her*. Here and now. Relentless, beautiful, intense, her whole being centered on that spot where his fingers and tongue were stroking and penetrating her.

He shifted again, changing the angle of his hand to place the pad of one thumb over the entrance to her anus. He didn't seek to enter, though she knew he could, knew he might later. For now, he was just— there. And she found the very suggestion so erotic, so sensual that her third orgasm was upon her moments later. Sweeter now, less hurried, less the frenzied clenching and more the relaxed flexing of her inner muscles as she welcomed his plunging fingers. She quivered around him, her cries now subsiding to low moans as the pleasure grew, swelled and overflowed again.

When she was still once more, her breathing returning to normal, Ethan slid his fingers from her body. He stood and reached for something. She heard the snap of foil and wondered if she should tell him she was on the pill. Not that that would matter, he would still use the condom, she knew that. A seasoned and regular traveler, he would never dream of doing otherwise and that realization saddened her momentarily. Was she one of many women he fucked whilst on his travels? She must be. Good sense told her that. She might not be as experienced as he was but that did not make her naive. And neither was she—any longer—the silly, idealistic girl who believed in happily ever after. Ethan's very experience and sophistication drew her to him and she was glad of them.

But even so...

"You okay, honey?"

Fleur opened her eyes to find Ethan watching her, his expression one of concern.

"Of course."

"You looked...troubled. I'm praying to any god that might be listening that you haven't changed your mind."

"I have not." Seized with sudden dread, she blurted out her next words, "Have you? Please, I never meant to..."

"Hush, love, we're fine. You're fine. Tell me, though, how long has it been since you've done this?"

Despite his assurances, panic rose in Fleur. Something was wrong. Why did he not just slide his cock into her? He was ready enough, his erection hard, solid. She could see that, could feel him at her entrance, nudging, positioned. Poised.

"Not long. Not really. Why do you ask?"

"You're tight. I don't want to hurt you."

"I am not a virgin. I was married."

"Is this the first time since your marriage?"

That would make it over ten years. She could do the sums and knew he would too. "No. There were others. While I was in Scotland."

"Others?"

"A couple. Not many, I accept. It was seven years ago. I have been busy, always working. No time for relationships."

He smiled. "I'm glad you managed to slot me into your schedule, sweetheart. Right then. We go slow and you tell me if I hurt you, yes?"

She just nodded, then gasped as he slid his cock into her. Just the head at first, pausing for her pussy to open and settle around him. His gaze never left hers, his eyes daring her to look away. She knew she would not dare to, her eyes locked on his unwavering stare. Instinctively she knew he was reading her response in her eyes, would know if he hurt her before she had a chance to tell him. She appreciated the sense of well-being this gave her. She felt cherished, treasured, utterly safe.

He pressed farther, another inch, another then another. It was tight, not comfortable, but slightly unnerving. He stopped, and she knew her eyes had shown her uncertainty. Not distress—he was being achingly gentle and Fleur knew this would be wonderful. Once her body accepted him, as it surely would. He lifted one eyebrow, silently asking the question 'Shall I continue?'

Fleur nodded.

He drove forward again, so slowly, so controlled, her pussy stretching to allow him entry. Her eyes never left his, and he studied her response as though looking into her soul. She felt totally connected to him, and not just in the physical sense, though that was now complete too, as he finally sank fully into her and went still. He leaned down to brush his lips across hers, his fingers in her hair as he trailed kisses along her jaw and around to her neck. He nuzzled her ear, nibbling on the lobe in a way she was coming to adore. He made no attempt to move, to thrust. He would wait. She knew he would wait until she signaled she was ready.

And she was ready. Now. She squeezed her inner walls around him, glorying in the sense of fullness, the solid length of him embedded deep in her, right to the hilt. He felt it, took his cue from her. Fleur gasped as he drew back and slowly, evenly sank his cock back into her. It was wonderful and quite sublime. She clenched her muscles around him, more sharply this time, and brought her legs up to hook her ankles together behind his back.

Ethan took his weight on his elbows and his knees, drew back and plunged. The thrust was hard, sharp. Fleur moaned and clung on, her pussy and legs tightening.

"You still doing okay?"

"Yes. Oh, yes. Please do not stop."

"Christ, girl..." His tone was low, guttural, almost a growl.

Fleur was fleetingly aware that his control was shattering, at last, then he set up a hard, fast rhythm and she stopped thinking at all. He managed to somehow angle his thrusts to lay the friction across her G-spot with every stroke, caressing her inner walls with a steady, punishing regularity that Fleur found quite breathtaking. She gripped his shoulders, digging her fingers into his flesh as she hung on, craving now, urging him to move faster, to fuck her harder.

"Please, I want... I need..."

Ethan paused only long enough to reach for her knees and pull them around, lifting her and placing her ankles against his shoulders now. This position allowed him even greater penetration, and Fleur was sure she could feel the head of his cock against her cervix with each long, hard stroke. She closed her eyes, her head flung back against the pillows, and let out a long, keening cry as she came. Her pussy flooded with wetness, spasming hard and gripping him like a fist. She could feel his solid width deep within, her anchor in a world suddenly gone dizzy and chaotic. He continued the onslaught as her cunt quivered and convulsed around him. All the while, he murmured encouragement to her.

"Come for me, sweetheart. Let me have it, all of it."

Yes, yes, all of it. Nothing held back. Fleur was utterly relaxed, totally his as the last waves of pleasure washed through her and finally dissipated. She was dimly aware that he'd driven his cock deep one last time, was holding still now while he twitched violently inside her. She was not sure, but thought she felt the moment his semen filled the condom, believed she could detect the warmth of the thick and delicious liquid inside her, evidence of a job well done.

Chapter Eight

"You still conscious?" Ethan nuzzled Fleur's hair from behind as he pulled her warm body to him, tucking her delectable little bum against his softening cock as they lay together on the bed, their panting now settled to a steady gasp or two. His arms encircled her, one hand on her breast. He could feel her heartbeat, the frantic pounding also steadying and slowing as her body came down from the high he'd driven her to. He felt oddly proud of himself.

"I believe I am."

"Ah, well that makes at least one of us, then." He pulled her closer, loving the scent of her. There was really nothing on the earth that smelled quite as heavenly as a just-fucked woman. And the lovely doctor Mansouri was one very well-fucked woman, even if he did say so himself. Christ, when had he ever had better? If he had, he couldn't recall it now. She'd been tight, which was always good, but her body fitted his like a glove. He'd known instinctively that this was not a regular occurrence for her, but still...

Seven years. And how did he get so lucky that she'd decided to break her famine with him?

Whatever, Ethan wasn't about to question his good luck. Vanilla sex this might be, but hell, he'd settle for that. She was exquisite, whatever her preferences. He also knew that, in time, if she ever plucked up the courage to explore that side of her nature, she could be a wonderful submissive. Fleur was responsive, courageous, determined to please and to be pleased. Add to that she was clever—always a massive turn-on for him—and she was so beautiful it actually winded him to look at her. How she hadn't been snapped up by some government official or bank executive—or even another doctor—was beyond him. She was a prize. And for this night at least, she was his.

"Are you tired?"

"Maybe. A little."

"Sore?" He'd been careful, he knew, but even so he had to ask. Seven years was a long time.

"No, sir. Not sore."

Sir? He started, but let that go, envying the man who might eventually demand such respectful surrender from her.

"You're staying the night. Here."

"Of course. If you want me to."

"Shit, don't you even think about going anywhere. I'm nowhere near done with you yet."

She rolled in his arms, turning to face him. "There is more? I thought... Are you not spent?"

Ethan chuckled, dropping his gaze to study her breasts. So far this evening they had been sorely neglected. He really should put that right before too much longer. "Spent? Not hardly. And I know you aren't."

"How do you know that? I feel—satisfied."

He noted the slightest hint of indignation in her voice and smiled to himself. Married she may have been, she may have even had a lover or two in the UK, but she had much to learn. Her education could start here. He itched to tie her wrists to the bed to commence her instruction in the noble art of serious fucking, but knew that would be a step too far. And in any case, she wasn't going anywhere. A little obedience training, though, might not go amiss.

"Kneel up, Fleur." His tone was low, still sensual, but hardening slightly. He was unable to do other as he issued his commands. He watched her eyes widen, her pupils dilate slightly. Wordlessly she scrambled up onto her knees.

"Lean forward and place your nipple between my lips. The right one first."

He held his breath, waited. Would she obey him? Fleur reached for him, her small palms on the sides of his head as she shuffled closer, leaning forward to position her right breast close to his waiting mouth. Just an inch or two separated them.

"Use your hand to guide it into place. Move forward a little more, all the way. Now, please."

Fleur did as she was told, cupping her breast with her right hand and leaning in to offer the swollen pink tip to him. His lips parted and she placed her nipple between them, gasping slightly as he tightened his mouth around it.

Fleur continued to hold her breast in place, but other than that, the show was now all his. Ethan scraped his teeth over the taut peak, flicked at it with his tongue before hollowing his cheeks to suck on it. He increased the pressure, her fingers tightening in his hair. He knew that with just a slight adjustment, he could close his teeth around the hard, pebbling nub fractionally more, and she would be hurting, hovering already on that thin line between pleasure and pain. He was tempted, but knew he wouldn't push her. She'd made her feelings known, and he would respect that totally.

But still, shit.

He released her nipple and glanced up into Fleur's face. Her eyes were closed, her expression one of pure sensuality.

"Now the other. Just the same please."

Without further prompting, Fleur released her right breast, and placed that hand on his shoulder to steady herself. She used her left hand to cup her breast, leaning toward him. He opened his mouth and she placed her nipple between his lips. She looked down, her attention focused on her breast and her task until she had it perfectly placed, then she flicked her gaze up to meet his. He watched her eyes darken as he sucked, her mouth open in a little 'O' as he nibbled, as he drew his teeth over the sensitive, swollen tip. It would be so easy to make her squeal, and in his heart, he believed she'd thank him for it. But not here, not now. Not today and not him.

He used the flat of his tongue under her nipple to press up against it, lifting the hard little nub against the roof of his mouth as he opened wider, taking more of her breast inside. Her eyelids fluttered down as she tipped her head backwards, gripping his shoulders with both her hands now. He wondered if he might be able to bring her to orgasm just through this alone. He suspected he might, but wanted to force the pace a little.

Fleur had subconsciously spread her knees apart as she'd maneuvered into position, settling herself for balance. Ethan slid his hand down to take her clit between his fingers. He tugged slightly, rolling it between his fingers and thumb. She jerked violently, but he felt the wetness spurt against his hand. God, she was so responsive. Where had she been hiding all this? How had she managed not to have half the males in Marrakesh panting at her feet?

He rubbed her clit, rewarded by the subtle gyrating of her hips as she sought more friction. He gave it, knowing exactly what would work, what would feel best for her. Watching her face, witnessing the myriad of expressions flitting across her features, he knew when she was approaching orgasm again. He brought her there, led her delicately and sensually right to the very edge of the cliff. Then he stopped.

Fleur gave a little mewl of disappointment, of protest, but Ethan allowed her no time to formulate the complaint.

"Turn around and lean forward. Lift your bum up for me."

If it occurred to her to hesitate, to ask why, she gave no sign of it. Obediently she shifted, leaning forward onto all fours as Ethan moved to kneel behind her.

"Spread your legs as wide as you can." He couldn't resist laying his palm over her tight buttock, caressing the smooth skin there. Her coloring was that of a rich latte, a beautifully even tone all over. He felt deeply privileged to be able to see her, all of her, to touch and savor. She shivered as he slid his hand down the furrow between her buttocks, tracing a leisurely path to her arse where he halted. He waited, half expecting some protest even now. He would have respected that. None came. Instead, Fleur wriggled her bottom under his hand, the urgent invitation unmistakable.

Never one to keep a lady waiting — well, not unduly — Ethan brought his other hand into the action. He grabbed a second condom and sheathed himself quickly, then positioned his cock at her entrance. He slid home, driving into her pussy deep and fast. He didn't set up a thrusting rhythm immediately, though, preferring to remain still, his cock buried in her to the hilt, while he reached around to rub her clit. She'd been close to climax before, so it didn't take long. A couple of deft strokes, and he felt her cunt contract around him, gripping hard, the waves of pleasure rippling through her inner walls and caressing his cock. Christ, he fucking loved that sensation. Did women know they did that? Some, perhaps. This one, undoubtedly not.

As Fleur's orgasm ebbed, Ethan started to move. He withdrew almost to the very end, just the head of his penis still parting her lips, before thrusting forward. He'd done gentle last time, now he was ready to ramp it up a bit. Not too much, she was still relatively new to this, but he fully intended her to know he'd been here. Tomorrow, she would be aware of him every time she moved.

He fucked her hard and fast, each stroke perfectly aligned to hit her G-spot. He hovered the pad of his middle finger over her clit and brushed it lightly with each stroke to remind her what more he could do for her, if she asked him. She need only say the word. He was sure she would, eventually. He could, would bring her back to the brink of orgasm and hold her there until she begged him to finish it. Meanwhile, he had another project in mind.

He withdrew his cock briefly, just long enough to slide his own fingers across the head, coating them with the slick moisture there. His fingers loaded with natural lubricant, he plunged his cock back into her, maintaining a fast, punching pace as he traced her tight little rear opening with his moistened digit. Her sphincter resisted his attempt at entry and he wouldn't mind betting she had never received this sort of attention before. He would be careful, but she was going to experience this.

He probed. Not hard, but enough that she would be aware of it. He twisted his finger against her entrance, teasing the ring of muscle, enticing it to open and allow him in. He felt her stiffen, saw her buttocks clench and smiled to himself.

Excellent. Just the reaction he sought. Interested anxiety. Apprehension, but no overt protest. He applied slightly more pressure, and the pursed muscle loosened. He slipped his fingertip inside, circling the inner rim. She relaxed further, and he was able to penetrate to the first knuckle. He waited, concentrated on fucking her relentlessly while she acclimatized to the intimacy of his latest intrusion. A sensual feathering of his finger along the length of her clit was all it took to bring her shuddering to a climax again, and as this release gripped her, he pressed his advantage once more. Her arse was quite unresisting as she sank into her orgasm. He inserted his whole finger easily.

Fleur moaned as her orgasm subsided, the sound low and breathy. He slowed his thrusting, preferring to direct her attention to what he was about to do with her arse. When she stopped panting, he started moving. He drew his finger back slowly then slid it home again, twisting in order to create more friction. She needed to feel this, really feel it, and know that he wouldn't hurt her.

"You doing okay, honey?" Good ethics demanded that he ask her. After all, he hadn't sought her permission for this

There was a brief pause, then, "Yes, I think. Oh!"

He couldn't resist delivering a swift thrust, deep and purposeful, to leave her under no illusion about who was indeed running this show. It was enough. He didn't want to scare or humiliate her. This was about erotic pleasure, intimacy, and maybe just a hint of submission. He kept his movements slow now, gentle and tender, alternating between sinking his cock into her pussy and his finger in her arse. His rhythm was solid, regular, calming almost, and he felt her steady under him as her confidence and delight grew. Again, she tightened around him, and this time he knew they would both climax. He was a controlled lover. He prided himself on making sure his partners, whether vanilla or submissive, got theirs first. But he had his limits and Fleur was pushing them.

He leaned in and rubbed her clit, harder this time, caressing her back to a final, powerful release. She came, crying out his name. He was mere moments behind her, burying his cock deep and holding still as his balls contracted sharply to eject the rush of semen. He grimaced as the last drops spurted, his whole body stiff as every nerve ending connected to his cock.

Fleur turned limp and sank down onto the bed as he slowly slid his finger from her arse, then his cock from her pussy. He disposed of the condom quickly in the en suite bathroom, stopping to wash his hands and check the temperature of the scented water filling the deep, sunken bath. Satisfied, he reached for the jar of rose petals left by the hotel staff on his instructions, and tipped the lot onto the surface of the water. He'd prepared the bath earlier, and now blessed the superb thermostatic controlled facilities in the Totally Five Star that had maintained the perfect water temperature for the last two hours while he'd tended to his companion's other needs — and his own.

When he re-entered the bedroom, Fleur was lying face down across his bed, her hair tangled wildly around her shoulders, covering her face. She remained perfectly still, her breathing slow and steady, and he wondered if she'd fallen asleep. Ethan stood for a moment, and admired her. It never failed to amaze him that a woman could be fucked almost to unconsciousness, yet still look untouched.

He lay down beside her again, combing the hair back from her cheek with his fingers. She gave a small murmur, turned her head toward his hand and kissed it. *Not asleep then, thank God.* Ethan's heart turned over, the sweetness in her gesture achingly tender. He hauled her into his arms and held her against his chest, her small, latte-colored body draped over his paler, harder form. She brought her arms around him, her breasts pressed against his torso. Her nipples had swelled to hard little pebbles and now pressed against his skin, and he loved that she remained aroused, even after the workout they'd had. He kissed the top of her head.

"Bath time, sweetheart."

She snuggled in further. "I cannot. I am too tired now. Exhausted."

Ethan just chuckled. "Allow me." He pulled her across his body and in one lithe motion rolled from the bed with her in his arms. Fleur gave a little shriek and grabbed him around his neck. She clung on, though he would not have dropped her. Not for the world. He carried her into the adjacent bathing area and simply strode down the steps into the bath of scented water. He sat, Fleur still cradled in his arms, as the warm ripples washed over them both. She let out a soft moan of appreciation as the fragrant little swells lapped around them, loosening her death grip on his neck.

Ethan took advantage of the moment to turn her so that her back touched his chest, his arms under hers, his hands clasped around her waist to hold her steady. He smiled as her small toes broke the foaming surface, a sure sign that she felt safe and secure in his grasp.

Neither spoke for several minutes, though an occasional sigh or shiver confirmed to Ethan that she appreciated his attention to her comfort. This was a pleasant enough way to round off an evening of perfect sensuality, but he had his practical side too. He fully intended a repeat performance in the morning, so he could do with Fleur not being too stiff or sore to respond with the enthusiasm he might hope for. A warm bath now would pay dividends later. And it really was very nice to simply lie here and hold her.

At last, Fleur turned in his arms. She trailed a row of kisses along his chin, finally reaching his mouth when he dipped his head to help her.

"I want to sleep. May I go to your bed now?"

Shit! His balls leaped to attention, his cock only fractionally behind. His intentions were clear, his planning meticulous, but the sweet submissiveness of the request was almost his undoing. Despite her obvious fatigue, it was all he could do not to lift her onto his dick right there and then and fuck her again. Hard. He didn't do that, though. Didn't even suggest it.

Instead, he listened as a voice, which must have been his, said "Yes, of course." He stood, hoped she wouldn't draw attention to the rampant erection now making itself disgracefully obvious, and offered his hand to help her from the pool. She took it and followed him up the steps out of the water, then stood perfectly still as he grabbed a pristine white cotton bath sheet from the bale beside the bath and wrapped it around her. The towel dragged along the floor as she followed him from the bathroom and back into the bedroom, and for a moment, she reminded him of a sleepy, impossibly pretty child. It was just a fleeting impression, though, for which he thanked God again given his plans for her in the coming hours. As she dropped the towel and slid between the sheets the brief glimpse of breasts and soft, rounded buttocks left him harboring no illusions. Fleur Mansouri was without doubt the loveliest woman who had ever done him the honor of sharing his bed.

* * * *

Fleur stretched, crinkling her brow in discomfort as the aches in her muscles asserted themselves. She felt odd, not entirely herself. She was stiff rather than in pain, but the differences did not lay there. Something else had changed, something fundamental.

She rolled to her side, and the movement brought realization of two key facts. One, she was naked. And two, she was not alone.

The warm, hard and undeniably male body stretched out alongside her was the trigger that brought the memories rushing back. Good, magical memories, memories to start her stomach fluttering and her pussy clenching all over again. Last night she'd slept with Ethan Savage, an English minerals engineer in her country for only a matter of days. She'd only met him herself two days ago, and here she was, snuggled up to his nude body in his huge bed, in one of the best *riads* in the Totally Five Star hotel.

They'd made love—twice—but she was not sure how many orgasms he had drawn from her quivering body on the route to this. It seemed he'd only to touch her and she would come. And he had touched her. Everywhere.

She shivered, the reaction a mix of delight and embarrassment as she recalled exactly how and where he had touched her, leaving no part of her body unmarked by his hands, his tongue, his lips. But it hadn't all been about the sex, not all about her body, and his. There had been caring too. After they made love he'd carried her to the bath, held her in his arms as she'd relaxed in the warm scented water, then he had wrapped her in a thick towel and led her to bed. To sleep.

Ethan Savage was different—like no one she had ever known, certainly not like any man. Even her father, supportive, tolerant and loving as he was, could not exude the sense of safety and security that flowed from Ethan Savage in waves.

A shift in his posture, a slight hitch in his breathing, and she knew he was awake too. Ethan rolled toward her and lifted his arm to haul her back against his chest.

"I hope you weren't thinking of going anywhere." His voice was a low growl. Fleur wondered if he always sounded so sexy when he woke. And if his cock was always quite so solid. Her anatomy courses in medical school has covered this aspect of male physiology so she knew that men invariably awoke with an erection, but she'd had little direct experience of it. She was beginning to think that was a pity.

"No. But I was thinking."

Ethan dipped his nose into her hair and inhaled. Despite her remaining tenderness, Fleur wriggled her bum against that impressive cock and wondered if he might be persuaded to…

Yes! With an almost effortless shift of his hips and arms she found herself face down against the mattress, her legs spread wide as he settled between her thighs. "Lift your bum up, love." He whispered the words into her ear as he reached over her to grab a couple of pillows from what had been her side of the bed. Fleur managed to obey, raising her lower body from the mattress sufficiently for Ethan to shove two pillows under her stomach. Now her hips were positioned much more conveniently for him, a fact illustrated as he slid a hand between her thighs to test her readiness for him. He plunged two fingers inside her, and Fleur groaned into the cotton sheet, squeezing her muscles tightly around him. The sounds of her wet readiness were unmistakable as he treated her to a couple of experimental thrusts. Fleur might have felt embarrassed, she was sure only yesterday she would have, but not now. Now she just wanted him.

And she was to have him, it seemed, with no further delay. The sound of foil snapping heralded his swift preparations, then he was poised at her entrance. She stiffened as he pressed forward, clenching her pussy around him to better feel and experience his entry. He drove his cock into her, fully sheathing himself in her cunt before reaching down to pull her knees forward, each one in turn. She was now kneeling, and he positioned himself behind her, between her widespread thighs. With his palms on her buttocks, he thrust a couple of times, by way of getting her attention she supposed, then he leaned around her to lay the pads of his fingers across her clit. He rubbed, soft at first then more firmly. Fleur clamped down hard, her pussy starting to spasm almost immediately. He seemed to know exactly how to touch her, how to get the response he wanted. This morning it appeared he wanted fast, hard and now.

His deft fingers demanded her response. His cock felt to be swelling and hardening yet more inside her, stretching her until she was sure she could not take any more. As she gasped in a heady combination of lust and disbelief, he started to move in earnest. His long, even, perfectly angled strokes wreaked maximum effect. His fingers on her clit did their part too, and it seemed to take just moments before she spun out of control again, hurtling toward orgasm. She heard breathy cries, dim, distant, that had to be her own, but it was difficult to focus on anything beyond the intense sensations he created in her pussy as he ground against her G-spot.

Lifting her hips farther, holding her body still for him, she silently begged him for more. He knew and found an extra gear. Fleur came, whimpering her delight as the waves of pleasure rocked through her. She clutched at the finely woven cotton sheet with her fingers, and at his cock with her pussy, gripping both as though she would never relinquish her hold.

Ethan seemed disinclined to drag proceedings out this morning. A couple of strokes after her orgasm had settled, he came too in a shuddering hot rush, the warmth of his semen seeping through the condom to make itself felt against her sensitive inner walls. One day, she thought, one day soon she would feel the warm wetness against her bare skin, filling her cunt.

But as reality reasserted itself, she knew that not to be true. The truth was, one day soon he would be gone. The day after tomorrow, in fact. His work here was almost complete. He might never have any reason to return.

* * * *

Propped up against the pillows, Fleur accepted the cup of tea Ethan offered her. They could have made it themselves, but he'd insisted on phoning room service, who had brought up a tray within minutes laden with aromatic Lady Gray tea, a *cafetière* for him, and a pile of breakfast pastries, rich and flaky and at just the right temperature. He'd also ordered various types of jam, a bowl containing small knobs of butter fashioned into delicate curls, a bowl of fruit salad and plain yogurt, a selection of cheeses and even an individually wrapped biscuit of Shredded Wheat.

"Well, I like it. It's the *only* cereal I like. Want some?"

Fleur shook her head—she had no intention of depriving him of the only breakfast cereal he liked. After all, he might need his strength.

They enjoyed their breakfast picnic-style on the bed, unconcerned at the crumbs liberally sprinkling the coverlet. When they had finished, Ethan shifted the tray to the floor and they lay back against the pillows, neither in any hurry to be anywhere.

"What time are you on duty today?" He reached for a stray lock of her hair and smoothed it back behind her ear as he asked her the question.

"Not until noon. What time is it now?"

"Almost ten. I'd normally have been up for four hours by now. You're a bad influence, Doctor Mansouri."

And I do not usually allow men I hardly know to slide their fingers into my anus. On a general scale of things, Fleur felt his influence on her had been the more telling. She kept that observation to herself, though, preferring to stick with the less personal for now.

"What are your plans for today?" She hoped her tone came across as light, undemanding. She had no wish to appear clingy. This was, after all, a casual liaison. Not her usual style, but as a one-off, it was shaping up remarkably well. She had no wish to spoil things.

"Another site visit, but that can wait until this afternoon. I sent some data to my head office in London yesterday and the results of my team's analysis should be back by now. I'll look those over, then I'll need to make one final check before settling in to prepare the final report for James."

"James?"

"James Conroy. The CEO of the hotel chain. He is who I'm working for, though he's a friend too."

"I see." Fleur recalled vividly the one occasion she had met the CEO of the chain, when he'd been here in Marrakesh. She'd found him a deeply unsettling presence at the time. Now, as she lay in Ethan's bed contemplating the last few hours and the couple yet to come before they went their separate ways for the rest of the day, she wondered if maybe she'd been too quick to judge. "I met Mr. Conroy once. Here at the hotel."

"Oh?" Ethan glanced at her, apparently aware that there was more.

"He… He seemed…quite stern."

Ethan quirked his lip. "I guess he could come across that way. He runs a mean hotel chain, though, so I suppose he'd have to be."

Fleur drew a deep breath. "No, I did not mean professionally. I mean, in his personal life." She stopped, uncertain what else to say, how to phrase this. Ethan's sharp glance at her across his coffee cup indicated that she had managed to get her meaning across anyway.

"Did he say something to you? About his personal life?"

"No, of course he did not. He would never discuss such a thing with his staff. I am sure of it."

"Me too. So, how come you know so much about how James spends his downtime?"

Fleur placed her cup on the bedside table, mortified. She was a doctor, so she understood patient confidentiality as well as any in her profession. She really should not have raised this matter and, right now, she had no idea what had gotten into her.

"I cannot say. I should not have mentioned it at all. It was very unprofessional of me and I must ask you to forget I ever said anything."

Ethan regarded her silently for a few moments, then shook his head. "If I couldn't see that it was upsetting you I might let it go, as you ask. But there's something on your mind and I want to know what it is."

"I cannot."

"Fleur, now please."

His tone hardened, becoming firmer than she had ever heard from him. Both compelling and troubling, the timbre in his voice made her uncomfortable, unsettled. And she knew that whatever her professional ethics, she was not going to be leaving this room until she'd told Ethan what he wanted to know.

"Very well. I will tell you. But please, do *not* repeat this. I would lose my job here if you do. And I need this work. It is just, you are his friend, and you are like him, I think."

Ethan nodded slowly. "James and I share many interests. This is true. And our lifestyles are not dissimilar in many respects."

Fleur inclined her head, realizing that he'd just told her, in not much code at all, that both James and he were Dominants. But she already knew that.

"Mr. Conroy came to Marrakesh some months ago, to visit the hotel. He was here for a few days, with a companion. A lady."

"I see. None of this is confidential, though."

Fleur nodded and continued. "The companion — I am afraid I do not know her name, though it will be in my notes — became ill whilst they were here. I had to attend her in their guest *riad*. She was experiencing breathing difficulties. It was an asthma attack, which I treated, and she was soon quite well again. In order to treat her, I had to examine her, which meant I had to check her respiration. When she raised her top for me to place my stethoscope on her back, I saw that she had been beaten. There were marks, several of them. Contusions, I would say, caused by a strap perhaps or maybe a belt. I saw them, and she knew that I had seen. Mr. Conroy was not in the room when I examined her. I asked her if she needed any help, if she was happy to remain with Mr. Conroy. She smiled at me, and she told me that she was never happier than when she was with Mr. Conroy. I thought at first she was scared of him, would not speak against him for fear of reprisals. But her face was not fearful. Her expression was one of calm. Despite her injuries, I believed she *was* happy."

Ethan listened without interruption. When Fleur finished, he didn't reply immediately. She sat on the bed, her body huddled as she waited for him to speak, to tell her she had no business repeating the private details of a medical consultation. Which was perfectly true, of course.

It seemed that medical ethics were not his primary concern. "You're right. She *was* happy. Would have been happy. As would you have been, if your brute of a husband had been more like James in his outlook. More like me, even. And that's what's really bothering you, isn't it?"

"I do not understand your meaning, Ethan." There was just the slightest tremor in her voice, more than a hint of defensiveness, but she heard it. Could he detect it too?

"You told me about your marriage, about how you wanted your husband to treat you—what you'd hoped for when you agreed to marry him. Instead, he accused you of being perverse, wicked, or some such thing. He proceeded to beat the crap out of you, and even though it's long since over with, and you've grown into a lovely, intelligent, successful woman, you still hide behind some pretense that being different, being what some might call kinky, is not acceptable. Am I right so far?"

"I... I..." To Fleur's horror, tears pricked her eyes. She never cried—well, she never used to, though she was making something of a habit of it recently around Ethan. But she had not for many years, and certainly not over this. As Ethan had said, those days were long gone. But the chance encounter with James Conroy and his seemingly contented companion had resurrected all her latent uncertainties and confusion, not to mention her deeply repressed longings. Many years ago she'd felt drawn to—something. She had wanted to explore it, discover the mysteries of what she now knew to be her submissive personality. But that had proved to be dangerous, terrifyingly so.

Buried for years, totally submerged under her sophisticated veneer of professionalism, she had not anticipated that she would ever be outed. She had even managed to disregard the evidence of James Conroy, until something in Ethan's quiet, assured manner had reminded her of him.

"Hey, come here."

His tone had softened. Fleur regarded him through tear-filled eyes, gulping back her sobs. It was no good. Despite her determination, ten years or more of pain had to erupt sometime, and it would seem that it was going to be now. Before she knew what was happening, she started to bury her face in her hands, just to be seized and hauled yet again onto Ethan's chest. She buried her face there instead, and sobbed as though her heart was breaking.

Ethan held her, his arms around her heaving shoulders, murmuring words of encouragement and comfort that she couldn't really hear but knew were there. Fleur clung to him, her rock right now, the one solid and certain thing in a tangle of confusion, of missed opportunities and roads not taken.

Eventually her sobs subsided, and Fleur was seized by panic and remorse. "Please, you will not tell him? It was private, I should not have told you. I should not have told anyone."

"Sweetheart, if you betrayed any medical confidences, they were those of his companion, not James. He wasn't your patient."

"No. But he is my employer, and he is your friend."

"James is my friend, but he can look out for himself. We won't talk about him anymore. I'm more interested in you."

"Me? I am no one, not that interesting."

"Now that's where you're wrong, sweetheart. You *are* interesting. I'd say you're fucking fascinating. Ever since I saw you on that bloody donkey of yours, I've hardly been able to take my eyes off you. Christ, was that only a couple of days ago?"

"I thought you were very handsome — and arrogant."

"'I'll take handsome. And I have my moments, I suppose, but arrogant?"

"You watched me, all the way down the road. You were staring. It is rude to stare."

"Yeah, I know. Like I say, I couldn't tear my eyes away from you."

"But when you took your sunglasses off, I decided you were nice. Polite, after all."

"The sunglasses? I don't get it."

"They were dark, very dark, and they hid your eyes from me. You were looking at me, but I couldn't see you. Then you removed the glasses and looked me in the eyes. I liked you then. And when you slowed down to drive past me, careful not to startle Agwmar, I thought you were more considerate than most tourists."

"I wasn't a tourist."

"I did not know that at the time. Then you drove away, and after a few seconds, I heard the screech of your brakes and a crash. I was so scared. I thought you might have been injured, killed even. I am a doctor, but had almost no medical equipment with me."

"You took excellent care of me."

"I tried to. You were extremely hard to help, Mr. Savage."

"So you've said already. Ah well, perhaps you saved me from myself."

It was on the tip of Fleur's tongue to return some witty, flippant comment, but she did not. Instead, she considered his words, their earlier conversation, the comfort he'd provided when she was distressed. Maybe she had saved him from himself. And perhaps he could return the favor.

Chapter Nine

"Are you staying at the hotel tonight?" Ethan asked the question after he had kissed her as they prepared to leave his *riad*—he to collect his hire car from the hotel underground parking area and she to open the day's clinic.

Both had dressed to face their day, she in her semi-formal dark trousers and neat blouse that she had brought with her yesterday evening in a discreet shoulder bag. She would put on her clinical tunic top when she reached the hotel medical facility. He wore his usual working outfit of jeans and a T-shirt. Fleur noticed his desert boots, and that after studying the communications he'd downloaded from his office in the UK he had packed several bottles of water from the hotel minibar. He looked to be gearing up to spend the day in the desert. She resisted the temptation to warn him to drive carefully.

"I finish working at ten o'clock this evening. I am not on duty tomorrow, as it is my day off, so I should go home. My parents will expect me."

Ethan simply nodded. It pleased Fleur that he made no comment about this, did not see fit to point out that she was thirty years old and entitled to do as she pleased. In the UK perhaps and in many other places that would be so. But here in Morocco she was careful to project the image that would most help her career. This did not include openly sharing the beds of passing European businessmen, no matter how appealing the prospect might be.

"I'll see you tomorrow, then, at your parents' place. You'd better let me have the address."

"I could come here to meet you…"

"I had the impression you were hoping to be discreet. How would that look?"

She knew he was right. "Very well. I will write it down for you." She found a hotel notepad on one of the hall tables arranged around the living area and jotted down the address of her family home. "Show this to the taxi driver. It is not far, but in Marrakesh traffic, it will take about fifteen minutes to get there. You will need to ring the bell at the gate."

He took the slip of paper, folded it and placed it in his wallet. "What time should I arrive?"

"Would late afternoon be all right? We tend to eat quite early."

"I'll be there. I'm going to miss you today. And I'll miss you even more tonight."

Me too. Fleur did not say this, though. Instead, she bowed her head and followed him from the *riad* and along the guest walkway leading to the hotel's central courtyard where they would go their separate ways.

* * * *

Despite the heat and the dust, Ethan's day should have passed quickly. Sociable by nature, he nevertheless enjoyed his own company. When he was out on site, alone, anywhere in the world, he prided himself on his ability to concentrate on the job in hand, to focus totally. He was known for it.

But not today, it would seem. Today, a rather lovely Moroccan doctor continually interrupted his concentration. Her voice, low and sultry. Her scent, which he was astonished to note, put him in mind of a light spring day at home. He recalled the way her skin felt under his fingers—smooth, with a tendency to shiver ever so slightly when he brushed past one of her more sensitive spots, like her ears or the backs of her knees. He especially loved the little sounds she made as she came and wondered if he would hear those again. Probably not. He wouldn't see her tonight, and tomorrow he would leave her at her parents' home. The day after that he was booked on a flight back to Heathrow.

He'd had no plans to return to Morocco for a while. He might have to revise his schedule.

After he had left her in the hotel courtyard, he'd intended to make straight for the car park. Instead, he'd found himself chasing down the formally attired head of the reception staff and asking him to recommend a local florist. A few minutes later, he'd completed his business and was on his way out to the desert again. He really needed to complete his fieldwork today if he was to keep most of tomorrow free for writing up his final conclusions and recommendations, and his dinner appointment. He might even get in a little pool time.

* * * *

For Fleur, the day dragged. Just when she might have appreciated an epidemic of Moroccan tummy or maybe a few poolside bumps and grazes, no one seemed to need her services. Her charges were the very epitome of rude good health and safety consciousness. Feeling somewhat superfluous, and with altogether too much time on her hands — time in which she might think on matters perhaps better left untroubled — she fell back on an overdue stock take of the medical supply cabinet. She busied herself ordering bandages and gauze, even tidied the medicine fridge in a final act of desperation. She almost wept with relief when reception called her to attend a woman who had experienced a dizzy spell in the bar, though she suspected that the sudden onset of symptoms owed much to over-indulgence in the local liquor. Even so, she managed to sport her most sympathetic expression as she recommended plenty of bottled water and a lie down out of the sun.

Fleur didn't know what she had to complain about. Usually a quiet day was a blessing, a chance to catch up on paperwork, check supplies, read the latest medical journals. And ordinarily she was a lot more tolerant of the foibles of holidaymakers than she felt today. She loved the hotel atmosphere, the multinational nature of it all, the constant coming and going, the chatter of different languages, the fascinating mix of cultures and traditions, all jostling around and generally having a good time together.

She could have easily found a job in the hospital where her mother was a senior pediatrician or in one of the other medical facilities in the city. Sometimes she wondered if her skills might not be better invested in caring for the local population, but she preferred the Totally Five Star. She was in her element here, enjoyed the hustle, loved meeting new people — interesting people who converged here from all corners of the globe. Her language skills were an asset, as was her gender on the whole. Most of her patients were women or children, so a female doctor was usually preferred. Although her initial contract was a temporary one, Fleur was optimistic regarding her prospects with the hotel chain — as long as she didn't screw up right royally by offending the CEO. She still couldn't quite believe she'd discussed his private life with another guest — his friend at that. Talk about professional suicide. Ethan had promised to keep her lapse to himself, though, and she trusted him.

Fleur's faith in Ethan was further bolstered when she called out "Enter" in response to a tap on her office door, to admit a young local man carrying a long, white box.

"Delivery for Doctor Mansouri."

She stood and strode around her desk, puzzled. She had ordered new supplies but they would not be delivered until tomorrow at the earliest. She checked the name on the delivery note, and took the proffered ballpoint pen to sign, accepting the package. As the door closed on the courier, she slid the lid from the box and gasped.

Dozens of lilies, all pure white, filled the box, topped by one exquisite crimson rose.

The scents bursting from the flowers were heady, delicate, yet they filled the small room instantly. Fleur's practical self hoped that no hay fever sufferers would be seeking her help today, while her romantic soul soared. *Ethan. Who else? They have to be from him.* Apart from her parents when she had passed her final medical exams, she couldn't recall that anyone had ever sent her flowers before.

There was a card, discreetly tucked among the blooms. She retrieved it, opening the small pale yellow envelope carefully to extract the tiny handwritten card.

Fifty. One for each hour since I first saw you. I couldn't resist the rose.

Fleur sank into the chair behind her desk, staring at the box lying open in front of her. Fifty hours. Was it really only fifty hours? Two days? For over ten years, she'd managed to keep the lid firmly slammed shut on her secret, wicked yearnings. And he'd managed to pry it off in just two days.

There was only one question left, she supposed. What was she going to do about it?

* * * *

As her shift ended, Fleur took off her doctor's tunic and hung it up neatly on the back of her office door. She picked up her box of lilies and her medical bag before exchanging pleasantries with the agency nurse, who would hold the fort until her medical colleague came on duty at eight in the morning. She herself was not due back for thirty-six hours, but would be here in time to say goodbye to Ethan as he checked out for his flight back to his usual life—a life that did not include her.

She made her way along the staff corridor, headed for the Totally Five Star central courtyard. From there she could hail a taxi to take her to her parents' *riad,* where a late supper would await her. Her mother was working all night, she knew, but her father would be there, keen to hear about her day. He would quiz her about Ethan, without doubt. Yvette had clearly taken to Ethan. She would not have invited him to their home otherwise, and by now, she would have told her husband all about him. There were no secrets between her parents.

The Mansouri household was by no means a typical Moroccan family, and Said Mansouri was far from the traditional Muslim father. Fleur knew he would have no real concerns regarding his daughter forming a relationship with a man not of his own faith. That said, her father was deeply religious himself and a man of no faith at all would cause him to raise his eyebrows. Fleur had seen no evidence to suggest that Ethan would meet her father's expectations in that regard, though, in fairness, the subject had never arisen.

Fleur had no reason not to go home, no reason not to want to sit and drink tea with her father, tell him all about Ethan Savage. Well, not quite all perhaps, but she knew her father would assume they were at least close. He would be too tactful to pursue the matter, but her mother would be more direct. They had that to look forward to when Ethan joined them for their evening meal tomorrow.

She had no reason not to leave, to get into her taxi and put the Totally Five Star out of her mind for a while. She might go shopping tomorrow, or perhaps play tennis. Her sister was always pestering her for a game. Or maybe she would read. It seemed a long time since she'd just put her feet up and relaxed with a good book. Her mother would no doubt like some help with the preparations for the evening, though Fleur was no cook, really.

No, there was definitely no reason at all not to head for home, but she still found herself settling into a deep sofa in one of the Totally Five Star lounges, almost deserted at this hour when most of the guests were in either the restaurants or the bars. She ordered a coffee and settled back to enjoy it — and to think.

It was true that she had only known Ethan Savage for a couple of days, but she felt closer to him than she ever had to anyone, even her family, beloved though they were. Ethan understood her, knew her most private yearnings and accepted her. He wanted her. He was not shocked at her failings, nor even surprised. She had told him of her marriage and he had taken her side. There was nothing of the condemnation she had feared, just contempt for her husband. Ethan seemed to regard it as sheer bad luck that she had found herself shackled to a man who had no understanding of her needs and had even suggested that had she married someone more like James Conroy or himself, her life might have been very different.

In this interlude of self-awareness, Fleur acknowledged that she had no quarrel really with her life, as it was, at least not in most respects. But some differences would be nice.

She had no quarrel with her home either, but was making no move to go there. Her father would worry, she really must let him know she was delayed. She pulled out her mobile phone to text him, but hesitated, unsure what to say. Why was she still here? When would she be home?

In truth, the only reason she wasn't on her way back right now was that Ethan was not there. He was here, at the hotel, but not for much longer. She would see him tomorrow, but they would not be alone. And she wanted to be alone with him again.

To make love? Yes, certainly that. But that was not all, she now acknowledged. She had unfinished—no, scratch that—unstarted business to settle. Despite what she may have told herself in the years since, her private desires and most secret longings had gone nowhere. They were still within her, buried deep but surfacing fast. Ethan had unsettled her, challenged her, and drawn from her a sensuality she had not dreamt she possessed. But he had done much more than that. He had reawakened possibilities that she had convinced herself no longer existed, at least not for her. If she did not explore them now—with him—she might never meet a man whom she trusted enough to take this risk with. Even when he left Marrakesh the day after tomorrow, as she knew he would, she would have this to remember, and perhaps something to build on.

But she needed him now, while he was still here. She needed him to show her what she had been missing, what she had denied herself for so long. And it had to be tonight.

Her decision made, Fleur tapped out her message to her father.

Staying at hotel tonight. See you tomorrow. Love you.

Said Mansouri must have had his phone in his hand when she texted as his reply was almost instantaneous.

Take care, ma petite. Love you too. Until tomorrow, then.

Fleur smiled and hugged herself as she placed her empty coffee cup back in the saucer. She could always rely on her papa. And now, perhaps she'd found another man she could put her trust in too. She was about to find out.

Chapter Ten

He might not even be here. He could be having a meal somewhere in one of the restaurants. Perhaps he was not even in the hotel at all. But somehow, she knew he was close by. She would have felt his absence if he was not. Still, Fleur hesitated at the door to Ethan's *riad*, her hand raised to knock. What if he had made other plans for tonight? He was not expecting her, so he might even have other company.

She dismissed that notion. He would not have sent her the lovely flowers if he could then so casually bring another woman back to his suite. She was sure of that, as she hugged the florist's box to her chest, a talisman of his esteem, if not his affection. But she thought that affection might not be too far off the mark. He seemed to like her and to care about her. He'd been kind, gentle, considerate, and something more besides, something she found harder to name. She thought she saw a tenderness in his eyes as he looked at her, an appreciation that went beyond lust.

Her own feelings for Ethan were quite incomprehensible to her at this moment and she had deliberately chosen not to examine them too closely. There would be a time for introspection later. Right now, she needed to see him, to talk to him. She needed to ask him.

She knocked on the door, quickly, before her courage failed her, then waited. Footsteps inside, soft, barefoot probably, as was the custom here. The door opened.

"Hey, hello you. Looking as delicious as ever. But I wasn't expecting you tonight." Ethan's smile of pleased surprise and genuine welcome reassured her.

Fleur's heart turned over. Relief, certainly, that he was pleased to see her, but it was more than that. She blurted out the first thing that occurred to her.

"Thank you for the flowers."

He tilted his head, a half smile on his lips. "You're welcome. I take it you liked them." He gestured to the box still clutched to her chest.

"Very much. No one ever sends me flowers."

"They do now." Still that smile, lazily sexy, as he leaned on the doorframe watching her.

"I wanted to see you again. Before tomorrow, I mean. Is this all right? Could I come inside?" She was babbling, she knew, realizing only afterwards how needy she sounded. She hadn't intended to crowd him.

He didn't seem to mind, just reached to take her bag from her. "Do you have a change of clothes in here?"

"No. I did not think."

"Ah, well, we need to make sure you don't get too rumpled, then. Don't want you looking a mess tomorrow. Maybe you *should* come inside and get undressed."

Her pussy clenched and moistened. Fleur knew she did not have long before she succumbed to the inevitable around Ethan Savage. Still, she managed what she thought might pass for a witty reply.

"That sounds most prudent, very forward-looking of you. But first, may I ask you something?"

He stepped back and beckoned her in, closing the door softly behind her. He placed her bag on the floor then turned and backed Fleur against the door, his hands on either side of her head, the flower box pressed between their bodies.

"What do you want to ask?" He settled his lips on her neck, her throat. Despite Ethan's considerate suggestion regarding tomorrow's wardrobe precautions, it was already too late to save her knickers. She would have to buy new ones at the hotel boutique and try to convince herself that the staff there might not draw the obvious conclusion.

"I want... I mean, would you...?"

"Probably. Is this a flying visit, or are you able to stay a while?"

"A while. All night."

"Ah, that's good. Very good."

He dipped his head to brush his lips over hers and, for a moment, Fleur forgot why she was there, forgot all about the important matters she needed to discuss with him. The one very important matter for which she needed his help. It was no good, she had to get the words out. He might not even want to kiss her after he'd heard her request. But she thought—hoped—he would.

"I want you to hurt me."

Ethan stopped, suddenly motionless, his lips still against hers. He lifted his head, a slight frown now on his handsome features. "I beg your pardon?"

"I want you to hurt me. Like James Conroy."

To his eternal credit in Fleur's view, Ethan made no pretense of not understanding her. He cupped her cheek in his palm. "Ah, your inner submissive fancying some fresh air, then. Is that it?"

Not quite the way she might have phrased it, but yes, he was right. Fleur merely nodded.

"I thought she would. Eventually. I just didn't expect it to be so fast."

"It has not been fast. I have wanted this thing for years."

"I see." He straightened, all thoughts of kissing now seemingly abandoned. "Come in and sit. Can I get you a drink?"

"I do not want a drink. Please, will you do it?"

Ethan regarded her silently for a few moments, clearly turning her suggestion over in his mind. His dispassionate expression made him appear cold even, and in that moment quite unlike the man she had thought him to be. Fleur's heart sank. He was about to turn her down. He would be kind about it, because he was no Youssef. Neither was Ethan a violent brute — he would find a polite and courteous way to refuse. But refuse he would. She opened her mouth to plead with him, ready to sink her pride for this one chance. Ethan stopped her flow with one finger, simply raised it to ask for quiet. And he got it as Fleur clamped her jaws shut.

"If this is what you want, truly want, then yes. I will. But first, we talk. So please, come in, sit and accept that drink."

Her head whirling at the ease with which he had seemingly agreed to this wild scheme of hers, Fleur followed Ethan across the foyer. He seemed to be heading for the living area, but changed course unexpectedly and led her into the courtyard instead.

He gestured to the low seat close to the babbling fountain and waited until she had settled herself there.

"Water? Juice? I'd offer you something stronger but I really think you need a clear head for this conversation. As do I."

"Water would be nice. Thank you." And her head was remarkably clear, considering.

So polite. Fleur was struck by the incongruity of the common courtesies, given the direction that this encounter was about to take. She hoped. She sat in silence as Ethan strolled casually back inside to return a few moments later with two glasses of sparkling water.

"Fresh from the chiller." He handed one to her then took his seat alongside her. "So, tell me."

"Tell you? I do not understand."

"Don't hedge with me, Fleur. If you want this to happen, you need to say it. Out loud. I'm reasonably certain I can provide what you need, but only if I fully understand what it is. So, tell me."

Fleur stared at the bubbles fizzing from the bottom of her glass to the surface, watched their effervescent sparkle for a few moments. "I want it all."

"All?" Ethan's tone was soft, even. He waited for her to elaborate.

"All." Fleur raised her eyes to meet his, gaining in confidence at his serious expression. She had his full attention. She drew in a long, steadying breath then went for it. "I want to feel powerless and cared for too. I want to hurt, to be forced to do things I never dreamed of—wicked, sinful things I never wanted before but now I do. Does that make sense?"

"Wicked and sinful. I'm liking the sound of this. So far, so good. Continue, please."

He smiled, and Fleur took encouragement from that.

"I want to be scared and excited at the same time. I want to be told what to do and whatever it is, I will obey. I want to *not* be in control, not be accountable for my actions, for my responses." She paused, hesitant, then continued, her voice little more than a whisper. "I want you to use me, to play with me. I want to be yours, no longer mine."

"I see. And do you want me to fuck you while I'm making you feel all this? Is that part of it too, for you?"

"Yes. Of course."

"I'm relieved, but there's no 'of course' about it. What you're describing is invariably sexual in my experience, but doesn't have to involve fucking. I needed to check. You said you want to be hurt. How would you like me to hurt you?"

Fleur took a sip of her water, raised her eyes to his. No point in mincing her words. "I want you to hit me."

"As in, slap your face?"

"No! Of course not. You would not do that... Would you?" She cringed, drew back from him as the realization dawned. Her memory rekindled the fear and revulsion of her marriage as though it were all happening again, right here and now. She'd been so sure that Ethan was different.

Ethan shook his head. "No, I wouldn't, so you can stop cowering over there. Despite what you might like to think, despite everything you just said about being forced to do things you never imagined you'd like, there would be no coercion in anything I might do to you. Nothing happens without your consent, and you can stop any time. Is that clear?"

"What if I don't want to stop?"

"Then we won't. I won't. Unless I decide you've had enough and that would be my call."

Fleur frowned, uncertain how she felt about that. But the main thing was that he had agreed. So far, he seemed ready to oblige her and Fleur was seized by a compulsion to make it happen, to make it real. Before he changed his mind. "So, can we start? Shall I get undressed now?"

"Christ, so eager. You scare me. You can certainly get undressed, but we start when I think you're ready. When the ground rules are clear and you've had my instructions. You've told me what you want, and I get that. Some details still need to be ironed out, but I do get the general idea. So now, I need you to fully understand and agree to what I want from you."

"Anything. Just, I need…"

"Tonight, love, you need good, down and dirty, sweaty sex and a serious conversation." Ethan's brow wrinkled as he heard her stomach rumble.

Fleur remembered that she'd not eaten since mid-afternoon and started to apologize.

He smiled wryly. "And maybe something to eat. It's hungry work, being a kink freak."

"I am not a freak. I just—"

"I meant no insult, Fleur. And if—when—we do this thing you seem so set upon, I daresay I'll call you other things you might find strange too. Get used to it. So, what would you like to eat?"

"I do not know. I am fine. Really." Her head was still reeling from being dubbed a kink freak, and that being oddly okay. Ethan might be able to make the seamless shift to food, but she could not.

"You *are* fine, if just the right side of skinny. You need to eat. Chicken Caesar salad, I think. I'll get them to send up a pot of coffee too. We won't be sleeping for a while."

He left her to do her best to unscramble her tumbled thoughts in the courtyard while he went to the hotel phone to order up room service. Fleur watched him stroll away from her, so self-assured, so confident. So terrifying. She trembled, her knickers quite beyond redemption now. This was going to be so good, *he* was going to be so good. She just knew it. She could feel it in her water.

Shit, when your luck's in, it just is.

How could just thinking about a woman conjure her up like that? The last person Ethan had expected to find when he opened his door was a gorgeous submissive looking for action. And the very submissive he craved, the curvy female body he had wanted to get his hands on since his eyes had first met hers out on that dusty road. She was here, now. Wanting him to hurt her. His instincts had been right all along. He'd correctly read the stream of signals she had been giving off unconsciously since the moment they had met.

His cock strained the front of his jeans and he reached to slip the button of his waistband, stopping himself just in time. His usual preferred costume for a scene was barefoot, bare-chested, and the button of his jeans undone. He liked his subs just plain naked. And tied up, of course. Gagged, perhaps, though he thought not with Fleur. At least, not yet.

His mind raced. He had to get this right. He liked to plan his scenes carefully, in meticulous detail. He was not a seat of the pants Dom—never had been. Accidents happened that way and he'd never relished the prospect of showing up in an accident and emergency department with an injured submissive he would have to explain to some stony-faced casualty consultant. No, not his style at all. Planning, preparation, careful adherence to the rules were what kept subs — and Doms — safe.

To the best of his knowledge, none of the hotels in the Totally Five Star chain offered a BDSM dungeon among the facilities to cater for the comfort and enjoyment of guests. Pity really, he might mention it to James. Not that he would have considered such a setting for Fleur. In any case, he instinctively knew that she would need privacy, seclusion, and very careful handling. A dungeon would have made some toys available, though, a few items of equipment that he might have found useful.

Useful, but not essential. A good Dom could achieve the desired effect without the theatrical setting and props. Submission was, after all, a state of mind, and as much could be achieved with words as with a whip or handcuffs. But his little Fleur clearly expected something more tangible by way of a challenge to her pain threshold, so he needed to come up with something. He would do a little more shopping tomorrow.

For now, though, he had other needs of hers to attend to. He called the Totally Five Star twenty-four-hour room service line and ordered the chicken salad, asking for a baked potato with prawns and creamy coleslaw to go with it. He was peckish too, so they could share. The efficient female voice at the other end assured him that the trolley would be with them in a matter of minutes, so he thanked her and turned to go back into the courtyard. Partway across the foyer, he stopped. Fleur was exactly where he'd left her, still clutching her glass, now almost empty. She looked tiny, frail almost. He had been right to insist on feeding her first — she could stand to gain a few pounds in his opinion. If she'd been about to become his regular sub, he would have insisted on it.

But there was nothing regular about any of this. Since he had first set eyes on her and everything she was, all she did had seemed distinctly irregular. She was not the traditional Berber peasant he had originally thought, far from it. Neither was she only the consummate medical professional, though she did a passable show of that. Under her smooth surface rippled wonderfully hidden depths that even she didn't understand, and he was about to get to explore those. With her.

His cock swelled and twitched relentlessly. Ethan ruthlessly subdued the drive to spread her on the tiled courtyard floor and fuck her senseless. At least, not until after the salad. Instead, he went to the fridge in his large living area and grabbed the bottle of chilled water before rejoining her in the courtyard. She glanced up when she heard his footsteps, a small, uncertain smile on her lovely mouth. He couldn't resist leaning down to lay a soft kiss on her lips.

"Okay?" He caressed her cheek, relieved as she turned her head to nuzzle her face into his palm. He'd managed not to scare her off so far. Still, he would need to make sure that she knew what he had in mind for her, in general terms at least, and that she consented to all of it. "Food's on its way." He sat next to her again and poured her another half glass of water. Hydration was good. Submission was thirsty work at the best of times, and especially so in thirty degrees of subtropical heat.

"Thank you. I am not interrupting your work, I hope."

"No. All done." He'd have managed to fit her in whatever. "I thought you were expected at home tonight. Will your family be wondering where you are?"

"I texted my father. He knows I'm staying here tonight."

"Here? You mean here at work? The hotel?"

"Yes. I think." She paused, recalling her father's somewhat enigmatic advice. "He told me to take care."

"Wise man. Though that's my department now. So, are you ready for me to tell you how this is going to go?"

Fleur nodded, her eyes widening. *Has she any idea how sexy that is? How utterly sensual she is?* He thought perhaps not and added that to his set of goals for her early education in submission.

"You're staying with me all night, yes?"

"Yes."

"That should be 'Yes, Sir.' Rule one, when we're alone, you call me Sir. Without fail. In company, Ethan is fine. Any questions on that?"

"No, Sir."

Ethan's lips flattened in quiet satisfaction. He hadn't expected any issues with the form of address, but her ready acceptance was promising, even so. He pressed on. "I expect you to obey me, to do as I instruct without argument. You can ask questions, seek clarification. It's important you understand what's required because I *will* punish disobedience or obstruction. Once we start, you are mine, in my hands. You said that earlier, and I intend to hold you to it, nothing less. Is that also clear?"

"It is, Sir. I accept those terms."

"Good. There's more, though. Do you know what a safe word is?" She was inexperienced he knew, but well read. She might have come across the concept.

Ashe Barker

Fleur nodded slowly. "Yes, Sir. I think so. If I want you to stop—"

"Not want. Need. If anything I do is simply too much, intolerable, you use your safe word. Not otherwise."

"Would I be punished for using it? Sir?"

"No, you wouldn't. If you need to stop, your safe word is there to get you out of trouble. You can have another signal for if you want me to slow down, or you need to talk to me, ask something. Or even if you think you might be about to use your safe word. I can help you. I *will* help you, but you need to tell me if you're struggling. I'm a Dom, which means I can be hard, stern, demanding. I don't compromise. But I'm not heartless, not cruel, not a bully. Always, this will be about what *you* want, not so much what I want. Does that make sense?"

"I… I think so. Sir."

A knock at the outer door to the *riad* caught both their attention.

"Ah, your supper. Hold that thought…" Ethan stood, and made short work of accepting the trolley of perfectly prepared food from the young Moroccan waiter at the door. He tipped him a generous handful of dirhams and declined his offer to set out the food for him. She hadn't said anything, but Ethan had the impression that his overnight guest might prefer her presence here in his suite not to be the talk of the Totally Five Star kitchens. He wanted the waiter out of the suite as quickly as he could decently manage it.

He wheeled the trolley into the huge living area and called out to Fleur, "Do you want to eat in here or outside?"

The answer came in the form of Fleur following him into the lounge and seating herself on one of the long,

172

low sofas. Ethan laid the plates of food on the low table in front of her. Room service had included all the necessary utensils so he just handed her a knife and fork.

"I ordered something for me too. I thought we might just share."

"Of course. It all looks delicious. Thank you very much." Fleur's stomach growled in agreement and this time she smiled with him. "I forgot to eat this evening."

"Oh? Busy day, was it? Did I hear a Sir then?"

"Oh! I'm sorry. Sir. Yes, of course."

He smiled to himself, enjoying her fluster. This boded well. In his experience, subs always got this wrong and always earned a punishment for it. It was a good way of breaking the ice, so to speak. He decided to lay his cards on the table now.

"Tonight, we just talk. And we fuck. I intend to tie you to my bed, and I have few things in mind I want to do to you. I might scare you a bit, embarrass you—a lot. I won't hurt you, though. You will have a good time with me tonight. I can promise that. Tomorrow, though, we settle any scores. After we enjoy a delightful meal at your parents' house, you are going to find a reason to return here, to the hotel. You will come here, to my suite, to wait for me. I'll have more precise instructions for you closer to the time, but tomorrow is when I'll punish you for any disobedience or failures to meet my instructions tonight. So far, you've earned a punishment for forgetting to call me Sir. I'll be keeping a tally from now on."

Her eyes widened, and she shifted slightly in her seat. He would be prepared to bet the entire not inconsiderable fee he would be charging James Conroy that her pussy was dripping wet by now.

"I see, Sir. What will my punishment be? Is it permitted for me to ask that?"

Christ, she's fucking delightful. "Yes, you can always ask questions. I may not always answer. On this occasion, though, I want you to know exactly what to expect. I intend to exact retribution on your bare bottom. I think two strokes for each offense. It would usually be more than that, but I'm making allowance for your inexperience. I expect you to make plenty of mistakes, though, so the numbers will rack up. So, you're at two already."

"With your hand? I suppose it must be. You don't have anything else here to use…"

Ethan chuckled, and even to his own ears he knew the sound lacked any hint of mirth. "With your hand, *Sir*. That's four so far now. You really do need to concentrate." He shook his head, his smile wry. "Oh, Fleur, you'll be amazed at what I can do to you with just my hands. My bare hands and your bare bottom." He watched her pupils dilate further, and knew she was wet. Wetter. Ah, yes, words could be so much more effective than actions, carefully chosen words, delivered at just the right time. And anticipation would build the effects in her head until the actual event could even seem tame. Not that he'd let her arrive at such a conclusion. He smiled sweetly at her. "Would you like a prawn?"

Fleur was so nervous she hardly expected to be able to eat anything, but the food was oddly delicious. It was a deceptively simple meal, the salad crisp and succulent, the chicken expertly seasoned and grilled to perfection. Ethan's choice of a potato with prawns and coleslaw was delightful too, and she accepted the forkfuls he kept holding out to her with polite thanks. She did not once forget to call him Sir. Whilst his promise of a bare bottom spanking was exactly what she'd been hoping for, her instinct was still to minimize the number of strokes. That said, she had a feeling he would achieve exactly the effect he wanted, making up in quality anything he felt may be lacking in quantity. His expertise was one of the main factors that drew her to him.

His superbly sexy chest and toned shoulders might be playing their part too. And that smile that made her knees buckle and her pussy cream. This was so much more than merely physical, though. Privately she acknowledged that he could do whatever he chose to her, tonight or tomorrow. The safe word was nice in theory. In practice, she did not imagine it would be required.

She was in. It was that simple.

Fleur laid her knife and fork beside the empty plate and reached for Ethan's too, intending to re-stack the trolley ready to wheel it back out into the corridor for the staff to whisk away. Ethan stopped her, again with that single raised finger.

"Time you were undressed."

Fleur looked at him, unblinking. "Of course, Sir. Shall I go upstairs?"

"No. I want you to strip here. Then stand still and let me look at you. I'll tell you when to go upstairs." The hardening in his tone was unmistakable, that timbre of command, the thread of steely resolve that demanded obedience. Fleur had to resist the impulse to drop to her knees on the floor in front of him. No doubt if he wanted that, he'd tell her. She lowered her eyes, murmured her response.

"Of course. I am sorry, Sir."

Ethan leaned back on the low sofa and regarded her quietly. She did not move, uncertain how to do this. Was he expecting some sort of seductive swaying, some sultry belly-dance display? She hoped not. She possessed no such skills. And wearing her professional trousers and blouse, she just was not dressed for it.

"Problem? I thought I explained that I expect you to obey my instructions immediately, or if something's unclear that you should ask. Why are you still sitting there?"

"I was not sure how you want me to do this, Sir. Should I be...enticing you? Entertaining you? I am not good at that."

"Honey, the sight of you undressing is going to entice me perfectly fine. Your nudity will entertain me. Have no fear of that. I don't want the dance of the seven veils. I just want you naked. So, if you could please stand and remove your clothes just as you normally would? You might like to fold them neatly, ready for tomorrow. Then, when you're naked, come and stand here in front of me."

That seemed clear enough. And she had undressed for him once already, yesterday, in the courtyard after their dinner together. This should be no more difficult than that. It was, though. This time Ethan was much less the passionate lover-to-be, and more the objective observer. Fleur felt exposed and vulnerable.

In a flash of lucid self-awareness, she realized that was exactly the point. He had played her masterfully. Just as she wanted him to.

Fleur stood, stepped away from the ottoman couch and started unfastening the buttons on her blouse. She looked down at her fingers as she worked. She had to because her hands were shaking so much she never would have managed the task otherwise. She pulled the blouse from the waistband of her trousers and slid it from her shoulders. As he had instructed, she folded it and laid it carefully on the seat of the sofa beside her. She deliberately avoided looking at Ethan as she unfastened her trousers and pushed them down to pool at her ankles. They were loose fitting and made of a soft, light fabric, comfortable to wear all day in a Moroccan summer. She bent to pick them up, shook the wrinkles from them and folded them too.

Now only her bra and disgracefully moist knickers remained. There would be no point placing her pants on the neat pile of clothing, they were fit only for the bin. Pity, they had been one of her favorite pairs, a pretty confection that matched her white lacy bra. Fleur reached behind her back to unhook the bra and quickly placed that with the rest of her things. She did not turn yet fully to face him, but was nonetheless acutely aware of his gaze on her breasts. They felt heavy — she was more than usually conscious of their fullness, her swelling nipples. Naturally slender, Fleur still managed to sport a few curves where it mattered. Her breasts might not be as large as many other women's were, but they were a decent shape. Ethan had seemed to appreciate them yesterday. And again this morning. Nothing had changed.

Who was she trying to kid? *Everything* had changed and nothing was the same any more. Fleur felt assessed, judged, and was suddenly afraid she'd be found wanting. Pleasing Ethan was the most important thing in the world to her right now. She chanced a peep in his direction.

"Looking good, Fleur. Just the pants now, please."

It was all she needed, the quiet encouragement, the affirmation. Fleur slid her briefs down and stepped out of them. Her impulse was to kick them away, under the sofa, but she bent to retrieve them. Sure enough, they were limp and soggy. She glanced at Ethan, wondering if he'd mind her simply dumping them in his rubbish bin.

"Give them to me please." Ethan's hand was outstretched, waiting.

Surely he couldn't mean... Why would he want these disgusting things? But obedience was coming naturally enough to her, and she stepped forward to drop the soiled lace into his hand. She watched in amazement as he laid her damp knickers flat across his palm, and lifted them to his nose to inhale the aroma.

"What a perfect little slut you are. We've only just talked about what's to happen to you, and your cunt's already drooling. Am I right, Fleur?" His tone was deceptively soft, seductive, at odds with the crudeness of his words. Not being a native speaker of English, many of the more coarse expressions were ones she was unfamiliar with. 'Slut' and 'cunt' fell into that category. Her medical training had equipped her with a clinical vocabulary sufficient for every eventuality and Fleur thought she knew what he meant, but she needed to check the translation.

"Sir, you use words in English I do not know. I am a doctor, I do understand the, the..."

"The plumbing?"

He lifted one enquiring eyebrow, and she noted that he now seemed to be absently running his thumb across the scrap of fabric in his hand.

"Perhaps. I meant the process, the biology. The anatomical facts. I think I may have heard... I am not sure about all of these words."

Ethan smiled. "Your English is better than my French. I'll teach you the words as we go along but don't repeat them in your surgery. Come here, please, and stand in front of me as I asked you to."

Fleur moved forward the couple of paces required to bring her immediately in front of him. She stood, determined to remain still but feeling awkward and very uncomfortable. Yesterday this had seemed natural, she'd actually enjoyed undressing for him. Today, despite his having agreed to do exactly as she'd asked him, she was on edge.

Fleur stepped back involuntarily as Ethan rose to his feet. Her nose was level with his shoulder, and she was once more struck by the heady male essence of him. He smelled of coffee, and of some sort of woody-scented cologne. But most of all he smelled male. She could not have described it, that musky, slightly tangy aroma that was unmistakably him. Her impulse was to lean in further, to bury her nose against his hard torso and just breathe him in.

Instinctively, though, she knew better than to move. He had told her to stand here. She would do that, just that, nothing else.

Ethan raked his eyes over every inch of her from her small, slender feet, her slim legs, her smooth mound and slightly rounded stomach, up to her breasts and their swollen nipples now verging on the decadent. His eyes reached hers and held her gaze for a few moments before he lifted one finger, twirling it to indicate that she should turn around to show him the rear view.

Fleur obeyed, standing still as he trailed one fingertip along the top of her shoulder, from arm to neck, then slowly down her spine. It tickled, but she willed herself not to move. He reached the base of her spine and continued on, down the furrow between her buttocks until he reached the tight little hole of her anus.

"Shall we have a little biology lesson, submissive style? Bend over, please. If you need to rest your hands on the table, that's all right."

Fleur's pussy clenched violently. It was starting. *He* was starting. Now. She had to move slightly to be able to place her hands easily on the table that pressed her bottom more fully into Ethan's hands. It felt strangely nice. She had no qualms about doing as he asked, assuming the position and even spreading her legs before he asked her to.

"That's good anticipation. Be careful, though. Usually, I'll tell you exactly what I want. Can you open your legs even wider, please?"

Fleur complied and was rewarded with a long, open-handed stroke across her pussy, from clit to anus. Despite her anxiety, she groaned aloud.

"When I refer to your cunt, I mean all of this. I'm not being specific. Pussy means the same. I'll use both words a lot. What would you call it?"

She thought for a moment, searching for the correct medical terms and translating those into English. Or was that Latin? She wasn't sure. "I would say vulva, Sir. Or labia majora. Labia minora. Perineum. Vagina."

"Ah, yes, very clinical."

"But I do know pussy, Sir."

"Excellent. We'll be talking about your pussy and your cunt. Which includes here, too." He slipped one long finger inside her, sliding easily through her entrance to bury the digit deep. He thrust twice before withdrawing to trace the outer lips on either side of her opening.

"Pussy lips. Clit?" He slid his finger forward to rub the swelling nub.

Fleur gulped, struggling now to hold still. "Yes, Sir, my clitoris. Clit. I am familiar with that word too."

"You'll be more familiar with it soon, sweetheart. You'll come to know it intimately." He swirled the pad of his finger lazily across the tip of her clit before working his way backwards to her circle her anus again.

"And here?"

"My, my anus. Sir. Oh!" Fleur jumped as Ethan slipped the tip of his exploring finger inside, now lubricated from his brief foray into her pussy.

"Arse to us, love. Do you like this?" He rotated his finger slowly, pressing gently to ease it past her sphincter.

"I am really not sure, Sir." Then, as an afterthought, "It does not hurt."

"It's not meant to. I will hurt you, a little perhaps, but not by accident. And not now. I intend to be very, very gentle with your arse, when I fuck you here."

Whether her unsteadiness was caused by his words or his actions, she had no idea. Fleur only knew she stumbled forward as her knees threatened to give way. Ethan slipped an arm around her waist quickly, holding her in position. His finger sank deeper inside her arse.

"Are you all right, Fleur?"

"I... I think I am, Sir. It is difficult to remain on my feet, though, while you do...that."

"While I finger-fuck your arse? Is that what you mean?"

"Yes, Sir. Oh…" She ground out the words as he withdrew his finger then plunged it back inside, hard.

"Did that hurt?"

"No, Sir." She braced her hands more firmly on the low tabletop, closing her eyes as his firm, rhythmic movements in her anus focused her attention totally. She pulled her lower lip between her teeth, biting down hard in her concentration.

Ethan continued to support her, taking most of her weight, she realized, as he thrust his finger in and out of her now unresisting arse. It felt good—incredibly good, in fact. Intimately wicked. This was in essence only the same thing he had done to her yesterday, but it felt different, more intense. And this time, she knew he would not stop at just a finger.

Fleur's arousal grew. She panted, squeezing her pussy muscles. She wished he would—what? Touch her. She wanted him to stroke her clit.

"Please, Sir, could you…?"

"What, Fleur?"

"I want you to touch me, Sir." There, the words were out. Well, he did say she had to articulate her needs. He had even taught her the words he preferred to use. She intended to prove a diligent pupil in the short time that she would have him as her tutor.

"Do you? Where? How?"

"My clit, Sir. Please."

"How polite you are. I always find it amazing how a finger in her arse will do wonders for a sub's manners. Not that you were ever rude, Fleur."

"Thank you, Sir."

"Unfortunately, I can't oblige you. My hands are full just now. I don't want you collapsing at my feet. Not quite yet."

"I... I see, Sir." Obvious, really. How could she not have realized this?

"But I've no objection if you want to touch yourself. I have your weight, you could do it."

"I don't know if I can, Sir. I mean, I don't usually..."

"Now might be an excellent time to learn. Stroke your clit, Fleur. Do it now."

Later, she would recall the subtle shift between permission and instruction. Subtle, but utterly compelling. Being told she could, if she wanted to, was one thing and she might comply. Or she might choose not to. But an instruction—now that was entirely different.

Do it now. The absolute authority in those three words flicked a switch in her brain, and without further ado, Fleur shifted to lean on her left hand. Her right she lifted to her throbbing clit, instinctively taking the swollen bud between her thumb and forefinger. She rubbed, squeezing lightly. The sensation crackled through her core, igniting her nervous system.

"Oh, Sir..."

"Did you know you could do that?"

"No, Sir. I could not, before..."

"I think you could. You just never have. Do it now. Do what pleases you. Enjoy."

Fleur needed no further urging. She continued to rub her clit, experimenting with side-to-side motion, then stroking from front to back. Her pleasure built and grew, her inner muscles clamping down hard. She slid her finger along her clit, back toward her pussy and carried on going, thrusting it between her pussy lips and deep inside her.

"Mmm, does that feel good?"

"Oh yes, Sir, it does. Thank you."

"Try a second finger too. More contact. Are you close?"

Fleur heeded his advice, slipping a second finger alongside the first. A good move, he was right. She remembered his question. "Close, Sir?"

"Close to coming. Orgasm."

"Yes, I am. Oh, Sir…" A wave of pure pleasure shot through her, setting her nerve endings alight. Fleur's legs were no longer supporting her weight at all, as Ethan tightened his arm around her and stepped up the pace of his thrusts. Fleur managed to synchronize her own movements to his, instinctively falling into step. She quickly realized that by pressing the heel of her hand on her clit she could create the friction there that she needed to make her pleasure complete. Moments later, her orgasm gripped and spun her, her senses whirling away as she clenched hard around her fingers and his, shivering uncontrollably.

The climax passed almost as quickly as it had burst upon her, leaving Fleur a little stunned. Whatever she'd expected as she'd knocked on Ethan's door, it had not been this. Or had it? She had told him she wanted to be made to do strange, unprecedented things, to be used, her body not her own. Was this not a taste of exactly that? It may have been her own fingers doing some of the work, but he had orchestrated the whole thing. He instructed and she obeyed.

"Upstairs now, I think." His voice seemed to come from a long way off. Fleur was dimly aware that he had withdrawn his fingers from her anus—arse. She pulled her own fingers from her vagina and braced herself fully against the table again, intending to make an attempt to stand upright. She was not optimistic, but if he wanted her upstairs…

Then it was all out of her hands. Ethan bent and slipped his now free arm under her legs and picked her up. Cradling her in his arms, he headed for the stairs.

He laid her on the bed, rolling her gently onto her back. Fleur opened her eyes to watch him move around the room. He went into the en suite bathroom, scene of yesterday's rose petal experience, and she heard water running. *He is washing his hands.* He came back into the room and she watched as he adjusted lamps and opened drawers. He seemed to be looking for something.

Scarves. The gorgeous cashmere scarves he'd purchased yesterday, to be exact. He found them in one of the drawers of the dresser and came toward the bed. He dropped them beside her, his eyes holding her gaze evenly. The question clear. He waited, allowing her the opportunity to back out even now.

She had no intention of doing so. Fleur lifted her hands, placing them behind her head, close to the slatted headboard, her invitation clear.

Ethan took a scarf and looped it around her right wrist. He secured it to the headboard, then repeated with the left. He slipped his fingers into the loops too, apparently testing them.

"Is that comfortable? It should be tight enough to keep you still, but not painful at all."

"It feels fine, Sir."

"Good. Close your eyes, please."

A blindfold. Fleur was less at ease with this, but lowered her eyelids obediently. The soft cashmere brushed her face as Ethan laid it across her eyes and reached under her head to secure it in place. The bed dipped beside her as he sat. She turned her head in the direction she knew he must be, her heart setting up a furious rhythm as nerves started to take over. She had wanted this, but the reality seemed more *intense* than she had anticipated. Not that she had allowed herself much time to contemplate what might be about to happen. She had just dove straight in.

He cupped her cheek, stroking her face with his fingers. The gesture was soothing, as she knew he intended. Soft lips brushed hers, the tip of his tongue tracing the shape of her mouth.

"I won't hurt you, but we need a safe word. Cashmere, I think. That's your word for 'stop'. And for slow down I think we'll have...fountain. Okay with those?"

"Yes. Those words are fine."

"Yes, *Sir*."

His tone was not in the least angry but she could clearly detect the thread of steel that told her she'd earned additional punishment. Fleur chewed on her lower lip, her nerves back with a vengeance. What had she been thinking?

"I apologize, Sir."

"That's quite all right, Fleur. You're learning and doing very well. We can settle everything tomorrow, as I promised."

"You are scaring me, Sir."

"You asked me to, if I recall correctly. Have you changed your mind?"

Fleur lay still, drawing in deep breaths, even, steadying breaths. She fought to bring her rampaging heartbeat back under control. She didn't want to change her mind, had no wish at all to stop. But this was hard, harder than perhaps she'd anticipated. She'd been fine until the blindfold, but now, in the dark, everything seemed magnified.

"No, Sir, I don't want to stop. But, could you take off the blindfold?"

"The blindfold stays. Do you?"

Silence.

Fleur gnawed on her lip again, her battle with herself rather than with Ethan, or the blindfold. Was she about to fail, right at the outset?

"Remember your safe words. Both of them. You can ask to slow down, ask me to help you." The low voice came from close by, the words murmured directly into her ear. His very proximity steadying her.

"Fountain," Fleur whispered the word, not sure what the outcome would be.

She shivered as Ethan trailed his hand down her chest, between her breasts to her stomach. There he rested his hand, his fingers lightly brushing her skin. "Tell me what scares you about the blindfold."

"I'm not sure, it makes me feel uneasy. Insecure."

"You are absolutely safe here, with me. Do you believe that?" He moved his fingers against her stomach again, reminding her of his presence at her side.

"Yes, Sir, I do." Her response was quick and certain. She *did* feel safe.

"So..."

"I am afraid of the dark, Sir. A little bit."

"A little bit? Are you always afraid or just when you're alone in the dark?"

Fleur thought about that and her response was an honest one. "I am always scared, Sir, but not so much when I am not on my own."

"Are you scared of the dark now? Right at this moment?"

She hesitated, then, "No, Sir."

"Why is that?"

"You are here, touching me, talking to me. I can feel you. I can hear your voice."

"Okay, so here's what we'll do. I'll be touching you and talking to you a lot of the time in any case, but if at any point you feel yourself panicking just say fountain. I *will* be here. I won't leave you alone, even for a moment, but if you need to hear me, to feel me, and know you're not alone, just ask me. So, can we continue?"

Fleur smiled, her pleasure genuine. When she had said she wanted to be pushed to do things she'd never thought possible, she had no idea she might also be taking steps toward conquering her lifelong fear of the dark. It seemed that submission was a many-faceted jewel.

Chapter Eleven

Ethan was aware the moment she started to relax, to believe in this, in him, and in herself. He didn't usually play with inexperienced submissives but he had on occasions, and he recognized that moment when fear and doubt might not fall away, exactly, but the reality of the situation came into the ascendancy. It was a sort of 'I'm here, this is happening, and I'm still all right' moment. Fleur had just experienced hers, though she may not recognize it for herself for some time yet.

Ethan's plans for the scene were pretty clear and his plans for tomorrow were crystallizing fast. When he'd told Fleur he wouldn't hurt her tonight, he'd meant it. Whatever she might say, she did not need pain on this first excursion into his lifestyle. No, tonight was for removing barriers, for conquering inhibitions, and perhaps a phobia or two. Tonight he would push back Fleur's boundaries to make tomorrow possible.

His intention was to lead her to a point where she would accept his touch without question or resistance, comfortable in her own skin and content to let him handle her as he pleased, to know her body intimately. They were already a long way down that road. She was an enthusiastic learner. Now he wanted her to become even more keenly aware of her body, its sensitivity, its power to bring her joy.

"Are you thirsty?"

Fleur shook her head. Ethan wasn't having that. She needed fluids. He reached for the bottle of water beside the bed and snapped the cap open. Fleur jumped, startled by the sound.

"What was that?"

"Just me opening a bottle of water. Here, take a sip."

"I am fine."

"Just a few drops." He placed the neck of the bottle by her mouth, trickling a small amount of the cool water onto her lips.

Fleur licked them quickly, swallowing the water.

"More?"

She nodded, and he poured a few more drops onto her lips. Her mouth opened fully so he placed the bottle in her mouth for her to suck.

"Enough?"

"Yes, thank you, Sir. I was thirstier than I had thought."

"I've noticed submissives tend to become rather dry-mouthed. Especially when they're new to the lifestyle."

"Is it a lifestyle? I had not thought of it in that way."

"For some of us it is. You'll have to make up your own mind. So, feeling calmer now?"

"I am, thank you, Sir."

"You're most welcome, Fleur. Ready to play?"

"Yes, Sir, I am ready."

"Okay, so here's how it works tonight. I'm going to touch you with my hands, my tongue, my lips, and if

Chameleon

you're very well behaved, perhaps with my cock. I won't hurt you. You have my promise on that. Your job is to lie perfectly still. I'm already helping you with that to an extent by tying you up, but you're not immobilized. Your legs are free and will remain so. You'll still have to concentrate on not moving. And—don't orgasm either."

"But I—"

"It won't be easy. We've already established what a slut you are. But you're going to try very hard. Exercise a little willpower—or won't power—whichever suits. By way of an incentive, if you manage not to come until I give you permission, I won't double your punishment tomorrow. If you do, then whatever spanking you've earned by then will be doubled—either twice as hard, or twice as many spanks. But I'm a generous Dom, so you can choose which it is. So, do you understand your instructions, Fleur, and the consequences of not obeying?"

He waited, watching the play of emotions across her face. Consternation, anxiety. Determination. She took her time considering her response, and he found he liked that about her.

At last, "I think I do, Sir."

Ethan smiled to himself, still resting his hand lightly in her stomach where it had been since her little wobble a few minutes earlier. Now he trailed it up, across her ribs and cupped her left breast in his palm.

"Beautiful. Your nipples are so hard and red like cherries."

He rubbed his thumb across the taut peak, and Fleur arched under his hand.

"I told you to remain still. Was that not perfectly clear?"

"I am sorry, Sir, I didn't realize—"

191

"If I want you to move, I'll tell you. Otherwise, you remain absolutely still. Any questions?"

"Have I...? I mean, is my punishment doubled now? Already?"

"No. That only happens if you come without permission. But wriggling when you've been expressly told not to will earn you extra spanks, as would any act of disobedience or forgetting your instructions. You've reached eight now."

He watched as her chest rose and fell and could feel the slight rise in tempo of her heart under his hand. She was starting to understand, he thought, that this would be far from easy.

"I see. Thank you, Sir—for explaining, I mean."

"You're welcome." He was amused to see her bottom lip getting another worrying as he returned to his task, rolling her hard little nipple between his finger and thumb. He'd promised her gentle, no pain, so he wouldn't squeeze, tug or twist, though he fully intended to do all of that and more tomorrow. To her credit, Fleur managed to lie perfectly still, even when he leaned in to take her nipple between his lips and scrape it with his teeth. He heard her gasp, though, and knew she was already struggling.

Pain was relatively easy to bear, he'd generally observed, with a little practice. Endorphins were a wonderful evolutionary gift to the BDSM lifestyle. Pleasure, though, was different. Endorphins were no help there. Pleasure just had to be mastered the hard way. Fleur was about to learn this.

Easing his long body onto the bed alongside Fleur, Ethan continued to tease her nipples mercilessly. He used his tongue, his lips, his teeth, his fingers to work the sensitized nubs ceaselessly as Fleur stiffened beneath his ministrations. She was a chaotic turmoil of mixed emotions. He could feel the tension in her body as plainly as the arousal apparent in her pebbled tips. She was utterly rigid, her body locked in place as much by the sheer force of her will as by his cashmere scarves. Her concentration was absolute, on him, his delicate manipulation of her body and her own determination to suppress her response.

From time to time, she whimpered, the sound somewhere between a sob and a moan. He hadn't instructed her to be silent so he made no comment on that. Perhaps tomorrow, though probably not—he found he liked her helpless vocalizations.

"Please, Sir, this is very difficult. How much longer will you want me to…?"

"Until I tell you differently. Or you safe word." He might have added some further instruction about accepting his treatment without complaint, certainly he would have had she been even slightly more experienced, but he felt on balance she was doing fine. And so was he.

Fleur continued to gnaw on her lip, her head tilted back as though seeking intervention from a higher power. She'd learn that *he* was the high power in this room. Unless she opted to take hers back, but he felt that unlikely.

Content that he'd coaxed her nipples to their fullest, hardest, most erect response, Ethan turned his attention to the rest of Fleur's body. She lay with her legs stretched out on the bed, her knees clamped rigidly together. He could have secured her ankles when he had tied her to the bed, forced her to part her legs, but he intended her to spread her thighs for him willingly. She would, he knew, if—when—instructed.

He nibbled his way down her slightly rounded stomach, dipping his tongue into her navel and swirling it round there. She drew in a sharp breath. He knew he was tickling her so he did it again. Her movement was slight, ruthlessly suppressed but still apparent to him. Again, had she been even slightly more experienced he would have called her on it, but on this occasion, he let it go. She'd be coming in the next couple of minutes anyway and as he had no intention of granting permission that would cause her enough trouble.

He continued on his journey south, reaching her smooth mound. He kissed it, trailing his tongue down the two creases making up the V at the apex of her thighs. He stopped, turned his head to see her face.

Fleur looked to be in pain, her expression agonized, an incongruous mix of passion and genuine horror. She knew that he knew, as soon as he touched her pussy, she would detonate.

"Open your legs, Fleur."

Her muscles relaxed slightly, but her thighs remained firmly closed. Ethan waited a moment, then, "Fleur, do as I say, and do it *now.*"

He'd always found the Dom equivalent of 'please' effective, especially if injected with just the right tone of stern, uncompromising command. Fleur was getting the full benefit of this now, and complied instantly. She even had the grace and good sense to bend her knees in order to offer him better access to her, though she had to know what the consequences would be.

Ethan shifted his position slightly to bring his shoulders between her now widespread thighs. He took his time, gazing at the sweetly moist and very pink pussy so obligingly displayed inches from his face. She was aroused, close to incoherent with it, her clit swollen, almost completely out of its protective hood. The lips of her cunt were engorged, plump and inviting, slick and wet. Leaning on one elbow, Ethan slowly drew the backs of his knuckles along her quivering slit, noting the extra droplets of moisture appearing there. He leaned in, blew directly onto her clit and watched as her muscles tightened. He blew again, and caught the merest twitch as she suppressed the urge to thrust upwards, seeking the friction she desperately needed.

"Don't move, Fleur," he maintained that implacable tone then leaned in to destroy her totally.

Two licks. Two long, slow, flat-tongued licks along the length of her cunt was all it took to send Fleur and her hard-fought-for composure spinning out of control. She gave a lurch, a small cry and was gone, caught up in a whirlwind of orgasmic fury as her body finally asserted its inevitable victory. Ethan slid two fingers into her, thrusting sharply to rub against her G-spot. Even though his instructions had been explicit, he had known she would lose this battle. It went against all he knew and felt to allow a woman's orgasm to be anything less than it could be. Not on his watch. She might not have had his permission for this release, but in the end, they all counted. He massaged her G-spot and finger-fucked her into oblivion, smiling to himself at how easy it had really been, despite her determination to obey his instructions. She was such a hot, responsive little thing.

Ethan carried on sliding his fingers in and out of her pussy, slowing the tempo as her body ceased its uncontrolled shudders. At last, she lay still. Ethan watched as she drew the tip of her tongue along her lower lip, a sign he was beginning to recognize as fear. She was afraid of him, afraid of the consequences of her lapse. He found he didn't appreciate this, not at all. Nervous apprehension was all well and good—he could work with that—but fear was counter-productive.

Ethan reached up to cup her chin in his hand, rubbing the pad of his thumb over her lips.

"You came, without permission."

"I am sorry, Sir, so very sorry. I tried and I just—"

"I know. It's hard, and I didn't let up. You did well to hold out as long as you did. I'm impressed."

"I... Thank you, Sir. But, what about my punishment?"

"I haven't forgotten. Don't worry about that. But that's tomorrow's problem. Right now, I want to fuck you."

"I see, Sir."

"Do you know why?"

"Why, Sir?"

"Do you know why I want to fuck you? Why I intend to do just that?"

"No, Sir."

"Because you're my fuck toy. My own hot little cunt for my personal use. Isn't that right?"

Fleur hesitated for a fraction of a second, then, "Yes, Sir. It is. That is right."

Ethan smiled to himself and rolled off the bed to stand beside it, looking down at the olive-skinned woman spread out, naked, tied and blindfolded for his use. Still fully dressed himself, he unbuttoned his shirt and drew it off his shoulders. Fleur obviously heard the rustle of fabric and turned toward him, her head tilting slowly from side to side as she sought a clue, any clue, as to his whereabouts. Ethan stepped slightly farther away from the bed and unzipped his jeans. He took a condom from his front pocket then slid his pants off his hips too, taking his boxer shorts with them, and watched as Fleur again turned her head toward the sound.

He moved a few paces to his left before ripping the foil open. She tilted her chin in his direction, following the audible clues. He unrolled the condom along his length.

He stood still, silent, fully naked now, and waited. It didn't take long, a few seconds no more, before she began to panic.

"Sir?"

Ethan remained still and perfectly quiet. He knew what he wanted her to do, what she needed to learn.

"Sir? Please, Sir…"

Silence.

"Fountain! Fountain, please, Sir…"

He was beside her instantly, his hands on her face, cupping her cheeks to hold her still for his kiss. He brushed his lips over hers and lifted one heavy thigh over her hips, wrapping himself around her. She was left under no illusion that she was not alone.

Fleur responded powerfully, opening her mouth as she sucked his tongue inside. Rolling fully onto her, Ethan positioned himself between her thighs, his cock nudging her wet and welcoming entrance.

"Please, Sir, I want you. I want this. Please…"

Ethan required no further encouragement, sliding into her with one long, swift thrust. Fleur arched toward him, thrusting her hips to meet his. He reached for her knee, drawing it up and outwards to more fully open her. Then he withdrew, waited a moment with just the tip of his cock inside her before plunging back into her. Fleur gasped with pure pleasure and she gripped him tightly with her inner strength. She'd been tight before. Now she was utterly exquisite. Ethan shifted his angle slightly to allow him more, deeper penetration. It was what they both wanted. Fleur brought her other leg up, unbidden, to match the one Ethan had positioned, and he started thrusting.

Ethan soon established his rhythm—crisp, sharp, incisive. He didn't intend for this to take long. There would be time later for more drawn out teasing and gentle finesse. Today he was going for a demonstration of what it meant to be submissive. He wanted her surrender.

He got it. Fleur's body accepted him as readily as her heart and her mind had. She was unresisting, totally giving, absolutely taken. Ethan fucked her hard, efficiently, pushing her swiftly toward her climax. As she hovered within reach of it, he slipped his hand between their bodies to rub the pad of his middle finger roughly against her clit, leaving her in no doubt of what he wanted, demanded from her.

He hurled her from one extreme to another, one moment forbidden to orgasm, the next it seemed compulsory. Fleur may have failed to obey the first time, but she did not the second. Her climax drew a long, low moan from her as her body spasmed sharply under the onslaught of Ethan's thrusting cock. Her pussy gripped Ethan's erection, her muscles contracting around him as he, too, hurtled toward his own release. He knew the instant Fleur passed the point of no return, and followed her gladly, his balls tightening and drawing up, ready. He rammed his cock into her one last time, hard and deep, and held his position as his semen spurted to fill the condom.

Fleur lay still beneath him, her breathing rapid, her lips slightly turned up in the beginning of a smile. Ethan reached for the cashmere binding her wrists and tugged at one end of the fabric. The knot fell away, freeing her hands instantly. He made similarly short work of the blindfold, watching, amused, as she blinked in the sudden light. Still inside her, he rolled to his back, wrapping his arms around her shoulders and hips to bring her with him.

Her hair lay everywhere, it seemed. He grabbed a fistful of it to draw it back from her face as she tilted her head to prop her chin on his chest. He noted that she still looked vaguely stunned but otherwise okay. If this had been a vanilla fuck, he would have asked her, made sure, but this time the rules were different. Now he waited, allowing her a few moments, no more, to collect her wits, then, "You may thank me, when you're ready."

Her eyes widened but just a fraction. "Thank you, Sir. I... I liked that — very much."

Me too, honey.

He treated her to a slight incline of his head. "You did well. Well enough, anyway. You only disobeyed me five times, so you've earned just ten spanks, would you agree with that?"

"I... Yes, if you say that, Sir, I am sure that you are correct."

"I am. As you know, you came without permission so your punishment is doubled. So I'll make this an easy choice for you. You'll accept ten stripes with my belt on your bare bottom, or twenty slaps with my hand. Think about it overnight and tell me tomorrow which you think you prefer."

Now her eyes did widen, and Ethan managed not to smile. If she'd looked slightly stunned before, the mention of a belt across her arse had completed the job. Tomorrow was going to be interesting.

Chapter Twelve

"Morning, gorgeous."

Ethan was clearly busy, seated on one of the low sofas in the living area of the *riad*, piles of papers spread on the coffee table in front of him. His laptop sat open on the seat beside him, and a half-full *cafetière* perched on the edge of the table. His cup sat on the floor. As Fleur entered, he put down the pencil in his hand and smiled across the room at her.

The friendly greeting reassured her. He seemed not to mind her disturbing him. Which was good, as she wanted to talk — or to listen. Anything, really, she just craved the contact with him.

She had awoken to find herself alone in the huge bed, though the side previously occupied by Ethan had been still warm. He would not be far away, and her impulse had been to find him, to be close to him again. She had slipped from the bed, hunted around for something to wear, as she felt self-conscious about presenting herself before him naked. At least, not without a direct instruction to that effect. Then she had left the bedroom to seek him out.

"Good morning, Sir," she offered the final word cautiously. Fleur was uncertain of the protocol for the morning after and in fairness, she was feeling more than a little confused right now. But of one thing she was certain. For her, the events of last night were still very much in the present—her pussy contracted sharply, just at the memory of it. But this Ethan, the efficient, professional Ethan, who concerned himself with maps and laptops and paperwork, might not be minded to continue their interplay from the previous evening. He looked too serious, too businesslike. He looked—detached.

"There's coffee in the pot. Or I could get some tea sent across for you by room service. What would you like for breakfast?"

You. "I am not hungry, thank you. But tea would be very nice."

Ethan got to his feet and strode to the side table where the hotel phone handset sat proudly. He ordered up a tray of Earl Grey tea, toast and croissants in more than passable French, she noted. He made a detour on his way back to his workstation to drop a light kiss on her forehead.

"You might get peckish later. After your spanking."

Ah, not so immersed in business, then. Fleur was conscious of the flush starting at her neck and creeping up her face. She had known that this was coming, but not quite so immediately. A spanking before breakfast? She had somehow managed to assume that her punishment would be administered later, after their return from her parents' home.

"You intend to do it now? At this moment?" Her voice sounded rather breathless to her ears. She hoped he would not misinterpret it as eagerness. Although, on the other hand…

He slanted a brief, inscrutable glance in her direction as he settled back on the sofa. "Who are you talking to, Fleur?"

She frowned, momentarily thrown. Then she remembered. "You, Sir. I apologize."

He simply nodded, accepting her apology. "I could administer your punishment now, which has just grown to twelve spanks, incidentally. You really need to concentrate, Fleur, but I'm confident a seriously sore bottom will help you enormously in that regard. I'll be giving you a memorable lesson, so I expect it to be effective. I'm happy to allow you to drink your tea first, though. You may prefer to do that sitting. You won't be sitting afterwards." He gestured to the sofa opposite him, inviting her to make herself comfortable.

Despite his ominous promises, Fleur found herself doing exactly that, arranging the lower hem of the shirt she had borrowed from his drawer carefully so as to cover as much of her legs as possible. She fully appreciated that modesty seemed somewhat misplaced between them now, and by the sound of it, it would be entirely shredded before much longer. But the habits of a lifetime die hard. She thought she caught a slight smirk on his handsome face, though that was gone as quickly as it had appeared. He made no comment on her appearance or demeanor, simply applied his attention to gathering his papers together.

"Please do not let me disturb your work, Sir." Her protest was quick and polite, of course, but it was offered as much to allow herself a few more minutes to contemplate her situation and immediate prospects.

"I can finish this later. For now, Fleur, you have my undivided attention. Did you sleep well?"

"I did. Thank you, Sir." *How polite we are.*

"Me too. You make a delightful bed companion, so soft and warm. It took some effort of will not to wake you up first thing and fuck you until you screamed. But you looked so peaceful."

"I...would not have objected, Sir."

"How accommodating. Perhaps later. In fact, definitely later. First, though, have you decided how you would prefer to accept your punishment this morning? I take it you *will* be accepting it?" He smiled pleasantly across the coffee table at her, one eyebrow raised expectantly.

She would, she had no doubt of that. And she was fairly certain she had made her decision regarding the manner in which she preferred to be punished. Fleur opened her mouth to speak, but was interrupted by a soft knock at the door.

"Ah, your tea. One moment, please." Ethan stood and went to answer the door.

She thought about moving from the center of the room in the hopes that she would be unnoticed by the hotel staff member, but recalled that Ethan had protected her anonymity yesterday and she was confident he would do so again. Her confidence was not misplaced as she heard him thank the waiter. He returned to the room carrying the tray, no doubt taken from the waiter in exchange for another handful of dirhams. He placed it on the table in front of her, on top of a large chart still spread out there.

"Please do help yourself. I think I'll stick to coffee." He poured himself another cup. She noticed he did not add milk this morning.

A minute or so later they were both supplied with drinks. Fleur took a first, tentative sip before lifting her gaze to meet his again.

"You were saying, Fleur...?"

Ah yes, a spanking or his belt? "Yes, Sir. I think, if it's all right with you, I would prefer you to use your hand, please."

"Of course. May I ask why you chose that?"

He could ask, certainly. She might struggle to answer. She knew she had to try, though—he would insist on that much.

"Because I am afraid. I am afraid of both, but less of you, of your hand. You will be able to control, to know…"

"Be under no illusion, Fleur, I will be in absolute control, whichever method of punishment you select. A spanking with my hand is not a soft option—I can hurt you. I *will* hurt you. I intend you to learn from this so it will be a memorable experience."

Fleur swallowed hard, her pussy clenching and dampening even as her heart sank at his words. She was experiencing a confusing, chaotic reaction, erotic lust tinged with a healthy apprehension. But she knew, in the very pit of her stomach, where dread was even now transforming into something else, that she would not back out. She wanted this, wanted to feel it, experience it, hurt from it and learn from it. And she wanted him. It was really very simple.

"I do understand that, Sir."

He regarded her silently for a few moments, seemed to be assessing. At last, satisfied perhaps that she did indeed understand her situation, he nodded briefly. "Good. We'll do this outside, I think. Come with me."

He stood and walked away from her, heading for the French window leading out to the internal courtyard. Fleur replaced her teacup on the tray before her and got to her feet. Silently, she followed him.

Ethan sat on one of the several seats arranged around the courtyard. He beckoned Fleur to him as she hesitated by the door, her back to the cool interior of the *riad*. It was already approaching thirty degrees outside and he had chosen a spot in full sun. She was sure this was deliberate to afford him an even better view of her bottom, unimpaired by shade. She moved forward to stand beside him.

"Are you wearing underwear?"

"No, Sir. I do not have any, apart from the pants I wore yesterday and they are no longer clean."

"I see. Would you like me to buy you some fresh ones? I'm sure one of the boutiques in the hotel can supply what you need."

She wondered what he would choose for her. "That would be very helpful, Sir. Thank you. I have the money. I would not expect you to pay for my clothes."

His sexy smile went some considerable way toward melting her insides entirely. Perhaps this spanking would not take long, then...

"Consider it a parting gift, Fleur. I'll see to it. Now, please position yourself across my lap and raise the shirt above your waist." He looked up at her expectantly. She knew better than to cause him to ask twice.

Leaning across his lap, Fleur lowered herself onto his knees. She wriggled a little, settling. The unfamiliar position felt oddly comfortable. She squeezed her buttocks together experimentally, though what she hoped to discover was somewhat beyond her in that moment. Remembering the rest of her instructions, she reached for the hem at the back of the shirt and lifted it to the small of her back.

The sun's warmth caressed her naked bottom, gentle heat that would shortly become searing—with or without the aid of Ethan's hard, heavy palm. The irrelevant thought fluttered through her consciousness that, as far as she could recall, she had never bared her skin in the full sunshine. Not totally, not like this. Ethan was certainly using all the props at his disposal to make this occasion special for her—unique, in fact. And she had a suspicion that he was nowhere near done yet.

Fleur squeaked as Ethan's hand connected with her buttock, though this was not a slap. He stroked her, the sensation erotic and tender. Her response was born out of surprise, not pain.

"You're trembling, Fleur. I know you can't be cold."

"No, Sir." She had already told him she was afraid, though she had felt calmer since he had asked her to lie across his lap. The connection, the direct contact with him both soothing and reassuring. This was another reason why she had opted for the spanking rather than his belt, though perhaps he would have put her over his knee for either. Maybe she should have asked...

"Do you remember your safe words?"

"I… Yes, Sir. But will I…? I mean, am I allowed to use them?"

"Yes, always." He paused but continued to caress her bottom slowly, pressing his fingers against the delicate fleshiness.

It felt wonderful. She would be content to remain there all day and let the sun burn her to a crisp if he would just continue to stroke her like this.

He spoke again, his voice modulated to that exact frequency that could turn her to jelly. "You won't need cashmere, I'm fairly sure of that. But fountain might be useful. Remember it, and use it if you need to. And, Fleur, you won't enjoy this. You're not meant to. It's a punishment and I'm about to hurt you. But it *will* be tolerable, just about. If, at any stage, you think it isn't, then you use that safe word. Do you understand me?"

She considered this for a few moments since it seemed only polite. Then, "Yes, Sir. You have made matters very clear. Thank you."

"Are you ready, Fleur?"

No. "Yes, Sir."

The first slap landed across her left buttock, hard and sharp, though not especially painful. The sound reverberated around the courtyard, echoing back from the tangled vines and bougainvillea tumbling from the trellises that ringed the inner space. Fleur jerked involuntarily, though she made no attempt to get away or to raise her hands to protect herself. She closed her eyes, gritted her teeth and waited for the next spank to fall.

Ethan did not draw matters out unduly and she was grateful to him for that. He spanked her solidly, alternating between her buttocks and not landing a slap in the same place twice. He had not asked her to count but she could not help doing so. Three, four, five.

The sixth slap was harder. She swore he was piling it on now — or maybe her skin was becoming more sensitive. She let out a small squeal, followed by a definite scream at the seventh. Ethan stopped.

"I'd prefer not to have hotel security come running, thinking you're being murdered in here. Could you be quiet, please, or would you like me to gag you?"

Fleur shuddered. She viewed the prospect of rescue by the Totally Five Star staff with even less enthusiasm than did Ethan. "I am sorry, Sir. I will try not to make any sound."

"I'd be obliged. Okay to continue?"

Fleur clenched her buttocks pitifully. Despite her words and her determination to endure her punishment without fuss, she struggled. And not even halfway there yet.

"Yes, Sir." And as an afterthought, "Please."

The next few slaps were dropped hard and fast onto her already smarting backside. Fleur continued to count them in her head, now grinding her teeth together to prevent herself from crying out. She was sore, really hurting, her bottom on fire. His hand was heavy, solid, tireless, and still she was nowhere near the finishing post.

Twelve. Thirteen, fourteen, fifteen.

"Oh, Sir, please…" She could not help the whimper of pain that escaped her. Ethan stopped again.

"Safe word or be silent," he said, his tone harsh and uncompromising.

Despite her best intentions, Fleur started to sob. She was disappointing him and disgracing herself. She should be able to manage this better, surely. It was only a spanking.

"Fleur, if you need me to stop for a minute you have only to ask. Say fountain and we can have a timeout." His voice was gentler now, and Fleur squeezed his ankle with her hand by way of acknowledgment.

"A couple of minutes, Sir, if you please."

"Of course. And would you like me to entertain you during this little interlude?"

"I do not understand, Sir."

"Spread your legs for me, love, and I'll show you what I mean."

What, now? Here? In the middle of…this?

"Fleur…?" Apparently so. Fleur obliged, opening her legs as wide as she was able in her current position. Her reward was a long, slow caress along the entire length of her pussy.

"Mmm, you may be squealing a bit but you're fucking loving this. Here's the evidence, girl." He used the flat of his hand to smear her own wetness across her bottom. Fleur winced at the contact but offered no protest. Ethan repeated the caress, but this time he maintained contact with her cunt, easing one long finger inside her. Fleur tightened her inner muscles around it, writhing furiously on his lap. She wanted friction. She needed him to thrust.

"What are you up to, girl? If you want something, you know to ask. Tell me what you need."

"More, Sir. I want more."

"More what? More fingers? Two, perhaps? Three, even?"

"Three, Sir." She saw no point in being less than direct. Her reward—three fingers firmly inserted into her desperately wet pussy. Ethan twisted them inside her, spreading them to stretch her, to press sensuously against her inner walls. It still was not enough, nowhere close to enough.

"Please, Sir, can you move your hand?"

"What, you don't like this?"

"I do. Yes, Sir, I do. But I need you to, to..." She hesitated, seeking the correct word. Would he understand if she spoke to him in French?

She was spared the problem.

"Do you want me to finger-fuck you?"

Yes, please, yes. She tried for a modicum more decorum, however. "Yes, Sir, I do think that is the phrase I was looking for. My thanks for that."

Ethan's answering chuckle was slow and sexy, and her pussy spasmed around his fingers. He withdrew them and plunged them back into her. Hard. He did it again. And again. Fleur stopped writhing and settled for deep, contented moaning. She lay still, giving herself over entirely to Ethan's skilled attentions. He brought his other hand into play too, feathering the tip across her clit. Fleur almost cried out again, this time in delight, but managed instead to shove her fist into her mouth. Ethan increased the pressure, very slightly, but enough to edge her toward orgasm. She knew she was about to come—and come hard.

Moments later, she arrived there, spinning, whirling, her senses scrambled. Her knuckles hurt from the pressure of her teeth, but still she clenched and trembled as the waves of pure pleasure washed through her. Even in the middle of a spanking— perhaps because it *was* in the middle of a spanking— he could still find her inner *poutin*.

As the tremors subsided and Fleur's senses returned to her, Fleur became conscious that he was talking to her again. She had missed his words, though.

"I am sorry, Sir. What did you ask me?"

"I asked if you were ready to continue. To complete your punishment. Another nine spanks to go, I think you'll find."

"Yes, Sir, that is correct. I am ready. And, thank you."

"Any time, Fleur. You have only to ask. Now, we finish."

She yelped as the next slap landed and she apologized quickly. She managed to remain near enough silent for the next four or five, though it was hard going. The final three were absolute agony, and Fleur started crying again by the time Ethan finally delivered the last one. He knew she was in tears, but this had made no difference it would seem, either to his determination to complete her punishment or to the severity of his spanking. Despite her discomfort, Fleur would have had it no other way.

The spanking finished, Ethan helped her to stand up straight. Fleur remained still, standing before him, her face wet with tears she made no attempt to wipe away. Her bottom was so sore that the merest brush of the fabric of her shirt was agony. She knew she would not be able to sit, perhaps for a long time. Even the slightest movement seemed impossible. How was she going to endure the meal with her parents? Surely they would be able to tell.

"Would you like to lie down? On your stomach, naturally."

Fleur nodded, though she was not sure she could get as far as the bedroom under her own steam. She needn't have worried. Ethan stood and, with one swift movement, whisked the shirt up and over her head to leave her totally naked. It was more comfortable, though. He lifted her, one arm behind her knees and the other bracing her shoulders, and carried her inside. He did not take her to the bedroom, though. Instead, he headed for the cool lounge area and deposited Fleur gently on the long padded ottoman. He helped her to roll onto her stomach and commanded her not to move, stating that he'd be right back.

He need not hurry. Fleur sank her cheek against the smooth fabric, her bottom smarting in the cooler atmosphere of the air-conditioned room. She was going nowhere.

Ethan returned in a few moments and sat beside her on the couch. "You did well, love. Twenty-four is a lot, for a first attempt. Even though I was taking it easy on you, I expected you to need more breaks. I'm impressed."

Taking it easy! Fleur made a mental note never to really aggravate him. Her delicate buttocks would not endure it.

"You'll feel the effects for a while. You're meant to. But this should help make you a bit more comfortable. Lift." He looped an arm under her shoulders and raised her from the couch, shifting along until his thighs were under her upper body. He lowered her gently back and Fleur nestled into him, her face turned away. She was aware of his erection close to her head, thick and solid inside his jeans, but he seemed disinclined to do anything with it right now. A pity, perhaps, but still she was glad of his restraint and consideration.

Fleur flinched as something cool and wet landed on her abused bottom. "Keep still, I'll be gentle. This should help take the sting out."

Fleur turned her head to see that Ethan had poured a generous puddle of body lotion directly onto her bum. He must have borrowed it from the hotel bathroom. He started slowly smearing it across her sore buttocks, not pressing hard, allowing the lotion to soak in naturally.

"You know, love—and I really should have mentioned this before—you have a truly beautiful arse. Or would that be *derrière* to you?"

"*Derrière* is a nice word, I think. I am not sure I care for arse."

"Well, I care for arse. I care very much for *your* arse, little Fleur. It would give me great pleasure to spank it for you again, should our paths cross in the future."

His words set off an unexpected surge of longing—or was it perhaps regret?—in Fleur. Their paths were unlikely to cross again. If she did submit to another spanking at some time—and she sincerely hoped that might prove possible—it would not involve Ethan Savage. She found that thought distinctly unpalatable, even though she had known from the outset that this would just be a temporary interlude, a moment of madness made possible in part by the fact that he would be gone within a few days and she would not have to see him again. Ever.

"That would be very nice, Sir. And so is that." She stretched languorously on the ottoman, rubbing her breasts against his leg. "Is this always how a spanking ends, even when it is intended as punishment?"

"Mmm, pretty much. Preparation is crucial, but aftercare is the clincher. How do you feel, Fleur?"

"I am fine, Sir."

"If you feel unhappy, sad, depressed, or even especially tired later, you're to tell me. Yes?"

"Of course, Sir. But I feel good. Very good. Even my *derrière* is not so sore now. You have an excellent bedside manner, Mr. Savage."

"And you, Doctor Mansouri, are an insolent sub who would do well to mind her manners. Remember the Eleventh Commandment—Thou shalt not take the piss out of thy Dom."

"My mother is the Christian in our household. I will be sure to check that reference with her, Sir."

"Ah, yes, I apologize. You're Muslim, yes?"

He continued to caress the soothing balm into her smarting skin as Fleur considered how to answer. She opted for the truth.

"No, not really, Sir. My father is Muslim, and my mother Christian. Roman Catholic, in fact. I am familiar with both faiths, and I have worshiped in the mosque and in the church. For myself, though, I doubt the existence of a god at all, though I would not say such a thing in my mother's hearing. It would cause her to offer up prayers to the Virgin for my immortal soul. This could continue for days. My father would not thank me for it either."

Ethan laughed loudly. "What an irreverent little slut you are. I'm looking forward to meeting your father. He sounds fascinating."

"My papa *is* fascinating. And he will like you."

"Let's hope so."

"*Insha'Allah…*"

"What does that mean?"

"It means God willing."

Chapter Thirteen

A slight movement on the ottoman caught his attention. Ethan looked up from his laptop to see Fleur stretch and start to turn onto her back. The pressure of the upholstery against her beautifully pink bottom soon put a stop to that. Her nose wrinkled and she shifted back onto her side, not yet waking.

She had slipped into a deep sleep minutes after their conversation about differing theological perspectives, not unusual in a sub who has just been soundly spanked. Ethan had waited until he was sure that she was out for the count before slipping out from under her and fetching a light sheet from the spare bedroom to drape over her body. Pity to cover her up, he thought, but the air con was fierce and he didn't want her becoming chilled. Not much chance of that, though. She had kept on kicking the sheet off, and after picking it up from the floor two or three times, he'd decided to simply leave it and enjoy the view.

Actually, he was enjoying everything about Fleur Mansouri. She had responded exquisitely to her first experience of a spanking, giving in to tears eventually as he'd expected, but not before her bottom had turned a truly stunning shade of crimson. She'd even managed a sweet little orgasm for him. She was a natural submissive and he was pleased that she had decided to explore this part of herself at last. His one regret was that he would not be here to see her unfurl fully, but he could be content knowing that he had helped to awaken her appetites, and had done nothing to dispel them. How she progressed from here was really up to her. He had no doubt she would find her way. She had so far.

She rolled again and this time her eyelids fluttered. Now she *was* waking. Ethan left his work and went to kneel beside the ottoman, brushing the mass of dark hair from her face. Fleur opened her eyes and looked directly at him—and smiled. A dazzling, joyful, genuine smile. A smile that screamed, 'Hello, welcome. I am truly delighted that you are here.'

"Nice nap?" He dropped a chaste kiss onto her mouth.

"Yes, thank you, Sir." She struggled to push herself up on one elbow. "How long was I asleep?"

Ethan glanced at his watch. "About an hour, maybe a little more."

"What time is it?"

"Nearly eleven."

"I should go, Sir. My mother will need me to help with preparations for tonight."

"I see. Okay, then. Would you like to shower first? Or maybe take a bath?"

"A shower would be best, I think, Sir. My *derrière* is still not quite recovered."

"Hmm, I note you've not forgotten to call me Sir since I spanked you, though. It certainly did the trick."

"Yes, Sir, and may I thank you for your efforts on my behalf? I think I would like that shower, please."

"You go ahead. While you're doing that, I'll see about getting some new underwear for you. I intend to keep your old panties as a souvenir."

Fleur carefully eased her legs from the couch and slid sideways from the seat, exercising great caution not to apply any undue weight to her bum. Ethan watched, amused, conscious that his cock threatened to burst out of his pants any time now. He had no doubt that at just a word from him she would turn and bend over the settee, completely obliging and utterly submissive, presenting her delightful little tush to him for his perfect enjoyment. And hers. But he could also see the stiffness as she moved, the fatigue in her muscles, despite her recent sleep. She needed a shower, then she needed to go home to see her mother. He would have her again soon enough.

He watched as she made her way across the room, still not entirely steady but good enough, and no longer mindful of her nudity around him. She turned at the bottom of the stairs, smiled at him and was gone.

* * * *

Ethan called up room service again and they ate a picnic-style lunch of harira, a traditional Moroccan soup made of chickpeas and lentils, a specialty of the Marrakesh Totally Five Star. They had huge lumps of the local flat bread to dip in it, and Ethan couldn't remember a meal he had enjoyed more. Fleur was relaxed and if her bum was still hurting, she gave no sign of it. She was, quite simply, beautiful.

"What time do you have to leave?"

"When we have finished our meal. I am sorry, but I must go. Do you mind?"

She seemed apprehensive, as though she almost felt she might be denied permission. He hoped he hadn't created such an impression. "I love your company but no, of course I don't mind. You were always free to leave at any time. And I'll be seeing you again soon."

"Yes, at my home. I gave you the address yesterday. It is just a short walk, perhaps twenty minutes from here, but you will not be able to find the way. Too many narrow streets in the city. If you ask for a taxi at the hotel reception and show the address, the driver will take you there."

Ethan suspected he might have managed to find the place on his own—he usually did and he'd visited a great many cities over the years. He could always ask if he got lost. But the huge bunch of flowers he'd acquired for Madame Mansouri at the same time that he'd ordered the lilies for Fleur would probably not survive the journey through the bustling alleyways of the medina. So, a taxi it would be.

"Shall I walk with you to reception?"

"I think perhaps not, if you do not mind, Sir."

Ethan did mind, up to a point, but he understood her reticence. He was leaving tomorrow and she would be staying. This was her life, her job. Her reputation mattered to her. She could do without the questions, the gossip. Her family sounded quite supportive from what he had heard of them, but they, too, might appreciate discretion. So he wouldn't be walking her to the hotel lobby, advertising their liaison for the entertainment of any interested colleagues and other guests. Instead, he contented himself with kissing her soundly at the entrance to his own suite.

He broke the kiss and stepped back from her. His expression inscrutable now, he picked up a white envelope from the hall table beside the door and handed it to Fleur. "While you were sleeping, I wrote down your instructions for later. Please read these and comply exactly with my requirements." He ignored her startled expression, leaning past her to open the door. She simply nodded, placed the envelope unopened into her bag and slipped away down the corridor.

Later, baby.

* * * *

The place was huge. Fucking enormous! He'd gathered that the Mansouri family were relatively wealthy, but this villa exceeded anything he might have imagined. He paid the taxi driver then did a double check of the address Fleur had given him. The neat handwriting on the slip of paper tallied with the name on the marble plate attached to the gate. This was definitely the place. *Dar Roumana,* House of the Pomegranate. Under the rather imposing name, in smaller lettering, he read, *Riad Mansouri.*

But this was not a *riad* in his view. A *riad* was the sort of place he was staying in. This was nothing short of a palace. Surrounded by a high wall constructed of a soft pink-colored stone, he could just make out the contours of the two-story house itself through the close-spaced vertical slats of the gate.

The gate itself was sturdy and solidly locked. No one would be getting in here without permission. Fleur had told him to ring the bell when he arrived, so he looked for one. He found it, a small discreet button to the right of the gate, under the nameplate. He pressed it and waited.

He didn't have long to kick his heels. Immediately after he'd pressed the bell, the massive gate began to slide slowly to the right. Seconds later, the opening was sufficiently wide to walk through, so Ethan did just that. He was greeted by the sight of a smartly dressed man, aged he thought in his mid-fifties, bustling down the wide steps at the front of the villa, his hand outstretched.

"*Monsieur Savage, Vous nous avez trouvé. Bienvenue chez nous. Je suis Said Mansouri.*"

Ethan took the man's proffered hand and shook it. "*Bonsoir, Monsieur. Merci pour l'invitation.*"

"Papa, we agreed to speak in English this evening."

Ethan looked up to see Fleur framed in the doorway to the *riad*, looking her usual stunning self. Whilst not dressed in Western style exactly, neither was she wearing traditionally Moroccan clothing. Her skirt hung at ankle length, made of swirling, soft fabric in various shades of blue. Her top was a fitted, waist-length wrap-over affair in a rich shade of yellow. She reminded him of sunshine. He was momentarily fascinated by her shirt, and could not help imagining his hands sliding inside it, parting the two halves of the front to reveal what he knew to be perfect breasts. He quashed such thinking immediately, entirely inappropriate for the present company.

As she trotted down the steps to join them, Ethan was conscious of how at ease Fleur looked. Not so surprising perhaps. She was, after all, in her own home. But it was more than that. He realized this was usually her way, managing almost effortlessly to transcend cultural norms and fit in anywhere. Whatever the situation, whatever the company she was in, she never appeared to be out of place. Her command of languages, her appearance, even her fluid attitude toward the spiritual side of life, all helped her to blend in. She was a chameleon, he thought, a human chameleon constantly adapting to her environment. And quite enchanting.

"I apologize, Mr. Savage, but you do speak French, I think. Is it not so?" Said Mansouri broke into Ethan's reverie.

"I do, of course. Enough to get by, though not as fluent as your English or that of your daughter." He turned to Fleur. "How delightful to see you again, Fleur. You look beautiful."

Her face reddened slightly, and Ethan wondered if her bottom were still sporting an equally pink aspect following his attentions earlier this morning. He imagined so. It had been a spanking with staying power.

"We are delighted you could join us this evening, Mr. Savage. Please, come in. Come in. My wife is inside, and you have not met my other daughter, I think." Said Mansouri took over the proceedings, ushering Ethan to precede him into the *riad*.

As he passed through the door, Ethan was struck instantly by the coolness of the interior, the place built to maximize comfort in this climate though no doubt assisted by efficient air conditioning.

Yvette Mansouri greeted him in the lobby, rushing forward with both hands outstretched. Ethan juggled the large bouquet of red gerberas, yellow roses and pure white chrysanthemums into one hand and returned her exuberant hug with his free arm.

"Ethan, how lovely. My little Lily is such an excellent judge of handsome men, is she not, Said?"

Her husband eyed Ethan critically, as though assessing that possibility. He apparently deemed it wise not to comment, instead turning to beckon another young woman to join their group.

"You have met my wife already. Here is the other lovely lady with whom I share my home, my youngest daughter, Yasmine."

Ethan greeted Yasmine Mansouri politely, noting that whilst the family resemblance was obvious, she lacked Fleur's innate grace. Yasmine's cool handshake, though, was confident and well mannered, and Ethan could easily see her as the professional lawyer described to him by Fleur. The Mansouris were an accomplished family.

"Madame Mansouri, these are for you." Ethan held the flowers out to his hostess, who accepted them with a smile.

"You should not have. You really had no need. But they are truly beautiful. Thank you." She kissed him on both cheeks in a fundamentally Gallic gesture. Ethan liked it, and noted that her daughter had displayed no such exuberance on first making his acquaintance. She had, however, made up for it since. Yvette rushed on. "Our meal is almost ready. Please, go through into the courtyard and make yourselves comfortable. I have laid out drinks there. Said, you must help Fleur to take care of our guest whilst I finish the preparations. Yasmine, would you help me, please?"

With her family organized to her satisfaction, Yvette Mansouri headed back into the interior of the villa, her younger daughter at her side. His instructions clear, Said took his duties as host seriously. He led the way into a spacious courtyard, a larger version of that in Ethan's own suite, of which he would carry fond memories. The inner courtyard at *Riad Mansouri* was a riot of floral color and splashing water features, statuary dotted around and plenty of seating arranged in small groups. Said led them to a delicately ornate metalwork table set with a jug of what Ethan assumed to be lemonade and half a dozen glasses. He urged Ethan to take one of the matching chairs. As he sat, Fleur reached for the jug, but her father forestalled her.

"No, you sit too, Fleur. I will pour. May I offer you some of my wife's homemade lemonade, Mr. Savage? Or would you prefer something stronger? I tend not to, but we do have wine, I believe. Or even a beer...?"

"Ethan, please. And yes, lemonade would be very welcome, thank you." Ethan had no intention of drinking alcohol this evening. Quite apart from his awareness that whilst this might be tolerated in a Muslim household, it would not be the norm here, he really wanted to maintain a clear head for later. He had big plans for Fleur, and alcohol had no part in them.

He leaned back to enjoy the chilled lemonade, conscious of the quiet presence of Fleur at his side. He wondered what excuse she had provided for her early departure this evening—and what she had thought of his instructions. He had no doubt that she would comply.

"I will be glad of your company this evening, Ethan. My wife is required later at the hospital, and I understand Fleur will be needed at the hotel too. This is what happens when you associate with the medical profession, Ethan. Always the sick have priority. Still, we will get along very well without them, I imagine."

"Yes, I'm sure we will." Ethan smiled noncommittally over the rim of his glass, wondering how soon after Fleur's departure he would be able to get away himself. His instructions required that she wait for him patiently, but even so, he did not want to waste too much of their only remaining evening together. Something told him that Said Mansouri would not be entirely without an inkling that he and Fleur would meeting each other later. What was less clear was how this enigmatic Moroccan would regard that possibility.

"So, I understand that you also work at the Totally Five Star hotel, Ethan?"

"In a manner of speaking. I'm a minerals engineer, doing some consultancy for the hotel chain. I am here just for a few days. In fact, I leave tomorrow."

"Ah yes, Yvette did say that your schedule is busy and that we are fortunate to have this evening with you. So, you met our little Lily at the hotel then?"

Lily? Ah yes, the family nickname. Ethan wondered how much she had already told her family of their first encounter, but he saw no reason to be evasive. "No, Monsieur Mansouri, we met in the desert. Fleur was kind enough to come to my assistance when I had an accident in my car."

"We are on first name terms, I am sure. Said, please. Ah, yes, the bruise on your head. I had wondered. I hope you are quite recovered."

"I am. Fleur took excellent care of me." Ethan had almost forgotten the small bruise still marking his forehead, the only remaining evidence of his accident a few days earlier. He touched his fingers to it gingerly. Perhaps his head injury could account for his uncharacteristic decision to get involved with a local woman. He didn't usually indulge in such unwise liaisons, but all sensible consideration had fled the moment that Fleur had made her wishes known to him on her first visit to his suite. It had never occurred to him to turn her down. He was cautious, not dead.

"So, what were you doing out there in the mountains? I am assuming it was close to Maman's farm that you met Ethan?" The second part of Said's query was directed at Fleur, but Ethan pricked his ears up. Ah yes, that farm in the foothills of the Atlas Mountains. Fleur had already given a brief explanation of her mysterious presence there but he would be fascinated to learn more.

"Yes, I was taking *Grandmère's* latest carpet to the trading warehouse in Tahnaout. It seemed like an excellent opportunity to give Agwmar an outing. He is getting fat."

"You were on that lazy beast? In all that dust and heat? What was wrong with your car?" Her father wrinkled his nostrils in distaste.

Ethan supposed at the prospect of his pristine daughter perched on top of the donkey on that arid, inhospitable road. He shared the older man's misgivings.

"Nothing was wrong, Papa, but Agwmar needed the exercise. And you know I enjoy the peace and quiet of the desert." Fleur placed her glass on the table and reached for her father's hand. "I was quite safe. Agwmar knows the way and I had on *Grandmère's* thickest cloak to keep the sun off."

"It sounds as though your journey was more eventful than you might have anticipated."

Now on this point, Ethan certainly agreed. And now at least he understood — or thought he did — why his lovely Fleur had been out there on that road, riding a donkey and dressed as a Berber peasant. It even made a sort of sense. His little chameleon, blending once more into her surroundings. She had not looked incongruous, so he'd never questioned her presence there. Indeed, he had been the one out of place. And as soon as their worlds had connected, the façade had slipped. At the beginning, she had been a puzzle, an enigma. Now, she just took his breath away.

"You are leaving us early, Fleur?" He turned to murmur the words, his voice deliberately low. He watched her face to gauge her mood now, now that the prospect of her true initiation into his world loomed large.

"I... Yes, I am, Si—Ethan." She was having to concentrate now on *not* calling him Sir. Oh yes, the spanking had done its job. Ethan's cock throbbed at the recollection of her delightful arse presented across his knee, the skin turning a bright and glowing pink as he piled on the slaps. She had weathered it well. He would be careful not to harm her, but depending on the state of her bottom, he might even repeat the treatment tomorrow morning, by way of leave-taking—if he thought she might like that. He had no intention of leaving her on a sour note.

"You were saying...?" he prompted her gently.

"Ah, yes, I have an—appointment—at the hotel. I need to leave as soon as we have eaten."

"My wife will be leaving then too. No matter, it will give us a chance to talk, to get to understand each other, *n'est-ce pas?*" Said Mansouri topped up all three glasses, smiling benignly at his guest. Ethan made a mental note to navigate that conversation with care.

The food was superb and appeared to have been prepared by Yvette and her daughters. He saw no evidence of servants at all during the evening, though he supposed they must have some domestic staff. It was inconceivable that the entire family held down responsible professional roles whilst also managing to maintain this place to the standard that he observed with no additional help.

Yvette served the meal, aided by Fleur and Yasmine. They began with an assortment of hot and cold salads that seemed to include every vegetable known to Ethan. The dressings were many, various too, some tart, and spicy, others bathed in sensuous olive oil. Every course included the delicious local flat bread. He had been uncertain whether to expect utensils, but it seemed that the French influence extended to this aspect of the meal and he was provided with the usual knife and fork. Ethan noted that Said made infrequent use of his fork, preferring to use the bread to pick up his food. He suspected Fleur and Yasmine might have followed suit but for his presence at their table.

The main course was a wonderful spicy lamb dish accompanied by vegetables, couscous and relaxed conversation. The meat fell apart at the nudge of his knife and Ethan wondered when he had last enjoyed a meal so much. Oh yes, that would have been earlier that same day, the harira he had shared with Fleur. He rather thought prolonged exposure to this family would have an impact on his waistline. As they ate, he learned of Said's work at the university as well as Yasmine's aspiration to become a top lawyer in the city. She was now just at the foothills of her career, but Ethan suspected she would achieve what she set out to do. He had the impression that she shared her mother's single-minded approach to life.

He thought that perhaps Fleur did too, though her approach was less direct. And he now understood that her natural enthusiasm, in at least some respects, had been severely curtailed by her experiences as a younger woman. He hoped her recent encounters with him had helped to dispel some of that, and that what he had planned for her later would build on those foundations.

The meal concluded with cups of sweet mint tea, copiously topped up as required. In a brief lull in the conversation, Ethan caught Fleur's gaze. He did not need to speak. She knew. With a slight bow to her father and another to him, she started to make her excuses.

"I am afraid I must leave you now. I am expected at the hotel. Please, I do hope you enjoy the rest of your evening." The final words were directed specifically at him.

Ethan wondered if the double meaning was apparent only to himself.

Yvette took her cue from Fleur, and the two of them rose to leave the table. Ethan's mouth watered as he watched Fleur glide from the room. When next he saw her, he expected her to look rather less self-assured.

Yasmine remained only a few minutes longer before also making her apologies and leaving to read in her room. She had an important meeting the following day and had not yet had an opportunity to acquaint herself fully with the relevant files. Ethan found himself alone with Said Mansouri.

"Are you sleeping with my daughter?" The older man's question took him by surprise, but Ethan knew better than to lie to him.

"I am, yes."

Said eyed him narrowly, though without hostility. "I see. Will you be sleeping with her tonight?"

"I hope to, yes." There was, of course, always the slim chance that she might even now back out.

"Yet you are planning to leave our country tomorrow. Will you be returning to Morocco?"

"I have business in London in the coming days. I may return. I had no plans to initially, but now, who knows?" Ethan was more than a little surprised to hear himself say this. He had not realized himself that he was contemplating coming back. But there it was. How interesting.

"Fleur has not had good experiences always, I am sure you will know this...?"

Ethan nodded. "She told me she was married, and that her husband is now dead."

Said shook his head gravely. "Yes, a terrible business. Not Youssef's death, you understand. That was not terrible. It was long overdue in my view. I have no sympathy for the dog. He hurt my precious girl. I might have killed him myself at one time."

Ethan pondered that, and considered the possibility that Said was warning him of the potential consequences if *he* were similarly careless with Fleur's well-being. He had no intention at all of harming her, at least, not in the manner that her father meant. As for emotional hurt, she had known from the outset that his was a flying visit at best. He fully appreciated that emotions could assert themselves to derail even the best-laid plans, but he would be careful not to create expectations where he should not.

"I understand he was a violent man. Please be assured, Said, that I am not." Ethan could deliver a decent whipping, fully consensual, of course, but he would never raise his hand to any woman in anger, and he was not a bully. He could and would make Fleur scream, but he knew she would thank him for it afterwards. Meanwhile, it was by now clear to him that Said was not about to play the paternal moral card, though he was clearly seeking reassurance.

Ethan was happy to provide it. "Fleur is safe with me, Mr. Mansouri."

Said nodded. "I believe that. It is clear to me that she holds you in high regard. Is that the right phrase? You will appreciate English is not my natural tongue."

"I take your meaning, even so."

"Fleur is old enough to make her own choices now. She is wiser than once she was. I want her to be happy. I want this for all my children."

Ethan nodded. They seemed to be at an understanding. "Yours is an unusual family, if I may say so, Said."

The older man nodded. "I imagine it is. We have found a way to get along well enough together, though."

"Indeed. Fleur tells me she was brought up to be both Muslim and Christian. I had not thought that possible."

Said's smile wryly. "I suspect it may not be. I would never ask any of my family to choose. We all find God by our own route, whatever name we call Him by. In truth, I fear my Fleur is a godless creature, despite her mother's most fervent efforts. My daughter's immortal soul remains a work in progress for Yvette, I think. For myself, I trust that she may find whatever she is seeking, be that God or some other source of fulfilment. We all need to have meaning in our lives. Would you not agree?"

Ethan did agree, and said so. He couldn't help thinking that if his own father had possessed the tolerance, wisdom and vision of Said Mansouri, and the ability to let go of old hurts, his own community in south Yorkshire might have been the richer for it.

"I think that perhaps you need to be returning to your hotel. Not that I am not enjoying your company, of course. It has been a pleasure to make your acquaintance this evening and I sincerely hope that we may meet again, perhaps when you are able to remain with us for longer…?"

Said's meaning was clear. Ethan smiled, inclining his head slowly. "You are right. I should be going. And yes, I hope we do have an opportunity to meet again. Thank you for your hospitality this evening, and please pass on my thanks to your lovely wife."

"Of course. I will telephone for a taxi for you."

"There's no need…"

"I would not hear of anything else. It will just take a few minutes. Please, have some more mint tea while I make the call." Said pulled his mobile phone from his pocket. Ethan reached for the teapot.

Chapter Fourteen

Fleur sat in her car, the engine running. The drive back to The Totally Five Star would take her no more than a few minutes at this time of night when there was much less traffic about. She just had enough time to reread Ethan's note, the one he'd given her as she'd left his suite earlier that day—his list of instructions for her. She knew it was vital that she get this right so it would be worth a final check. She retrieved the white envelope from her bag and pulled out the one sheet of paper inside.

It was written on the thick, cream-colored hotel notepaper, the writing neat and precise. Like Ethan, she reflected. She read slowly.

Fleur

You will return to my suite and let yourself in. You have a staff passkey, I daresay, but if not, please inform me of this and I will arrange access for you. You may bring such items as you will require for an overnight stay. In addition, if you have any anti-inflammatory creams or lotions you might find those to be of use. No other pain relief will be permitted.

Please bring the cloak you were wearing when I first met you in the Atlas foothills or, if that is not available, one that is similar.

On arrival at my suite, you will undress and leave your clothing neatly folded and out of the way. You will not require it until you leave tomorrow. If you wish to take a shower, you may do so. Naked, you will then wrap yourself in the cloak. When I arrive, I expect to find you in the courtyard, kneeling, nude but for the cloak that will cover your head also. Your hands will be on your thighs, palms turned upwards. You may use a mat from inside the riad, if you wish.

Please make sure you have plenty of water to drink prior to my arrival, but, of course, no alcohol.

During our evening together, you will be allowed to speak only in response to a direct question, or to seek clarification on any instruction I may give. Of course, you may use a safe word at any time, and you will be free to leave at any time should you choose to. You will keep your eyes downcast unless specifically instructed otherwise. You will not touch me without permission, and you will obey any instruction I give you without delay or protest.

If you have any questions or concerns, may I suggest you make a list of those and I will address them at the start of our scene.

Ethan

Curt and to the point, Ethan's note was quite explicit. Accordingly, in her overnight bag on the back seat she'd stashed a change of clothing for tomorrow and the cloak he had specifically requested. She did have the one from their first meeting, now freshly laundered and free of the dust from the desert road, and she had carefully folded it at the bottom of her bag. She had packed some toiletries, though she knew the Totally Five Star would be able to cater admirably for any and all of her requirements. She packed no nightclothes. It seemed clear that these would be superfluous. The only other items she had with her were her toothbrush, a couple of tubes of non-steroid anti-inflammatory cream borrowed from her medical bag, her hairbrush, her purse, her glasses and her phone. And she had also brought with her an intricately hand-woven Berber carpet. It was about thirty inches in width and forty or so in length, and was neatly rolled on the back seat next to her bag.

Content that she had overlooked nothing, she pulled out of the parking bay at the rear of *Dar Roumana* and headed for the hotel.

Back at the Totally Five Star, Fleur made for the underground car parking area and pulled up in her own bay marked 'Doctor'. She hoped that none of the security staff would consider it noteworthy that her car was here whilst she was ostensibly off duty, but that was a risk she would take. Fleur made her way quickly through the modern and well-lit corridors, happily encountering no one, and let herself into Ethan's guest *riad*. She closed the door softly behind her and glanced around.

It was clear that the maid service had been in since she had left soon after lunch. The cushions in the lounge area were all perfectly positioned, the flowers refreshed. She knew without looking that the minibar would be restocked, the towels fresh and fragrant, the toiletries replenished. Upstairs, Ethan's bed would be expertly made up and sprinkled with petals or something equally sensuous. She imagined they might soon undo that bit of good housekeeping, though on reflection she was not entirely certain. Her previous experiences with Ethan had not made extensive use of the bedroom.

She did not know how long he would remain with her family after she had left, and she had already devoted more than enough time to checking and re-checking her instructions. Whilst not afraid of Ethan — certainly not in the sense that she had feared Youssef's temper — neither did she relish the prospect of starting this evening's scene having failed to meet his expectations. She did not want him to punish her if she could avoid that so she was conscious of the need to hurry, to prepare herself for his arrival.

Fleur stripped where she stood by the door. She folded her things neatly and placed them in a drawer in the lounge area. The cloak she left out on the ottoman where she had slept earlier that morning, ready for use later. She laid the carpet next to it, still neatly rolled up. She put her toothbrush in the bathroom off the main bedroom, casting a longing look at the huge bath as she passed. Ethan's note had said she was welcome to shower, so perhaps he did not intend to return imminently. Might she have time to use the bath?

She decided it was wiser not to indulge in a bath but she did turn on the shower jets and stepped quickly under the spray. Afterwards, she smoothed generous amounts of Totally Five Star body lotion into her skin, finding the aromatic citrus scents both erotic and invigorating. After showering and glancing at the clock, it shocked her to see that it was already close to ten in the evening. Certain that she did not have much more time before Ethan returned, Fleur tidied the bathroom after herself and hurried downstairs again. This time she draped the cloak around herself, careful to arrange it so it fully covered her body and her head. Through long years of practice, she was able to ensure that it would stay in place without undue fussing on her part. She knew instinctively that Ethan would not take kindly to a lot of shifting and rearranging of her clothing, such as it was.

She picked up her carpet and walked purposefully out into the courtyard where she unrolled the rug and laid it on the mosaic tiling beside the central fountain. And there she knelt, to wait.

Footsteps, faint but becoming clearer. Getting closer. Fleur's breath hitched. She shifted one last time, intent on ensuring that she was flawlessly positioned. His first glance at her had to be perfect, or as much so as she was able. She thought she had obeyed his instructions to the letter. Now was to come the acid test.

The lock clicked and the door opened. Fleur concentrated on not turning her head. *It is him. It must be him. It has to be.* The footsteps sounded like Ethan's and she simply felt his presence fill the *riad*.

The footsteps approached her from behind and still she did not turn. Her posture was just as directed, straight and motionless. She held that pose, her eyes downcast but her ears attuned to every minute sound. She breathed in deeply through her nose, was sure she could detect his unique essence, that woodsy blend of spice and fruit. His cologne? Or just *him*?

The sound of footsteps became more muted. He had kicked off his shoes, in deference to local tradition, she supposed. But still she could hear him, the clink of a glass, the rattle of ice cubes. He was close by, behind her, saying nothing but watching. Seeing. Assessing.

Evaluating.

Fleur's pussy clenched, the internal twist almost painful in her apprehension. Had she missed something, some detail? Had she been careless? She thought not, but still…

"You look adorable."

Fleur let out her breath, only now realizing that she had been holding it. She was not sure if she should answer. His instructions were that she remain silent unless spoken to, unless asked a direct question. He had spoken to her, though not a question. Nevertheless, she opted to reply.

"Thank you, Sir." She kept her tone low, her eyes fixed on a point a few inches in front of her knees.

Footsteps, then Ethan came into view. Or his feet did. Bare, as she had surmised. They now provided the focus for her gaze. He had nice feet, Fleur thought, long and straight, tanned, as though he kicked off his shoes often. They stopped right in front of her. She sensed his gaze on the top of her bent head but knew the cloak concealed her entirely. She also knew that he was perfectly aware that she was naked beneath it and what her nude body would look like, feel like. Taste like. He had sampled her extensively already so she should have no surprises left for him.

"You have obeyed my instructions?"

"I have, Sir. I hope I have done correctly all that you have asked."

"At first sight, I think you have. How did it feel, Fleur, to obey me, even though I wasn't here?"

"It made no difference, Sir. I did as you told me, exactly as you instructed."

"And if you had found yourself unable to complete any part of my requirements? What if you hadn't had a cloak to hand? What if your knees had become stiff from the hard floor?"

Still she stared at his feet. "I do not understand, Sir. Your instructions were clear—this cloak or one similar. And to kneel until you arrive. Why would I do otherwise?"

"Look at me, Fleur."

She tilted her head back to raise her eyes to meet his. Warmth resided there, approval. And lust, she was sure, though his expression gave nothing away. He didn't smile, but neither did he scowl. He could intimidate her, and his very presence, their relative positions—she on her knees and he towering over her—all conspired to emphasize her submission to him. But he did not exploit that now. Instead, he quirked his lip in the faintest of smiles.

"Do you have any questions or comments before we begin? You will have limited opportunities to ask them later."

Fleur thought about this for a moment. "Do you intend to gag me then, Sir?"

"No, probably not. Unless I think your screams are likely to bring the hotel staff running to your rescue but I'm hoping it won't come to that."

"I see, Sir. So why…?"

"I won't allow you to speak without my express permission. You may well scream and certainly, I expect a few whimpers, gasps, moans. Those I take as read. But I'll be doing the talking, not you. So if there is anything you need to ask me or tell me, do it now, please."

Fleur thought for a moment, then, "Will you tell me what is going to happen? What you intend to do? What I need to do?"

"Not up front, but I will explain everything as we go along. You won't need to do anything apart from obey me."

This was not exactly the response Fleur had hoped for, though it was what she had been expecting. She knew she would take the passive role here, that she would not get to direct their play, but there was one thing she particularly hoped for. If she were to request it, she realized it must be now.

"Please, I would like to start by sucking your cock, Sir. I want to swallow your semen. If that would not undermine your other plans for me, of course..."

"I see. Topping from the bottom already, little Fleur. I don't usually take requests."

Fleur dropped her eyes to study his feet once more, unaccountably disappointed. "No, Sir. I should not have asked. Forgive me."

Ethan reached for her chin, tipping her head back up with his fingers. "I asked you to look at me, Fleur. Don't look away until I tell you to. I didn't refuse your request and I had planned to fuck your gorgeous mouth later. I have no objection to bringing that forward. Do you have any other questions for me? Anything worrying you? Anything else you'd like me to do? Or not do? I may not agree to all your requests, but if I know that something bothers you or especially interests you. I *will* take that into account."

"I... No, Sir. I am happy to do as you think best."

"That's good. Have you had something to drink?"

"I have, Sir. You instructed that I should."

"If you want more water at any time, please ask me. If you need me to stop, to slow down, use your safe words — nothing else will help you. That's it. So, is everything clear?"

As much as it is going to be. "Yes, Sir. Perfectly."

"Then, you may start when you're ready."

Ethan released his grip on her chin. He unbuttoned his cotton shirt and slid it from his shoulders to drop it onto the tiled floor. He then placed his palms on each side of her head, on top of the cloak covering her hair. He made no move to undo his trousers. A few moments passed before Fleur realized that this was clearly her task, her part in the proceedings.

"May I, Sir?" She reached tentatively for his waistband, her eyes fixed on his.

"Please do." He stood perfectly still, gazing down at her. He made no move, did not seem to intend to sit. His height meant that she would have to strain upwards to properly take his cock in her mouth, but that did seem to be his intention. So be it.

Fleur slipped one hand from beneath her enveloping cloak. She released the button on his waistband and drew down the zip. The fabric parted to reveal dark blue boxer shorts made of some shiny, soft fabric. Possibly silk. He seemed a silk sort of man, she decided, smooth and sensuous. And for tonight, he was hers. Or perhaps more properly, she was his.

Or perhaps it made no difference at all.

Using both hands now, Fleur tugged on the elastic waistband to draw it down and release his cock. She looked up at it, solid, thick and jutting toward her forehead. It had an arrogance about it, a sense of certainty. She found it impossible to disassociate the cock from the man and perhaps that was pointless in any case. Both were powerful, both exuded strength. Both brought her to her knees. Exactly where she wanted to be.

Shuffling forward slightly on the narrow rectangle of carpet, Fleur cupped Ethan's balls in one hand whilst she wrapped the other around his broad shaft. She drew her hand up his length, observing the droplets of clear fluid already emerging from the slit. Her medical training would dub this the stagola, though she imagined he would be able to supply an earthier name for it. No matter, she was not kneeling at his feet in any sort of medical capacity. Lifting her hips a little and stretching her body, she leaned forward to lick the slick beads of moisture from the head of Ethan's cock. She licked her lips straight after, noting the slight saltiness. Every man's semen tasted different. She knew that, though her direct experience was not extensive. Ethan's tasted delicious, so she leaned in for another sample. This time she used the flat of her tongue, lapping across the whole of the smooth, pink surface of the glans.

Ethan tightened his hands around her head, his fingertips pressing against her skull. She took that to be a sign that all was going well and leaned in farther to take the entire head of his cock between her lips. She had to open her mouth wide, swallowing franticly at the unfamiliar sensation as her mouth was full of him. Still the only movement from Ethan was his hands, now defining small circles in her scalp above each of her ears. He made no sound.

Fleur drew her lips back along the head, almost expelling Ethan's dick from her mouth entirely. She waited a few seconds, the tip of his cock resting between her lips, then she leaned forward to drag it inside. She took more of his length this time and was gratified at the way his cock distinctly twitched as he sank into her. Encouraged, she did that again, and once more for good measure. Each time she drew all of the head and more of the shaft in, her hands holding him steady whilst she moved her head and neck up and down. Soon the muscles in her neck started to ache, but she continued, loving the salty taste flowing over her tongue. She swallowed hard and the taste filled her throat too.

Reaching the limit that she could manage with her mouth, she used her hand around his shaft to pump him, increasing the pressure as he jerked sharply under her ministrations. She used the hand cupping his balls to massage him, tentatively at first but gathering confidence as Ethan's labored breathing made his approval clear.

Fleur continued to control the action for several more minutes, rewarded by Ethan's guttural moans and occasional murmurs of "Holy fuck" and "Christ, yes." As she tired and slowed, he took over.

"Let me, love." He now held her head still whilst he used his hips to thrust his cock into her mouth, the strokes fast, though not deep. She knew he was being careful not to penetrate any farther than she had already shown him was acceptable, manageable, and she appreciated his consideration. At first. She wondered, though, was sure that had she still been directing events she would by now be taking him deeper. She raised her eyes to his, the request there, though she could not express it. Ethan saw and understood.

"More?"

Fleur gave a slight nod, then closed her eyes as Ethan picked up the pace, lengthening his strokes as she had requested. The head of his cock hit the back of her throat and she fought back the urge to gag at the unfamiliar intrusion. She managed to suppress her natural reflex and accepted his firm thrusts, loving the savory tang of his pre-cum as it slid down her throat.

Then, almost without warning, he was there, about to come. Fleur felt the tightening in his balls as she caressed them, closing her fingers around the solid roundness. Gripping her head tightly, his hold almost brutal, he delivered the final, deep thrusts. Then he stilled, his cock quivering at the back of her throat and Fleur's mouth immediately full of warm, tangy semen. It was slick, smooth, easy to swallow. She cleared it quickly and breathed hard through her nose, but could still feel some escape and dribble slowly down her chin. She could have wiped it away with her hand but chose not to, instead concentrating on gripping and pumping his thick shaft. Instinctively, she hollowed her cheeks to suck hard on his cock, rubbing the flat of her tongue along the underside of the head to lap away the last few droplets. She swallowed those and lifted her eyes again to meet his.

Ethan relaxed his grip on her head and eased her back from him. His cock slid out. He took a piece of the fabric of her cloak and lifted it, meticulously wiping her chin. Then he smiled at her, his devastating ninety-watt smile that would crumble her knees if she were not already on them. Fleur smiled back, her gaze perhaps slightly watery as the emotion of the moment seized her. She felt utterly used and completely elated. In a sudden flash of self-awareness, she knew that his was what she was born for.

Ethan? Yes, perhaps they might have been together, in another life. If he and she were different people in another place.

But *this*, certainly.

"Are you done calling the shots, little sub?"

Fleur kept her eyes lowered but her voice was strong and clear. "Yes, Sir." *For now.*

"Stand up, then. Slip the cloak back from your shoulders and show me your breasts."

Fleur did as he instructed, allowing the fabric to slide from her shoulders and down her back, using her hands to gather the cloak in front of her stomach. She was nude from the waist up and stood absolutely still as Ethan perused her breasts carefully. Despite his obvious appreciation of her body in all their previous encounters, this seemed different to her, more detached somehow. She hoped for some generous comment, some signal of approval.

"Very pretty, but of course you know that. Do you have sensitive nipples, Fleur?"

That might pass for approval, more or less.

"I believe so, Sir." She was uncertain whether she should raise her gaze to his as they spoke. He had instructed her not to do so unless specifically given permission, so she opted for caution now and continued to stare at the floor.

"Then you'll love what comes next. Or maybe not. We'll see. I intend to clamp them. You *will* squeal for me."

If he thought this was so, she was not inclined to disagree. Further, she was inclined to wonder how he thought to achieve this feat. Ethan might be a natural optimist—she had no reason to doubt it—but nevertheless it seemed unlikely that he would have brought nipple clamps with him on a business trip to Morocco. And as far as she knew, no such items had been added to the merchandise available for purchase in the Totally Five Star souk, that wing of the hotel that catered for all shopping requirements in traditional local style. If sexual fetish accoutrements had suddenly appeared on any of the traders' stalls she was sure someone would have alerted her, in a professional capacity, if for no other reason.

Ethan interrupted her puzzled musings, apparently not requiring any further comment from her just at this precise moment. "You will remain quite still until I tell you otherwise. You can make sounds if you want to. I'm sure you will, in fact. But if you move, I *will* spank you. Then we start all over again. Is that clear?"

"Yes, Sir."

"Good. I'll want your cunt later, but for now, can you fasten the cloak at your waist and place your hands in the small of your back, please?"

Fleur did as he asked, repositioning her hands as directed. At last, she took the risk of lifting her gaze. He met her eyes and made no comment.

"Clasp your fingers around your wrists." He paused for a few moments to allow her to do that. "I'm going to want you to maintain that position. I'm happy to leave it to you, but if you think you might struggle, I could tie your hands in place. Some inexperienced subs prefer that—it keeps them from incurring too many punishments as they're learning. I've told you what the consequences will be if you move. So, which would you prefer? I'm going to hurt you. It won't be unbearable but it *will* be tough. You *will* struggle. But I can help you if you want me to."

Fleur took just a moment to decide. "Tie my hands please, Sir." There was a time for bravado and this was not it. She had no wish to find herself on the receiving end of a punishment spanking if she could avoid that. Ethan was offering her a reasonable certainty of success, provided she managed not to scream her safe word at him. She was fairly sure she would not be doing that.

He nodded and strode away, back into the cool interior of the *riad*. He returned moments later with one of the cashmere scarves he had purchased from the souk. He stopped behind Fleur and looped the scarf around her wrists a couple of times. He tied it off and slipped two fingers underneath.

"Wiggle your fingers, please."

She did.

"Fine, seems good. I'll be checking but if that starts to hurt, you tell me—or if your hands feel numb."

Seemingly satisfied, he returned to stand in front of her, his attention now fixed on her nipples. Fleur tugged against the scarf binding her wrists, not that she wanted or expected to be able to get free, but instinctively she felt compelled to check. The bonds were secure, comfortable, but no movement was possible. Fleur's pussy moistened, her arousal heightened by the sense of helplessness induced by being tied. She knew Ethan would release her in a moment if she asked him to, but being bound and held in place made her imminent submission so much more real. Her head started to shift between the sense that this was a game, that they were just playing, and the chilling reality of being tied, half naked, and utterly vulnerable.

She was sure her nipples must be peaking decadently, but she could not tear her gaze from his face to check. Neither could she suppress a shiver as he reached for her right breast, cupping it in his hand, as though testing the weight. He rubbed his thumb across the nipple, raising his eyes to meet her gaze.

"So hard already, and pink. Like a pebble. Still, I think we can do better."

His gaze dipped again, and this time Fleur's followed. She watched curiously, as he took her swollen peak between his finger and thumb and squeezed, tugging slightly. The pressure was light, and despite her apprehension, the sensation one of pleasure. He increased his grip, pressing the hardened nub between his fingers. Fleur instantly found herself hurtling into that place where pain and pleasure mingle before pain suddenly wins out. She jerked and stepped backwards.

Ethan released her immediately, his gaze flashing back to hers. Now his eyes were cool, stern, clearly unimpressed.

"Were my instructions in any way unclear? I told you to remain still."

"It… You hurt me."

"I told you I would."

"Yes, Sir."

His tone was curt and hard enough to crack rocks. Fleur did not think he had used such a timbre with her previously and found that she did not like it one bit. Her insides seemed to shrivel at the displeasure she detected in his voice. She could not believe she had failed so completely and so soon.

"I am sorry, Sir. Please, may I try again? I can do it, now that I know what to expect."

Ethan nodded once, his features still a harsh mask. "Very well. But I won't continue if you struggle or try to fight me, or try to escape. You have no need to resist. This is not about me forcing you to endure something you hate. You do it, *if* you do it, by your own choice. If it's too much, if you don't want this after all, just say your safe word and we're done. Is that clear?"

"Yes, Sir, I am sorry. I do understand."

Fleur had backed away from him as he spoke. Now he lifted his hand to beckon her to stand right in front of him, resuming her previous position. Fleur obeyed immediately. Ethan held her gaze as he took her nipple between his fingers again, this time pressing and twisting hard. Pain radiated out from the tortured nub. Fleur gasped, pressing her lips together to keep from crying out. He could not have failed to see her struggle but Ethan was merciless, ratcheting up the pressure until she could no longer contain her squeal of pain.

"That should do, I think." He held her nipple tightly between his finger and thumb, but didn't squeeze any harder. Fleur panted, trying to breathe through the discomfort, and managing, just about.

Ethan slipped his free hand into his pocket and pulled out a length of ribbon. The color caught her eye, a deep rich blue. The narrow strip was perhaps a quarter of an inch wide, woven from a shiny satin. Irrelevantly, Fleur noted that he might well have acquired this toy at the hotel bazaar after all. Ethan draped it across Fleur's erect and swollen bud, wrapping it tightly around several times. The delicate strand did not look like an instrument of pain, but its innocuous appearance belied its performance. As Ethan pulled it tight around the distended nub, Fleur let out a sharp cry. The pain proved intense. Her knees began to buckle as Ethan tied the ribbon off in a small bow. He swung an arm around her waist quickly to steady her.

"Are you okay?" His tone was low now as he pulled her close to his own body, holding her up until she was able to support her own weight once more.

Fleur was glad of his help, and after a few seconds, she nodded.

"I am. Thank you for your assistance, Sir. It was just a bit of a surprise at first. I did not expect a ribbon to be so...compelling."

"I told you yesterday, Fleur, the tools of BDSM can be very simple. A scarf, a length of ribbon. A few ice cubes."

Fleur glanced up sharply. "Ice cubes?"

He lifted one eyebrow but said nothing further as he drew a second length of blue ribbon from his pocket.

This he draped across her left shoulder as he reached for her remaining nipple and started to apply the same pressure he had to the first. Fleur gritted her teeth and managed not to cry out until the last moment, as he started to wrap the ribbon around the swollen, pebbled nub. He pulled the length of tape tight, his gaze holding Fleur's. At last, apparently satisfied, he tied the ends into another small bow and stood back to admire his work.

"Blue suits you."

"Thank you, Sir." She managed to force the words past her gritted teeth, wondering if her legs might be about to collapse under her.

"Stand still and straight. You can do this, Fleur. You *want* to do this. Don't you? Look at me and tell me." His tone was firm, unyielding, his words carefully chosen and effective.

She *did* want this, and his sharp, uncompromising reminder of that fact was sufficient to stiffen her resolve, not to mention her knees. "Yes, of course, Sir." She stood before him, raised her eyes to meet and hold his gaze. "Thank you, Sir."

"You're very welcome, Fleur. Are you hot?"

The question came seemingly from nowhere. Fleur blinked in confusion. "Hot, Sir?"

"I promised you ice. I think here would be a good place for it, don't you?" He lifted his hand to flick her tightly bound right nipple, stroking the pad of his thumb over the deep pink portion protruding beyond the ribbon.

"Oh, Sir..." Fleur swayed toward him, despite her determination not to falter. The caress had felt intense, almost painful, but not exactly that. His touch was more tormenting than hurting.

"Mmm. I think so." He turned to pick up his glass of iced water, shaking the cubes against the wine flute. Fleur recalled the clinking sound she had heard as he arrived, but surely that was so long ago now, and in the warmth of the night, the ice would have melted.

Not so. He held the glass before her face and she saw the cubes still very much intact. There were a couple of inches of chilled water too, but plenty of solid ice left. In any case, there was an icebox full of ice cubes in the minibar fridge, should his supplies run low.

"Here, take a sip." He held the glass to her lips, tilting it so that she could drink some of the cool water. It trickled down her throat.

"Thank you, Sir." She genuinely appreciated the refreshment, had not realized how thirsty she was. With just a lift of one eyebrow, he offered her more. She accepted, conscious of the ice cubes nudging her lips as she drank.

"Enough?"

Fleur nodded, watching him apprehensively.

Ethan's grin became sardonic now. He glanced at the water feature in the middle of the courtyard and gestured Fleur toward it. Specifically, he led her to the rear of it where the surrounding wall was higher, almost chest height for Fleur. Ethan placed his palms on either side of her waist and lifted her easily onto the wall, bringing her bound nipples more or less level with his mouth. Looking down at him from her lofty but exposed position, Fleur appreciated instantly what he intended to do next.

As she watched, he tipped the glass to his own mouth, taking an ice cube between his lips. He sucked on it briefly, rolling it around his mouth before gripping it in his teeth. His eyes were not on hers, though. He was intent on her right nipple, now throbbing painfully under the satin ribbon imprisoning it. He leaned in and Fleur braced herself, expecting to feel the cruel, frosty bite of the ice cube against her skin. She did not, though. Instead, he seemed to slide the ice cube into the side of his mouth and instead drew his chilled tongue over the sore nub.

It felt—*wonderful*. Soothing yet revitalizing at the same time. The pain created by the tight ribbons added to the sensation, gave it an edge, a delightful yet wicked frisson she could never have imagined. Overwhelmed momentarily, she leaned forward to lay her cheek briefly against the top of his head.

Ethan straightened, his smile soft. "So, not so bad as you imagined, little sub?"

"No, Sir, not at all bad." She lowered her eyelids, leaning back slightly to raise her breasts for his attention. "This is beautiful, it feels so good. I thought, hoped perhaps, but…"

"We continue then?"

"Yes, please, Sir."

Ethan repeated the treatment for her left nipple, sensuously soothing away the discomfort of the binding. Fleur sighed as his tongue caressed her distended tip, loving this more with each stroke, this bittersweet mix of pleasure and pain, the two sensations inextricably tangled together.

Ethan switched his attentions back to the other side, and this time he did apply the ice direct to her skin. Fleur shivered but continued to press her breast toward his mouth, offering, begging.

At the same time, she became aware of a cool sensation on her naked back, and realized that this was the spray from the fountain behind her. Ethan edged her a little closer to it. Fleur rolled her shoulders, conscious that her body was stiffening now, her hands still bound awkwardly. She considered asking him to release her, but soon forgot as another wave of delicate, erotic sensation washed through her. Ethan had taken an ice cube in his right hand and was now applying that to one nipple whilst he continued to tease the other with the ice in his mouth, lightly swirling the hard, glinting cubes over her delicate peaks.

He paused for a moment to glance up at her. "Tell me what you're thinking now, Fleur."

"I am thinking, I am… I do not believe I *am* thinking, Sir."

Ethan's low chuckle was sexy. "Wise girl. Thinking can be overrated. Sometimes it's better just to feel. Tell me what you're feeling, then."

"I feel that I want to orgasm. May I, please?"

"You may."

Moments later, Fleur did. She was grateful for Ethan's restraining arm that prevented her from toppling backwards into the cool water rippling behind her as her motor control failed in the throes of a long, slow, undulating orgasm. Her climax seemed to roll back and forth through her sensitized nervous system, lazily picking her up and rocking her before gently depositing her back on earth. Ethan lifted her from the wall and turned her so that she leaned against him, her back to his chest. She writhed in his arms, oblivious now to his earlier command that she remain still. He did not remind her of it. She moaned, the sound low and formed deep in her throat as he pressed the ice cubes to her quivering peaks to draw every last tingle from her.

Ethan lowered them both to the floor as Fleur's legs eventually gave up the struggle to remain upright. At last, she lay still in his arms. Ethan tossed the remaining piece of ice into the ornamental pool with a soft splash and reached down to release her wrists. He pulled them in front of her, gently rubbing them to ease out the stiffness.

"You liked that?"

"I did, Sir. Very much. I had no idea..."

"So now that you do, now that you know how good that felt against your nipples, shall we try something else?"

"I... Yes, I think I would like that." Fleur suspected she might have an inkling what he had in mind.

"Would you lie still, do you think? No tying you up this time and spread your legs wide for me? How about if I suck your clit until you scream for me to fuck you, at the same time as I slide ice cubes into your hot pussy. And you are such a slut, so I know you *will* be hot. How quickly would my ice melt, do you think?"

"I... I do not believe it would take very long, Sir."

"Me neither. And when the ice has all melted, and your cunt is lovely and cool and very, very wet, then I'll fuck you. Hard. You *will* see stars. You *will* scream. So, how does all that sound to you?"

"It sounds a little bit terrifying."

"Yes. And?"

"A lot wonderful."

"So that's a yes, then?"

"It is, Sir. A yes."

As he murmured his delightful suggestions in her ear, Ethan had been untying the bows around her erect nipples, his fingers deft and sure as he loosened both tight ribbons at once. He unwound the blue satin, allowing the blood to rush back into her hard peaks. Fleur let out a shriek, the pain unexpected and sharp.

"Sorry, love. This soon passes, though." He took her nipples between his fingers to squeeze and massage them, easing the blood flow back to normal. Fleur stiffened but quickly relaxed as the pain dissipated. A few moments passed before Ethan lowered his head to whisper into her ear again, "Shall we go inside?"

Fleur nodded, fisting her hands in the folds of the cloak still draped around her waist.

"I think we can leave that here, don't you?"

Again, she nodded, pulling the folds free to drop the cloak onto the tiles at her feet. Naked now, she turned to Ethan. He lifted her in his arms and carried her across the courtyard.

Chapter Fifteen

Inside the *riad*, Ethan made a detour to the fridge that housed the minibar. He snatched a glassful of fresh ice cubes from the freezer compartment and thrust it into Fleur's hand.

"Go upstairs to the bedroom. Get a thick towel, two perhaps, from the bathroom and spread them on the bed. Then I want you to lie on the towels and wait for me, your legs open as wide as you can. Questions?"

"No questions, Sir."

He said nothing further, just tilted his head in the direction of the hallway. Fleur took the hint and bolted for the door to the stairs. Ethan's voice followed her.

"Put some pillows under your bum."

In the bedroom, she wasted no time. She placed the glass of ice cubes on the small table beside the bed and went into the bathroom for towels. She found two huge fluffy bath sheets and grabbed both. She folded them in half and laid them across the center of the bed. She stood back, then thought better of her work so far and pulled the towels off again. She heaved the

Ashe Barker

light quilt from the bed and dropped it on the floor, then remembered the pillows and grabbed a couple to place on the mattress, about halfway down the bed. She replaced the towels directly onto the mattress, covering the pillows too. She had a suspicion that Ethan's plans for her could be messy and there was no point wetting the bedclothes more than strictly necessary. It would only cause talk among the housekeeping staff and she preferred to avoid that.

Fleur lay on the towels, her hips lifted by the pillows, loving the feel of the thick woven cotton on her bare skin. Not a prude by any means — or so she liked to think given her medical training — still she had not experienced so much personal nudity for as long as she could recall. Patients did not count. It felt decidedly pleasant, comfortable, uninhibited. And intimate — very, very intimate.

A step on the landing beyond the bedroom door caused her to shift her position fast to place herself exactly as she had been instructed. Her legs bent and the soles of her feet facing each other, she allowed her knees to fall to each side, opening and exposing her pussy as Ethan entered.

He strode across the room, still wearing just his jeans, zipped but unbuttoned. He stood at the foot of the bed and looked at her. He said nothing at first, just ran his gaze over her, from her face — perhaps only very slightly flushed, she hoped — to the tips of her toes. He lingered a long time at her pussy, seemingly taking in every detail. Fleur should have been nervous. Just hours before she would have found his cold, slow perusal unnerving, would have reached for something to cover herself, in all probability. No, there was nothing of the probable about it. Certainly. Now she did not do that, nor did she experience any

256

particular wish to. She lay still for his scrutiny and found that she loved the feeling that he was examining her, appraising her. She was sure of her body, confident in him. She liked him to look at her, reveled in his admiration, and the lust he made no attempt to disguise. His erection might split his jeans before much longer.

"I think your inner slut's emerging. Christ, girl, you look hot."

"Yes, Sir. But we have ice…"

Ethan chuckled and glanced at the glass on the bedside table. "So we do, slutty sub. I'm thinking you seem eager to get on with this."

Fleur smiled, more for herself than for him. Amazingly, she was incredibly eager. Her pussy kept clenching violently and she could have sworn her clit had swelled to about three times its normal size. It seemed all he had to do was look at her and she dissolved in a pool of hot lust. Oh yes, she would be needing that ice.

Ethan sat beside her on the bed. "I won't tie you up, but I do expect you to remain still." He paused and lifted one eyebrow as he waited for her response. Fleur noted that his tone had shifted again. It was a subtle change, but unmistakable. He was done teasing. Now things would get serious. A familiar fluttering started in her lower abdomen, a slight but insistent quiver that she realized was her body's instinctive reaction to his dominance. She was in. She wanted this, but still, she was scared — just a little but enough.

If I'm not scared it would not count, right?

Swallowing hard, she watched as he reached for the glass containing the ice cubes.

"So, we both know where these are going, right?"

Fleur merely nodded.

"Your legs are fine, keep them spread wide like that. You can put your hands behind your head I think…" He watched as Fleur complied, then inclined his head to signal approval. "So, are you warm enough? I can turn the air con down if you like."

"I am fine. Thank you, Sir." Fleur's earlier confidence began to waver now. She wished he would just get on with it. In her experience—limited though that admittedly was—anticipation was far worse that the actuality of all this. Of course, he knew that perfectly well, which was why he was drawing this out.

"Good. Let me know if you need anything changing. I want you to be comfortable." He shook the glass, clattering the ice cubes inside. Fleur heard the soft splash too and knew that they were just starting to melt. Ethan glanced at her. "Well, perhaps not comfortable exactly, but I wouldn't want you to catch a chill. Mmm, I think these are about ready, not too cold. We wouldn't want them sticking to you, would we? That could be very unpleasant." He took a cube from the glass, holding it between his finger and thumb.

"Would you like this one?"

Fleur nodded.

"Open your mouth, then."

Surprised, she did. Ethan popped the ice cube between her lips and she sucked on it, savoring the chill. Again, she hadn't realized how dry her mouth was. But Ethan had. Ethan always seemed to know. She rolled the ice across her tongue then held it between her teeth as she ran her tongue over it. Cool liquid slithered down her throat and she swallowed greedily.

"Nice?" His voice was low now and thick like velvet.

Fleur nodded, her cheeks working as she sucked on the melting ice.

"Let me have it back now, please." He leaned in and laid his mouth over hers. Immediately Fleur parted her lips and allowed him to slide his tongue into her mouth to retrieve the ice cube. He took it from her and held it in his teeth as he traced the outline of her lips with it. Her pussy quivered, desperate now for— what? She wanted him to touch her, of course, but more than that. She wanted him to challenge her too, to shock her. And she wanted him to hurt her. The more delicately he teased, the more desperately she craved the intensity of real pain.

Oh yes, he was good at this.

The ice cube suddenly landed in her mouth again, and Fleur sucked on it hard. It was smaller now, shrinking fast in the heat of her mouth. In no time it reduced to a mere sliver, then disappeared entirely,

"More?" Ethan offered her a second cube, holding it between his finger and thumb.

Fleur chewed on her lower lip then nodded. This time, though, Ethan popped the ice into his own mouth before leaning down to kiss her again. Fleur opened immediately and he dropped the ice between her lips, following it with his chilled tongue. He swirled the coolness around her mouth, the cube clinking gently against her teeth. He did not allow her to keep it, though, not this time. He caught it on his tongue and rolled it back into his mouth, then began a long, slow journey south.

He started at her neck, drawing the ice along her skin, leaving a wet trail in its wake. Fleur tilted her head back as he marked a cool path across the front of her throat and continued on across her shoulder. She shivered and could not prevent the slight wriggle as he moved it down under her upraised arm. It was cold but more than that, it tickled. She had anticipated all sorts, had admitted to herself that she actually craved pain. She had not expected him to tickle her. But he did and she squeaked.

"Problem, Fleur?" He stopped his lazy exploration of her body, the ice cube safely lodged in his cheek as he spoke to her.

"No, Sir. It is just — that tickles."

"Ah." He did not elaborate, just returned to his task.

Her nipples still stood erect, though they had softened a little since he had carried her from the courtyard. Ethan soon brought them back to a solid, swollen hardness as he wrapped his cold lips around them and sucked. His touch now was infinitely gentle, so erotic she thought she might weep. Despite his firm instructions, she thrust her hips forward.

"Slut. Be patient. Your cunt will get plenty of attention, all in good time. You really don't want to be earning a spanking right now, do you? That said, an ice cube or two in your arse. Now that might be fun…"

Fleur squeaked again. "I am not moving, Sir. I swear."

"Coward. Maybe after I've fucked your arse, you'll be more agreeable to my suggestion. We'll see. So where was I?"

He managed to resume his place without further input from Fleur, who concentrated fully on keeping perfectly still as he drew his wet, icy pathways back and forth across her torso. Her breasts and nipples received particular attention but so did her navel as he dropped the small remnant of an ice cube into it and left it there to melt. The chilly water trickled across her stomach and down her side onto the thick towel beneath her. Fleur shivered, though she thought not with cold. Even so, Ethan went to the thermostat to adjust the air conditioning before dipping his fingers into the glass for another ice cube.

Now his trail took in Fleur's legs. First, the right one. He explored her inner thigh, her knee, her calf, leaving a slipstream of icy wet skin. Fleur ground her teeth, determined not to shift an inch, though she had had no inkling that her ankles were quite so sensitive. He reached her foot and there he chose to linger. With the sole of her foot turned toward him, he used his fingers this time to tease her with the ice. He drew it across the ball of her foot and her heel. Then he tucked it between her toes and reached for another ice cube to start all over on the other side.

Now he covered the path in reverse, trailing the ice over the side of her left foot until her toes involuntarily curled and flexed. He slipped a cube into his mouth then sucked on her big toe. Fleur let out a small yelp, once more overwhelmed by the sheer eroticism of his play. He seemed to be in no hurry, though she knew the main event was yet to come. Or was it? Everything he did, every place he touched her became an erogenous zone—her heel, her instep, that little hollow at the back of her knee.

Slowly he made his way back up her inner thigh, studiously ignoring her throbbing pussy. He had not touched her, at least not there, but she was convinced that her cunt was glowing. Her limbs ached from the sheer tension of holding still, every muscle tight and poised, every nerve ending standing at attention. Her stomach muscles clenched hard, her shoulders rigid with anticipation. And still he played—teasing, tempting, promising.

Fleur forgot to breathe as he reached the top of her inner thigh and traced the crease between her leg and her pussy with a half-melted cube. He brushed her outer pussy lips, as though by accident. Fleur closed her eyes and considered praying. Her mother's influence at work, without doubt, though there was nothing of the Blessed Virgin about this.

She shrieked, whether with relief or delight, or perhaps sheer exhaustion, when he at last laid his cool lips against her pussy, an ice cube held between them. He traced her outer lips, caressing them with his freezing kiss.

"Oh, oh… Sir." Fleur managed to drag in a breath, caught between earth-shifting arousal and the sharp intensity of the ice against her heated skin. Ethan circled, spiraling inwards, and she knew it would be mere moments now until…

"Argh!" Fleur let out a scream, unable to contain her response. Ethan might have been concerned at the prospect of hotel staff rushing to investigate, but he gave no sign of it. He continued to torment her pussy with the ice, using his tongue to ease it from his mouth and between her pussy lips. He pushed it right inside, following with his tongue. He licked at the ice inside her, nudging it farther into her pussy as her inner walls closed around it.

Reaching with his tongue, he pulled the ice back out and into his mouth, then slid it back into her pussy. He fucked her with it, slowly, so gently, the sensation intense. Fleur gripped his tongue and the ice tightly, squeezing hard with her inner muscles and wriggling now, despite his instructions. He growled, his warning clear. She stiffened, forcing herself to remain motionless as he continued to slip the ice in and out of her cunt.

"Please, Sir, I want to come."

"Not yet. I'll tell you when."

"Sir, I cannot…"

"You can. You will. Do as you're told or accept the consequences."

Fleur groaned to herself as she struggled to suppress her response, grateful that at least he was not yet carrying out his threat to suck her clit until she screamed for him to fuck her. In fact, she might just scream anyway.

Ethan selected another ice cube and inserted that into her pussy along with the first one, now almost melted. He licked away the chilled water as it trickled from her, though Fleur was sure the towels would be soaked in any case.

"Bring your knees up to your chest please. I want your arse now."

"But I haven't… I mean, you said…"

"Do it, Fleur. Now, please."

She chewed her bottom lip but did as she was told, lifting her bottom to expose her tight anus for his use.

Fleur whimpered as he slipped two long fingers inside her pussy, pushing the ice deeper inside her as he twisted his hand to coat his digits in her moisture. He would be using that as lube, then.

He did. His fingers were slick as he inserted them into her arse, and cool from the ice. This felt strange, alien, but Fleur offered no protest. He withdrew, then plunged back, full length this time as her arse opened to accept him. Her head might resist — her body had apparently ceased to do so. Fleur moaned, the pleasure almost overwhelming her now. Her resolve not to orgasm without permission started slipping away in the face of such a determined and effective assault on all her senses. Her pussy was cold, freezing, yet hot too. And full. She squeezed down on the ice, felt it soften and shrink inside her. She wanted more, so she asked for it.

"I need… It's gone. Going."

"Allow me." Ethan's fingers remained in her arse as he reached with his other hand for another ice cube. He popped that in his mouth while he opened her pussy lips with his cold fingers, then leaned down to insert the ice. He eased it between her inner lips then pushed it deep with his fingers.

"Another, I think. Yes?"

Fleur nodded, beyond speech now. Ethan sucked a second ice cube briefly before slipping that into her cunt to follow the first one, gently pressing it inside until her pussy lips closed to hold it in place.

"I think another, just one more, here. Between your sweet, pink lips. You *will* feel the cold from this last one but I promise to lick it for you."

He did not wait for her to reply, and moments later, he eased a third ice cube between her pussy lips. That one he left in her entrance, her lips stretched tight around it. He was right—the cold was intense, excruciating. Fleur might have whimpered her protest or her desperate plea to allow her to orgasm. She did neither, just lay there, still, obedient. Drowning in sensation.

"Open your legs again, love." His fingers remained deep in her arse. Her pussy now felt packed with ice, though she knew there were only two ice cubes inside her, with the third one stretching her entrance. She was aware just of the solid hardness inside her rather than the cold. Her tissues numbed, except for her pussy lips where the ice still inflicted its freezing burn on her. It did not occur to her not to obey, and she spread her legs obligingly. She knew that he would lick her clit now, and that she would not be able to repress her reaction to that. She would come, and powerfully, regardless of his instructions. Then he would punish her. It was inevitable. She should simply accept and be done with it.

"You have my permission to orgasm now."

"What?" Dazed, she needed to check. Perhaps she had imagined...? Maybe she was delirious, or delusional.

"Come. Now." He leaned in and wrapped his cool lips around her clit. He flicked it with his tongue before taking the swollen, throbbing bud between his teeth. He nibbled it, sucking lightly.

It was enough — more than enough. At the first touch of his lips, Fleur started to orgasm, the release surging up from somewhere deep within to crackle at her clit then pulse outward through her body, the waves of her climax radiating outwards to every extremity.

Her pussy pulsated, gripping the ice inside her in a sudden, heated rush. It was melting — fast — the wetness gathering in the now-soaked towel beneath her hips. Fleur did not care. Her body rocked and lurched, her head spinning from the conflicting sensations assaulting her. She was cold, she was hot, she was solid, she was melting, she was full, she was empty. He was fucking her with ice, with his fingers in her arse.

"Ethan, Sir... Oh, oh!" she cried out, incoherent as the power of speech deserted her. He seemed to know anyway, and firmed up his thrusting in her arse at the same time as he extended his licking to include the ice lodged between her pussy lips. He worked at it, pulling it in and out to match the rhythm of his fingers in her anus as she unraveled under him.

At last, spent, she lay still and quiet, the ice now completely melted inside her. Ethan slid his fingers from her arse. He dropped a quick kiss on her mouth before standing and walking into the bathroom. Fleur watched him go through half-closed lids, knowing he would return in moments. The sound of running water followed, then he came back, drying his hands on a small towel. He had another larger towel, a bath sheet, over his arm.

"Lift your bum."

She obeyed and he pulled out the wet towels and the pillows, dumping the lot on the floor with the long-ago discarded duvet. He laid the fresh towel on the mattress, and Fleur settled herself on it.

"I want you to fuck me. Please." She made her appeal hopefully. He looked satisfied enough with the proceedings so far—he might be taking requests. And by her reckoning, he must be overdue an orgasm or two himself.

"I think you mean you want me to fuck you, Sir."

"Yes, Sir. But I don't want you to spank me. I'm sorry. I won't forget again."

"Too late. You know our rules. I want you on all fours, now."

"Please, I am sorry, truly."

"Now, Fleur."

Her mind reeling, all Fleur wanted to do was be held tight, preferably with his cock buried deep inside her. She wanted connection, closeness, not discipline. One look into his implacable features, though, and she knew she would get only what he chose to give, and right now he had a score to settle. Reluctant, feeling maybe even slightly resentful, she shifted to position herself for her spanking.

"Five strokes, I think. But I'm a generous Dom and you've pleased me this evening. So you can have an orgasm between each slap. How does that sound to you, little subbie?"

Fleur almost sobbed with relief. He knew. He cared about her and he knew how she would be feeling right now. He was not about to leave her hanging, disorientated and unhappy. She should have known, should have *really* known her Dom better than that.

"It sounds very good, Sir. Thank you."

"Ready?"

"I am, Sir — oh!"

The first slap landed on her right buttock. He was not pulling his punches today, or if he was holding anything in reserve in recognition of her inexperience, he was considerably less restrained than yesterday. The slap hurt, the pain quickly swept away, though, by the wave of pleasure as he applied a long, slow, open-handed caress to her pussy, from front to back and lingering around her still unresisting arse. He teased her opening, dipping his fingertip inside and running it around the entrance to loosen it further.

"This is mine. Later, yes?"

"Yes, Sir." He would not hurt her. She knew that. She was relaxed with this.

With his finger still working her arse, he reached around with his other hand to stroke her clit. He intended her to come and fast. He rubbed the swollen nub hard as Fleur sank her face into the mattress, moaning in delight. Her release this time came swiftly, peaking sharply as her senses scrambled. She gyrated her hips, squeezing around his probing finger.

"Sir, I want you inside me, please. Now, Sir."

"Since you ask so nicely. First, though…" The second slap landed on her left buttock. Fleur welcomed it, knowing what would follow

The sound of foil tearing, and the snap of latex were the confirmation that he was about to grant her request. He moved behind her, and Fleur lifted her hips and spread her thighs as wide as she was able. She could have wept with sheer joy as he entered her, smooth and fast, right to the hilt in one long stroke. He held still for a moment to allow her to stretch around him, to adjust and accept. His cock felt huge and hot as he filled her greedy, welcoming pussy, though she knew that was just because her inner walls were still chilled from the ice. Even so, it was a delightfully tight fit. The temperature soon equalized, and he began moving, thrusting slowly but quickly picking up a rhythm. Fleur stretched her hands out on the mattress in front of her, grasping at the cotton sheet, taking great fistfuls of the fabric and holding on.

"This is going to be hard. Feel free to scream." His voice was rich and low, rolling over her as he drove his cock deep. Fleur rather thought she might take him up on his offer and try to explain it to hotel security later, if it came to that.

Her pussy tightened and gripped him. She thrust her hips back to meet his strokes, increasing the friction she craved. As ever, his aim was accurate, connecting with her G-spot each time he plunged forward. He leaned over her, reaching around and under to lay the pad of his middle finger over her clit, circling and caressing the throbbing nub.

Within seconds, she hurtled toward another climax, gasping his name and pumping her hips furiously. Ethan matched her rhythm, sinking his finger deep into her arse to fill her completely as she convulsed around him. As her orgasm subsided, he inserted a second finger alongside the first, thrusting and swirling to open her sphincter even wider. He straightened and released her clit. The third slap fell on her unresisting left buttock, and Fleur was not sure she even felt it.

She did feel his cock withdrawing from her cunt, though, and turned her head in surprise. She was sure that he had not come. She would not have missed that.

"Now here." He slid his fingers from her arse and placed the head of his cock at her relaxed rear entrance. He pressed forward. "Open, love. Let me in. Push back toward me when I tell you."

Fleur could only nod, increasing her death grip on the sheet between her fingers.

She felt his cock ease its way into her arse. Inch by inch, he was slow, infinitely gentle, her body extensively prepared and receptive. She could do this. She knew she could. The sphincter was already slackened and as he pressed forward, her entrance opened further to allow him through. She dimly heard his murmured command to press back now, and did as he asked. Fleur groaned, her submission complete as he slid home.

His cock seated fully inside her arse, Ethan held still again, trailing his fingers in delicate patterns on her shoulders as she quivered in stunned silence. This had been easy, much easier than she had imagined. As everything seemed to be, with Ethan. She would probably never have contemplated any of this with a Dom who was other than a very temporary fixture in her life, but even so, she would miss him when he was gone. She would *really* miss him.

"Okay, love?" His tone was gentle, as were his hands, caressing her, soothing, reassuring.

Fleur nodded.

"Good. Sit up then, I owe you at least another orgasm. Or was that two?"

She turned her head, unsure what he might mean. In any case, she had lost count, whether orgasms or slaps.

He reached for her, his hands under her shoulders as he pulled her upright into a sitting position. "There are lots of excellent reasons for sticking your cock in a sub's arse, but the best one I can think of is that it gives you access to all of her. So, what do we have here then?"

He shifted on the bed, turning them both until Fleur found herself facing a mirrored wall. Reflected there, she sat astride Ethan's thighs, her breasts and stomach a shade or two darker than his tanned skin. His arms lay around her waist, but as she watched in the mirror, he lifted his hands to cup her breasts. Her nipples were still swollen and hardened further as he rolled and tugged at them. His grip was firm, and although she would not have described it as gentle, it was exactly right. She threw back her head, resting it against his shoulder. Ethan cupped her chin and turned her face to his. He kissed her, his tongue exploring her mouth, dancing with her tongue. Fleur reached for his face, laid her palm across his cheek then ran her fingers back through his hair.

He was utterly wonderful, this Dom she had found out in the desert.

He broke the kiss, smiled at her, and winked. "You are one sexy little peasant, Fleur."

"And you are one persuasive Englishman, Sir."

"Mmm, you weren't such a hard sell, once you got the idea in your head."

"Are you calling me a slut again, Sir?"

"Yes, probably. Do you mind?"

"No, Sir. But you still owe me a climax. Or two. We sluts are particular about these matters."

"We Doms are too. I'm so glad we find ourselves on the same page, then. I think it's time you did some work, though. You have exactly two minutes to bring yourself to orgasm."

"I have to do it myself?" She craned her neck to look him in the eye.

He smiled at her, but his expression was determined. "You do. And you're wasting time."

"But…"

"Have I been unclear in any way? Or perhaps you've changed your mind. Do you not want an orgasm after all?"

"I do, Sir. Of course I do."

"Then why are we still discussing this? You have one minute fifty seconds."

Fleur knew by now when he was serious and when he might be joking. He was deadly serious in that moment and she had better make some progress. She reached down with her right hand to slide it between her legs, her target the throbbing clump of nerve endings pulsing there. She drew her fingertips across her clit then took it firmly between them. She thought Ethan might well have squeezed if he were pleasuring her right now, so she did the same. The result was electric. She gasped in wonder that she could create this sensation for herself. Well, not entirely for herself, she acknowledged, but pretty close. She continued to roll her clit firmly between her fingers, tugging lightly, then more firmly as her arousal built. She would not be requiring anything close to two minutes.

Her orgasm took mere seconds to build and overflow, starting as a soft but insistent tingle low down in her abdomen, building quickly to an overwhelming surge that rushed up to sweep her away. Her body clenched hard, gripping Ethan deep within her, then her muscles went limp. He tightened his arms around her to hold her upright as the current of intense pleasure flowed through her body. Fleur threw her head back against his shoulder, her eyes closed as she savored every crackle and tingle, every soft convulsion until her climax was spent.

"Nice work, little sub, you did well. I felt that too. Now, though, it's my turn."

He eased her forwards until she was back on all fours, then he withdrew his cock until only the tip remained inside her arse. His thrust forward was hard and deep, but her body was totally ready and accepting. The stroke was long and pleasurable. Fleur moaned her bone-deep approval as she flexed her fingers in the sheet beneath her.

"Sir, I…" Her words trailed off—she really had nothing to say at that moment.

"I won't hurt you. I promise." Ethan's voice was low and gentle, his words murmured beside her ear as he withdrew to thrust again

"I know that. Oh…" Fleur gave up any attempt to communicate, at least not verbally. She would do any further talking with her body. Ethan seemed to be of the same mind because he turned his attention to delivering powerful, deliberate strokes into her arse, each one angled to be smooth, comfortable but filling her totally. Fleur knew he was stretching her, that she was straining to accept, but managing anyway. And the pleasure was beyond imagining, the intimacy total. Her surrender complete.

Ethan gave a guttural moan, swore softly, and the warm rush of semen filled the condom. He had not made good on his threat to put ice into her anus, but even so the heat of him now was intense and Fleur whimpered despite her delight at the proceedings. Ethan held still, his nose nuzzling the back of her neck as his climax peaked, then subsided. "Are you all right, little sub?"

"Yes, Sir. I am perfect," she managed to whisper the reply, wriggling slightly under him.

"You are, certainly. Do I still owe you a slap or two? Perhaps an orgasm?"

"I am not sure, Sir. I lost count."

"Better safe than sorry." He slid his cock from her arse and quickly removed the condom. He tied it off and dumped it on the floor on top of the wet towels. Just as Fleur was about to move onto her side, he dropped the final two swats onto her bum in quick succession. She yelped and turned to him, her expression accusing.

"I was not ready. I thought—"

"A deal's a deal, girl. You wouldn't like me to short-change you, now, would you? I believe that's just one more orgasm I owe you, then we're quits. Unless you know better?"

"I would not dispute this with you, Sir, but I doubt I can manage another orgasm this night."

"Wise girl. You'll make a superb submissive, though you must learn to let your Dom be the judge of what you can manage. Despite your unwarranted skepticism, I think we'll play very nice for this last one. Roll over onto your back."

Fleur did as she was told. It never occurred to her that she might do otherwise. She spread her legs, expecting Ethan to use his mouth to bring her back to boiling point again. He did not. Instead, he knelt between her legs and lifted her hips onto his thighs.

He smiled at her, his expression knowing. He was planning something, she was sure of it. When was he ever not?

As she watched, he leaned behind him to grab his jeans from the floor, and extricated another condom from his pocket. Fleur's eyes widened. Surely he couldn't? Not so soon?

Apparently he could. His erection had subsided hardly at all, she realized as he snapped the foil and unrolled the latex to sheathe himself. He guided the head of his cock into her pussy, slipping into her moist heat with ease. Fleur gasped, expecting it to be painful after so much intense activity, but it was not. Once there, seated to the hilt, he made no attempt to thrust. Instead he gazed down at the point where their bodies joined, tracing her stretched opening with his fingers.

"You're so beautiful, Fleur. You take my breath away."

"It is you. You are the breathtaking one, not I."

"We'll see. If you want me to stop, you have your safe word. Otherwise, enjoy. You have my permission to come as hard and as often as you like."

Before she had any opportunity to reply, he trailed his finger along her clit, from the back to the front. Her own ministrations faded to insignificance in comparison with such exquisite and perfect stimulation. Fleur stiffened, thrusting her hips involuntarily.

"Ah, you liked that, then? Are you still of the opinion that you can't manage another orgasm for me?" His words may have been slightly mocking, but his tone was deadly serious. He intended to wring every last drop of pleasure from her before he would allow her to sleep. Fleur found she had no real quarrel with that plan.

"No, Sir. You were right, I believe."

No further words were exchanged. None was necessary as he feathered his fingers across her sensitive bud. He was unhurried and skillful, seemingly knowing just how much pressure to exert, when to stop and let her draw breath and when to push her mercilessly toward climax. Fleur came again, could not help it as he teased and caressed her. His erection was hard, wide and solid inside her, but he didn't move. Fleur loved the sensation of fullness he created for her, squeezing her inner muscles tightly around him as each shiver of delight shook her body.

"That feels so good, little sub. When you come, I share every quiver, every little convulsion of yours. Come for me again, Fleur."

She obeyed, her body carried along on a sensuous wave over which she was powerless. Nor did she have any desire to exert even the slightest control. She was his, had been from the moment he came into the *riad*, and now he had her entirely.

He owed her one orgasm and he delivered three. Four perhaps. Spent at last, Fleur opened her eyes to gaze up at him. "Cashmere." She whispered the safe word, but he was clearly expecting it and slid his fingers from her now exhausted body.

"At last we're agreed. You really can't manage any more. Just this now…" He leaned over her and straightened his legs. Two quick thrusts later, his hot semen filled the condom, and at last, he was done.

Chapter Sixteen

Fleur woke to an empty, though not yet cold, bed. She thought she might be able to smell coffee, or hoped she could. Her stomach grumbled. Breakfast would be welcome. Sounds came from somewhere in the *riad*. The clink of a cup perhaps, and running water. Footsteps, drawers opening, a soft scrape here or the thud of a case hitting the tiled floor. The sounds of someone packing to leave.

Today. He would leave today, to return to his home in London. Well, he might live in London. She realized she was not sure, had never asked him. But he was certainly leaving the Totally Five Star, and soon. She raised herself on one elbow to look at the time displayed on her phone beside the bed. Ten seventeen. Thinking back over the events of the previous night, she was not sure just what time he had finally accepted that she had had enough and allowed her to sleep. Two o'clock, maybe later. She thought she had slept for perhaps eight solid hours. She had needed it — she felt delightfully refreshed now.

And quite desolate.

He was going. Really going. She had known he would, but still it hurt. He would be checking out in a couple of hours, three at the most. She would probably never see him again. Despite the pain of separating, it was good, surely. That had been her plan, her rationale for allowing herself this incredible interlude, this snatch of time from an otherwise ordered, businesslike and for the most part unexciting existence. She could permit herself this, *had* permitted it, because the madness was temporary and would never happen again. It couldn't. No one knew of her outrageous behavior, her uncharacteristic abandonment of all scruples, of anything remotely resembling inhibition or proper modesty. No one except Ethan, and he would be gone.

She would stay here. She would build her career in medicine. She intended to remain in Morocco. Her family was here. She was happy in Marrakesh, though she could move to one of the other major cities at some stage, if she chose to. Casablanca perhaps, or Tangier. They were important tourist hubs too. She could do well catering to the thousands of visitors who came to enjoy the North African sun and a bit of Arabian mystique, but more often than not ruined the ambience with too much beer or by carelessly swigging unbottled water. Oh yes, tourists always needed a doctor, and one who spoke several European languages was particularly in demand. She would be just fine.

On that optimistic note, she swung her legs from the bed and made for the en suite bathroom. She used the loo, brushed her teeth quickly, pleased that she had had the presence of mind to leave her toothbrush to hand. She did what she could to straighten her hair though Ethan's comb was woefully inadequate for the task. She had her own hairbrush somewhere but it was probably downstairs with the rest of her things, including her clothes.

She had slept in the nude, of course, and as she wandered back into the bedroom, she realized that the only clothes there were Ethan's jeans from yesterday. She had been wearing only her cloak when he'd arrived and that had been discarded somewhere downstairs. She tugged the duvet from the bed and wrapped it loosely around her body as she left the room, heading for Ethan, for her clothes, and for food. In that order.

"Morning, pretty lady. Did you sleep well?" He glanced at her from across the living area, pausing in the act of folding his clothes and laying them in his holdall. He was neat, she noted, meticulous, probably a frequent traveler and he had the preparations down to a fine art. His possessions were arranged around him on the two low sofas. He only needed to place everything in the bag and he would be good to go.

"I did, thank you." Fleur surveyed his progress from across the room, unaccountably desolate that he would be leaving without her. *Where did that come from?* She had never expected him to ask her to go with him, would have said no in any case. Her life was here, with her family, her career.

"Good. I didn't want to wake you. I had breakfast sent across. Just croissants and a selection of cold meats, cheese, that sort of thing. Some yogurt too, I think. And fruit juice. Help yourself. Would you like coffee or shall I phone room service for some tea?" He gestured in the approximate direction of the still-crowded breakfast tray and resumed his packing.

"Just coffee will be fine for me." Fleur felt distinctly not hungry, despite her growling stomach of a few minutes earlier. That had been then, before she'd remembered.

"I'd prefer you to eat, if you would, please. Just a glass of juice and a croissant if that's all you fancy. You do need to eat, though. I can't leave stripes across your bum on an empty stomach."

"I beg your pardon?" Fleur stared at him, her stomach clenching now and her pussy dampening disgracefully.

"You heard. Food. Now." His tone suggested that this was as close as he would be getting to 'please'. Fleur clutched the duvet to her chest and headed for the tray.

She was conscious that Ethan watched her select a couple of slices of meat, a piece of cheese and pour herself a glass of orange juice. With a brief smile in his direction and offering no further comment on the proposed stripes, she took her plate and drink out into the courtyard, and sat on the stone bench encircling the fountain. Her bottom was still slightly tender as she placed her weight on the hard stone seat. More of his attention there would leave her uncomfortable for days. She supposed that was his intention, his legacy to her, so to speak.

Ethan continued to stow his luggage neatly while she nibbled on her breakfast, forcing herself to eat for no better reason than that he had instructed it. She smiled at him as he approached her, a cup of fresh, steaming coffee in his hand.

"For you." He handed her the cup. She nodded her thanks and placed it beside her on the bench.

"Would you like to join me? Do you have time?" She watched him hopefully.

He did not take a seat, apparently preferring to lean casually against the wall surrounding the fountain. "I have plenty of time. I won't be checking out for a couple of hours at least. I just wanted to get stuff done before you woke up. You have my undivided attention now, Doctor Mansouri."

"I see. Thank you, Sir." Fleur knew by his tone, his demeanor, by some indescribable quality that he could inject into the exchange that he was talking to her as her Dom. It was important that she respond accordingly.

"You will go upstairs and find a ruler in my bag. The rucksack I use for site visits." He paused.

Fleur nodded to signal her understanding. She knew which bag he meant.

Ethan continued, "Then you will come back down here and bend over for me. Here, I think. You can lean on that seat you seem so fond of. Lose the quilt, obviously. I'm thinking ten strokes on each side, including the backs of your thighs. It'll hurt. You won't be able to sit for a long while afterwards. The marks will be visible for days. Something to remember me by…"

"I see. Thank you, Sir." She shifted uncomfortably on the bench, conscious of her now seriously wet pussy. She *was* truly a slut. She must be, she reflected, to become so aroused at just the description of a serious beating. Still, she intended to make the best of this while he was still here.

"Now, Sir?" She placed her still half-full plate beside the coffee cup on the bench.

"Finish your breakfast first, Fleur. And your coffee. Once I have your bottom the way I like it, I'll allow you to suck my cock before I fuck you again. So, those are my plans for you this morning. Do you have any questions? Or comments?"

"No, Sir, it all sounds perfectly straightforward." Fleur picked up her plate again and continued to nibble at the remaining slice of meat. She finished it then drank her coffee. She carried her plate and empty cup back inside as she went to obey his instructions.

The rucksack contained three rulers of varying lengths, two made of plastic and one from metal. Fleur selected the metal one, a foot in length, and returned with it to the courtyard. With just a sideways glance at Ethan, she placed the ruler on the bench before she dropped the duvet into a heap on the tiled floor. She turned her back on Ethan, leaning forward to place her hands firmly on the stone surface.

"Is this all right, Sir?"

"I'd prefer your bum to be raised up a little more. I want to see your buttocks and thighs, please. I like a nice clear shot, and I intend to lay these stripes very accurately for you. Nice and symmetrical. Maybe if you rest on your elbows…?"

"Like this, Sir?" Fleur adjusted her position as suggested, her bottom now prominently displayed for Ethan's attention.

"Perfect. I see you chose the metal. Why not the plastic? That might have been less — severe."

"I was hoping for a lasting impression, Sir. I thought metal might be more suited to that purpose."

He chuckled, the sound low and sexy. "I see. I expect you're right. Do I need to remind you of your safe words?"

"No, Sir, I have not forgotten them." And she had absolutely no intention of making use of them.

He leaned across her to pick up the ruler, the front of his cotton shirt brushing her hip. Fleur relished the brief contact as he straightened and took up his position behind her and slightly to her left.

"Hard and fast, this time. I'll keep count. Please try not to make any undue fuss, and if you need time out, just say so."

"Of course, Sir. Thank you." Fleur shifted her feet, parting her legs slightly to increase her stability. "I'm ready."

Despite her confident statement, the first stroke still took her breath away when it landed square across her right buttock. Fleur hissed in pain but did not move. She braced for the next, expecting the pain to blaze across her left buttock this time. It did not. Ethan continued to lay the strokes across her right side, each one immediately below its predecessor. By the time he reached five, Fleur was struggling to contain her cries. On six, she whimpered. On seven, she let out a low squeal.

"Quiet, girl. Do you need something to bite on?"

Fleur shook her head quickly, determined to manage this.

"The last three will be on the backs of your thighs. This is the really painful bit."

Fleur groaned inwardly, wishing she had not been so hasty in rejecting his offer of help. She did not have long in which to reflect on her mistake, though. The next stroke seared her upper thigh and Fleur could no longer hold back her tears. The next two strokes followed in rapid succession as she wept silently, her entire body jerking with each stroke.

"I'm liking the effect so far. Your skin is quite delicate. The stripes are really vivid. Are you okay to continue or would you like a break?"

"N-no, Sir. Please continue." Fleur wanted this to be done with now, but it was with some effort that she remained in position, offering him her other buttock for the same treatment.

Ethan shifted slightly to the left, positioning himself. The first stroke on her left buttock landed across the widest, fleshiest part. It was less painful than the final two or three on her right side had been, so Fleur was able to relax slightly. Ethan continued to lay the stripes just as he had on her right side, dropping each into place with unerring accuracy. Despite her mounting discomfort, Fleur could not fault his skill. This second batch seemed easier, less excruciating. Perhaps she was becoming more accustomed to the assault on her senses. Perhaps the release of endorphins was coming to her aid. Or maybe he had reduced the intensity of his strokes, though she could think of no reason why he would. She found herself able to relax into the sensation, finding a perverse pleasure in the pain. Somehow, her body, or perhaps her brain, converted the agony to create something different, something...other. It was not pleasure, not quite, but very nearly. As near as made no difference.

The individual strokes blurred, became one continuous sensation. Fleur felt somehow detached from what was happening, as though she was watching this from somewhere close by. She could hear the whistle of the ruler as he swung it, and the sharp crack as it made contact with her bottom, but the pain became muted, dispersed. Fleur was vividly aware of her pussy, which was wet and throbbing, aching to be touched. She widened her legs in invitation, not even caring if he caught her sensitive clit or pussy lips with the ruler. But, of course, he would not. He was far too accurate in his task.

She lost track of everything—her surroundings, the continuing onslaught—even her desperate need to be touched took on an ethereal quality. She heard a low, insistent buzzing now, as she seemed to float on some buoyant cushion of air, oblivious to the pain as each blow fell. When she looked back on this later, she would say that events seemed to go into slow motion, the edges of everything blurring, sounds muted, muffled. She felt to be floating, though she was conscious of the cool tiles under her bare feet.

Long, timeless moments passed. A voice, low and seductive, commanding her.

"…now, Fleur."

What? Who?

"I have you, love. Open your eyes and look at me."

No, not yet… Soon.

"Now, Fleur. Look at me. Can you hear me?" His voice was low, soothing, not shouting but insistent. He must be obeyed. She had to…what?

With his hand on her face, he stroked her hair back. The other lay on her stomach, his arm around her, supporting her. Fleur turned her head toward his voice, forcing her eyelids open. Ethan. Ethan was there, his face close to hers, his wonderful deep blue eyes soft, warm. She might drown in them. Perhaps she already had. He smiled, the expression etching sweet lines at the edges of his eyes. His face softened, gentled.

"Back with me, love?"

Fleur frowned, confused. She had a sense that something had happened, something she should know about but couldn't quite recall. There was an uncharacteristic fogginess wrapping itself around her brain. She was confused, disorientated, her memories not quite her own. She felt somewhat good, though. Yes, on reflection, definitely good. And safe. Warm but not uncomfortably so. She reached for Ethan, the one solid feature in an otherwise shifting world. She caressed his cheek with her palm, noting the slight scratch of stubble. He had yet to shave this morning.

Yes, morning. It *was* morning. She was with Ethan in his *riad*. In the courtyard of his *riad*, to be exact. She tried to stand, straightening her arms to push herself up and immediately winced. Her bottom was on fire, there could be no other explanation for the searing pain now spreading across her skin.

"Oh, oh, that hurts..."

"My work here is done then. Well, nearly done. Can you stand, do you think?"

Of course, why would she not? Fleur tried to do just that, only to stagger violently as a wave of dizziness hit her. Ethan tightened his arm around her and pulled her upright, slipping his other arm behind her knees to lift her off her feet. He turned and carried her inside, across the living area and up the stairs. In the bedroom, he laid her on the bed, face down. He left her briefly to return with his ubiquitous bottle of water. He snapped the top open and held it to her lips. Fleur did not even start to protest, just took it in her mouth and sucked greedily.

Her recollection of the events in the courtyard began to reassemble, the pieces slotting together quickly. He had been striping her bottom with a ruler. A metal ruler, which she had helpfully brought from his site kit because that was what he'd instructed her to do and she was in the habit now of obeying Ethan. Twenty strokes, ten on each side. He had almost finished, but something had shifted, changed. He hadn't finished but had done something else instead. Something that had made her feel odd, disconnected from herself and from the pain. It had hurt, was still hurting. She could hardly move, but for a while back there, she had felt nothing. Or nearly nothing—a sort of tingling, as though the vibrations were reaching her through cotton wool. It was odd and she did not understand.

"You hit subspace, love. Was it good?"

Subspace? Fleur turned her face toward Ethan as he now crouched beside the bed. He smiled but did not seem at all perturbed by whatever had just taken place.

"What? What happened? What did you do?"

"I saw that you were dropping so I slowed down, gave you plenty of time to sink. You were out of it for maybe five minutes or so."

"Out of it? I do not understand."

"Subspace, Fleur. A sort of trance brought on by your response to the pain stimulation and the rush of endorphins. Not all submissives manage it but you just did. I'm told it's good."

Good? Fleur frowned, considering. *Yes, good would not be too far wide of the mark.* The experience had been strange, but not unpleasant. She'd felt relaxed, as though nothing mattered. Vaguely euphoric. As she examined the sensation, and with the not inconsiderable benefit of hindsight, she came to the conclusion that she would have no objection to repeating it. It *had* been good.

"Yes, Sir, it was. It is, I mean. Very good. It was—interesting. I had not expected that to happen. Is this thing, this subspace a regular occurrence?"

"It can be, with a receptive sub and a Dom who knows which of her buttons to press."

And that, she supposed, would be her problem. Ethan clearly could manage to hit the correct buttons, but he would not be here to do so. She might have to wait a long time for another Dom with similar skills to cross her path. Fleur pulled herself up short. What was she thinking? She had known from the outset that this would be an isolated incident, a brief and never-to-be-repeated experience. Subspace was simply a bonus she had not anticipated, a good experience to file away and savor later. After Ethan had gone.

Fleur turned to her side and propped herself up on one elbow. She smiled at Ethan, suddenly overwhelmed by a rush of grateful affection for him. He had shown her what she had wanted to see and so much more besides. He had been, quite simply, superb.

"Now it is my turn."

"Your turn, little sub?"

"To pleasure you. Is that what you would call it?"

"I expect I would. You have so far. Do please feel free to continue."

Fleur reached for his zipper and pulled it down. She took her time, her gaze fixed on his, and was pleased to see his pupils dilate. "You said that I was to suck your cock, Sir. Is that still your wish?"

"I see no reason to vary my instructions at this stage."

Fleur nodded as she released his straining erection from his jeans to wrap both her hands around it. She shuffled to a kneeling position, taking care not to settle her weight on her still incredibly sore thighs. Leaning forward, she tilted her bottom upwards, the tender skin throbbing in the warmth of the room. Ethan wore a knowing expression. He fully appreciated her discomfort. He was equally conscious of her delight in it, her exultation that she had accepted the beating without protest, her body's involuntary descent into subspace her additional reward. Fleur winced with every movement, but relished the burning sting across her tender buttocks, the proof that she was alive. The irrefutable evidence that she could feel, and that it was possible to steal such wicked pleasure from pain.

She lowered her lips to nuzzle the head of Ethan's cock, opening her mouth around it as she pumped both her hands up and down the length of his shaft. She closed her eyes to concentrate on her task, lapping his salty juices with the flat of her tongue. The taste was familiar now and uniquely Ethan. He had not said she was to swallow his semen, but she would. She wanted to, every drop of it.

She continued to pump his shaft with one hand and used the other to reach for his balls. She caressed them, soft at first but firmer as she heard his muffled groan. Ethan shifted on the bed. He now lay beside her as she knelt at his left hip, bending to her task. She snuck a glance at him. His eyes were closed, his right arm flung across his forehead. His left hand reached for her to caress her sore bum. He had to be doing that deliberately. Fleur was convinced of it. Not that she had any objection. Her stripes were his handiwork. He was entitled to fondle them, surely.

She scraped the swollen head of his cock with her teeth, cautious not to apply too much pressure. So far, he seemed perfectly delighted with her performance, so she leaned in to take more of his erection into her mouth. Fleur sucked, hollowing her cheeks around the solid, smoothness, loving both the feel and the taste of him as his arousal built.

"Fucking hell, girl. Do that again."

His growled command caused Fleur's pussy to convulse and moisten even as she widened her mouth to repeat the suction. She did it harder this time, allowing her teeth to sink just that fraction deeper. Not much, not enough to…

"For fuck's sake." He grabbed her leg, his large hand tightening around her thigh just above the knee. "Open your legs, girl. Wide. Now."

Fleur obeyed, her own strangled moan caressing his cock as Ethan's fingers slid deep inside her waiting pussy. He thrust, once, hard, then added a third finger. Fleur could hear sounds of her own wetness as he plunged his fingers inside her. She squeezed him, tightening her fist around his shaft to pump hard, matching her rhythm to his.

Ethan twisted his hand inside her. He continued to finger-fuck her hard, rubbing her G-spot with each stroke. Fleur knew she would come and it would not be long. She was determined not to be the first this time, though she suspected she would have little to say about the matter. Even so, she used the flat of her tongue to press his cock against the roof of her mouth then leaned in farther to suck him to the back of her throat.

Ethan's moans became more frenzied, thrusting his hips upwards to meet her strokes. His fingers inside her were equally determined as he plunged and withdrew, hard, fast, deep. Fleur's response bubbled in her lower abdomen before boiling up, rushing to fill and overflow as she prepared to tumble helplessly into her orgasm. Ethan stilled a moment before Fleur passed the point of no return. His growl seemed to be dragged from the back of his throat an instant before his semen filled her mouth. Briefly distracted from her own response, Fleur swallowed quickly and continued to work her throat as the spunk continued to spurt. Mercifully, Ethan seemed unable to come and finger-fuck simultaneously so she had a few seconds of respite to savor the flow of salty liquid slipping down her throat. His climax passed quickly and he started to work her with renewed determination. It was a matter of moments before Fleur came too, her cunt pulsing and contracting around his digits.

Ethan had his hands in her hair, gripping her scalp and lifting her head from his cock.

"You did well, girl. I'm thinking you enjoyed yourself too?"

Fleur turned to look at him, her smile sleepy now, and more than a little smug. "Yes, Sir. Thank you."

"Thank me by getting on all fours. In the middle of the bed. Now, please." His expression was stern despite the encouraging tone of his words. Fleur wasted no time in assuming the required position, knowing what would come next. His itinerary had been perfectly clear after all, and thus far, he had stuck to it. Now he would fuck her and she knew he would make a good job of it. He always did.

This might be the last time, in fact it almost certainly would be. She knew this, accepted this, and fully intended to carry the memory with her for the foreseeable future.

Ethan stood and removed his jeans, already loose around his hips. The bed shifted as he knelt behind her. Fleur lifted her bottom, her knees spread as wide as she was able. Her buttocks still throbbed beautifully, a sensation intensified as he caressed her skin with both hands, separating her cheeks. "Christ, you are so fucking gorgeous. Your arse is glowing, and your tush is pink and so wet I could drown in it. Are you hot, little slut? Are you desperate for this?

"Yes, Sir. Please be quick. I do not want to wait."

"But you will, won't you? If I tell you to."

"Please do not ask that of me. Not this time. I want you, now. Please, Sir…"

His response was to sink the full length of his cock into her pussy. Fleur let out a scream as her elbows gave way and she sank her face into the duvet, her bottom raised in welcome. Ethan said nothing, his cock doing the talking for him now as he withdrew and plunged back into her. He set up a brisk rhythm, slapping his body against hers with each stroke. Fleur's cries of pleasure were muffled by the bedclothes as she tightened around him. Her grip was fierce, her hips gyrating to increase the friction. She wanted and needed more, though, and reached for her clit. Ethan was there ahead of her.

"Let me, sweetheart."

His tone was gentle now — she might have thought affectionate, though that would have been fanciful. Still, this was a fairy tale type of moment so maybe a little fantasy was not out of place. His caress was pure bliss, unerring and accurate. He flicked her bud with his fingertip before laying the pad of his thumb over it and rubbing in easy, soothing circles.

Fleur came, moaning her delight into the duvet, her cheek flattened against the mattress. Ethan did not stop. He continued to thrust into her, maintaining the soft pressure on her clit as he brought her back to the brink again. He held her there for a few moments before one firm rub sent her hurtling back into her own private orbit. This time she screamed aloud, her body convulsing around his cock. Ethan held still until the crisis had passed, then resumed his steady rhythm. He picked up the pace now, his own pleasure starting to assert itself. Still he did not let up on her greedy clit, rubbing and massaging relentlessly until she clenched and screamed again. This time he was with her, sinking deep one last time and holding still, the head of his cock nudging her cervix as he came too.

Chapter Seventeen

Dressed, showered, her hair neatly brushed and arranged into a plait, Fleur perched on the edge of a sofa to watch as Ethan completed his preparations to leave. Her own overnight bag was already neatly packed and now waited by the door. He glanced at her, his hair still damp from the shower and slicked back from his face. He smiled, and she noted that the expression reached his eyes. His gaze was warm, and yes, perhaps affectionate would not be too wistful a conclusion to arrive at.

Fleur's evolving feelings for him were a mystery to her. She had not expected to be so sad that he was leaving. She had always prided herself on her pragmatic approach to life. His departure had always been on the cards, so why should it distress her now that the moment had arrived? She was determined not to examine those feelings, at least not yet. Right at this moment, she needed to be cool, collected, not clingy and needy. However much she might wish he was staying, he was not. He had a life and so did she. Their paths had crossed and now they were going their separate ways once more. It had been good, better than good, but it was ending. It had to end, and it had to be now.

"Will you be eating here, at the hotel, before you go?"

Ethan pulled the zip around his travel holdall as he answered, "No. I planned on a late lunch at the airport. After I've checked in."

"What time is your flight?"

"Sixteen ten. If it's on time, I should be back at Heathrow by around half past seven or eight o'clock this evening."

"Do you have far to travel after that?"

He shook his head. "An hour or so, that's all."

"You will be glad to be home?"

Now he regarded her, his expression quizzical. He took his time in answering, "Not especially."

Fleur did not reply, uncertain how to interpret his remark. Ethan hauled his case over to the door and left it alongside her bag.

"The porter can bring that down for me later. I'll be checking out in about half an hour. You don't have to leave, though. I can ask housekeeping to delay coming in for a while."

Fleur stood. She ran her palms down the front of her loose cotton slacks, smoothing imaginary creases. "No, I should be leaving too. I will go now, if you do not mind. I prefer to say goodbye here. In private."

"I understand, and of course I don't mind." He came to stand in front of her, his smile distinctly sad. Fleur dropped her gaze, unable to bear the sweet pain of this inevitable end. She had promised herself that she would not cry, would do and say nothing to make this parting any more painful than it needed to be. She was determined not to make a fool of herself now.

Ethan cupped her chin with one hand and tilted her face up. He used the thumb of his other hand to wipe away the tears now forming, then dipped his head to kiss her eyes, first one then the other.

"Tears, love? You'll miss me, then?"

Fleur gulped and nodded. She could find no words at that moment and hoped he would not press her for them. He didn't.

"I've enjoyed meeting you, Doctor Mansouri. Very much. And not just for the obvious reasons. You're a remarkable woman."

"I am glad too, that we met. You have inspired me. And you have helped me in ways I had not imagined, could never have dreamed..."

"If I've been of service, please be assured that it was a pleasure. Hey, I even find myself developing a fondness for donkeys. Who would have imagined that?"

"Agwmar is an appealing beast..."

"Fleur..." His expression turned serious now. "Please take care of yourself. Be happy. And safe. Promise me that."

"I will. I will try, at least. And you must do the same."

"I have a gift for you, something you might like to keep, to remember me by."

"There is no need..."

"No, but I want to. The cashmere scarves, the ones I bought in the souk, despite your attempts to thwart my bargaining prowess. I'd like you to have them. They're on the bed."

Fleur smiled. The scarves were indeed lovely. "Thank you. I will retain fond memories of them." That those memories were mainly associated with being tied naked to his bed, blindfolded, she chose not to elaborate on just now.

"Good. While we're on the subject of fond memories, I have a request too. Something of yours I'd like to keep, if I may."

"Of mine? Yes, of course. What is it?"

"Your cloak. The one you were wearing when I first saw you and again last night. Could I have that, please?"

She stared at him incredulous. She had expected him to request a lock of hair, or even her underwear. "You want the cloak? But it is old and not even mine. I borrowed it from my grandmother."

"Would she mind you giving it to me, do you think? I'd be happy to pay her for it, or send her a replacement."

He seemed to have his heart set on the tatty old cloak. *There really is no accounting for the vagaries of sexy Englishmen.* "I am certain she will not object. I am surprised, though, that you would want such a thing. It has no value."

"It has value to me. I can have it, then?"

"If course. It is in my bag. I will get it for you." She hesitated, then, "I… I have another gift too. Something I brought with me intending you to have."

"Oh?"

"It is in the courtyard. I will show it to you." She turned and headed out of the French window into the inner garden. She stopped beside the fountain where her handmade carpet still lay on the cool tiles. "I made this. It took me over a year to weave. It is mine, but I want you to have it."

She turned to see Ethan staring in wonder at her carpet. It was a nice piece of work. She had been proud of it when she'd completed it, almost ten years ago now. Traditionally all Moroccan girls were taught to make the beautiful handcrafted carpets, though many of those sold to tourists were now mass-produced. In the past, it had been considered an essential requirement prior to marriage that a young woman should make a carpet to present to her husband's family. It seemed to her appropriate that Ethan should have this one.

Each Berber carpet was unique, designed and stitched by the girl herself, and usually incorporating a deliberate mistake in the pattern. This would be put there on purpose, a sort of signature to mark the work as her own. Fleur's eye was drawn to the slight flaw in the design running around the border, one bird's wing a fraction longer than the others. No one but her would ever pick it out, though she might tell Ethan about it. If he asked.

"This is lovely. But it's too much. These things are worth a fortune."

"It is valuable, yes. But like the cloak, its value is perhaps not monetary. I want you to take it with you. Please accept it. Keep it. Put it in your house and think of me sometimes, when you look at it."

He turned to her, took her face between his hands and kissed her mouth. "It's a beautiful gift. Truly the most perfect thing anyone ever gave me. I'll treasure it. Thank you."

Fleur heaved a relieved sigh. She had not been entirely certain that he would accept her gesture. He might not fully appreciate its significance, but he would at least know that it was a part of her and he would take it with him.

"It is not perfect. It is not meant to be. Let me show you." Fleur knelt on the rug, her position so reminiscent of last night that her knickers were already becoming wet. This was not to be, though—not now, not ever again. "See here, the bird at the edge. This wing is a little too long, not exactly like the others. It is done on purpose."

He crouched beside her, peering at the woven bird. "Yes, I see it now. Such a tiny thing, you'd have to know what you were looking for."

"Yes, that is the idea." She reached into the back pocket of her pants and pulled out a folded piece of paper. She handed it to Ethan. "You can show this at Customs, at the airport. The paper says that this carpet is a gift. The customs officers often ask how much was paid and you may be charged import duty. The paper may not be accepted as proof, but I have written my contact details on it, here at the hotel and at my home, so they will be able to check. If you do have to pay duty, please let me know and I will do what I can to have it refunded to you."

Ethan pocketed the paper and stood.

Fleur also got to her feet and bent to pick up the carpet. She rolled it quickly and held it out to him. "It should fit in your bag, I think."

"I'll make sure it does, even if I have to leave half my clothes behind. Thank you."

"Thank *you*, Sir."

Ethan smiled and went back into the *riad*. He returned a couple of minutes later, without the carpet but he was carrying the scarves, neatly folded now. He handed them to Fleur. "I'll swap these for the cloak, then?"

"Of course." She clutched the scarves to her chest and rushed past him, hurrying to her bag waiting by the door. She rummaged quickly, tucking the scarves inside and pulling out the cloak. She handed it to

Ethan, who had followed her. He held it briefly to his nose.

"Mmm, it smells wonderful. Fresh and incredibly sexy."

"I will tell my grandmother you said so."

"I suspect the scent is yours, unless you're telling me that sensuality runs in your family."

Fleur considered making some other witty and perhaps flippant remark, but had no appetite for it. Tears again blurred her vision. She wanted to remember him clearly.

"I must go."

"I know."

"Do not forget me."

"I think that's unlikely. You're extremely memorable, Doctor Mansouri."

"I... Thank you."

"Remember me to your parents. They're remarkable people, with a truly exceptional daughter."

"You are very kind."

"And you, Fleur, are absolutely fucking gorgeous. I've loved spending time with you. Thank you for being here."

Fleur had no further words. This was hard, much more painful than she had imagined. She needed it to be over.

"Goodbye." Her voice came out just a whisper, because saying the word aloud was just too awful. She reached up on tiptoe to lay her lips against his, the touch soft and light, a kiss of parting rather than passion.

Ethan closed his arms briefly around her then loosened them as she broke the kiss and bent to pick up her bag. She reached for the door handle and opened the door. She stepped into the corridor then turned back to face him. She touched her fingers to her lips and blew the last kiss to him from the distance of a couple of feet. He winked and blew her a kiss back, leaning casually on the doorframe. He smiled, his grin sexy and somehow totally male. That was how Fleur wanted to remember him.

She walked away down the corridor. She did not look back. Neither did she hear the door close behind her.

At last, she reached the corner, conscious of his gaze still on her retreating back, and she remembered having felt the same sensation when she first passed him on that dusty road just a few days ago. This was infinitely more unnerving. She drew in a breath and turned the corner. Out of sight, she clutched her bag to her chest, and made no further attempt to stem her tears. She started running.

Shit.
Fucking, bollocking shit.
Ethan watched the small figure marching away from him. Shoulders stiff, head up, spine ramrod straight, resolute to the core. She'd been close to tears when she'd blown him that last kiss—he fully expected her to be sobbing by now. But she wasn't. Somehow, she had managed to hold herself together. He had to hand it to her—she had grit. And determination. Her performance as his submissive over the last twenty-four hours had demonstrated that well enough. She had been absolutely superb, despite her inexperience. He had gone easy on her, to be fair, but only at the outset. Whilst he had not forgotten that she was a novice in the art of submission, he had found her to be a natural and had soon ramped up the intensity of their scenes to match her needs.

He had played with countless submissives over the years and had had one or two significant relationships in and among. There was something special and distinct about Fleur, though — something he found difficult to name but was keenly aware of, even so. She seemed set apart, not like anyone he had met before, whether as his submissive or in any other way.

He had not thought for a moment that she would agree to scene with him. That would have been beyond his wildest expectations. That she should do so, and with such enthusiasm and aptitude, beggared belief.

Women like Fleur Mansouri were a rare treat. Submissives like Fleur even scarcer, more precious. He hoped her experiences with him would not be her last in this lifestyle, though the thought of her gorgeous body exposed for the attentions of some other Dom left him feeling less than impressed. She was his. *He* had discovered her. *He* had introduced her to the pleasures of pain, the wicked delights to be had from a decent spanking. But she was delicate and she needed to be handled sensitively, fully appreciated. She deserved no less and her response had both astounded and delighted him. Another Dom might not realize her subtleties, might not take sufficient care of her. He did not like that thought, not in the least.

He watched as she reached the end of the corridor, where she hesitated for a moment. He thought she might be about to turn around, possibly even come hurtling back down the corridor and into his arms.

I wish.

She did nothing of the sort. She turned the corner, heading purposefully for the central foyer then presumably the hotel clinic. He seemed to recall that she was not on duty for a while yet but she had dressed for work. He didn't think she intended to return home first. He might even be able to see her again before he left, just one last time.

He stepped back inside the *riad* and closed the door, firmly rejecting that notion. Saying goodbye once had been hard enough, for both of them. She certainly wouldn't thank him for forcing the ordeal on her again, and he wasn't entirely sure he could go through it either.

He picked up the hotel phone and dialed reception. In true Totally Five Star style, the call was answered by the second ring. Ethan made arrangements for the porter staff to collect his luggage and ordered a taxi to be outside the front entrance in thirty minutes. That just gave him time to help himself to a refreshing drink of sparkling water from the minibar, which he took out into the courtyard. He leaned against the fountain, remembering the beauty of this space when Fleur had been in it. And felt the desolation now that she was not.

He finished his drink and headed back inside. He picked up his hand luggage, did a final check for his passport and tickets, more out of habit than any real sense that they might not be where they should be. He patted his back pocket to check that he had the room key card to hand, and felt the crinkle of the folded paper Fleur had given him. He smiled to himself as he pulled it out and unfolded the single sheet. Although written in French, he could understand enough of it to get the gist. And sure enough, she had managed to give him her phone number, at work, at home, her mobile too. He pulled out his own phone and quickly transferred the details. If he needed to show the document at Customs, he had no way of being sure he would still be in possession of it at the end of his journey. Better not to take the risk.

He hadn't intended to return to Marrakesh, but his plans could easily change. He had a suspicion that they already had. He would want to know how to contact her if — when — he came back.

Thirty minutes later, he sat in the back of an air-conditioned taxi. He glanced over his shoulder as the car pulled away from the hotel entrance. Despite his resolution, and hers, he wondered if he might catch just one last glance, one final fleeting glimpse of his beautiful Berber princess. It wasn't to be. He turned to face the front again as the taxi slipped into the teeming noisy chaos of the city traffic, leaving Fleur Mansouri behind.

Chapter Eighteen

Three weeks. Three long, endless weeks, and no word from him. None. Nothing at all.

He could have phoned or texted, if only to let her know he had reached home safely. Not that he had said he would, nor had she asked this of him. It was just... Well, he could have—he knew how to reach her. All the details had been there on that paper she'd given him. He must have realized.

Maybe he had forgotten her already. Maybe he was not missing her or didn't as much as she missed him. Which was far, far too much, she was quite certain about that.

It was not meant to feel like this. Her brief fling with Ethan was only ever going to last for a few days, a passing thing at best. An experiment, perhaps, just a way to find out if what she had always thought might be true. Of her. Ethan had offered her an opportunity, and she had taken it. Grabbed it. With both hands. She was fast realizing that he had offered far more than that. He had offered her safety, caring, security, and she had gladly accepted the entirety of his gift.

The first few days had been the worst. She had barely functioned, just managing to drag herself through her daily routine. Home, sleep, hotel, work, home, sleep, hotel, work — and so it went on. And on and on. Fleur told herself it would pass, this heavy, sad mood of hers. It was to be expected, perhaps, after the intensity of the experience with Ethan. She made it her business to read about the psychological aspects of BDSM and convinced herself that she was suffering from sub-drop. Perhaps she was, and if so, the right course of action would be to seek out her Dom and ask for his support. She was entitled to it.

But her Dom was gone. She could not contact him, because although he had her phone number, she did not have his. And even if she did, would he welcome a call from her? Perhaps not. Probably not, in fact. He would be back in the UK, immersed in his everyday life by now, and a call out of the blue from some distraught, depressed ex-lover would be the last thing he wanted.

No, she was on her own. She would get through this. There was no alternative, really.

By the end of the first week, she had convinced herself that she was managing, improving even. Her appetite remained non-existent but she no longer burst into tears for no good reason. A grumpy or over-fussy patient, a late delivery of pharmaceuticals, even the news that her favorite brand of deodorant was temporarily out of stock at the Totally Five Star boutique had been enough to plummet her into a fit of weeping. By some stroke of luck, she'd contrived to keep her fragile state of mind a secret, at least at work. At home, it was a different matter.

Yasmine was normally more than a little self-obsessed, but even she could not miss Fleur's dismal expression, her moping, her general misery. Fleur's parents were worried, and it took them precisely one look at her stricken expression when she arrived home late on the evening of Ethan's departure to work out what the cause was. Her mother made no bones about tackling the matter head on.

"You are in love with this Englishman, *oui*?"

"*Non, Maman. Il est parti et…*"

"Yes, I know he is gone. That is the problem, *n'est-ce pas*?

"It is not a problem. He was only ever to be here for a few days."

"A few days—*cela suffit*. It is enough to fall in love."

"I am not in love with him. I never was. I liked him. I enjoyed his company. I miss him, that is true, but…"

"But nothing. Do I look to you like a fool? Does your father? We know you. We know what we see. We care about you."

Fleur had no answer to that. She settled for weeping instead, her face buried in her mother's smart silk jacket. Her mom stroked Fleur's hair, muttered the usual nonsense about getting over it, he might come back, she could always call him, it might help to talk…

Fleur knew she could not contact him, and as far as she could make out, there was nothing that would help. She was alone, again, and would stay that way.

Said was less direct, but equally concerned. Fleur saw the pain and confusion in his expression, the frustration that on this occasion there was nothing he could do to put things right for her. There would be no marching in and snatching her away from the source of her unhappiness, not this time.

On her first day off work following Ethan's departure, Fleur found it difficult to convince herself that it was truly worth the effort of getting out of bed.

Her father appeared in the bedroom doorway, a tray of her favorite lemon tea in his hands.

"Thank you, Papa, but I am not thirsty."

"Tea is not for thirst. Water is for thirst. And for washing, I daresay. Tea is for conversation."

"I do not want to talk either."

"No? Then I will talk." He placed the tray on a low table and brought it alongside her bed. "May I?" He did not wait for her answer before seating himself beside her and reaching for the teapot. He poured two small glasses of tea and handed one to Fleur. She took it wordlessly, sipped the steaming liquid as she watched him over the rim.

"He is a fine man, your Ethan. I liked him."

"He is not my Ethan."

"He was, for a while at least. You slept with him, yes?"

"Papa!"

"Ah, you do not deny it. He did not either. You were together that night, after you both left here." He shook his head gravely as he sipped his tea.

"It was not like that."

"Like what, my daughter?" He smiled at her, not a hint of reproach in his expression.

"It was not what you are thinking."

"What am I thinking?"

"That I should have... That I might... I do not know. You are angry?"

"Do I look angry?"

"No. You look — sad."

"I am saddened that my girl is unhappy."

His girl. Ethan called her 'girl', but it had not the merest hint of the paternal about it. This was so very different.

Her father continued, "I want you to smile, to enjoy your life, however you choose to live it. As I say, I like Ethan. As do you."

"But he had to return to England. His life is there. He is not coming back."

"Is he not?"

Fleur just shook her head, the tears flowing once more. Said made no attempt to stem their flow, just drank his tea calmly and waited. Eventually Fleur raised her tear-ravaged face and managed a watery smile. "He will not be back, Papa. Never."

"Never is a long time. Who knows what could happen? God has his ways and you may meet your Ethan again, *Insha'Allah*. Next time it might be different."

Fleur smiled. Her father's rare flirtations with invoking the will of God tended to be reserved for when he had exhausted all more practical courses. He was clearly at a loss, and so was she.

Another week dragged past, sluggish, monotonous. Fleur's existence seemed more bleak with every passing hour, every endless, meaningless day. She persuaded her mother to phone the hotel and tell them that she was ill, having convinced herself that she just needed a few days of peace and quiet at home to pull herself together. The manager at the Totally Five Star sympathized, said he had noticed that she seemed off color and insisted that she take as long as she needed. The other locum doctor would take her shifts, and the regular incumbent of the post was due back in a few days.

That last snippet of news should have dismayed Fleur. Her post was a temporary one, and she was by no means certain that the hotel would wish to retain her services long term. She loved this work—or she had. The apparent kindness of the hotel manager was code for 'Take your time, we don't really need you.' She really should do something about negotiating a permanent role, or a transfer to another hotel perhaps where locum cover was required.

All that would require energy, though, and at least an appearance of enthusiasm. She could muster neither. She took to her bed again.

"Your grandmother is unwell. She has asked if you could call on her today—or tomorrow, whichever is more convenient for you." Yvette called the words over her shoulder as she headed out of the door.

Her mother was on duty at the hospital all day and would not be back for at least twelve hours. Her father was away on business and, of course, Yasmine was occupied elsewhere. With the exception of the local woman who came in three times a week to clean and polish, Fleur would have only her own company to enjoy all day. Ordinarily that prospect would not bother her. She might even welcome the solitude. She liked to read, to listen to music, sometimes just to walk the souks and bazaars of Marrakesh and soak up the atmosphere of her beloved city. Having time to herself was a gift.

But not today. Fleur dreaded the silence, the emptiness of the day yawning ahead of her. A drive out to the mountains and a couple of hours of her grandmother's idle chatter would be pleasant. Therapeutic, perhaps.

Fleur adored her grandmother, she always had. The feeling was mutual.

Yvette and her mother-in-law had never been close—the differences in culture and outlook, not to mention their religious beliefs, had proven insurmountable over the years. They did agree on what they had in common, though—their shared loved of Said, and in time of herself and her siblings. This had been enough to maintain a fragile peace. If her mother thought Tilleli, the elder Madame Mansouri, required a visit, this did not bode well. Fleur hoped that the old lady was not seriously ill as she dug in her bag for her car keys.

An hour later, she bounced slowly over the dust track leading from the main road up to the farm that had been in her father's family for generations. It was a large property, and prosperous, but her uncle, who now ran the place, seemed unwilling to invest in a proper access road. Her grandmother also insisted that things were fine as they were—those whom she wanted to see could find her well enough. Change and modernization were not welcomed here in the mountains, and for her part, Fleur was glad of it.

The final leg of her journey took about fifteen minutes of cautious maneuvering, easing her city-loving Opel between the pits and furrows of the unpaved road until eventually the low, white-painted buildings of the Mansouri farmstead came into sight. The place seemed to glitter in the midmorning sunshine, the light glinting off the roof-mounted solar panels and water system. Fleur pulled up about a hundred meters away and parked her car in the shade of a couple of olive trees. She would walk the rest of the distance and be glad that she had made the effort when it was time to leave and her vehicle was not baked to a crisp. She hated trying to drive when the steering wheel was too hot to touch with her bare hands.

She got out of the car and did not bother to lock it. There was no need here. She started to pick her way across the dry, hard soil surrounding the property to be greeted by a loud bellow coming from her left. She turned to see Agwmar, tethered beside an outbuilding, also benefiting from what shade was available. She smiled. Her grandmother refused to part with the elderly animal, even though his useful days were long gone. The Mansouri agricultural machine no longer used donkey power to haul the plow or transport produce to the markets, but this old boy continued to live out his days here, munching oats and languishing in the shade. Fleur turned and made a detour to say hello.

Agwmar lowered his head as she approached, his ears pricked forward to be tugged and tickled. He knew what to expect from her and nuzzled her pocket for the usual treat of a polo mint or perhaps an apple, if he was especially lucky. Fleur had not thought to bring any fruit, but fortunately for the donkey, she did have a packet of mints in the bottom of her bag. They may not have been scrupulously clean, but he seemed ready to overlook that failing on her part as he munched happily.

"So, old man. You had a lift home, yes? I am sorry I left you, but I had to drive that idiot Englishman. It could not be helped."

The donkey tossed his head, which Fleur interpreted as a nod. "Good, I knew you would understand. How is *Grandmère*?"

Agwmar stamped his front hooves in the dust, seemingly irritated that the supply of mints appeared to be drying up. Fleur patted his neck, then flung her arms around him, burying her nose in his coarse mane. She breathed in the warm smell of him, the smell of her childhood, the aroma of comfort and security, and of timeless certainty. And now Agwmar evoked other memories too. She associated him with that fateful meeting on the mountain road, just a few weeks ago.

She had murmured to the faithful donkey the whole way as they had ambled slowly down the tarmac. She had complained to the faithful beast about the manners of some people as she had eyed the lone tourist parked at the side of the road, the man who had watched their progress every inch of the way. She had thought him rude and she was sure Agwmar shared that view, but at the last moment, the stranger had taken his sunglasses off and she had seen his eyes. She had changed her mind then and simply thought him beautiful. She had said as much to Agwmar, who had not disagreed.

"He is gone, old friend. He left and he is not coming back. What am I to do now?"

The donkey nuzzled her shoulder, his low snuffling sounds sympathetic but offering no persuasive answers. He seemed to be as much at a loss as was she.

"I need to go. *Grandmère* is ill, I understand. I have come to see her. And you, of course." She kissed the donkey's flat forehead, giving his ears a last affectionate tug. "I will see you before I go, though, and maybe we'll go out for a walk. You are getting fat."

Agwmar's answering snort may or may not have been agreement, but Fleur was fairly certain he would welcome a change of scene. "Later, lazy beast." She managed to locate one last mint in her bag and used that as a parting bribe before resuming her cautious journey up to the farmhouse.

The door stood ajar when she arrived, as was usually the case during the day. People came and went the whole time, her grandmother, her uncle and his noisy family. Two adult sons, her cousins, worked the farm with him and lived in several of the buildings scattered around the main house. Her grandmother did not lack for company, but still she had asked for Fleur to visit.

"Bonjour, c'est moi..." Fleur called out as she entered.

The entrance was empty. Fleur pushed open the door to the large kitchen, the heart of this house, to find that unoccupied also. Next, she looked in the living room. Still no one. She turned at a sound behind her to see her grandmother trotting through the door, a bucket of freshly gathered eggs dangling from her hand.

"Ma petite! How lovely to see you. I was not expecting you..." The old lady placed the bucket on the floor and rushed forward, arms outstretched. Fleur had a moment to note that the elderly Berber woman looked as hale and hearty as Fleur had ever seen her before she was engulfed in a strong hug. Her grandmother might be a lot of things, but ill was not among them. At least, not right now.

At eighty-seven years old, the elder Madame Mansouri was more frail than she had been, though still reasonably fit. She attributed her ongoing rude good health to hard work, an obedient husband and strong sons. She left most of the work on the farm to the younger members of her extended family, but still managed to keep her hand in. The regular supply of eggs was her main contribution these days. The rest of her time was spent weaving her intricate carpets, drinking tea, and complaining about her infidel daughter-in-law, though the pastime had become less frequent over the years.

"How long have you been here? I was just out collecting my eggs. You should have phoned. I would have sent one of the boys to meet you at the road. That fancy car you insist on driving is no good for here in the mountains. You did drive up here? I did not see your car outside…"

Fleur smiled in spite of her solemn mood. Her grandmother could always lift her spirits just with her incessant barrage of chatter. "I just arrived, *Grandmère*. I left my car down under the olive trees. I stopped to chat to Agwmar. He looks to be getting fat."

"Idle beast. I should have him melted down for glue but I doubt anyone would have him. He does nothing but eat all day."

Fleur knew full well that her grandmother had delivered Agwmar as a foal the same year Yasmine was born. He had been a sickly baby and her grandmother had hand-reared him. There was no way he would ever be melted down for glue. He would end his days here, a pampered pet, and eventually be buried somewhere on the property. Sentimentality was not normally a trait among Berber farmers, but an exception had been made for this particular donkey. Fleur was glad of it. She adored him almost as much as she did her grandmother.

"They told me you were ill."

"They?" Madame Mansouri picked up her bucket.

Fleur followed her into the kitchen.

"My mother. She said you asked for me to come and visit you. I was worried."

"Ah." The old lady nodded, as though understanding had suddenly dawned.

Fleur wished that she shared the sentiment.

"What does that mean—ah?" She started to help her grandmother to sort the eggs by size, picking up a damp cloth to wipe any dust or other unsavoriness from the brown shells. It was a task she had done countless times.

"It means ah. That's all. Would you like some tea?"

Fleur knew better than to press for an answer. It would come, eventually. "Yes. I'll make it."

The old woman nodded and continued to sort her eggs.

Fleur poured the tea then sat at the kitchen table to drink hers. Her grandmother continued to bustle around the room, placing the eggs in large trays in a huge refrigerator, then washed her hands copiously before eventually taking a seat. Fleur knew better than to hurry her grandmother. She waited, topped up her tea and gazed around the familiar farm kitchen.

Despite the remote location, the farm was relatively modern. The Mansouris had never been fond of roughing it when they didn't have to. They had installed electricity as soon as the technology had become reliable, and a good water supply meant that they had more than adequate plumbing. On the few occasions Said had tried to persuade his mother to come and live with them in the city, she had pointed out that he could offer her nothing that her home of almost seventy years could not. She was staying put. That was not to say that she did not enjoy coming to stay at *Dar Roumana* once or twice a year, if only to torment Yvette. The two of them bickered endlessly, and Fleur reflected that it was blessed relief that they did not live together permanently. No doubt her father shared that view, though he never uttered it out loud. Fleur also knew, without a shred of doubt, that if it came to it, Said would take Yvette's side. He always had. That was why they worked so well. Tilleli Mansouri knew it too, knew her youngest son and was perfectly well aware that his wife and family were all important to him. So she never pushed too hard. Just enough to keep life interesting, and Yvette on her dainty little toes.

"So, tell me about this Englishman of yours."

Fleur splashed her tea over the rim of her glass as she set it heavily back on the solid table. "What? How do you know about that?"

Tilleli did not even deign to answer, just regarded her granddaughter solemnly from under lowered brows. Eventually Fleur answered her own question.

"Right. Maman. That is why she told me you were unwell and that I needed to come here. She thinks I should talk to you."

"Does she? Why would she think that?" Tilleli was giving nothing away.

"Search me. But she told you, did she not? About Ethan?"

"That is his name then, this Englishman who has broken my granddaughter's heart?"

"Yes. No! That is, he *is* called Ethan, but he has not broken my heart."

"Yvette tells me that he has."

"And when did you ever agree with her? If my mother tells you it is Tuesday, you would consult your diary."

"I do not have a diary." Tilleli reached for the sugar.

"*Grandmère*, please…"

Fleur's tone became beseeching, and Tilleli recognized the despair for what it was. She abandoned the sugar bowl and instead stretched her hand across the table to take Fleur's fingers in hers.

"Your mother and I argue—we always have and will continue to do so. It makes us happy. You cannot begrudge either of us our little pleasures, surely? But we have never quarreled about anything that really mattered, certainly not about you. If Yvette tells me your heart is broken, then it is broken. And if she sends you to me, it is for a reason. So, tell me."

"*Grandmère*, I…"

"Tell me, *ma chère*." The old woman's voice had gentled. Fleur reflected that she was facing Tilleli Mansouri at her most persuasive, the family matriarch for whom the welfare of her brood surpassed all other concerns. She knew this was the Tilleli who had accepted a non-Muslim marriage for her son, because she could see how much he loved the young French doctor with the laughing eyes. Said Mansouri had made no secret over the years of his gratitude for his mother's influence. She had hoped for the best and convinced her husband to do the same. Despite their outward hostility, Fleur was sure that Yvette had not disappointed her mother-in-law. The old lady doted on her grandchildren. No surprise then that Yvette had known where to turn for help.

Fleur gazed at the old lady she adored, her vision blurring as her tears, never far from the surface, filled her eyes. "I love him, *Grandmère*…"

Tilleli squeezed the hand she still held, encouraging Fleur to continue.

"I love him, but he has gone."

"Your mother tells me you no longer have your carpet. It used to be on the wall in your room at *Dar Roumana*. It is no longer there."

"I gave it to him. I wanted him to have it."

The old lady nodded, aware as Fleur was of the significance of the traditional gift.

Fleur continued. "I gave him your cloak too. He asked for it."

"Was he cold then, this Englishman?"

"No, of course not. I swapped the cloak for some cashmere scarves."

"I see. You drove a hard bargain then. I am proud of you. And now he is gone, you say?"

Fleur nodded, her tears still flowing unchecked. "I knew he would leave. He never promised me anything else."

"But?"

Fleur looked up, saw the love and concern etched in the lined brown face opposite her, the faint smile, the dark, wise eyes that knew Fleur so well, saw her so clearly.

"But we come from different worlds. He is English. He runs a company, his own company. He is an engineer. He travels all over the world. His life is nothing like mine."

"How so?"

"Is it not obvious? I just explained."

"You described an individual not unlike your father in many ways—or your brothers perhaps. None of them are English, of course, but as for the rest…"

"It is not the same."

"But it is. Anas is a businessman, Omar travels and lives abroad. How is that different? You studied in England yourself."

"Scotland. I studied in Scotland, *Grandmère*."

"You are splitting very narrow hairs, *ma petite*."

Fleur sighed and tried another tack. "I belong here, and he does not. He never could."

Fleur raised her voice now, but Tilleli was not letting up.

"How can you say that? How can you be so sure of who belongs where? Does this Ethan speak more languages than you do? Is he better educated? Richer? What do his family do that yours does not?"

"His family?" Fleur said. "What does that have to do with anything?"

"You tell me. You are the one so convinced that we are what we are and we belong in one place and not another. Surely you, more than anyone, would know that is not true."

"Me? Why would I know that? What are you saying?"

Tilleli released her hand and sat back in her chair. She watched Fleur quietly for a moment or two as she stirred the sugar into her now-cooling tea. She narrowed her eyes, as though remembering something from long ago.

"I was born not two kilometers from where we now sit. I have lived in this house, run this farm since I married your grandfather nearly seventy years ago. I could have left. I was never trapped here. Even when times were hard, and we were not always prosperous. There were bad years, but we still wanted to be here. We both wanted to stay. Your grandfather is long dead now, but I choose to stay. Ahmad was my eldest son and he chose to stay also. Said did not. Even if he had not married your mother, he would have left. His future was in the city, if not Marrakesh then somewhere else. He is an academic, so he belongs in the university. He is a teacher, so he would never have been content to work with his hands. It is good that we are not all alike. The farm could not support more in any case, and your father left to make his life elsewhere. I am glad he stayed nearby, but I never regretted his decision to leave here and I do not believe he did either. He did well and so did your mother. They brought up four beautiful children, who now must find their own places."

"I have a place. It is here, with my family, with you. I can practice medicine here. I belong here."

"Yes, you do. But not only here. You have a rare gift. Perhaps it is your parents' legacy to you, to all of you. You can belong anywhere you choose. You have skills that will be in demand wherever you choose to go, and you speak several languages so you can easily fit in. You were brought up a Muslim, but you are Christian too. Somehow." At this, the old lady paused to shake her head, seemingly incredulous that such a bizarre combination could exist but the evidence was sitting before her, sipping tea at her kitchen table. "You are a chameleon, Fleur. You change to suit your environment. You wear Western clothes and speak your perfect English, and you are not out of place in that hotel where you work — or any hotel anywhere in the world, I should think. Or you could work in a hospital as you did before, but it does not have to be here."

"Are you saying I should follow Ethan? Go to England to find him?"

"Is that what you want to do?"

"I am not sure. Perhaps." She hesitated, then, "No. I could not do that. He would not expect that of me. We had no such agreement."

"Agreements can change. Expectations can change."

"I cannot chase Ethan. Not to his home. It would not be fair."

"Yet if he were to return to Marrakesh, you would not consider it amiss of him."

Fleur considered that for a moment. "No, I would not."

"Then perhaps he too would be pleased to see you again. Surprised, but pleased."

Fleur shook her head. "I could not. I just could never do that." She looked across the table at Tilleli, resolution etched in her grandmother's expression. On this, she would not shift.

Tilleli shrugged. "Then, may I make another suggestion?"

Fleur looked up. Tilleli's tone was serious now, and Fleur had the distinct impression that her grandmother had given this situation some careful thought before embarking on this conversation. Fleur nodded. "If you have another suggestion, I would like to hear it."

"France. You could go to France. Yvette has relatives in Paris, I seem to recall. You have an aunt, cousins. Surely there will be a Totally Five Star hotel in Paris. Perhaps you could work there."

"Paris? France? But... Why...?"

"Correct me if I am wrong, but is there not now a direct rail link between Paris and London? How long does it take to get from one to the other? Three hours? Four, perhaps? It is practically on the doorstep. Less time than it would take to get to Tangier, yet you would not consider that journey too far."

"Paris? You think I should move to Paris?" Fleur knew she was repeating herself, but the possibilities were only now beginning to drop firmly into place. Tilleli was right. When was she ever not, in fact? But this... This was pure genius. Paris was indeed easily reached from London and the reverse was true too. There was a Totally Five Star there, just off the Champs-Elysées, she seemed to recall, or failing that, she might find work with another hotel chain. Her medical qualifications would be accepted anywhere, and she spoke fluent French. It was a perfect solution.

Also, there was another factor to consider—one she would never say aloud to her grandmother. Some things were too personal, just not for sharing, however close the relationship. Paris, like London, had a BDSM scene. She wanted Ethan, but what if he was not for her, would never be hers? In a major European city, a capital city even, she would be able to explore this aspect of herself further, at her leisure. She had first recognized these yearning years before, but in Paris she would be able to experiment with this lifestyle she had only now begun to properly understand. Marrakesh would offer her no opportunity to play. If she stayed here, she would never be free to grow.

And what of Ethan? Paris would be near enough to open up possibilities, but not so close to seem pushy or to force his hand. That would not do. She could not live with herself if she caused him embarrassment. He had been careful to spare her any discomfort, had been the soul of discretion whilst he was here. She owed him the same consideration. She was as certain as she could be that he had no one else, no regular girlfriend or, perish the thought, a wife. She was not sure how she knew that, since they had never discussed the matter, but she was quite positive. Even so, he may not want to see her again, whether in Paris, London or anywhere else. She had to accept that possibility. What was more, she had yet to track him down, though she had a notion of how she might manage that.

Already she was planning, already she knew she would do this. Thanks to Tilleli, she saw a solution now, a way forward. She had to try.

Chapter Nineteen

Fleur left the Mansouri farm a couple of hours later, having first taken Agwmar for a much deserved stroll down to the meadow at the end of their property where an underground stream bubbled clear and cool up from the parched land to form a shallow pool. He loved to roll in the water there—he always had—and if she was honest, Fleur found it no hardship either. The pair of them were more or less dry by the time they returned to the farm and she left the donkey in his stable with an extra helping of oats in return for his wise counsel.

She drove back to Marrakesh, straight to her parents' villa where she showered and changed her clothes. She phoned the hotel and made an appointment to speak to the head of human resources later that afternoon.

* * * *

"We will be very sorry to lose you here at the Marrakesh hotel, Doctor Mansouri. Are you sure we cannot persuade you to reconsider?"

So much for her services being surplus to requirements. Fleur thanked the smart, middle-aged man on the other side of the desk for his kind remarks but explained that personal circumstances meant that she must consider moving on. She wondered if there might be other opportunities within the chain, perhaps in France? She had family there, in Paris actually, and it would suit her to relocate there, if at all possible. She did not add that if Totally Five Star could not accommodate her requirements, she would resign her position with them and move to Paris anyway.

In the event, that was not required. She received a call the next day from a man who introduced himself as Pierre Rivaux, in charge of human resources at Totally Five Star's Paris hotel. Monsieur Rivaux had received Fleur's request for a transfer and wanted to check out some details before confirming the move.

Fleur could not believe her luck. Details? Confirm the move? Was it really to be so easy? So simple? It seemed so. Monsieur Rivaux sought clarification on Fleur's medical credentials, needed the names of three references, since this was to be a permanent rather than a locum position, and required details of her passport. Accommodation could be made available at the hotel, or Fleur could make her own arrangements if preferred. The salary was comparable to what she had earned as a locum, with an allowance for the additional costs of living in central Paris. The position was currently unfilled, so she could start at her earliest convenience. Subject to settling any remaining contractual details, would Fleur be prepared to take the job?

Monsieur Rivaux had to ask, but as far as Fleur was concerned, the offer was ideal. She accepted the post on the spot, and two days later flew to Brussels to hammer out the contractual details. She agreed on a start date some two weeks after that. Yvette wept at the airport, but Fleur could not help noticing that she and Tilleli stood side by side at the doors to the departure lounge as they waved her off.

The Paris Totally Five Star was magnificent, one of the flagship hotels in the group. Fleur could not believe her luck that she was there, and so quickly. It had been less than three weeks since she had thought of the idea—or rather Tilleli Mansouri had and convinced her that she could do this. She spent the first couple of days settling in, getting to know the staff in Paris, and the medical facilities offered at the hotel. Her post had been unfilled for a month or two so there was a backlog of paperwork to clear, a stock take of medical supplies to be undertaken and orders to be placed with the various suppliers. The small team of nursing and ancillary staff had managed to keep the medical facility ticking over, but Fleur needed to assert herself, establish her leadership. This took time, a few weeks of concerted effort, and more or less round the clock activity on her part before she felt she had made the place her own.

But now, she was there. She was established. Time to put the rest of her plan into motion.

Seated on the settee in her staff apartment at the Paris Totally Five Star, Fleur dialed the number she had obtained from the hotel chain internal telephone directory. As ever, the phone was answered before the second ring.

"Is it possible to speak to Mr. Conroy, please?" Fleur injected her most polite tone into the request. She was sure he was there. She had checked. Her newly elevated position among the ranks of the Totally Five Star senior staff in one of their premier sites meant she had access to executive diaries and she knew James Conroy was in his London office right now. Hopefully he would not be in a meeting, but even so, she might be able to get him to call her back—or at the very least find out when he would be free.

"Who's calling, please?"

"Fleur Mansouri, Chief Medical Officer, Paris." *A lofty title. It sounds impressive enough.* She picked up a pencil, ready to jot down the time when she might be able to book a call to speak to the CEO.

"Doctor Mansouri, how can I help you? I trust the new accommodations in Paris are to your liking?" The strong male voice on the line came as a bolt from the blue. She might have asked for Mr. Conroy. She did not expect to get to talk to him at the first attempt.

"Oh, yes, yes, they are. Perfect. Thank you."

"Good. I've heard excellent reports of your work so far. That outbreak of so-called salmonella in the restaurant there could have been a disaster for us."

"It was not salmonella, Mr. Conroy. The guest was suffering from Crohn's Disease, but the local media picked up on the story and drew the wrong conclusions."

"I know that, but the negative publicity could have been serious. I appreciate your prompt actions in speaking to the press and scotching the rumors."

"It was nothing, sir—just part of my job. It was fortunate that I was able to convince the guest to confirm my explanation."

"Fortunate? Hardly. You were very persuasive, I understand. We always appreciate initiative. Too many employees think they need to ask first and act later. You took charge and headed off the problem before it got out of hand. Anyway, I'm sure you didn't phone me this morning just so I can sing your praises. How can I help you?"

Now for it. Fleur drew a deep breath. "It is a personal matter, sir."

"I see. Go on." His tone sounded slightly guarded.

"I wonder if you could let me have contact details for Ethan Savage. I understand he is a friend of yours."

There was a pause, then, "Ethan Savage? Do you know him, then?"

"Yes, sir, we met when he was in Marrakesh a few weeks ago. He was doing some work for you, I understand, relating to the site of a possible new development."

"I've seen Ethan a number of times since then. He didn't mention that he had met you."

"No, sir, he would not have done that." Fleur knew she was not handling this well. All earlier warmth had drained from the voice on the other end of the phone. James Conroy's tone was now clipped and formal.

"It was a casual acquaintance, then?"

Hardly. "No, sir, it was not. But still, it was personal and I would not have expected him to discuss it."

"I see."

By his arctic tone, she believed that James Conroy did see something, but it was not the truth. She hoped. Her liaison with Ethan had meant a great deal, to her certainly. And she believed it had been significant for him too.

"Please, Mr. Conroy, do you have the number? I would very much like to contact Mr. Savage."

"If Ethan wanted you to have his phone number, I daresay he would have given it to you. I'm not in the habit of giving out my friends' personal details."

"I do appreciate that, Mr. Conroy, but I was hoping you might be able to make an exception."

"I'm sorry, but no, I can't do that. I could…"

Fleur interrupted him. "Please. I would not ask but it is important to me that I speak with him." She knew she sounded desperate but was unable to help it.

"Doctor Mansouri, you must realize this is impossible. If it's any consolation, I wouldn't give your phone number to just anyone who rang me and asked for it either. But if you like, I could—"

"I understand. I apologize for having bothered you. Good day, Mr. Conroy." Fleur ended the call, mortified. She had known there was a good chance that James Conroy would refuse to divulge the information, but even so, she was bitterly disappointed. Her next recourse would be to go through Ethan's office. She would find a number for the head offices of Savage Geo. Ethan must have a personal secretary. Perhaps Fleur would be able to find out his email address and send him a message. Yes, that would be best. It was all she could think of right now.

Sighing, she checked the time. Nine thirty in the morning. She had a meeting at eleven and would be covering the hotel clinic from two. Just time for a coffee then she might take a shower before work. Maybe later, if she had a few spare moments, she could check the Internet for Savage Geo. Perhaps James Conroy was right. Certainly he had implied that Ethan had not given her his number for a reason.

Perhaps he had deliberately withheld it. Without a doubt, he had had every opportunity to contact her in the weeks since he had left but had chosen not to. Should she leave well alone, not risk the humiliation of having him tell her not to bother him, that he was not interested in further contact?

Fleur dismissed that notion. She was determined to speak to Ethan, to tell him she was in Paris and would very much like to see him again. He could only say no. She got up and headed into her tiny kitchenette to put the kettle on.

* * * *

By four in the afternoon, the first rush of medical problems had subsided. Fleur had bandaged a sprained wrist, prescribed antibiotics and painkillers, and had one guest transferred by ambulance to the local accident and emergency department—she suspected appendicitis. Now her surgery was quiet and at last, she had some free time to pursue her own pet project. She Googled Savage Geo.

The headquarters were in north London, but the company had sites in Sheffield and Edinburgh too. She wondered where Ethan was based. The company website gave a contact phone number, but that was intended for potential clients, she suspected—not for frustrated submissives wanting to rekindle their acquaintance with the whip hand of the chief executive. This was not going to be easy. She considered her options—not extensive—and decided that perhaps the best thing to do would be to call the one contact number there was and ask for Ethan's office. She might get passed around a bit, but eventually she would find herself talking to his secretary. She glanced at the clock and wondered what time it was in London. Were they an hour in front or an hour behind? An hour behind, she thought, so that meant it was still very much the working day in the UK. She had plenty of time.

A knock at her door interrupted her as she started to dial the number.

"Come in." Fleur replaced the handset, expecting to see another unwell guest come through the door. She did not expect the motorcycle courier who stepped into her consulting room, resplendent in his black leathers, his crash helmet tucked under his right arm. In his left hand, he held a package, neatly wrapped in brown paper.

"Parcel for Doctor Mansouri."

It did not instantly strike Fleur as incongruous that the courier spoke to her in English.

"I am Doctor Mansouri."

"Good. Could you sign here please?" The courier thrust a clipboard in front of her.

Fleur took the proffered pen automatically and signed, wondering what on earth this could be. The package looked to be soft, and the plain wrapping was not typical of pharmaceutical companies who usually emblazoned their wares with their logos.

"There's a letter too. My instructions were to deliver both this and the package personally. Good afternoon, ma'am."

"What? What instructions? Who…?"

It was too late. Leather Man had already closed the door behind him on his way out. Fleur glanced at the white envelope in her hand and picked up the package. It was soft and squashy. It bent as she handled it. She put it back on her desk and slid her thumbnail under the flap of the envelope.

She pulled out one sheet of paper, handwritten. The message was short and to the point.

Tonight. 10:30 pm, room 301. You know the drill.

She ripped the brown paper from the package. Out fell her grandmother's cloak.

How did he know? How had he found her? James Conroy — it had to be. But why? The CEO had been quite adamant that he would not help her, insisting that he could not divulge Ethan's address.

She thought about what he *had* said. Exactly. James Conroy had not revealed Ethan's contact details. But as soon as he had finished talking to her, he must have wasted no time in getting in touch with Ethan himself and telling him that Doctor Mansouri, the recently appointed doctor in charge of medical services at Totally Five Star Paris, was keen to speak to him. Ethan had done the rest.

She wondered if Ethan had hired the motorcycle courier in England and had him make the trip all the way to Paris to deliver the cloak in person. He must have, and it would have cost a fortune. Her stomach quivered at that thought. And to arrange to meet her tonight? That spoke of dropping everything and coming as soon as he knew she was in Paris. Within reach. More butterflies took flight inside her.

Room three zero one must be right here in the Totally Five Star. The third floor was where the finest suites were located. Her Dom was sparing no expense. The cloak made his intentions perfectly obvious, which might be interpreted as slightly presumptuous of him. After all, she had not had any opportunity to tell him why she wanted to talk to him. How could he be so sure that she wished to rekindle their previous relationship?

On reflection, though, he was *not* presuming too much. He was her Dom and therefore not presuming anything. He would command and she would submit. That was how it worked. It remained the case that she could refuse if she chose to. He would have no way of knowing until he arrived in room three zero one whether she had accepted his summons. If she did not want to play, she just need not turn up.

And pigs might fly around the Totally Five Star rooftops. Of course she would be there. This was what she had dreamt of for the last few weeks, the one thing she wanted more than anything and had feared she might never have again. Oh yes, she would be there, naked except for her cloak, kneeling in room three zero one. The perfect submissive, waiting for her Dom.

* * * *

She slipped into the suite on the third floor at twenty past ten. She had showered in her own apartment and dressed in just jogging pants and a loose T-shirt. She had not bothered with underwear. It had not seemed worth it. Her hair was freshly washed, dried and caught back in a loose ponytail. The cloak was rolled under her arm as she let herself in ˙with her staff passkey. She had just a few minutes to prepare herself. He would not be late, she was sure of it, and she must not be either. She preferred not to commence their reunion with a punishment.

The suite was predictably large, a central living area with a dining alcove, and two bedrooms leading from it. Both bedrooms were beautifully appointed in the elegant yet understated Totally Five Star style. Fleur assumed that she should wait in the master bedroom but she undressed in the living room, preferring to leave her clothes neatly folded and out of sight. This had appeared to be Ethan's preference in Marrakesh, so she would do the same here. She left her T-shirt and sweatpants on the sofa, freed her hair from the ponytail, and wrapped the cloak loosely around her nude body.

As soon as she entered the bedroom, she knew she had selected the correct place in the suite. This was where Ethan expected to find her in just a few minutes. The room was dominated by a huge four-poster bed. At the foot of the bed sat a solid wood blanket chest with a number of items arranged on the polished top. She glanced at those, intending to examine them more closely later. For now, her attention was seized by the priceless object spread on the deep pile carpet beside the chest. Her own hand-woven rug, the one she had knelt on in the courtyard the first time she had submitted for Ethan and had subsequently presented to him, her precious bride's gift. The fact that he had brought it here perhaps indicated that he understood the significance of the gift, and accepted it.

Fleur stood on her carpet, flexing her bare toes in the closely woven pile, the cloak clutched tight at her throat as she gazed at the selection of objects scattered on the polished oak chest. She stretched out her hand to touch the items, picking up each in turn. First, Ethan's business card, classy and discreet, understated in cool pearl gray with the writing embossed in a darker shade. She took in the office direct dial and mobile numbers printed on the front below his name, then turned the card over to find his home number and what she assumed must be his home address handwritten on the back. There could be no doubt now that he wanted her to have his contact details.

She put the card back and picked up an airline ticket wallet. This puzzled her. She opened it and drew out a single ticket, one way, from Heathrow to Marrakesh Menara Airport. What could this mean? A not so subtle hint that she should return to Morocco? She studied the ticket more closely and saw that it was for a flight in just over one week's time, and the booking specified a seat with extra leg room. Her own diminutive five foot four hardly called for such specifics. Ethan stood a good foot taller, on the other hand—his legs were long and he probably liked to stretch them out in comfort. This ticket was not intended for her. It was for him. He had made arrangements to return to Morocco. The wallet contained the booking confirmation and receipt, which proved that the booking had been made three days earlier, clearly prior to James Conroy's intervention.

When he had left her at the Marrakesh Totally Five Star, Ethan had had no plans to return, she was sure of that. He would have said so if he had. Something had changed his mind—or someone.

Fleur replaced the wallet, the ticket and other documents safely stowed inside. The rest of the items on the chest were fairly straightforward. Two pairs of handcuffs, a set of nipple clamps, a spanking paddle, a cane, a suede flogger, a tube of lubricant and a vibrating dildo. She picked up the dildo, pressed the switch experimentally. It whirred to life.

"You didn't think I'd forget the batteries, did you?"

Fleur whirled on the spot. Ethan stood in the open bedroom doorway, casually elegant and jaw droppingly sexy in black jeans and a plain white T-shirt. He was barefoot, which made her think he had been in the suite the entire time she had been exploring. She stepped forward, on the point of running to fling her arms around him. He halted her movement with one finger, imperiously lifted.

"It's thirty seconds after ten thirty. Why are you not kneeling?"

That voice…

"My apologies, Sir." Fleur dropped to her knees immediately, her head bowed and her pussy dripping. She arranged the cloak around her, pulling it up to cover her hair. Then she remained motionless, waiting.

She felt rather than heard his footsteps as he approached her from behind. She let her eyelids drift closed and she almost purred in contentment as his large hand rested on her head, his fingers spread to caress her softly.

"You are one seriously lovely woman, my little Fleur. It's been too long."

"Yes, Sir, much too long. You were coming back? The ticket…"

"I was."

"To see me?"

"Of course to see you."

"I thought you had forgotten about me when you did not telephone or send me an email. I gave you my number." Fleur snuck a peek upwards but he was still out of her line of sight."

"Eyes down, girl. You know the rules." His tone had sharpened.

Fleur lowered her gaze immediately.

Ethan gripped the edge of her cloak and drew it away from her face, revealing her loosened hair. He slowly combed his fingers through the dark softness.

"I would never forget you, Fleur. I'm sorry if you were upset. I should have kept in touch. I intended to surprise you but you beat me to it. I'm glad you did, though. If it's any comfort to you, James is very impressed, even if you did hang up on him. Your fame precedes you." His voice had gentled again, soft and low and so sexy she thought she might melt.

Fleur gulped and concentrated hard on forcing some semblance of coherence into her words. "I should apologize to him. I was extremely rude. I realize that. But I am very pleased to see you, Sir." It was not much, but the best she could manage while he was caressing her head so seductively. Her pussy spasmed wildly. In moments, she would be begging him to fuck her.

He stepped around to stand in front of her. "James is a big lad, so I expect he'll survive it. If you open your eyes and look up, you'll be able to see just how pleased I am to see you too."

Obligingly Fleur did as he suggested and found his huge, thick erection just inches from her nose. She smiled as her pussy moistened even more in response.

"Do you like what you see?"

"I do, Sir." *Understatement of the century.*

"I intend to fuck you, hard and deep, and this time I don't care how much noise you make. I intend for you to scream, little Fleur. This room is soundproofed. There's no danger of alarming the staff here if you become too vocal."

"I see, Sir. That sounds most—convenient."

"I thought so. Knowing your tastes, I brought some toys with me this time too, a few little bits and pieces to help keep you amused. Do you like them?"

"I am not sure, Sir. I like some of them, certainly."

"Ah yes, the vibrator. You'll have to earn that, though. And, of course, there is the little matter of you being late, despite my clear instructions. We do need to deal with that before anything else, I think."

"Late? I was here on time, Sir." She could not keep the note of indignation from her voice.

"All the more reason for being in place, kneeling on the rug, at the time *I* specified. Instead, I come in here to find you still tinkering with my little playthings. You've earned yourself a good, hard spanking, girl."

Fleur shuddered in glorious anticipation. He was right, and she offered up thanks for it to whatever god might be listening to her. "Yes, Sir, of course. Thank you."

"The paddle then, on your bare arse. Ten strokes, with some real bite, I think, to make the lesson memorable. Then, I cuff you to the bed and the fun really begins."

"Yes, Sir."

"Stand up, please. Remove that rather fetching cloak and hand it to me."

Fleur got to her feet, proud to be able to do so with a reasonable degree of grace. She slid the cloak from her shoulders and swung it around to drape it over her arms. She offered it to Ethan. He took it from her and folded it, his movements slow and deliberate. He laid the cloak on the chest with the rest of the paraphernalia he had brought, then he turned to Fleur.

"Stand straight, shoulders back. Look me in the eye, girl, and be proud. Your body is beautiful, so show it off to me."

Fleur realized she had been slouching, her hands clasped in front of her stomach. She had been nervous, and he saw it immediately, dealt with it. There were tears in her eyes as she met his gaze.

Ethan came to stand in front of her, his smile gentle. "Turn around for me, girl."

She did so, turning slowly. "God, I love your arse. I never forgot how soft it felt under my hand, especially when it had been heated up a little." He caressed her right buttock, causing her pussy to dampen further.

"Sir, I…"

"Be quiet. Unless you want to safe word, or I ask you a direct question, don't speak from now on. Is that clear?"

"Yes, Sir."

"Good. Go to the bed and lie across it, face down, your bum at the edge. Put your arms out to your sides, at shoulder height."

Fleur did as she was told, kneeling beside the bed before positioning herself on it just as instructed. She turned her head to see Ethan pick up the spanking paddle from the chest. He came to stand behind her.

"Ten strokes, hard. I won't draw this out. I want it over with fast. You can scream, make as much noise as you like, but I don't expect you to move until I've finished and I tell you to get up. Is that understood?"

"Yes, Sir." She could detect the slight tremor in her voice and was sure he would too.

"Is your safe word still cashmere? And fountain for slow down?"

"Yes, Sir, still the same."

"Use them if you have to." He paused then continued, his tone softening, "I know you're frightened, but this will soon be over. You *can* do this, Fleur. Trust me."

"I do trust you, Sir."

"Good. Try not to tense. It makes it more painful for you if you do and it robs me of the pleasure of watching your bum ripple. Are you ready?"

"Yes, Sir."

The first slap landed hard and sharp across her left buttock, closely followed by a matching blow on the right. Fleur screamed, and despite Ethan's advice, she tensed, hard. Ethan ignored her cries and continued to land the strokes in rapid succession. He had not asked her to count, but she found herself doing so anyway. Her shrieks of pain subsided as her body acclimatized to the sensation, converting it to something resembling pleasure.

"I do believe I've discovered a pain slut. Maybe I'll need to find other ways to punish you in the future. You're enjoying this too much."

"I am not sure I—"

"Open your legs, girl." The Dom tone was clipped and cool, the command irresistible.

Not that Fleur had any real objection to his instruction. She parted her thighs.

Ethan dropped the paddle onto the bed beside her and slid one long finger deep inside her pussy, swirling it around to test her moisture. "Christ, girl, you're fucking drenched. And so tight. Such a slut. So sweet."

"Thank you, Sir. Please, will you fuck me?"

"Oh, yes. Eventually. You're still owed three more strokes, though, before we can proceed to that. I think you can take those right here, on your hot pussy. Just here, I think, where the lips are all swollen and sensitive. Yes?" He drew his palm along her pussy to indicate exactly where he intended to spank her.

Fleur groaned, her response a mix of pure lust laced with just a hint of terror. "If you think that is best, Sir."

"I do." He slid his finger from her cunt and picked up the paddle again. Fleur closed her eyes, amazed at how relaxed she suddenly felt as she lay still, her tender pussy lips exposed for him to slap.

"Oh! Ooh…" Fleur's moans were muffled by the thick duvet under her as she buried her face in the downy softness. The sensation created by the first slap direct across her pussy was incredible. Pain, yes, but with an oozing soft center of wicked pleasure. It put her briefly in mind of a decadent hand-made and very expensive chocolate, the sort her father occasionally bought for Yvette as a special treat. Bitter and dark on the outside but revealing a soft, rich filling of sweet cream, delicately flavored and utterly delicious. The second stroke landed in the same place and she screamed, though she really did not know whether with pain or pleasure. She lifted her hips, silently begging, her throbbing, wet pussy aching for the final slap.

Ethan thrust three fingers deep inside her, finger-fucking her mercilessly. The first stirrings of a powerful orgasm tingled deep inside her cunt, quickly gathering pace as he plunged his fingers in and out of her tight pussy. She was there, almost, when he pulled his fingers from her. Frustrated, Fleur sank her face into the mattress, wondering what her additional punishment might be if she were to plead with him when he had expressly forbidden her to speak unless asked a direct question.

The third stroke was delivered direct to her clit, hard and sharp, the intensity of the slap sending shock waves through her already shuddering form. It was enough, more than enough. Her orgasm seized her, the waves of pleasure undulating unchecked as she shivered and writhed on the bed. Ethan placed his fingers inside her again, working her G-spot to prolong the climax. Fleur clutched at the cotton bedding beneath her hands, curling her fingers into the expensive Egyptian fabric as she rode out her release.

As her orgasm died, Ethan withdrew his fingers. Fleur lay still, expecting to be instructed to stand up, or perhaps to roll over onto her back. Instead, she flinched as Ethan gently parted her pussy lips with his fingers, then whimpered in surprise as something cool and hard entered her. The dildo. He had said she must earn it. It seemed that he now considered her deserving. She groaned her approval as the vibrator whirred into life inside her, the pulsating waves massaging her inner walls.

"Is that good?"

"Oh, yes. Yes, Sir, it is." Fleur gyrated her hips as she squeezed hard, gripping the dildo tight within her pussy and savoring its smooth, alien presence.

"That's the lowest setting. Would you like me to turn it up?"

She could only nod, gasping her thanks as he increased the intensity of the vibrations.

"Enough, I think. Maybe that'll keep you quiet through this next bit."

Next bit? Fleur's curiosity was soon satisfied as he spread her smarting buttocks to expose her anus, and the cool locating gel hit her rear hole. Ethan spread it around, working a little of it inside. Fleur considered protesting but had no real appetite for making a fuss. Not when the delightful sensations inside her pussy were distracting her so effectively. And really, he was not hurting her. It was a little embarrassing, no more than that. Not even embarrassing really, more— intimate. She liked intimate, could become accustomed to intimacy with Ethan Savage. Given the chance.

"Will you stay?" The words were out before she had time to think, to consider if now was really the right time.

"I beg your pardon."

"Not forever, I realize that. You have work, and so do I. But for a while. And will you come back?" Once she'd started, Fleur found she really needed to know. She had to have his answer.

"Do we need to discuss this now?" As if to punctuate his point Ethan slid his finger inside her arse, the sphincter relaxing under his determined probing. He did not pretend not to understand what it was she wanted to hear from him.

"Oh, Sir, that feels…" Fleur stopped, allowed herself a few moments to savor the gorgeous feelings he evoked in her. Then, "Please, I would like to know."

"I thought I told you not to talk."

"Sir, please answer me. Please."

Ethan sank his finger farther into her arse as he reached around with his other hand to stroke her clit. Fleur teetered on the point of orgasm once more, hovering on the very edge of oblivion but determined to have her answer.

Again, she asked. "Please, Sir, I need to know you won't leave me. Not this time."

Ethan sighed, and relented. Or perhaps he always intended to provide the assurance she was seeking. "I won't leave you—or at least, not for long. We won't be together all the time. We can't be. I'll go home to London, and maybe you'll come with me sometimes. But I'll come back here often, if I'm welcome. Perhaps we'll both go to Marrakesh, to visit your family. I'd like that."

"I would like to see your home in England too, and you will be very welcome here. And in Marrakesh."

"So, this sounds like a plan. I mean to do all I can to make this work between us and I expect you to do the same."

"I will, Sir."

"Excellent. Now, will you please concentrate on what's happening here or do I need to find a more challenging way to focus your attention?"

"That won't be necessary, Sir. What you are doing is just perfect."

Epilogue

From: Ethan Savage
To: Fleur Mansouri-Savage
Date: 23 April 2014
Subject: Your recent dispatch

My darling,
I fully appreciate your fondness for leather. Indeed, I share it. That corset, however, took leatherwork to an entirely new level and left little enough to the imagination.

Certainly your surprise package did not tax Mrs. Beauchamp's powers of imagination one iota, nor those of anyone else in the mail room this morning. I am confident that you brightened up their days considerably, but have to concur with Mrs. Beauchamp's view that in future such packages would be better marked private and personal. As you know, Mrs. B has worked for me for over twelve years. She is an excellent PA and I am accustomed to heeding her advice. You might consider it also.

But back to that corset. It really is very nice, and I look forward to admiring it to full advantage at the earliest opportunity. I will bring it to Paris with me later this week and hope not to find myself explaining its finer points to some dour-faced douanier at customs.

I do truly commend your choice. What the corset may have lacked in substance, it definitely made up for in inventiveness. I particularly appreciate the cunning design of the lacing that allows the garment to expand as required.

And this brings me to my next point. I understand from James that you were in your office again this morning dealing with some crisis or other. I know you take your promotion to Chief Medical Officer at TFS Paris seriously and no one is more proud of you than I am. Well, Tilleli perhaps, though that goes without saying. You have proven your worth many times over, so you have no need to continue to demonstrate your powers of organization. James assures me that he has your maternity cover in hand and all aspects of your work are being perfectly covered by your locum. You can safely leave everything to the estimable Doctor Sahid, and I am going to insist you do so from now on.

For the next two months, I want you to remain in our apartment with your feet up. You are to lift nothing heavier than a teacup. I hope I make myself entirely clear, girl, but if you are in any way uncertain as to my requirements, please do not hesitate to say so and I will clarify. I'm sure I do not need to remind you of the consequences if you do not obey me in this matter. I may have decided to refrain from the spankings you so richly deserve for the duration of your pregnancy, but you have already found orgasm denial not to your taste and I daresay you have no wish to deepen your understanding of it. So heed me in this. Please.

I should be back in Paris the day after tomorrow, but if I can get away earlier, I will. In the meantime, take care of yourself and our baby. You are both very precious to me.

I love you.

Ethan

P.S. If you happen to talk to your grandmother in the next day or so, please congratulate her on the safe delivery of her latest foal. And whilst I am flattered that she thinks sufficiently highly of me to want to name the little chap in my honor, please try to convince her otherwise. Savage is not a suitable name for a donkey. Perhaps you could convince her that my middle name is Neddy…

About the Author

Until 2010, Ashe was a director of a regeneration company before deciding there had to be more to life and leaving to pursue a lifetime goal of self-employment.

Ashe has been an avid reader of women's fiction for many years—erotic, historical, contemporary, fantasy, romance—you name it, as long as it's written by women, for women. Now, at last in control of her own time and working from her home in rural West Yorkshire, she has been able to realise her dream of writing erotic romance herself.

She draws on settings and anecdotes from her previous and current experience to lend colour, detail and realism to her plots and characters, but her stories of love, challenge, resilience and compassion are the conjurings of her own imagination. She loves to craft strong, enigmatic men and bright, sassy women to give them a hard time—in every sense of the word.

When she's not writing, Ashe's time is divided between her role as resident taxi driver for her teenage daughter, and caring for a menagerie of dogs, cats, rabbits, tortoises and a hamster.

Ashe Barker loves to hear from readers. You can find her contact information, website details and author profile page at http://www.totallybound.com.

Totally Bound Publishing